SUNDAY IS A GOOD DAY TO **DIE**

DAVID ELIE JR

Foreigners

Published by Foreigners Publishing, LLC
1621 Central Ave Cheyenne, WY 82001

Foreigners
Unleash Your Imagination!

For use of the material in the book, foreign and subsidiary rights, contact info@foreignersbooks.com

ISBN: 978-1-7375046-4-1

Cover Design: Nabin Karna

Cover Images: Pixabay.com

To all those who serve, and their loved ones who support them.

PROLOGUE

Five years ago

THE BALLROOM OF THE posh Chateau des Rés was filled. For the first time in decades, all the group members were reunited. A precarious situation, as the enemies of the Consortium had multiplied in recent years. Gone were the days of ruling the earth unencumbered. Worse, their existence was exposed. Though mainly the stuff of conspiracy theorists and sensationalists, the group's effectiveness hinged on being inconspicuous. The matters at hand warranted such a measure. But did it warrant summoning the Council as well? Robert Russo made the call, insisting it was necessary. But was it? Only Primus would determine that. Robert knew this was one of the few situations where he could lose his position and life. But he couldn't let these thoughts weaken his confidence because, to them, he was Quartum, the one point of contact between the seven men of the Council and the Consortium.

"Ladies and gentlemen, this assembly is now in session," he said from the podium. His pristine silvery hair, upright posture, and emerald eyes exuded confidence and entitlement. "Incumbent upon us today is the duty passed down to us from our predecessors, to maintain the perpetuity of the human race and the supremacy of our fraternal orders." He paused to sip a glass of water while glancing through the audience, marveling at the power gathered in this room.

All eyes and ears were fixated on him, paying attention to his every word. *Let's make them wait a little bit more*, he thought. The pause lasted for about five seconds but felt like an hour.

"Our Preservation mandate has reached a crossroads. The growth of the world's population can no longer be contained by our conventional means." Though his lips moved, his eyes observed every inch of his audience. Half the room had no clue what he was about to propose. A third showed discomfort; they sipped on their water, moved on their chair, or crossed their arms. Some of the more prominent members were closed with skeptical looks on their faces. But the elder members had an air of resignation as if they knew this was inevitable.

He planned to capitalize on the elders' understanding and willingness to make the tough choices. But would that be enough? The Consortium had maintained its dominance due to the induction of several younger members part of the new millennial dynasties. The most notorious being the president of FacedIn, which was by far the largest social media platform in the world. Those platforms were an invaluable tool in assessing the psychological profile of unsuspecting subjects. The new members were influential due to their capacity to sway the masses, but were unused to the hard decisions that came with this position of power.

"Within the next five years, the world population will pass nine billion people, then ten billion. At this point, the world's carrying capacity will be reached, and we will all be at risk of extinction." He knew this sounded alarmist and unsubstantiated, but he would do his best to make them see the light.

"In the past century, we have been hard at work to curb the growth of the population, but we have failed to slow the pace to a sustainable growth rate. In 1804, the world's population reached one billion. It took over 120 years before it reached two billion. Now, we add a billion every twelve years. At this rate, the Earth will run out of resources before our children or grandchildren come of age. Our dominance, our very existence, is now threatened. The World Health Organization estimates-"

"Excuse me, Mr. Quartum, but how do you suggest we deal with this situation?" The tall behemoth said from the back of the room. Oil Tycoon Jim Altman built the world's largest energy conglomerate through mergers and acquisitions.

"That is why we are here. The floor is open for deliberations," Quartum replied with an unexpressed sigh of relief. The speech was over, now the solutions.

A hand rose.

"Prince Albertsen, you have the floor," Quartum said, authorizing the Swedish royal to speak.

"We have for many centuries controlled the births of our region by indoctrination. Our families are not forced to limit their reproductive output, but they do so willfully. This has been very effective," the prince said.

"Unfortunately," Quartum replied. "Those techniques have not proven effective in the developing world. Dr. Girard, would you like to comment on that?"

Epidemiologist Dr. Marc Girard, the prominent World Health Organization assistant deputy director, was reputed for his medical breakthroughs.

"Yes, thank you. In fact, we are victims of our success. We have gained trillions of dollars in pharmaceutical sales and reduced mortality rates.

Contrary to our expectations, some third-world nations did not adopt the reproductive restraints of the West. Therefore, they live longer, and their offspring have higher survival rates."

"Have you tried indoctrination?" the prince asked.

"Yes, we did. But their ancestral beliefs and a lack of economic opportunity create an environment prone to breeding."

"So, what's the solution?" Jim Altman blurted.

"Come on, Jim! Do you have to ask?" the chairman of the Senate Foreign Relations Committee, Senator John Woods, said. A former three-star general, one of the few who have served in the Afghan, Iraq, and Syrian wars.

"This is just a segue to a war plot. Which country do you want us to invade this time?"

"Let's not jump to conclusions, Mr. Woods," Quartum said to squash any wave of dissent. He tried to redirect the conversation and dismiss the subtle insubordination of the senator. "Yet that's a good point, but would a war benefit us?"

"With all due respect," Erika Kaiser, former chancellor of Germany and director general of the World Trade Organization, said. "Let's be realistic. No war is going to curb the issue at hand. We need something more like an epidemic or forced sterilization."

"That would need to be a massive epidemic, and would we be able to contain it to the desired areas?" Dr. Girard said. "This would prove to be the more challenging aspect of an epidemic, but it can be done with some preemptive measures."

"How many casualties could we expect from such a strategy?" the prince asked.

"Approximately fifty million."

"Dr. Girard, aren't you being overly optimistic?" The voice came from Septime, the seventh member of the Council. Their words were few, but their words mattered most.

Dr. Girard knew he had but a few moments to explain his theory. "I understand the skepticism, but this can be accomplished with a genetically modified virus whose symptoms mimic a well-controlled disease like the flu. The modification would have to prolong the incubation period, maximizing exposure and transmission."

Septime did not reply, but his facial expression seemed to be content. Prince Albertsen spoke up. "It sounds like a good plan."

"A good plan?" Senator Woods said. "Are you serious? Ladies and gentlemen, wake up! It's one thing to play puppeteers with politics and fancy ourselves the masters of the markets, but you're talking about killing what? Fifty million to two billion people! Are you insane?" He took a deep breath as silence fell in the room. Regaining his composure, he continued.

"All I'm saying is there's got to be a better way to control the population than killing that many people at once." In an attempt to backtrack from his spontaneous outburst, he followed with a proposal more in line with the group's tenets. "Maybe we can mitigate the effects of the growth with genetically modified food, cheap to manufacture and easy to distribute?" As he felt the attempt to backtrack had failed, an unexpected voice of support rose.

"That could be a more viable option," Erika Kaiser said. "The cost wouldn't be as steep as a war, and the risk would be significantly less than an epidemic." She had been known to express eugenic views. Her more equitable approach was a departure from her historical stance. Quartum was a little taken aback by the turn of the conversation. Maybe she wanted to save her longtime friend. Maybe she thought that her position as the head of the World Trade Organization shielded her from reprisal. Or maybe she thought her unwavering allegiance to the group gave her such a status that could offset the affront made by the simple senator. Regardless, he had to regain control at once.

"Ladies and Gentlemen, as much as these solutions seem more humane, they will ultimately fail in accomplishing our preservation mandate."

He waited and watched for any signs of dissent. John Woods' facial expression was unmistakably opposed to anything he would say, but the question was, would he voice that opposition, or would he, in the interest of self-preservation, keep quiet?

"An epidemic at best will cause fifty million casualties," he said. "As horrific as this will sound, and believe me, it is horrific. The consequences of failure will be far worse for all of humanity. We have implemented several policies in our countries that have worked and curbed the growth rate. But those policies have not worked elsewhere. As a result, people who do not value life outnumber us. Once the Earth's resources become depleted, you can expect chaos and waves of uprisings so powerful that they will wipe us away. When that's done, their lack of understanding will cause them to self-destruct. We must act now!" His tone now firmly conveyed a sense of urgency and destiny, some sort of sacrifice for the greater good. "My friends, time is of the essence. We must act now. And we must do so decisively!"

John Woods was sickened. After years in the military and politics, he could smell manipulation miles away. Playing the Washington game was one thing, but the extermination of even part of humanity was another. He had won several uphill battles in the military and on Capitol Hill, but this one would be the hardest. Nevertheless, the stakes were too high to let go, and sometimes, one had to sacrifice oneself for a just cause.

"Listen to yourself! 'They will self-destruct.' Who are you kidding? All we're doing is preserving our lifestyle, and that's fine. But how can you justify the killing of millions, worse, billions of people? Cause it looks like that's what is needed for your so-called 'preservation'. I'm sorry, but this won't pass!"

"We understand your point, Mr. Woods," Tertius said. "Yet the nature of our organization mandates tough decisions. If you are uncomfortable with our proceedings, maybe it's time for you to reconsider your affiliation."

Quartum feared this would happen; Tertius intervened. He was responsible for the ARM. The tactical operatives executing the bidding of the group with unrivaled efficiency. They were deployed in extreme cases to deal with obstacles to the group's agenda. Their victims included Kennedy and his son, John Jr.

"Or maybe it's time for the group to reconsider its purpose," Woods said. "I'm pretty sure I'm not the only one here who thinks that killing billions of people is insane." He scanned the crowd. No one dared look him in the eye. "Really? You all are cowards. You know that I'm right! In that case, I would like to put a motion on the table for a secret vote." This was his only chance. If enough members felt the way he did but were afraid, a secret vote would grant him the support needed to overturn the Council.

"In this case, let's prepare the ballots," Quartum said.

Before they could follow through with the order, a hand signaled the crowd; it commanded immediate attention. Primus, the head of the

Council, seldom seen at the meetings, even more rarely spoke, uttered one word.

"War."

1

THE CONVOY

In the near future

Fordo, Iran, 125 miles south of Tehran

"WHAT IS OUR ESTIMATED arrival time?" Dr. Hiro asked, the newest member of the team of inspectors from the International Atomic Energy Agency.

"We should be there in twenty-five minutes," Mahmoud, the driver, said.

"I must say, your country is nicer than I thought," the Japanese inspector said, turning to Suri.

"How did you think our country looked?" she replied, perplexed and amused.

"I don't know, more desert, less city. Donkeys, camels, you know?"

"Well, glad you like our country," she said politely, wondering how someone with such high degrees could have little education.

"You know what else is nicer than I thought?"

"Watch your next words carefully, son," Israel's ambassador to the International Conference on Disarmament, Elisha Zvili, said.

"So, what else is Nice, Mr. Hiro?" she said.

"The landscape, of course, the landscape is breathtaking."

"Indeed, our landscape is very nice," she replied. Elisha, the diplomat, chuckled in his beard, yet Azael was not amused.

In the passenger seat, Azael, the chief of security, remained quiet and endured a pretentious scientist making small talk to his beloved.

Her tawny skin, hazel eyes, and wavy black hair tended to overpower even the strongest of men. He understood why she would enthrall the Japanese prodigy. As a world-class scientist, Dr. Hiro could relate to her intellect in a way he never would be able to. In his mind, he wondered if that would be a problem in their relationship. But he couldn't worry about that now.

The Sayeret Matkal operative was assigned to this mission to provide security and gather intelligence for the Israel Defense Force. He was to protect and observe. He heard a thump, then a whistling sound from afar, getting closer.

"Rocket!" he screamed while yanking the steering wheel, taking Mahmoud, the driver, by surprise but narrowly dodging the rocket. The deflagration shook the vehicle off its track, flipping it on its side. Mahmoud's head hit the cracked window. The convoy stopped.

Everything was whirling around Azael. The sky was at his feet. The ground was at his head. With a sudden surge of power running through his veins, he jumped out of the vehicle, using it as cover.

"Get them out of the car now!" he shouted to the driver while shooting in the direction of the rocket.

"Take them in gamma," he ordered.

The four SUVs had been left half empty precisely for situations where, if one vehicle is disabled, the others could take the passengers. The rest of the security detail, Azael's brothers-in-arms, took defensive positions behind their respective vehicles. Armed with Uzi-Pro submachine guns and rifles, they retaliated against an enemy they could barely pinpoint.

"Are you okay?" Mahmoud asked his three passengers.

"I think we're fine," Zvili replied. "Suri, are you okay?"

"Yes, I'm fine," she replied in a shaken voice, still assessing if all her limbs were functioning as usual. They were.

"Hiro, how about you?" Elisha asked.

"I think I broke something. I can't breathe. We're going to die!"

"Calm down. If you want to survive, you must keep it cool," Mahmoud said. "If you can move, get out the back door and quickly hide behind the vehicle."

While trying to regain their balance and orient themselves, the passengers crawled to the back door.

"Is everyone okay?" Azael asked as they reached his side.

"Yes, we're all fine," her voice comforted him. She was unharmed.

"Okay, run to the third vehicle. We will cover you."

"But they're shooting at us," retorted a traumatized Hiro.

"If you don't go now, they will kill you! Run as fast as you can! Go now!" He signaled Eliab, the security detail for the third SUV of the incoming civilians. In concert, they shot towards the mountain flank, hoping to slow down their attackers. Azael ran alongside the IAEA envoys to provide a window for the inspectors to safely pass. "Rocket!" he screamed while tackling them to the ground.

This time, the projectile hit its target. The black SUV flew from the ground and burst into flames midair. It landed back on its wheels, scorched and disfigured. Eliab lay on the floor, lifeless.

Azael looked back only to see the blazing vehicle overshadowing his brother-in-arms' body.

But no time to mourn. The soldiers knew too well the dangers of their mission. He saw the three civilians in harm's way, on the floor, shaken by the blast but alive. His glare locked with hers. Terror filled her eyes. Her stare cried out for him to save her. For a second, they were alone in their minds, holding each other in the comfort of their arms.

The moment was cut short by the sound of gunshots and commotion getting louder and louder. He lifted his eyes and scanned the surroundings. A few yards to his left, the two remaining SUVs were driving back toward the civilians. He turned his attention to the right and saw several all-terrain vehicles and pickup trucks with armed men brandishing machine guns, RPGs, and machetes. Time was running out. Their only chance was to return to the vehicles and hope to evade the attackers long enough to make it to the city.

"Get up! Get up! Run towards the cars as fast as you can! I will cover you!" he shouted.

"What about you?" her mouth said, betraying her heart's true concern.

"I will be fine, ma'am," he replied as professionally and distantly as he could. In a strange way, his words comforted her. His voice seemed to be saying, *"This is not the end. We must still maintain the anonymity of our love."*

For one of Iran's leading nuclear scientists to fall in love with an Israeli special force would certainly mean prison or even death for her perceived betrayal. He would be sidelined and relegated to a desk job pushing papers of no consequence.

"Run now," he asserted with a firm yet gentler tone.

She pulled herself together and sprinted towards the vehicle while the other security details headed in the opposite direction, to Azael's side, hoping to create a protective tunnel affording the civilians a small window to escape the attackers.

"Rocket!" They hit the floor again. This time, the rocket hit the first SUV of the convoy. It stood scorched and disfigured in the middle of the road. Forcing the second and last SUV standing to come to a screeching halt.

The hordes of assailants were now upon them. As chaos broke loose around her, the shouts and the myriads of gunshots, Suri looked around for a comforting presence. As she turned around to look for the man she loved in secret, one shot rang louder than all the others as she witnessed the unthinkable, unbearable sight of the man she loved falling to the ground. She screamed inside her heart, but no words came out of her mouth. No one could know her affection for this man, not even in the face of death. He lay there lifeless. *How could this be?*

Everything around her went dark as the militants bagged her and tossed her into a van.

Azael laid on the ground, holding his breath, hoping the assailants believed they succeeded in killing him. Every fiber of his being screamed, *"Get up and fight! You can't stay there and do nothing! Are you a coward?"*

But his head cooled him down. Outnumbered and outgunned, any outburst would lead to his undoing. More importantly, he might be the only lead and the last chance to save the hostages, to save Suri.

2

AN HONEST WOMAN

Fort Benning, Georgia, in the Columbus Metropolitan area

"THANK YOU FOR COMING to share this special moment with Maddie and me. Before we start, my dad, General Boykin, will say a few words."

Topher was used to operating under extreme pressure, but today, he was as anxious as any other. This little prelude by the general granted him time to breathe and compose himself. The general stepped forward to address the guests. His presence commanded respect and admiration.

"Thank you, son. I would like to take a moment to honor the memory of a special man. As you know, Senator John Woods has passed away from heart failure. He was one of us. I had the honor to serve with him in Iraq and Syria. He was a man of courage and integrity." The general paused, reminiscing in his mind.

"He saved my life more than once," he choked up for a second. "Sorry, but enough talk. We came here to celebrate." He lifted his glass. "To John Woods!"

"To John Woods," echoed by all.

"Thank you, Dad. Okay," Topher said, taking a deep breath. He addressed Maddie's parents. "First, I would like to thank you for raising such an amazing daughter. Mrs. McAdams, you have modeled for her what it means to be a military wife, and I am grateful. General McAdams, you have shown me what being a man of honor and a provider means. You've been my instructor, a mentor, and a second father to me. I am forever indebted to you for all you've done for me and all you've been. So, today, I respectfully ask for your daughter's hand in marriage."

"Topher, my boy, we didn't fly across the country to say no." Mr. McAdams said, teasing. "In all seriousness, I couldn't hope for a better man for my daughter. I had my eye on you through BUD/S. Little did I know you had your eye on my baby girl. But I'm glad you did. You've been takin' good care of her. So yes, you can have her hand."

"Thank you, sir. It will be my honor to care for your daughter for the next one thousand years."

"My dear," interjected Mrs. McAdams. "You're already part of our family, and we couldn't be prouder of you two."

"Thank you, I appreciate that," Topher said. He then turned to Maddie. She wore a white dress with blue flowery motifs matching her eyes. In awe of her natural beauty, his heart started pounding in his chest, his palms were sweaty, and his body temperature rose.

"Maddie, we have known each other since we were kids. You went from being an annoying brat to a not-so-annoying brat to a pretty cool brat when you guys moved out west. Then, I went out west for my BUD/S training. When I saw you again for the first time, the general's daughter, you were different. Something changed. Yes, the braces were gone, and your hair was flawless, but how you cared for others got me hooked on you. You're kind and thoughtful; you can brighten a room with your smile." he paused. "As my very best friend and the mother of my son. You carry me through the demands of my work and take care of Ryan while I'm away weeks and months at a time." Bowing down on one knee, the soldier asked a simple question, "Maddison McAdams, will you marry me?"

"Huh? No! absolutely not!"

The unexpected response caught him off guard, and his body temperature went through the roof. His mind raced, asking himself ten thousand questions, *"What does this mean? How do I turn this humiliation around? Is she leaving me? Is she moving out? What about Ryan? Where did I go wrong?"*

"I got you!" she laughed. "Of course, I'll marry you, Mr. Christopher Boykin!" Everybody in the room laughed in relief. She got down to his level and locked her lips with his. "Yes, I would be honored to be Mrs. Boykin."

As he passed her finger through the diamond ring, he smiled in relief, but his glare flared with a revenge prank. She could read his mind saying, *"Oh! My revenge shall be swift."* She would have to be on her guard. It wouldn't be today, but it would be planned carefully. For right now, they celebrate their love. She repeated the kiss to rebuild his bruised ego.

"All right now!" Shouted an over-enthusiastic guest. Topher rose back to his feet like a lion, wounded yet victorious. He roared, "Whoo-hoo! Guys, we're getting married!" A rare outburst from the cool-headed soldier. "Now, I'd like to ask Kyle to give a few words and give grace for the food."

"Hey, everyone, who would have thought?" Kyle said. "Topher and Maddie are getting married! I guess miracles are possible after all!" He smiled, looking at Maddie and then back at Topher. "If there ever was a match made in heaven, it's this one. Maddie, you're the most positive, outgoing military wife I know. You're always there when someone is in need. I know that you'll take good care of my brother. Topher, since we were little, you had my back in the schoolyard. Later, you bailed me out a few times when I was acting up. With God's help, I'm convinced you will be a great husband as you've been a good brother. Let us pray." All closed their eyes and tilted their head forward out of respect. "Dear God, we thank you for this special moment. We pray that you bless Topher and Maddie in this new step in their lives. Bless the food, Amen!"

All echoed, "Amen!"

"All right, guys, time to eat!" Maddie said, her stomach growling and her feet sore from her day's marathon towards perfection. Every detail mattered. For the first time, she allowed herself to pause. Scanning the room, etching her mind with the faces, their smiles, the laughter, the love. The group wasn't big, but it was strong. All bound together with a sacred cord of duty to the country. Active duty, special ops vets, their spouses, and siblings they were all related to the covert Delta unit of the military in one way or another. They shared an unbreakable bond. They were family.

"Thank you, Kyle, for coming," Topher said. They had different views on how a relationship should be managed. Though younger, Kyle was more old school.

"I wouldn't have missed it for the world. You finally decided to make her an honest woman!"

"Something like that," Topher said. Before the brothers could engage in another heated discussion on the meaning of life and the proper way to conduct oneself, Topher's mobile device vibrated, and his demeanor changed. His focus shifted. He scanned the room and made eye contact with several other guests. They nodded at each other; they were the soldiers of his unit, Special Operators Sigma.

"You got a mission?" Kyle asked.

"Yeah, it's urgent," Topher said, realizing the futility of his comment. They were always urgent and classified.

"So, you're leaving now?"

"Yeah, I got an hour to pack and make it to base."

"I'll leave you to it then. Be safe." He gave him one of those hugs that transpired deep-seated affection without displaying weakness. As they broke, Topher's eyes locked with Maddie's as she made her way to him with Ryan on her tail. They both knew what was about to transpire. He hated those moments of separation. Ryan was older now and would start to notice his absence.

"They called you in?" Maddie said.

"Yes, we have to report to base in an hour," Topher replied.

"They really know how to time these things," she exclaimed in humor. Topher could feel the frustration. She wasn't complaining; she knew what she had signed up for when she decided to love a special operations guy. Yet it would've been nice to have this special moment with him and their friends.

"Yeah, I know. I'm sorry about that. I'll make it up to you when we come back."

"Just make sure you come back before the wedding, Mr. Boykin."

"I will!"

"You should say bye to Ryan. I'm about to send him to bed anyway."

"Roger that," he said, kneeling towards his son.

"Hey buddy, Daddy will be gone for a while, but I'll be back."

"Daddy, you going to work."

"Yes, Daddy is going to work."

"You gonna catch the bad guys?"

"Yes, Ryan, I'm going to catch the bad guys, so they don't hurt anyone. Are you a bad guy?"

"No, Dad. I'm a good guy!'

"Okay, then, take care of your mommy, okay?"

"Okay, Daddy."

"Give me a hug." He gave him a big bear hug. Getting back to his feet and turning to Maddie, he said, "Okay, honey, I'll check in as soon as I can."

They kissed, and she rested her head on his chest for a moment. He kissed the top of her forehead and softly pulled away. "Okay, I love you. Be safe," she said.

Topher took his to-go bag and headed out.

3

THE LAIR

IT WAS EARLY MORNING, but everything was pitch black. Her eyes were wide open, yet unable to see through the black bag her captors had put on her head. Her hands were tied, and her heart was in pieces. The image of her beloved shot down to the ground was plastered in her mind. Yet, she tried to pay attention to her surroundings, listening for peculiar sounds, counting how many turns, and what the total length of the trip was. As she gained some control of her thoughts, the van stopped.

She heard the window come down. She figured it to be the driver's.

"Did everything go as planned?" a man asked.

"Yes," replied the driver."

"Take them to building four, then be on your way. Payment will be made as usual."

The window went back up without a reply from the driver, as if he heard what he wanted to hear. Suri was perplexed. They spoke Farsi with peculiar accents, but she couldn't pinpoint their origin. It sounded like a Pashto accent, but were they Afghans, Pakistanis, or something else? Exhausted, she was trying to piece things together. Maybe that guesswork would give her an edge when the time came to escape or recount the story to the authorities.

A few moments later, the van came to a stop. This time, the engine was turned off, and the doors opened.

The young Japanese genius had no frame of reference for what was occurring. Blinded, bound, and bereft of hope is not how he envisioned this mission going. Inside him, pandemonium, fear, anger, and bravado boiled until his molten entrails erupted.

"Where are you taking us? It's not too late for you to stop this madness. We're international diplomats. You're making a big mistake!"

Without missing a beat, a henchman cooled him down with the back of his machine gun, striking his abdomen.

"Be quiet, you fool," the henchman said.

"Dr. Hiro, are you okay?" Suri said. "Do not hurt him, you savages."

Before she could place another word, her captor struck her. The air fled her lungs. She paid little attention to the pain in her diaphragm. She had a more pressing crisis, breathing. A few endless seconds passed until the oxygen flowed through her system again.

Elisha knew this type of outburst would not accomplish much. Yet he was also tempted to antagonize the guards to become the bad guy. He felt a sense of responsibility. Being the eldest, he had lived a good life. But Suri was young with so much promise. If anyone had to pay the ultimate price, it would have to be him first.

He was ready to lay his life on the line to save the others. *Hopefully, things would not go that far,* he thought to himself. But for that, he had to strategize. He now knew the henchmen had a short fuse. He knew who was the first to act; thus, he was probably not the leader, just a hot-tempered brute. His flow of thought was broken by the sudden current pulling him to the unknown in a succession of crashing waves. Pulls and pushes, thrusting him to their destination. One final push and he found himself on the floor, disoriented. The blind bag snatched away, giving way to a blinding light. It took a few moments for the hostages to adjust their vision.

The terrorists, armed to the teeth, rushed the hostages through warehouse number four somewhere in the industrial district of Pardis City in the Tehran Province.

"Listen up!" Ahmed said in very good English. "If you do as we say and your governments cooperate, we will do you no harm. Otherwise, we will not hesitate to do what we must to get our demands met."

Suri couldn't stop thinking it was a lie. They would still be killed once the terrorists were done propagandizing. Somehow, they had to find a way to escape. Time was scarce, as their captors would certainly try to make a statement to show their resolve. A question haunted her every thought, *who would die first?*

4

THE INITIATION

Twenty-four years ago

QUARTUM WAS QUITE PERPLEXED as he sat down with this twenty-six-year-old internet mogul.

"Are we really inducting a kid, known for disseminating information to the masses, in the world's most secretive and powerful organization?"

Yet the Consortium felt like the opportunity was too great to pass. The new technologies, their connectivity, and the blind following of the masses had created the perfect tool for them to steer the public in whichever way they pleased.

This was a gamble, but one they were willing to take. The founder and president of the FacedIn platform had been very cooperative with authorities ever since the platform came under fire for enabling foreign powers to influence Western elections. He came to understand the burden that rests on his shoulders. The information being shared on his social network had real-life impacts. Old friends were found, new ones were made, crimes were solved, terrorist plots were thwarted, and recruits could be found to join any cause. What better cause could there be than ensuring the longevity of the human race and the dominance of the Old Order?

The meeting pleased Laurence Boseman. Thinking of it as another adventure. He had heard about the Consortium for a long time, and he thought it was the stuff of conspiracy theorists. But he became intrigued with the organization and all the mystery surrounding it. He came to view induction amongst the world's elites of the elite as the ultimate achievement. He already had more money than a small country at twenty-six years old. Influence and fame were his. What else was there? The answer came when Quartum courted him. The opportunity to effect change at the highest levels.

Being part of the secretive group would allow him to impact the world in ways not even world governments and international bodies such as the UN and the WTO could imagine. He would be rubbing shoulders with the real power brokers of the world, those who control those who control the world.

"So, do I have to cut a finger and sign with blood?" he asked.

"No, Mr. Boseman, we are not that type of organization," Quartum said, amused. "No blood is required for your induction, only for your departure," he said smiling, as if he meant it as a joke. It was a possible outcome, especially for someone yielding such power with so little life experience. The Council had to put in place a special contingency plan just for him in case he defected.

Quartum continued.

"If you are willing to join forces with us, you will meet the members of the Consortium. Every member yields power in a sphere of activity necessary for maintaining proper world order and ensuring the longevity of our planet. Your contribution to the group will be to keep our actions off the radar and tell the public what to consider important."

Laurence thought he understood, but for good measure, he thought to ask.

"So, you want me to scrub the internet clean of anything related to you?"

"Not quite. There is already quite a bit of chatter about us. This is inevitable, but nothing accurate and nothing actionable. We want to keep it that way."

"What makes you think I can do that?"

"We know you already do. You almost cost us the last election."

"How so?"

"All the searches relating to our guy were negative. While the ones for his opponent were positive."

"You wanted Rodriguez to be in power?"

"Actually, our first choice was Garrett, but we hedged our bet with Rodriguez."

The tech mogul was a little surprised. Garrett and Rodriguez were career-long arch-rivals. They couldn't be further apart on the political spectrum. How could they both be in the Consortium's pocket?

"How? Garret and Rodriguez are like staunch enemies."

"You see, Laurence, we're not a political party. We are a group concerned with the preservation of the World Order. Whoever occupies the White House, or the Kremlin, is incidental as long as they give us what we want when we want it."

"What if they don't?"

"They always do. The last one to go off-script was Nixon. We put an end to his presidency quite amicably, actually."

"So, Rodriguez is part of the Consortium?"

"Not quite. We find that it's easier to find compliance when one doesn't realize they are complying. They fight harder for what is important to us when they think it's important to them. They are more effective when they believe it's their cause."

Hiding is admiration and a sense of jealousy for not being the architect of such a system.

"So how did I almost cost you the election if both sides were in your pocket?"

"Rodriguez almost lost his primary battle because of a tape going viral."

"But then Schumacher bowed out due to health issues," the light lit in Laurence's mind. *Everything is calculated in advance. Nothing is left to chance. They hedge their bets in more ways than one.*

"Exactly. Members of the group understand it's easier to cut the legs off a soon-to-be viral video than to manufacture a believable health crisis strong enough to force out one of the most driven and stubborn politicians there is."

"So, Schumacher wasn't really sick?"

"Let's just say he might have started the campaign healthy as a bull, but when he announced his departure, he was as truthful as can be."

"You mean you made him sick?"

"I mean, we did what we had to do to ensure a certain outcome beneficial for the greater good."

"That sounds like a lot of work. Why not just kill him?"

"A martyr engenders more sympathy than a quitter. A martyr can have a successor to the cause. A quitter just goes away quietly."

"I see. Very clever. It looks like you have this down to a science. What do you need me for? So far, it sounds like you want me to be your own personal SEO—Search Engine Optimization. Techniques companies use to land on the first page of Giggles."

"I know what it means."

"An organization of your magnitude can impact internet traffic on its own."

"You're right. We have more plans for you." Quartum sensed that Laurence could be easily bored and would need constant stimulus to keep him busy. He thought to himself, *"That kid probably has ADD or some other mental trait making him both a genius and unstable."*

"I'm listening," Laurence said, leaning forward, eager to hear the next word coming out of his counterpart's mouth.

"We want you to be our main source of recruits."

"Isn't that your Job?"

"I'm not talking about The Consortium."

"What are you talking about?"

"We have several organizations doing work for us, knowingly or unknowingly. These organizations are vital to our objectives. We need constant manpower for them."

"What organizations are we talking about?"

"This is privileged information; do I count you in?"

"You had me at hello."

5

THE PREPARATION

Kim Il Sung Square, Pyongyang, North Korea

ONE HUNDRED THOUSAND SOLDIERS ready to die, perfectly lined up. Looking out the window onto the plaza, Chairman Kim was pensive. Staring down at the thousands of young men and women willing to die for their nation, willing to die for his dynasty.

In the past, he would not have entertained doubts. As the supreme leader, his will was, by definition, the right thing to do. He had grown weary of death and conflict. As the heir to the Kim dynasty, his path had been laid out before him. He spent his life consolidating his power at the expense of family members. Whether they showed signs of weakness, like his uncle dozing off during a meeting, or they posed a threat to his authority.

But after all those years, he grew more concerned with the power of life and death. In a real sense, he felt like the father of the nation. All those soldiers were his children. Could he send them to slaughter?

"Chairman, the guests are ready," an aide said.

"Okay, thank you."

Yet the prospect of reunification had never been so bright. There was something in the air. The generals and the troops were reaching a boiling point, ready to explode. He feared they would explode either way. Inside the country and drive him out, or outside the country and drive out the South Korean impostors. Their guards were down after decades of negotiations and goodwill gestures. They had become weak-willed and spoiled by Western thinking. But more importantly, he had some powerful allies now.

"President Chen, I hope your stay is pleasant," he said to his guest of honor.

"It is remarkable, Chairman. Thank you for your generous hospitality."

The two heads of state shared a warm handshake. The chairman peeked over the shoulder of his counterpart and saw the second delegation from another powerful ally.

"It seems I am late?" the Russian president said.

"No, you are right on time, President Lazarev. It is good to have you," Chairman Kim said.

"It is good to be here. It is a shame that this hasn't happened more often in the past," Lazarev said.

"Indeed, we hope we can do this again," Chen continued.

It was a powerful image unseen before. The presidents of China and Russia attending North Korea's military parade was a strong message to the West: *We stand united*. In the past, both countries would send heads of parliament or other dignitaries to the parade. But not this year. This year, they were sending a clear message, not only to the West but to Kim Jong-Soo. *We will stand by you in your quest for reunification, even to the point of war.*

The Chairman felt empowered by their presence but even more by their policy. In defiance of American sanctions, his two powerful neighbors had opened trade routes for his country to do business with the Eurasian Bloc.

"Gentlemen, it's time," the petite Korean assistant said. She exuded confidence and humility as she led the way for the guests of honor.

President Chen and Lazarev knew the North Korean Military parade was very special, but they were not ready for what they were about to experience.

A sea surpassing one hundred thousand people roared in jubilation when they reached the balcony overlooking the parade. It was deafening and impressive. The three men returned the favor by holding their hands up as a sign of victory and salute to this multitude.

The jubilation was as potent as the onslaught of a tsunami. President Chen was humbled by such overwhelming devotion to the Chairman's government. His own country could only achieve compliance of its people with economic prosperity. This dynasty had done it while overcoming UN sanctions and international ostracization.

The Chairman politely let go of his guests' hands and stepped towards the podium. He extended his hand in a gesture demanding silence. A stillness invaded the square. More impressive than the shouts was the rush to hush. In a fraction of a second, a deafening silence took over the historic square.

"My children, we have come far together. This flag, our pioneer founder, and our forefathers will be our light as we claim our victory. You are our future. And our future shines as bright as the stars in the night and the sun in the noontime. Your dedication will ensure that our country remains powerful and prosperous. You will make us proud!

The crowd erupted once more. Kim Jong-Soon took his seat as the Supreme Ruler of the people, the closest thing they have to a god.

6

THE CALL

Fort Benning, Military Compound

CHATTER FILLED THE ROOM while the soldiers were awaiting the top brass' instructions. The room, recently renovated with state-of-the-art holo-conference and surveillance technology, was a far cry from the old dingy briefing rooms.

This allowed the Secretary of Defense and the Secretary of the Army to spread the Delta Units across the country. Having this elite group only in one location, even one as secure as Fort Bragg, seemed ill-advised in this day and age. Terrorists were bolder. Warfare evolved in space and cyberspace. Long gone were the days when the homeland was safe from significant attacks. They feared the wars fought abroad would eventually be fought at home, so they took measures.

The room had three holographic platforms: one used for surveillance feeds, the second for communication with operatives in the field, and the third for communication with military and political officials, generally in Washington, DC.

Right now, they were streaming the news. CNBC, FBN, and CBSN were all streaming muted. Graphs, anchors, and headlines were all mashed together in the background. But a headline caught Chad's attention.

"Hey, can you turn on the volume?" he told the technician in attendance. The action prompted the attention of the team.

"Today, the World Bank confirmed what the Chinese government had been touting for months. China's economy is now the largest in the world, surpassing the US for the first time in modern history. This raises the question: Is the US still the world's top superpower? Here to discuss with us is Dr. Bradley Stevens, an economics professor at the University of Massachusetts."

"What does it matter?" Andy asked.

"It doesn't matter cause we have the most bombs," Max responded.

"It matters because if you have the most money, you can buy the most bombs," Cecilia Kennedy said. "You can buy bigger bombs. Don't underestimate the sleeping giant."

"I agree," Chad said. "If they have the biggest economy, how long until they get the biggest weapons? They already have the biggest army."

"Topher, what do you think?" Max said, diverting attention to their Sergeant Major.

"I think it doesn't matter for now. We have a five-decade head start on them. But it will in the long run. CK is right. More money equals more weapons. So, it's just a question of time before they catch up. We can't let that happen."

"How can we stop that?" Andy asked.

"We have to reclaim the number one spot," Chad said.

"And how will you do that?" Max asked.

"We have to rebuild the economy. Build businesses, innovate."

"So, your solution is a lemonade stand?" Andy quipped. They all chuckled. Chad fired back.

"Oh man, don't sleep on my grandma's lemonade recipe. That's a billion-dollar company right there. Maybe I'll let you work for me."

"I can see Andy in an apron asking, 'What can I get for you today?'" CK piled on.

"What you can get for me today are hostages," General West said as he entered the room with Colonel Yang and Undersecretary Thurman of the State Department.

Yang took center stage.

"Lady and gentlemen, twenty-four hours ago, a UN Convoy was attacked in Iran. Part of that convoy were scientists from a joint task force of the IAEA, the Israeli, and Iranian governments. Dr. Suri Mirzakhani, Dr. Elisha Zvili, and Dr. Hiro Ohira. They have been taken hostage. Responsibility for the attack has been claimed by a militant group going by the name *al-Saalihin*, meaning 'the Righteous'. They are demanding that all sanctions against Iran be lifted, or they will execute a hostage every forty-eight hours."

The undersecretary picked up.

"As you can imagine, that's not a viable option. There is no way the president will lift sanctions. Israel considers the kidnapping of its diplomat an act of war. They believe the terror group to be acting at the behest of the Iranian government. Their war cabinet is meeting to determine the best course of action as we speak. As far as we're concerned, we need them free. They represent our best hope for peace in the region."

"What's the status of their security detail?" Topher asked.

"The security detail agents were all found dead except Azael Azoulay," General West said. "He is MIA. We do not know his whereabouts, if he survived, or if he died, or even if he wasn't part of the attacks."

"Do you think it was an inside job?" Chad asked.

"At this point, we just don't know," Yang answered. "But what we do know is where they're being held. Satellite imagery with drone surveillance has them in the industrial zone in Pardis City, eleven miles northeast of Tehran. We also know that they are vital to our national interest in the region. You will go in as Navy Seals. Your mission is to extract them with no traceable footprint. Upon extraction, you will head to Camp Buehring in Kuwait. From there, the hostages will be debriefed and sent to Israel. You will return home."

"The president thanks you for your service on behalf of our nation, and he will monitor your progress," Thurman said.

"Wheels up in one hour," Yang said. "Your gear is waiting at the armory. Tactical will be conducted in flight. You're dismissed."

7

A SLIGHT MISTAKE

Fifteen years prior

Department of Life Sciences at the University of British Columbia, Vancouver, Canada

"I REALLY DON'T WANT TO deal with them." Dr. Earhardt said.

"I did it last semester. This time, it's your turn." Dr. McMaster said.

"Correction. Last time, I won the toss. This time, I will win again!" Dr. Earhardt said as she looked towards the stack of work piling up on her desk. "At least, I hope."

"Come on, not too long ago, you were one of them," Dr. McMaster replied.

"That's precisely the point. I just left those years. I am not trying to go back."

"So, you'd take analyzing dangerous pathogens over touring the campus with aspiring candidates?"

"Yes! I'll take the viruses any day! Come on, flip that coin!"

She handed him a Loonie, the gold-colored one-dollar coin featuring a serene waterfowl, the tail side. That bird was somehow a source of anxiety for him. The only sight of comfort was the picture of his beloved Queen Elizabeth II, the head's side.

"That's a shame! Heads or tails?"

"Heads."

The senior doctor threw the coin in the air with fierce edge-over-edge rotation. The randomness of the outcome couldn't be more certain. The highly decorated researchers held their breath. The currency reached the apex of its ascent and went into its descent. McMaster reached out and caught the coin with his right hand in mid-air, slapped it over the back of his left hand, and held the position for a second or two. He removed his hand and revealed the result.

"Ah! It's heads! Enjoy your tour, professor!" Dr. Earhardt said.

"That's not fair, two out of three?"

"Na-na-na, It's a one-time deal."

"You're ruthless. You know, I remember when I gave you the tour."

"And look how I turned out," she said. She continued in his British accent. "See, you do a marvelous job, my dear!" Back to her Canadian accent, "Now, if you'll excuse me, I believe we have samples awaiting my attention. Have fun!"

She grabbed her binders and walked away.

"I could have flunked you, you know!" Dr. McMaster said.

"Bye-bye!" She continued to walk off, waving him goodbye.

He grabbed the phone on the desk and dialed the executive assistant.

"Hi, Laura, I will give the tour today."

"Dr. McMaster, you lost again, hey?" Laura said.

"Yeah, I did. I swear this Loonie is tricked. Would you please let me know when they're ready for our department?

"Yes, sir."

The scientist hung up the phone and sat at his desk to squeeze in some work before the group's arrival.

In the lab

Enthused by her victory, Dr. Earhardt looked forward to some quality time analyzing samples and making progress in developing a one-size-fits-all flu vaccine. All the viral mutations and variations made it seemingly impossible to develop one vaccine for all strains. But she was not deterred, embracing the challenge. Surely, there would be a financial reward and perhaps scientific immortality. Being recognized amongst great minds like Marie Curie or her daughter Irene Joliot-Curie was certainly appealing, but her drive was rooted in a deeper desire to save children.

"Okay, guys, let's see if we can save some children's lives today," Dr. Earhardt said. "Derek, did you log the samples?"

"Yes, Dr. Earhardt. They're all in."

"Okay, let me see your chart."

He handed her a binder with printouts of the content of their recent shipments categorized by viral class, originating laboratory, and health threat level.

"Alright, let's start with this batch from the CAP," she said.

"Okay, you got it," Derek responded.

Derek walked to the viral containment unit, pulled out a tray with viral samples, and placed it on her workstation.

"Thank you, Derek," she said.

An hour later

"Here is the atrium. It seats 170 people and is perfect for individual study and group studies," Dr. McMaster said.

The words came out of the doctor's mouth automatically; his thoughts were on his work, and he wondered when this nightmare would be over. Then a voice was heard; it was first in the back of his mind and then came to the forefront.

"Sir, is this when we get to eat the free food?" Kevin said.

"No, young man, that will be in the cafeteria. Just a little bit more to go."

"Okay, this is long!"

Dr. McMaster kept his cool and carried on with his tour. The thoughts in his mind were louder than his voice. They asked, *Why in the world would we offer free food to these ravenous predators? Hopefully, one of them will become a worthy scientist one day."*

A tap on his shoulder brought him back to reality. He turned to see who tapped him. It was Derek.

"Sir Dr. Earhardt is requesting your immediate presence. She said to keep the children in the building and not let them leave. We might have a code orange."

The renowned scientist kept a straight, pleasant face and turned to his visitors.

"Well, how about that? Food is ready. Please follow me to the cafeteria."

They walked for about five minutes into the mess hall.

"Feel free to take whatever you want. It's all included in the tour. Please stay here, and I will come to get you in an hour to complete the tour," Dr. McMaster said.

The excited pupils were too starved to discern the lie McMaster was feeding them. They rushed to the counter while he turned back to Derek.

"I didn't know those vouchers were all-you-can-eat," Derek said.

"They're not. Consider it a payback to the administration. Tell security to discreetly close this place down. We don't want a panic until we know what we are dealing with."

"You got it, sir."

They parted ways. Derek headed to the security desk while Dr. McMaster headed back to the lab. His mind was racing, running through all the different scenarios. What could cause Erika to stop everything and call for a shutdown of the facility? Since they first met on a similar tour, he knew she was special. Back then, she was just Erika; now, she was a doctor in microbiology and virology, one of the best.

As the elder doctor approached the lab, two lab assistants approached him with hazmat suits and masks in hand.

"Oh! This is bad," he said.

"This is just a precautionary measure, sir," Jonathan said.

They entered the changing room.

"Please sit down here. We'll suit you up first, sir, and we'll follow you shortly," Nadine said.

The trio quickly geared up the professor, making sure every inch of his being was sealed off. The procedure normally takes thirty minutes, but the urgency of the moment dictated that they perform the task in ten minutes.

"You're all set, sir."

"Thank you, Nadine."

Dr. McMaster entered the room, headed towards Dr. Earhardt, and searched for her eyes behind the protective glasses of her suit. Through the glare, her stare wasn't one of panic but one of someone with a very serious concern.

"What are we dealing with?" Dr. McMaster asked.

"Come take a look," she answered.

She stepped aside from her station, ceding him her seat.

"What am I looking at?"

"This is one of the unidentified viruses we received from the CAP."

"Okay, were you able to identify it correctly?"

"See, that's the problem. It's not one of the cataloged viruses."

"How do you figure?"

"I ran them in the system. And I can tell you it's an influenza virus."

"Which strand?"

"That's the problem, the strands changed."

"What do you mean?"

"I mean, within a few minutes, it mutated."

"What? Show me."

"Just take a look. You can see for yourself. It has been mutating right before our eyes."

"That's impossible! Those mutations should take weeks or even months. That's not good."

"But wait, it gets worse."

"How?"

"I ran an analysis of its biosafety level. I think it's level four."

"Oh, dear God!"

"The way it's rapidly mutating, I think we might be dealing with our first level five."

They looked at each other intently, trying to process the information. She broke the silence with the obvious question.

"So, what do we do?"

"You alert the CAP. If they sent it to us, they might have sent it to the other labs in the network."

"Whoa! That's more than two dozen of them!"

"Indeed, thirty labs spread out across the whole world. We'd better act swiftly. Offer them our assistance in everything they need."

He walked to the intercom.

"Nadine, Jonathan, do not come in here. Nadine, get the Public Health Agency on the line. We'll need them to come and enact a full containment protocol. Jonathan, relay back to Derek and security. Tell them to shut down the whole campus!"

The young assistant needed clarification.

"Sir, you mean to shut down the building?"

"I mean, shut down the whole peninsula. Have them stop traffic in and out of this area, starting from Granville Street forward. Close down all the bridges, especially the Arthur Laing Bridge. Don't let anybody get anywhere close to the airport."

"Okay, I'm on it!"

With everyone taking care of their assigned duties, the time came for Dr. McMaster to take care of his. The elderly man's heart was racing a little faster; he wished it hadn't come to this. Over his distinguished career, no such thing had ever occurred, at least not to this magnitude. He had dealt with several pandemics and similar situations. He dealt with SARS, H1N1, and COVID-19. But this had the potential to be far worse. It required immediate action. He got to the lab's telephone unit. He pressed the speaker mode.

"Please get me the office of the prime minister."

"Yes, sir, one moment, please."

As he waited for her to get back on the line, he rehearsed how to break the news. But like most bad news scenarios, he figured he'd have to give it to her straight.

"Sir, I have the prime minister on the line."

"Thank you, Laura."

"You're welcome."

"Madam Prime Minister, I hope all is well."

"All is well, Dr. McMaster. You caught me between sessions. What is the matter?"

"Ma'am, I thought it necessary to give you a heads up. We received a routine viral shipment from the CAP."

"Refresh my memory. Who's the CAP?"

"The Center of American Pathologists"

"Oh, okay, keep going."

"Okay, the shipment was supposed to contain a routine influenza virus for studies and assessment of detection readiness. Instead, it contained something we have never seen before."

"What do you mean?"

"Dr. Earhardt, whom you've met, found that this virus mutates almost instantly and, under current standards, would be classified as a level four threat, which is the max, but from what we can make of it, it should be a level five."

"God help us!"

"Indeed, ma'am. We have initiated a full lockdown of the peninsula and call on the Public Health Agency to enact a full containment protocol."

"Good! How can I help?"

"Ma'am, we are still ascertaining all the facts. However, there is a strong likelihood that this virus was sent to about thirty labs around the world. We will need the full weight of Canadian diplomacy and your relationships to get all of them back."

"Absolutely! All those samples must be retrieved and destroyed."

"And Ma'am, you might want to loop in CSIS."

"They're already on this call. They'll coordinate with the CDC, FBI, and CIA if need be."

"Oh, I see."

"Thank you for your diligence, doctor."

"Of course."

"And doctor, let's keep a lid on this situation. Worse than the virus, is the panic that would ensue if the information were to go public. So, we will get a handle on it. Our office will take care of the press."

"Yes, ma'am."

He hung up with the prime minister and headed back to Dr. Earhardt.

"Just got off the phone with Camden. She'll do what is necessary to get those samples back to the CAP. What did they say?"

"They were shocked. I can't tell for sure, but they seemed embarrassed, like a kid caught with their hand in the cookie jar. Regardless, they issued a recall notice to go out today. How do you think this happened?"

"How do you think?" He paused. "It's a bioweapon. They were indeed caught with their hands in the cookie jar. A chemical weapons cookie jar."

"So, you think they manufactured it to be some kind of flu-like chemical weapon that somehow got mixed up in their orders and sent us the wrong one?

"That's what it looks like."

"Shouldn't we tell somebody?"

"Only if you want a premature death. Besides, I can guarantee the CSIS already knows. So, we don't tell anyone, we let them handle the press."

"So, what do we do now?"

"We make sure no one talks to the press. We let the Public Health Agency address the media. We fall in line with their story. And we hope and pray that all those samples come back."

8

THE SEARCH

Golpayegani Hospital, Fordo, Iran

"THEY ARE STILL SEDATED, sir," Dr. Farhad said.

"When do you expect them to wake up?" Detective Zarif said.

"The driver should wake up any moment now. As for the other two, they were in a very bad condition. It will be several hours until they wake up."

"It's days like these that make me lose my hair!"

"I understand, sir. We are doing everything we can—"

"I don't think you understand, Dr. Farhad. The Foreign Ministry is breathing down my neck. I'm getting calls from the president's office. I need to talk to them now. Wake them up if you have to!"

"With due respect, sir. You don't understand. If we wake them up before time, it will hurt them, maybe even kill them. Do you want to add to the death toll? These three are lucky to be alive. Now, Detective Zarif, like I said, the driver should be waking up soon."

"Sir, sorry to interrupt, he's gone," Nurse Zamani said.

"Who's gone?" Dr. Farhad said.

"The driver, Mahmoud Hosseini."

"How can this happen? I thought you said he was sedated?" Detective Zarif said.

"He was. He must have woken up?" Dr. Farhad said.

"Well, obviously! Where is he?"

"Don't worry, detective, he couldn't have gotten far. He is probably still disoriented, trying to get home."

"Wait, sir, there's more," The nurse said.

"What is it?" Dr. Farhad said.

"His wife just arrived."

"Have her wait in the waiting room while we find her husband. And have security look for him. He should still be in the hospital."

"Yes, sir."

"Hold on. When was the last time you checked up on him?" Detective Zarif said.

"Fifty minutes ago, Detective," the nurse replied.

"So, he could be long gone by now?"

"Sir, there's no way he got far with the amount of sedative in his body," Dr. Farhad said. "He's most likely still in the hospital. Nurse Zamani, tell security and take a few other nurses with you and find him!"

"Yes, sir, right away."

"Do you have a functioning surveillance system?" Zarif said.

"Yes, of course," Dr. Farhad said.

"Can we take a look at the footage?"

"Yes, follow me."

The pair headed to the security center.

"Mostafa, did Nurse Zamani talk to you?" The doctor asked the security officer.

"Yes, doctor, she did. We are looking for him right now. So far, no luck."

"Don't look for him now," Zarif said. Look for him about an hour ago and trace his movements."

"Okay, let's see. This is his room's hallway. Rewinding to an hour ago," Mostafa said.

"Wait, stop," Zarif said.

"Yes, I see him," Mostafa said.

"Where is he going?" Dr. Farhad said.

"Excuse me. I'm very sorry to disturb you, Doctor. But Mr. Hosseini's wife is getting restless. She wants to see her husband."

"Tell her he's undergoing treatment and will come out soon," Dr. Farhad said.

"Don't do that. Bring her here instead," Zarif said.

"What, we can't do that. This is a restricted area," Farhad said.

"I know, but who can tell us where he might have gone better than his wife?" Zarif said.

"We don't know that he left. He might still be here," Farhad said.

"Sirs, he exited the building," Mostafa confirmed.

"Nurse, bring her here," Zarif ordered.

She looked at her boss, and he nodded. She stepped back out at a hurried pace.

"Where is he going?" Zarif asked.

"We lost him! He's out of frame," Mostafa said.

"Don't you have cameras covering the rest of the area?"

"No sir, we only cover the hospital grounds," Mostafa said.

A few moments later, Nurse Zamani returned with the restless guest.

"Sir, this is Mrs. Hosseini," she said.

"Thank you for coming, 'ma'am," Dr. Farhad said.

"What is going on? Where is my husband?"

"That's what we need your help with," Zarif said. "Less than an hour ago, he left the building. Take a look." He stepped to the side to give her a clear view of the screens. And turned to the head of security. "Rewind it for her."

"Yes, sir," Mostafa replied.

"Here he is when he's about to exit...and here he is outside," Detective Zarif said, pointing to the man on the screens.

She stepped closer to the screens, looking attentively. Her eyes squinted, a frown developed, the tension in her jaw muscles intensified, and she was puzzled for a moment.

"That's not my husband!"

"What?" Zarif said.

"That man is not my husband."

The detective looked at the doctor, the nurse, and back at the doctor.

"Then who is this?" he asked.

"I don't know, but that's not my husband! Where is my husband?"

Nurse Zamani grabbed the phone and dialed an extension.

"Can you bring me Mahmoud Hosseini's admission file? I'm at security."

"So, ma'am, you've never seen this man?" The detective sought confirmation.

"Never! What is going on? Where is my husband?"

Confused, distraught, she paused. Her eyes widened; they swelled with water, and her hand covered her mouth.

"Oh no, he is dead! He is dead, isn't he?"

"Let's not jump to conclusions. Where is that file?" The doctor said, feeling the pressure mounting tenfold. *How could we have the wrong guy? Was it a clerical error? Did the mayhem caused by their arrival create so much confusion that the staff mixed files? Maybe her husband is one of the other patients?*

"It's coming, sir," Nurse Zamani said as she wrapped her arm around the grieving spouse. "Don't worry, ma'am, I'm sure it's all just a misunderstanding. Everything is going to be alright."

The detective couldn't stand still too long, so he commanded the security officer.

"Go back to when they were admitted."

"Yes, sir," Mostafa tinkered with his equipment. "Here you go, sir." All the screens were synchronized to the same timecode. "This is when the ambulances arrived, sir."

"Thank you." He turned to the wife and adopted a more compassionate tone. "Ma'am, I know this is hard, but can you see if any of the patients is your husband?"

Nurse Zamani disapproved, but before she could raise her objection to Mrs. Hosseini's being subjected to an excruciating exercise, the doctor nodded to her to let it go.

Mrs. Hosseini wiped the tears off her face. She tried to focus on the blurry images as she pierced through tears.

"I can't tell for sure, but none of them look like my husband." She tried to find a point of reference, an article of clothing she might recognize, but to no avail. Sorry, I don't know, I don't know."

"It's okay, ma'am," Nurse Zamani said.

The door opened.

"Excuse me, you asked for Mr. Hosseini's admission file?" a nurse said as she handed the files to Nurse Zamani.

"Yes, Fatima, thank you." She opened the file to the picture ID. "Ma'am, is this your husband?"

"Yes, that's him. But that's not the man you showed me."

Nurse Zamani looked at her boss.

"Maybe the files were mixed up at intake?"

"Can we go visit the rooms of the other patients?" The detective asked. "We won't ask any questions. We just want to confirm their identity."

The physician was reluctant, worried about the safety of his patients.

"Yes, of course, but only to confirm identities."

"Thank you, doctor. Mrs. Hosseini, would you come with us, please?"

She felt a glimmer of hope. "Yes, detective."

They set forth on what felt like the longest journey of their life. For Dr. Farhad, the integrity and reputation of his establishment were at stake; the detective needed answers for his superiors, and Mrs. Hosseini needed her friend, the love of her life, to be alive. To be there. They made it to the first room. The patient was still unconscious from the anesthesia. A breathing mask partly covered his face.

"Ma'am, is this your husband?" While asking the question, Detective Zarif took the file folder and opened it at the picture ID to ascertain the answer for himself.

She looked with hope in her heart. But reality set in.

"No, that's not him".

"Okay, let's see the other one. Lead the way, doctor."

"This way," the doctor said.

They headed out on an even longer journey to the second patient. When they arrived at the room, Mrs. Hosseini froze before entering.

"It's okay, ma'am, you can come," the doctor said.

She stepped into the room and made her way to the bed. She looked at him, her head tilted down, her eyes closed. Her demeanor betrayed the answer.

"It's not him." Nurse Zamani immediately put her arm around her.

"It's okay, we'll find him," The detective said. "Let's go check the morgue."

"Okay, this way," the doctor said.

Time stood still as their legs moved one after the other towards their final stop for answers. As they entered the waiting area, they could feel the chilling current.

"Dr. Farhad, how can I help you?" The attendant said.

"We are looking for one of the victims of today's attacks." Taking the folder from the detective, he showed the attendant the picture of Mr. Hosseini.

"Hum, I think that would be this one," He opened a sliding drawer. They all gathered closer. Mrs. Hosseini made it to the side of the drawer. She took one look at the corpse and fell to her knees in pain and agony.

"Oh no! Oh no. Mahmoudi, Oh Mahmoudi!"

Nurse Zamani got down by her side and tried to comfort her.

"I'm so sorry for your loss."

Dr. Farhad turned to the detective for the next steps, but he had already walked out, dialing his cell phone.

"It's Zarif. Give me the chief, please."

"Right away, sir...sir, here is the Chief," Dispatch said.

"Zarif, what have you found about the attack?"

"Sir, we have a man on the loose."

"What do you mean?"

"I'm at Golpayegani. One of the survivors of the attack left the hospital. He was misidentified as a driver. We just found out the driver is dead. So, we have no idea who that individual is. We need a citywide search. We don't know if he is a friend or a foe."

Namak Neighborhood, Tehran

"How long till we make it?" Azael asked.

"We are right around the corner, sir," The driver said.

His face was placid, almost aloof, but his mind was racing, analyzing, strategizing. His heart, just like his body, was hurting. The painkillers were wearing off, but the physical pain was secondary. Only one thing mattered: find Suri before it was too late.

The driver pulled over to the side of the bustling street in the heart of the district.

"Here you are, sir. If you liked the service, please give me a five-star rating in the app."

Azael didn't linger nor look back, avoiding any eye contact. With his body halfway outside the car, he replied,

"I sure will. Thank you very much."

He set his sights on the Golestan Gym. He observed from a distance, looking for patterns, cameras, and breakdowns in the security system. The facilities looked like they had seen better days. Even so, it was crowded.

Only one employee was manning the front desk. He stepped away for a brief moment. It's all Azael needed to slip through to the male locker room.

The space was narrow, with wooden benches facing faded green lockers. Two patrons were in the locker room. One gentleman in his mid-twenties was sitting on the bench putting on his running shoes. And a middle-aged man was combing his hair and fixing himself to leave. To the left, a corner revealing three unused stalls. He took the one at the end. Finally, a moment of privacy. A time to breathe, a time to assess his stitches. He took off his shirt and gently probed his chiseled right pectoral muscle. He thought *they did a good job, the surgical compound works wonders.* Still, he needed to be careful; in any extreme situation, this wound could reopen.

About two minutes later, the locker room was finally empty. The young man was about his size. Azael sped to the locker. In about fifteen seconds, the three-number combination lock was unlocked as if he already knew the code. He took the clothes but was careful to leave the wallet, watch, and other valuables, but he took the cash. He headed back to the stall, changed his attire in the blink of an eye, and dumped his clothes in the garbage can. Casually, he headed towards the front entrance unnoticed.

Once he passed the threshold, he picked up the pace. He looked around, but there were no cabs to be seen. The subway would offer the cover of a crowd, but there were too many cameras. A rideshare would leave an easy trace. Walking would take hours, hours he didn't have. Every minute mattered. Every second that passed could be Suri's last. He could steal a car, but that would activate the authorities. *"This is Tehran. There must be a cab somewhere,"* he thought to himself. He looked around, and his fate turned as the yellow vehicle turned the corner. He waved at the cab.

"Where to?"

"Elahiyeh Shopping Center, please."

"Yes, sir. Are you a diplomat?"

Azael was not looking for a conversation, but being rude could have the adverse effect of making him memorable. *Let's play along for now.*

"No, I'm not."

"Oh, okay, what do you do for a living?"

Azael could see this conversation going on for the whole ride, but he had to cut it short.

"I'm a sales representative."

"Oh, wow, what do you sell?"

"Clothes."

"Oh, do you work for a big fashion brand?"

"No, we just sell uniforms for plant workers. By the way, what do you think of the Iranian selection this year? Do you think they'll make the World Cup?"

"Ah, man! I think the selection has some good players but needs more to advance further. You see..."

The words became jumbled one after the other. The special forces agent's strategy was to keep him talking about nothing significant. So, when they parted ways, his remembrance would be nothingness.

Seventeen minutes elapsed. The conversation centered around the Iranian football team. Just as fast as it started, it was over.

"We are here, sir," The cab driver said.

"How much do I owe you?"

"Two hundred thousand rials"

"Here you go. Nice talking to you."

He handed over the cash without hesitation. He hurried out of the vehicle.

"Thank you, be safe!"

"You too, sir."

A fast right, giving his back to the driver. He walked with his head down towards the luxurious building entrance until the cab was out of sight. He continued on foot to the Statesmen Suite apartment building.

The security was rudimentary; he could go with a direct approach and take out the security, but he'd rather be discreet. The security was tailored for approaching cars but ill-prepared for pedestrian threats.

He walked on the sidewalk towards the back of the building. There was a delivery truck parked at the service entrance. He slipped through undetected by the staff. He headed to the eighth floor using the staircase. He opened the door and peeked through the hallway. The coast was clear. He walked with confidence while looking towards the ground. Third door on the left, in one seamless movement, he put his hand in his right pocket, took out a bump key, inserted it in the keyhole, gave it a bump, unlocked the door, and entered the apartment.

He figured he had about two hours before his target came home. The apartment was classic Persian decor with a colorful bronze-themed rug, brown chairs and sofa, and a wooden coffee table in the middle of the living room. Abstract paintings on the walls and a tint of frankincense filled the air.

Azael felt his strength leaving him. The adrenaline from the day was wearing off. He needed a moment. Per his estimation, one hour should be enough; he had probably had two before his unwitting host came home.

Toward the back of the living room, the hallway led to the bedrooms. He headed to the guest room, which had been set up more like a study than a bedroom. A desk in the back of the room was overshadowed by a bookshelf embedded in the back wall. To the left of the room was a futon opposite the TV. The window let in some light through the curtains. The sound of the street was barely noticeable. He sat on the futon, thinking about his next move. The adrenaline subsided, and his upper eyelids connected with his lower eyelids. In the blink of an eye, forty-seven minutes later, he came back to consciousness, staring down the barrel of a gun.

"What are you doing here, stranger?"

The adrenaline resurged, and instantly, his senses were at their peak. In one fell swoop, he maneuvered his head and body away from the weapon. With a swift hand strike, he swiped the gun from his assailant's hand and turned it on him.

"You're getting soft," Azael said. "Too much embassy food?"

They both laughed.

"Me getting soft? I found you snoring on my sofa," Nikolas said.

Azael put the gun down, and they hugged.

"It's been so long," Nikolas said, putting his two hands on Azael's shoulders.

"Way too long, Nikolas. Take it easy; this thing still hurts." He pointed to his shoulder.

"Gunshot wound?"

"Yes."

"So, you were in this attack earlier?"

"Yes, I was."

"Were you doing the attacking or the defending?"

"Security detail for the IAEA."

"Oh no! Suri! She was in that delegation?"

He nodded.

"I'm so sorry. Is she...?"

"She was alive when they took them."

"What are you planning to do?"

"I'm going to find her."

"That's not going to be easy."

"I have to. If I don't find her, I'll find them, and they'll wish they were never born."

"How can I help?"

"I need to know everything there is to know about them. Who are they? What do they want? Who is their leader?"

"All I know so far is that it's al-Saalihin. Don't worry. I'll activate my sources. We'll find her."

"Thank you. Do you have a secure line I can use?"

"Yes, of course, hold on."

He stepped out of the room for about thirty seconds. He came back with a slim satellite phone.

"Here you go," Nikolas said while handing over the phone.

"Thank you," Azael said.

Azael dialed a number out of memory.

"Denris International, my name is Alona. How can I help you?"

"Hello, my name is Obed. Something is wrong with my order."

"What does it do?"

"That's the problem. It does nothing."

"One second, let me connect you with technical support."

The line plays, holding music for a brief moment.

"Technical support, my name is Ben. How can I assist you?" The male voice on the line said.

"My device has sustained water damage," Azael said.

A sigh of relief sounded on the other side of the line.

"Azael, you're alive!" Aluf Tishbi said.

"Yes, sir, I survived."

"It's good to hear your voice, son. How about the rest of your detail?"

"As far as I can tell, none made it out. I sustained a gunshot wound to the shoulder, but I'm operational."

"Where are you right now?"

"I'm in Tehran on the trail of our attackers. I secured some logistical support from an ally."

"Who?"

"Nikolas Scherzinger"

"Good."

"What do we know so far?"

"Well, so far, we know that they're a part of al-Saalihin. Their demands are ridiculous in nature."

"Any word on their location?"

"We think they're somewhere in Pardis. But we're working on confirmation. These guys are pros. So, satellite wasn't useful."

"How confident are you about the intel?"

"Very."

"Okay then, that's where I'll start."

"Azael, there are two things you should know."

"I'm listening."

"First, a group of American Navy Seals is on its way."

"Okay, what's the second?"

"Elisha Zvili is one of the architects of our modern nuclear arsenal. It could be catastrophic for our nation if they find out who he is. We can't let that happen. The higher-ups are exploring the possibility of a preventive strike against Pardis once we can pinpoint their location."

"What? They can't do that!"

"They can and they will. The only peaceful way out is for you to find the hostages before they do. I have to go. The meeting is about to start."

9

PREEMPTIVE STRIKE

Tel Aviv, Kirya Compound

TENSION PERMEATED THE CONFERENCE room as the military officers and civilian members of the general staff took their seats. Aluf Boaz Tishbi sat down, perplexed about what was about to happen.

He looked around the room. The main table placed in front of the room was still empty. One of the benefits of being in a semi-circular room was that one had a clear line of sight of everyone. The faces and postures spoke loudly to him. The room was quiet, with none of the usual chatter.

Aluf Sharon Piles, head of the Eastern Command, was crouched on the table, holding his chin and covering his mouth. Right next to him was Aluf Deborah Wiseman. She had a look of resolve and confidence in the face of crisis. *Is it sincere, or is she overcompensating? If so, for what?*

While the thoughts were still on his mind, Aluf Zechariah Ben-Zamir, chief of the general staff, made his entrance with the deputy chief of the general staff and the commanders of the Army, the Air Force, and the Navy.

The officers and civilians rose to attention to salute their superiors. Aluf Zechariah didn't allow them to be at ease rather, he stood at attention himself. The air was sucked out of the room when Prime Minister Ya'aqov Dahan entered, accompanied by his military secretary, the director general of the Ministry of Defense, and the foreign minister. They walked decisively to their assigned seats at the head table, joining Aluf Ben-Zamir and the commanders.

Prime Minister Dahan signaled softly with his right hand,

"At ease."

Everyone sat. Their bodies were at ease, but their minds were at full attention.

With a simple nod, Prime Minister Dahan signaled Ben-Zamir to start.

Ben Zamir, the top official of the Israel Defense Force, nodded back at the prime minister and turned to his audience.

"Ladies and gentlemen, thank you all for being here. As you all know, an IAEA convoy was attacked earlier today in Iran. We believe the scientists and diplomats are still alive. They are being held hostage as bargaining chips. One of the hostages is Elisha Zvili."

The elders in the room gasped.

"For those unfamiliar with Dr. Zvili's significance, he is one of the architects of our modern nuclear program. All the major strategic advancements of our defense system for the past forty years have been in some way related to his work. He is the reason we are a twenty-first-century military power. If his abductors realize who he is, our national security would be irreversibly compromised."

"And whose idea was to let our top scientist in enemy territory?" Tishbi blurted out, forgetting the decorum of such a meeting.

"There will be plenty of time for recrimination, Aluf Tishbi," Prime Minister Dahan said. "Right now, we must determine a course of action."

Prime Minister Dahan didn't have time for back and forth. He continued.

"So, what are our options?

Zamir retook the floor.

"We have three options, Sir."

All ears, Dahan leaned forward.

"Option one, let it play out and hope that we can retrieve the hostages through diplomatic means. Option two, we send our special operators to execute a rescue mission."

"Sorry to interrupt," Aluf Wiseman said. "Per your indication, if they break Zvili, our very existence is at risk. We can't take that chance with option one. As for option two, do we have their exact location?"

"No, Aluf Wiseman, not yet. We know they are in the Pardis sector, but as for their exact location, we are still working on it."

"So, what's option three?"

"A preemptive strike on the Pardis region. We are confident we can narrow down the location to one block. We could take that block out. It being an industrial zone, the civilian casualties would be minimal if done at night. We estimate no more than three hundred people would die." Zamir said.

"That includes the hostages?" Aluf Wiseman asked.

"Yes, ma'am, including the hostages and their abductors." The silence in the conference room was deafening. The greatest military minds in the Middle East understood the gravity of each option. Prime Minister Dahan felt it necessary to make sure everyone grasped the stakes. Maybe it was the academic in him or his remembrance of the battlefield.

"Just so we are all clear." He took a deep breath. "If we go with option one, we might get the civilians back alive but face the risk of terrorist attacks or even military attacks tailored to cripple our defenses. Thus, we are giving our enemies a shot at what they have wanted for centuries, our extinction."

He looked across the room in the eyes of his commanders.

"If we go with option two, the time needed to pinpoint the hostage location and mount an effective rescue might be enough for the abductors to find out who Zvili is and what he knows. That's if they don't already know. In which case, we're back at number one whether the mission is successful or not."

He leaned back on his chair.

"Which leaves number three. A preemptive strike on one block with low population density."

He leaned forward again with elbows on the table, two hands clasped together as if he was about to pray.

"This is a de facto declaration of war on the Iranians."

"Yes, sir, but at least it would be a battle we are ready for. We've prepared for that contingency for decades. We're not prepared for someone taking down the very foundation of our defenses." Zamir said.

The prime minister turned to his foreign minister.

"How do you think our allies would react?"

She cleared her throat.

"It's hard to tell, sir. Surely, the Americans would help. The Saudis might as well. Bahrain and the Emirates would most likely be dragged along and on the front lines of a full-out war."

He turned back to Ben-Zamir.

"Can we prevail by ourselves if we need to?"

"It would be a tough war, but we would prevail. If they get their hands on Zvili's knowledge, victory would not be assured."

"Casualties?"

"We estimate that the preemptive strike leading to war will cost one hundred thousand Israeli lives. A war fought on their terms with advanced knowledge of our defense architecture would lead to a catastrophic outcome with losses potentially in the millions."

Placid in his facial expression, Prime Minister Dahan looked around the room. He saw that they trusted him to make the right call, but he trusted them to pull through victory in the end.

"I think we all know what needs to be done. Prepare the strike, do it covertly, but get it done. Schedule a call with President Rodriguez. God help us all."

All started to gather their file folders. Tishbi did so as well, but a battle waged in his mind. The information he had could change the outcome and save thousands or even millions of lives, but though the room is filled with top security clearances, he is not convinced they can all be trusted. In the wrong hands, this information could jeopardize their competitive advantage. But if he kept quiet, they would chart a course of cataclysmic proportions.

"Excuse me, sir. I apologize. Can I talk to you in private, please?" Tishbi said.

The prime minister and his entourage were surprised, even annoyed, by the request. But the prime minister obliged.

"Everybody, leave us," Dahan said.

Most of the contingent exited the room. Only the prime minister, Aluf Ben-Zamir, and Aluf Wiseman stayed in the room.

"What's on your mind, Aluf Tishbi?" Dahan asked.

He hesitated still and thought to himself, *they are the Chief Executive, the Chief Military, and the Chief Intelligence Officer. If I can't trust them, who can I trust?*

"Sir, there might be a better way. It's a long shot, but under the circumstances, it might prove to be a better option."

"We're listening," Dahan said.

"We have an asset on the ground."

Their eyes widened, and their attention piqued.

"An elite special operator. He was in the convoy but somehow survived. He is currently awaiting orders in our safe house in Oudlajan. He is one of our best. If he locates the hostages, I am confident he can rescue them."

"Who is that operative?" Wiseman asked.

"Ma'am, for his safety, I would rather keep that to myself for now, if you don't mind."

"I do mind. How can we assess the odds of success if we don't even know who's on the ground? And how dare you withhold the identity of one of my guys?"

"Ma'am, I mean no disrespect, but I can't. The convoy's itinerary was need-to-know only, yet it leaked to al-Saalihin. Somebody betrayed us."

"You're being a little paranoid right now," Ben-Zamir said.

"Sir, with all due respect, our men are the best in the world, but we can't take that kind of chance with our national security," Wiseman continued.

"What we can't do is plunge headfirst into a war you know full well could cost us everything! Not if there's another way! This guy can get it done! We just have to give him enough time!" Tishbi said.

"Time is not something we have right now!" Wiseman said. "You're asking us to put the fate of our nation on the shoulders of someone we don't even know?"

"No, ma'am, I'm asking you to trust me!"

"Sorry, Tishbi, but that's not enough."

"Fine, his name is Arnon Saban, Mistaravim."

She made a quick phone call.

"Send me everything you have about Arnon Saban to my secure line. Do it now, thank you."

"Sir, I think we're wasting time. We should proceed with the plan without delay." Ben-Zamir said.

Wiseman's phone vibrated. She took a rapid look at the encrypted file.

"This is indeed one of our best. At first glance, his record is both impressive and impeccable."

"How long until we are ready to strike?" Dahan asked.

"Our timetable is twelve hours to send the strike force, alert our personnel, and be ready for retaliation," Ben-Zamir said.

"Okay, your operator has twenty-four hours," Dahan said to Tishbi.

"Sir, I think that's a mistake!" Ben-Zamir said.

"I know how you feel. But if he can get it done, countless mothers will not have to bury their sons and daughters. Twenty-four hours, make sure he has what he needs." Dahan said.

Ben-Zamir's facial muscles tensed up, but his mouth uttered,

"Yes, sir."

"Thank you, sir. I would like to run point on that operation if that's okay," Tishbi said.

"That's fine. You three can coordinate your resources to give our guy the best chances possible." A subtle knock on the door.

"Sorry to interrupt, sir," the aide said.

"That's okay. We were done."

"You're scheduled with Washington in thirty minutes."

10

POWDER KEG

White House, Situation Room

"LADIES, GENTLEMEN, IN APPROXIMATELY ten hours, Israel will strike Tehran Province in the Pardis district," President Rodriguez said. "Iran will retaliate. The question is: how? What are the ramifications and risks to American interests and our allies in the region, primarily Israel?"

"Mr. President," General McIntyre, the Chairman of the Joint Chiefs of Staff, said. "In the event of a direct, overt hit to Iran, we can expect Iran to launch an all-out war. This will rapidly devolve into a regional war."

"Run it for me."

"After a direct strike on their territory, we estimate that Iran will retaliate in kind. Since they do not share a border, initially, they will try to destabilize Israel with rocket attacks from their proxies in Lebanon and Syria, which would prompt Israel to counter with attacks on those neighbors. In turn, Israel will try to launch operations from the UAE and Bahrain. This might explode the tensions in Yemen, at which point the Saudis would have to get involved to protect their interest."

"Casualties?"

"Impossible to determine, sir, in the hundreds of thousands if not millions."

"Any way to prevent that?"

"The only way to prevent a full-on Middle Eastern conflict is for Israel to stand down or for us to step up with overwhelming force."

"Sir, if I may."

"Go ahead, Steve."

"Could you leverage the prime minister and maybe convince him to stand down?"

"That's doubtful. They are dealing with an existential threat. There's no deterring them."

"Can the strike be covert?"

"General McIntyre?"

"The timeframe we're dealing with doesn't afford us the time necessary to plan such an operation."

"Mr. President, with due respect," Steve said. "If Israel decides unilaterally to launch an attack against Iran, why are we being dragged into it?"

"Steve, no one is being dragged into anything. But we must be proactive in the event the situation devolves. So, we're looking at our options."

"We send them billions of dollars each year. They should be able to handle it on their own. But the truth is, they can't. They know we're going to bail them out."

"Mr. President, if I may," Kate Simmons said. "It's not about bailing people out, but ask yourself, are you okay with a scenario where millions of people die? We've been there before, where we stood by and let people solve their issues. What happened? A million Rwandans killed, and six million Jews killed until we put an end to it. This is a powder keg. If we let this thing play out, we might have a nuclear conflict on our hands, and then what? We must nip it in the bud now!"

"What about our boys?" President Rodriguez said.

"General Dunn?" Chairman McIntyre said.

"Thank you, general. They are en route to the location where we believe the hostages are being held. They are meeting up with an Israeli asset on the ground. Their operational window is seven hours. If they succeed during that timeframe, we will avoid this conflict. Pass that time, we'll pull them out for their safety."

"Let's hope they can get it done," Rodriguez said.

"Sir, sorry to interrupt."

"What's the matter, Sarah?"

"Permission to speak freely?"

"Granted."

"North Korea just launched a full-scale attack on the South."

11

SEVEN HOURS

"TECHNICAL SUPPORT, MY NAME is Ben. How can I assist you?"

"My device has sustained water damage."

"Where are you now?" Tishbi said.

"I'm in Pardis," Azael said.

"The Americans are on their way. The authentication is in your inbox."

"Understood."

"Azael."

"Yes, sir."

"You remember Arnon Saban?"

"From Mistaravim?"

"He's dead."

"How did he die?"

"I killed him."

"What? How?"

"I threw him under the bus to protect you. Our military is compromised at the highest levels. I'm not sure who, but they're in the inner circle. I needed to buy you some time. So, I told my superiors that he was our asset in Tehran. Next thing you know, the Iranian Revolutionary Guard shows up at his location. He didn't stand a chance."

"How much time do I have?"

"You have seven hours left. Then they'll level Pardis."

"That's not enough! I need more time and more manpower."

"All you have are the Americans. They're not sending anyone else. I risked everything to get you those hours. I wish I could have convinced them to send a unit, but that wasn't possible. Someone wants this strike to happen no matter what."

"I don't need Americans; I want one of our teams. We can get it done faster and more effectively."

"That's all I can do, Azael. If you want help, that's all you'll get for now," He paused. "I beg of you. For the sake of all that is good in this world, please do not fail."

"I won't." They hung up. Azael thought to himself, *"I can't fail. All that is good in my world is her."*

12

INFILTRATION

Boeing C-17 Globemaster V Over the Caspian Sea

THE ROAR OF THE engines had become silent, white noise no longer noticeable.

"Everyone, gather up. Let's run this thing one last time." Topher, code-named Wave Runner, said.

"Let's do it!" Andy, code-named Eager Beaver, said.

Spontaneously, they surrounded the holographic table displaying a 3D rendition of the neighborhood and building where the hostages were being held.

"From the top." Cecilia, code-named Mockingbird, said.

With a hand gesture, Cecilia contracted the holographic rendition to show a wider range of the Iranian territory from the Caspian Sea to Khojir National Park.

"When we fly out of here, we'll adopt a loose formation until we hit Chalus," Wave Runner said. "There, we'll regroup and refuel bodies and equipment at the safehouse. After thirty minutes, we fly out straight to Pardis, which is about seventy miles out. With good winds, that should be thirty to forty minutes at the most. Our rendezvous point is right here, about two miles from our target location. At that point, we reassess the data. If we are a go, Chad, you take overwatch on the Khomeini building. Stay sharp and keep us golden."

"Roger that," Chad, code-named Green Arrow, said.

"Andy, you head to the transformer up the street and turn off the lights for the whole block."

"You got it, boss," Andy said.

"Max and CK, you're with me," Wave Runner continued. "Firearms are a last resort. Take the enemy out the old-fashioned way. For proper weight balance, CK, you got Zvili, Max, you have Dr. Hiro, and I have Dr. Suri. They might not be ready to get flown out on a flyboard. If that's the case, for their safety, knock them out."

"What do we do about the Israeli guy they want us to work with?" Green Arrow said.

"We don't have time to babysit anybody," Wave Runner replied. "We get in, get out! Watch each other's backs, find the hostages, get them back to their families, and we get back to ours."

"I'm sure he'll be real cool with that," Andy said.

"Okay, fine, he's yours, Beaver. He'll cover you at the transformer."

"Oh, come on!"

"You're the only one. We don't have an extra flyboard suit. Chad is on overwatch and weighs more than you. We have the hostages. So, he'll have to tandem with you."

"Peachy!"

"Once we have the hostages, we fly out in flock formation. Chad, you take point. Andy, you cover the rear. We head to Marmazand, eighteen miles south. Transport should be awaiting us to take us to Buehring Base in Kuwait. Any questions?"

"No, we're all good," Chad said.

"Alright, suit up," Topher said.

Custom-made Vantablack suits equipped with a Stealth Adaptive Flight Enabling System (SAFES), commonly referred to as flyboards. They were more of a hybrid between a jetpack and a flyboard to be used as needed. The stuff of movies in the early 2000s, they were now a prized possession of special force units. Most operators gravitate to the flyboard mode for ease of use and increased maneuverability. Unique to the US military is the capacity to transition in flight.

They looked at each other with complete trust and commitment to the mission.

A voice is heard over the PA system.

"Sigma Team approaching drop-off location. Current altitude is 9875 feet. Confirm team readiness."

"We're ready," Wave Runner said, turning to his team. "Helmets"

State-of-the-art Mission Assistant Artificial Intelligence Devices (MAAID), also referred to as the helmets, provide enhanced vision and hearing capabilities with real-time Artificial Intelligence predicated on the individual's security clearance.

The cargo hold hatch opened to the dark night with the moon as the sole light source.

"Let's do this," Wave Runner said.

Without hesitation or reservation, they ran to the edge as lions toward their prey and plunged into the emptiness of night one after the other.

"Flyboard mode," Could be heard several times over the comms.

"Status Report," Wave Runner requested.

"Green Arrow, all good," Chad said.

"Milkshake, all good," Max said.

"Mockingbird, all good," CK said.

"Eager Beaver, all good," Andy said.

"Wave Runner, all good," Topher said. "We have two hours until our first touchdown. Enjoy the beauties of the Caspian Sea."

"Y'all should try the daytime overlay. It's impressive," Chad said.

"Thank you, Green Arrow, but I'll stick with Night Vision," Andy said.

"Watch out, Beaver, you might want to be nice to your future boss when you end up working at his lemonade stand you guys have going on," Mockingbird said.

"Really? And you wonder why we called you Mockingbird?" Andy said.

"You guys called me that because you have mommy issues and felt like you had to give me a girly name," she replied.

"Guys, we have incoming," Milkshake said.

"Roger that, Milkshake," Topher said. "I see them. Two MiG-29 Fulcrum heading this way. Team Descend a thousand feet fast!" Wave Runner said.

Immediately, they took a nosedive as though they intended to crash but redressed in perfect sync, almost as if they were engaging in an airborne nocturnal choreography.

"You think they're here for us?" Andy said.

"Possibly," Milkshake replied.

"Maybe our plane entered their airspace?" Arrow said.

"No, we didn't, but that won't stop them from shooting it down. Wave Runner to homing pigeon, you have incoming. Two MiG-29 Fulcrum. Do you copy?"

"Copy that Wave Runner ascending to 35,000 feet," the pilot said.

As they flew through the Persian airspace, they were fully aware of the enemy craft's locations, battle readiness, and offensive posture.

"Green Arrow to Home Pigeon. Hostile's weaponry is unarmed."

"Roger that, Green Arrow."

"Confirming hostile aircraft have disengaged," the pilot said. "Hostiles redirected Southwest bound. Sigma Team, it's all you now. Godspeed."

"Roger that," Topher said. "Team, keep it steady, and maintain a wide distance."

Topher was known for his astute tactical mind and propensity to overdo it. The team was virtually undetectable by any radar system and by the naked eye. They blended perfectly with the night, but he would not take anything for granted. He would rather overdo it than underdo it. He lived by the motto, *stay alert, stay alive.*

Pardis, Iran

This building, under construction, was the ideal base of operation. It provided shelter from the elements but also from prying eyes. Azael had been observing the comings and goings for hours. He had the city all mapped and had narrowed down the potential locations. He had a plan. His burner phone vibrated.

"Hello," Azael answered.

"Somebody ordered repairs?" the voice said.

"Yes, my roof is leaking." He replied.

"Okay, we can send a technician. What kind of roof do you have?"

"It's a roof full of infested pipes."

"Wave Runner confirming contact with Gazelle. We are approaching your location. We have you on the ninth floor, correct?"

"Correct."

"We're coming in straight through the north side."

"Understood."

"Team, activate quiet mode," Wave Runner said to his team.

The Flyboard's sound emission drastically decreased to a faint hum. As they made their approach, the night was peaceful, the street was calm, and they could land next to a bystander and take his life before he realized they were even there. Their suits blended perfectly with the dark of night. They were no noisier than the nightly breeze. They entered the wall-less structure at the ninth level. The floor of what would become a small office building was pitch black, with only the moon as a light source. As their flyboard devices sensed the ground beneath their feet, they automatically split in two and espoused the ankles of the soldiers, freeing the feet to walk. When looking closely, this mode revealed four small propellers per leg, allowing them to fly and make a quick exit if needed. This flight mode was only for critical situations, as the full power could damage their feet. Upon landing, they automatically adopted a pentagon formation, Topher (Wave Runner) at the point, Max (Milkshake) and CK (Mockingbird) covering the flank on both sides, Chad (Green Arrow) and Andy (Eager Beaver) covering the rear, assessing if their entrance went unnoticed as planned. Firearms drawn, they inspected their surroundings, watching for hostiles while looking for a friendly. They sported SIG Sauer MCX LVAM, a.k.a. *Black Mamba*, muzzled.

"You won't need that right now," a voice said.

Out of a shadowy corner, hands halfway in the air, Azael revealed himself. He was of medium build, just an inch short of six feet. His hair was dark, and his eyes were deep brown. He was wearing an unassuming outfit that Nikolas had provided for him. They lowered their weapons.

"Gazelle, as you called me," he said.

"It's your national emblem, isn't it?" Topher said.

"Not my choice."

"I'm Wave Runner. This is Mockingbird, Milkshake, Green Arrow, and Eager Beaver."

In a split second, Azael analyzed his new partners. Wave Runner was a couple of inches taller than him. He had light brown hair with blond streaks. The suit made his weight hard to assess. Mockingbird, her light caramel skin and black hair made it hard to pinpoint her ethnic profile. She could be South American, Middle Eastern, or mixed-race. As the sole female in this elite unit, she would not only be physically capable, but she most likely brought a particular set of unique skills to the table. Milkshake was the same height as him. Slick black hair and meticulous goatee professed an attention to detail. Green Arrow's darker brown skin, low haircut, and demeanor hinted at African American heritage. His rifle was different from the rest of the team; clearly, the group's sniper. Eager Beaver, a couple of inches shorter than him. His ginger beard, stocky build, and code name signaled he was a force of nature. Despite their varied background, they moved as one. This could be either an asset or a liability to the mission, to save Suri.

"Good to meet you," Azael said. Can we get started?"

"Sure, here are the plans."

Topher noticed an area where Azael had laid some plans. He figured it would be as good a makeshift command center as any. He walked there as the others followed in lockstep. Azael sensed the hubris but had no time for pissing contests. He followed as well. On the table was a sketch of the small town.

"Milkshake, prep the Cube," Wave Runner said.

"Already on it."

Max placed a holographic projector on top of the map. Not bigger than a holophone, those devices came in handy, providing three-dimensional views of the field of operation.

"Give it about ten seconds."

After a short moment, a three-dimensional schematic of Pardis hovered over the table. It was fully responsive to physical gestures or voice commands.

"Alright, time is short. Let's run it real quick. Green Arrow, you take position at the Khomeini Building. Eager Beaver, you have the transformer station right here. Milkshake and Mockingbird, you're with me. We'll infiltrate the building where they're being held. The latest heat signatures show ten bodies on the fourth floor. Seven in motion, three stationary. These, we believe, are our hostages. By going through the roof, we might be able to get them and get out unnoticed. Gazelle, you'll be teamed up with Eager Beaver."

"I'd rather go in."

"No offense, but you're wounded, and we don't have an extra suit for you. We're here to get the hostages out safe and sound. We don't want to lose you in the process."

Azael was taken aback for a moment. *How did Wave Runner know about his injury? Shared intel, or astute observation? Was he losing his edge?* This might be true, but it didn't matter anymore. For them, this was just a mission. For him, it was his life.

"None taken, regardless of whether I'm going in. You can either help me or stay out of my way!"

Immediately, Chad, Andy, and Max's senses became more alert. Chad's hand slid subtly next to his side weapon. Andy peeked at a stack of two-by-fours, thinking *this would be perfect to knock some sense into this dude.* Cecilia had a better idea.

"Guys, we're all on the same team and want the same thing." She turned to Azael. "Sir, if you're here right now, it's for sure because you're amongst the best. We've been training together for four years now and know each other better than our families. What we don't know is what we're facing. That's why we need you and Beaver to cover our backs if things get heated. Can we count on you?"

Azael knew the psychology she used to get her desired outcome. His sole desire was to save Suri. He'd play along for now.

"Okay, it's your game, your play."

"Milkshake, can you bring up the hostage's profile?" Chad said.

Milkshake found an odd request from their resident sniper. He knew his brother-in-arms' work ethic, so he didn't hesitate for an instant.

"Here you go," he said.

A 3D holographic canvas of data and pictures of the three scientists hovered over the table. Chad was analyzing more than the images, more than the data. He sought the truth.

"Okay, I'm good. Thanks," Chad said.

"Okay, so we're all good?" Topher said, looking around the room.

"We're good," Milkshake confirmed.

"Okay, check your gear, make sure you're in stealth mode. We're out in five."

Chad tapped Topher on the shoulder as they went apart and signaled him to come aside.

"Let me talk to you real quick."

"Yeah, what's up?"

"I think we might have a problem," Chad said, looking at Topher straight in the eyes and glancing at the room, making sure no one was observing them.

"What do you mean?"

"That Israeli guy."

"Yeah, what about him?"

"I think he has a thing for one of the hostages?"

"What makes you say that?"

"You see, the guy has been through hell, but he's still here wanting to go in the line of fire."

"Okay, keep going."

"He said, 'I'm going in! You can help or get out of my way.' That's personal, not operational. When I asked Max to pull up the hostages, I observed him. There was that look in his eyes. I guarantee you he's involved somehow. If I had to guess, I'd say it's the lady. I think he's in love with her."

"Hum, that would be a problem, but we don't know for sure."

"Trust me, I'm telling you."

"Alright, keep an eye out. But we have to focus on the mission. We'll take out anyone who gets in the way of that, including him. If he becomes a problem, you know what to do."

"Roger that."

"Alright, get ready. We're moving out."

A few minutes later, Topher signaled the team to gather. He led the way to the edge of the floor to the would-be windows that had yet to be put up. They lined up along the threshold. The night was quiet. The city had little light. The moon lit up the caliginous sky. Topher looked down nine stories below, and nobody was in the streets. He looked at the cityscape. No one appeared in their window. He lifted his gaze to the sky, analyzing it. It seemed luck was on their side. Scattered clouds covered the moon, providing the perfect cover of darkness.

"Let's go!"

They flew out, each towards their designated post. Chad headed straight up, using the building as cover as long as possible to reach the Khomeini Building. Topher, CK, and Max flew straight to the top of their target location. Andy harnessed Gazelle, headed to the transformer station.

"This is Green Arrow, setting up shop."

Chad assembled his Barrett MRAD Mk 24 rifle, which was fully synced with his suit. The Khomeini building being the highest in town, the sniper had a clear line of sight of the whole *theater,* as they called it.

"Eager Beaver in position."

"Okay, we're going in," Topher said while Max disabled the door's security.

He opened the door. Topher went in first, weapons drawn. CK followed, and then Max closed the door behind him. They ventured down the pitch-black staircase leading to a service door. The door was metallic, most likely bulletproof. Topher stepped to the side with his back against the wall to make room for Max. CK did the same on the opposite wall. As Max got to the door, he examined it with the assistance of his enhanced device.

"It's wired. Probably an alarm," he said.

"Can you disable it?" Topher asked.

"Yeah, it should take me just one second."

Max reached inside the right-side utility pocket of his suit and took out a small device no bigger than a lighter. He took another scan of the door and placed the magnetic device in the top right corner of the door. He proceeded to pick the lock.

"Here goes nothing," Max said.

Silence, no blaring alarm sound. He opened the door. Topher peeked inside with caution. His night-vision scan didn't detect any activity. He stepped in weapon first. CK was right behind him. Max followed, closing the door slowly to avoid making any noise. Their steps were decisive but silent. The floor looked like the office space of a manufacturing plant. They reached the end of the floor to another stairwell. If their data was correct, the hostages would be two stories down. Max looked at the door. It was clear. As they opened it, their night vision switched to standard. The light indicated that they might encounter foot traffic. Steadily, they went down to the fourth floor.

"If our scans are accurate, this is where they should be," CK said. "I have them about twenty-five yards in. And only seven other people, all considered hostile."

"Eager Beaver, do you copy?" Topher said.

"I copy."

"It's time for lights out."

"Roger that. Bedtime!"

The lights of the whole block went out. Their night-vision mode automatically re-engaged.

"Let's go!" Wave Runner said.

They went in hot. Three hostiles were sitting at a table using a cell phone to create some light while their colleague checked out the outage. Before they could realize what was going on, they each had a bullet in their heads. The first one fell forward, slamming into the feeble table, making a raucous alerting the other abductors. Two came from the left side, and CK took them down before they could draw their weapons. Max took down another two from the right. Topher took down the last one, further off toward the windows. They swept the area, making sure they didn't miss anyone.

"Clear," Mockingbird confirmed.

"Clear," Milkshake followed.

"All clear," Wave Runner said, while heading to the makeshift jail door leading to the heat signatures. "All hostiles are taken down, breaking into the holding cell."

Azael held his breath, counting on the moment they would be reunited. He hoped she didn't suffer during this ordeal. But he knew she was tough. Whatever her captors threw at her, they would overcome it together. Max picked the lock as fast as he could. They went into a room with three small beds with people on them.

"US Navy, we're here to take you home." Wave Runner said.

No response. They got closer, only to find dead bodies with small heaters.

"Wave Runner to Sigma Team. The friendlies are dead. I repeat, they are dead."

Azael's heart sank within him. The world around him spun out of control. He couldn't tell if he was standing or sitting. He lost all sense of balance. For the first time, he considered the possibility that he had failed her, that she was gone.

"Conducting identity verification," CK said.

"Green Arrow to Sigma Team, you better get out of here! We've got company."

Andy grabbed Azael and slammed him to the ground to avoid detection by the raging pickup truck filled with militants armed to their teeth.

"I have four pickups closing in on your location on all sides," Arrow said. "Your only way out is by air."

"Let's head back to the roof. Let's go!" Wave Runner said.

Milkshake was the first one through the door out of the holding cell. Gunfire rang out. He fell back into the room. CK reached over to him to close the door. To their surprise, there was blood.

"Argh, I'm hit," Milkshake said.

"How?" CK asked.

Max looked at his left shoulder and assessed his wound.

"I don't know how this ripped through the suit, but I'll be okay," he said. The bullet was nested between the suit and Max's flesh. He temporarily removed the damaged section of the suit, pulling the bullet out of his shoulder. "Argh!" The bullet fell to the ground.

Topher bent down and picked up the crushed projectile.

"Armor-piercing bullets,"

"Let me patch you up," CK said. She reached into her utility belt for an antiseptic coagulating ointment to stop the bleeding and prevent infections. She then applied a surgical patch over the wound.

"This should hold you over until we get out of here," she said. "You're lucky the suit took most of the impact."

"You have a weird idea of luck," Max said. "But thank you." He made several shoulder movements to assess his condition.

Topher looked down at him.

"Can you shoot?"

"You besta believe that."

Almost instinctively, Topher reached down while Max reached up and got back on his feet.

"I count fifteen heat signatures closing in," CK said.

"We have to get out of here fast, or they'll be a lot more," Topher said.

"What are you thinking, boss?" Max asked.

"Let's run an Alley Hoop," Wave Runner said.

"Perfect, let's do it," CK said.

She activated her flyboard in stealth mode to reach the ceiling and removed a tile to access the floor void.

As soon as she made it in, Max opened the door slightly, just enough for Topher to slip through the barrel of his gun and fire a few rounds, and immediately closed it back. Which prompted an instantaneous downpour of bullets. Steadily transforming the door and wall into concrete Swiss cheese.

"CK, what's your status? We're sitting ducks out here!"

"Almost there, boys!"

Once she reached the furthest point behind their enemies, she quietly descended from the ceiling.

"Mockingbird in position," she said.

"Ready when you are," Topher replied.

She grabbed a stunt grenade the size of a C battery and lobbed it over the unwitting assailants. The flash bang of the explosion disoriented them, just enough for Topher and Max to make their way out. The muffled sound of their shots told the story in about fifteen seconds, fifteen bodies dropped to the floor.

"Wave Runner, I'll drop as many as I can," Arrow said. "But you have to get out of there now! You have the whole Revolutionary Guard coming up." Arrow said.

"Roger that," Wave Runner replied.

Chad started shooting down at the mob, storming the building. But his efforts only dented the wave of militants storming the building.

Andy got up, thinking it was safe to do so after the Trucks passed. As he got off the ground, he looked up and saw what appeared to be a mere flicker in the night sky.

"Arrow, watch your six!" He said.

Chad, lying down in sniper position, turned around to an unmanned drone staring him in the face. He activated his thrusters, propelling him off the roof and allowing him to dodge the bullets by a nanosecond, but knocking him against the roof's edge.

He fell several floors before regaining control. The drone made a semicircle maneuver to re-center its target. Though slightly disoriented from the bumping against the roof's walled edge, he knew he didn't stand a chance in open space against the machine. He grabbed his handgun and shot at the window glass on the side of the building. He flew through the bullet-cracked window into the office building. He crash-landed and hid behind a desk as the drone sprayed the room with bullets. Chad knew his best chance to take down the drone was to disable the rudder. When he heard a break in the shooting, he took his turn and aimed solely at the rudder. The drone destabilized and crashed to the ground.

"Eager Beaver, we have to bail them out," Arrow said.

"Way ahead of you. We're coming in hot! "

Andy and Azael were running towards the line of fire. Chad was about to take flight towards the building when he detected five drones approaching the area.

Inside the Building

"Clear," Topher said, patrolling to the left of the holding room. Max patrolled the right side.

"Clear."

CK was by the stairwell.

"Okay, guys, we have to get out of here. I can hear them coming," she said.

"Okay, Team, let's exit to the rendezvous point," Wave Runner said. "Mockingbird, Milkshake to the southern window. We'll take flight from there." CK was the closest to the window.

Topher continued, "Mockingbird, make a hole, will ya?"

"With pleasure." She fired several rounds at the window, shattering the glass.

"Okay, let's go flock formation."

Topher and Max ran towards the window to take flight. CK was already in hover mode, ready to fly out. She had her weapon in hand, fixating on her teammates to synchronize her flight with theirs. She mentally counted down to when they'd reach her, *five, four, three, two—*

"Abort! I repeat, abort!" Chad said. "You are surrounded by drones."

Topher and Max stopped, and CK pulled back from the window.

"From where I'm standing, I count five," Chad continued.

"Green Arrow, can you take them out?" Topher asked.

"I can if I get back to my rifle on the roof. I'd have to get back there through the stairs. It'll take five minutes."

"That's five minutes we don't have," Milkshake said.

"I can give you five minutes."

"Who was that? Was that Gazelle?" Wave Runner asked.

"Yes, that's Gazelle," Azael said. "Eager Beaver, and I will buy you those five minutes, but it won't be a covert operation anymore."

"There's a crashed drone in the middle of the street. I think this stopped being covert a while ago," Chad quipped.

"Okay, come with me," Azael said to Andy.

Azael jogged to a parked Utility Vehicle CJ-6, an older pickup truck version. It had two barrels of flammable material in the cab. Azael was unsure what was in there, but environmental concerns would have to wait. They kept a low profile as they got by the vehicle.

"What's your plan?" Beaver asked.

"Two words. Car bomb."

"Got it."

"You smoke?

"Nah, but I have fire. Standard operating tool."

Azael picked up a sizeable rock and smashed it against the driver-side window. He unlocked the doors and got the lighter from Andy.

"Help me pour some of that on the passenger seat," Azael said.

They grabbed one of the barrels, unscrewed the knob, and poured some on the seat.

Azael continued as they put the barrel, still three-quarters filled, back in the truck's cab. "I'll drive. When we get in striking distance, I'll light up the seat to create a cloud of smoke on my signal, drop a grenade in the cab, and we jump off."

"Nice, I'm starting to like you."

Azael got in the driver's seat and hotwired the car.

"Okay, you're ready?" he whispered through the broken window.

"Yeah, I'm all set."

They drove off. He was holding the steering wheel with his left hand while holding the lighter in his right. This maneuvering was painful and strenuous for him, still weaker from the gunshot wound on the left shoulder. No amount of pain was going to quench his resolve. He was totally focused. Beaver was lying low in the truck cab.

"Okay, get ready."

He held his breath, dropped the lighter, turned on the beam lights, and said:

"Now!"

Andy dropped the grenade. They jumped out of the rolling vehicle. The beam lights and the smoke attracted the militants' attention and the drones'. The Israeli soldier's aim was impeccable. The vehicle crashed right into the entrance of the building and exploded. The deflagration reverberated throughout the building. Even Chad felt it.

"What was that?" Chad said.

"Your five minutes," Andy replied.

"Alrighty then!"

Chad ran up the stairs and got back to his sniper rifle on the roof.

"Okay, I'm in position. Let's hunt some drones," he said.

Chad could see three in his line of fire. He could take all of them out before they realized the first one was taken down.

"I have eyes on three. North, northeast, and northwest. Does anybody have eyes on the other two?"

"Negative," Andy said.

"I see their heat signature on the south side of the building," CK said.

"Okay, keep your eyes on them. And Beaver, keep your eyes on me, brother."

"I got you."

Bang! Bang! Bang! Three shots straight to the rudders, three drones going down to the ground.

"Green Arrow, they're heading your way," CK said.

"Let them come!"

Back inside

Topher and Max had barricaded the stairwell door, but they knew it wouldn't hold the militants out much longer. They were bracing for the firefight.

The first few through the door got hit. But the next few got through and were able to set defensive positions to exchange fire. Bullets were flying everywhere when they heard a crashing sound followed by another one.

"Drones are down; your coast is clear," Chad said.

Upon hearing that, Topher grabbed his second stunt grenade and threw it at the militants. Upon detonation, the trio returned to the shattered southern window and took flight.

"Everyone, fly out!"

Outside

Andy strapped Azael to himself.

"Are you good?" Andy asked.

"Good to go," Azael replied.

They flew out.

13

WHEN IT RAINS...

White House, Situation Room

"OKAY, LET'S GET STARTED," President Rodriguez said. "General, where are we with the Korean situation?"

"The Northerners are pounding the South with artillery and missile attacks. Special ops units are conducting targeted hits on high-value targets." The Chairman of the Joint Chiefs, McIntyre, said.

"What about our troops on the ground?"

"They have not engaged yet, sir. It seems the North Koreans are going out of their way not to engage."

"Why is that?"

"Most likely, they're signaling that they don't want to fight us. That their conflict is only with the South."

"Sir, if I may," Vice President Steve Emmerich said.

"Yes, Steve."

"Maybe that's a good thing. If the North isn't attacking our personnel, maybe we should let them figure out their own path forward. They are the same people. It's a family dispute we have little part in."

"Are you suggesting we do nothing?" President Rodriguez asked.

"What I'm suggesting, Mr. President, is that they are engaged in a conflict that's really a civil war co-opted by international powers. Us in the South and the Communists in the North. I think it might be best in the long term that they duke it out and self-determine."

"Steve, you're kidding, right?" McIntyre said.

"No, general. I'm not kidding."

"Do you realize how many people would die?"

"I do. But look at us. We had our civil war, and we lost six hundred thousand people, but we're better for it. We wouldn't be the country we are today if the British or the French had stepped in. I say let them figure it out. They'll be better for it."

"They aren't fighting with muskets and bayonets. A lot more people will die."

"I know, general, but at least they won't be Americans dying."

"I can't believe this. Mr. President, doing nothing is not a viable option. The conflicts we ignore have a way to come and bite us in the back."

"I understand that, General. But our people are leery of those never-ending wars. I ran on that very issue. Would you have me renege on my promise? Could we provide the south with weapons and logistical support?"

"Sir, I understand your pledge to the American people. But sometimes events unfold beyond our control and require us to rise to the challenges of our time."

The general took a deep breath, looked around the room, and found very few allies.

"If we renege on our promise to our ally, South Korea, it will signal to all our friends that they cannot trust us and to our enemies they need not fear us. The consequences would be beyond repair. China would invade Taiwan, Iran would attempt to obliterate Israel, and Russia would attack NATO allies. World Peace would be upended, destabilizing markets and world security, and eventually wreaking havoc on the home front. This would be the ultimate betrayal of the American People."

"Sir, if I may."

"Yes, General Dunn."

"I would like to echo the Chairman of the Joint Chiefs. Our troops are sitting ducks right now. If we pull them out, it would be viewed as an act of cowardice. They won't last long if we don't send reinforcements. The North not attacking them is just a ploy to gain time. We must act now."

"I hear you," President Rodriguez said. He pivoted to a different topic. "How are we doing with the hostage situation in Iran?"

"I'm afraid I have bad news, sir," Dunn said. "Our boys met with their Israeli counterparts on the ground. They attempted a rescue, but it turned out to be an ambush. They knew we were coming."

"Any casualties?"

"No sir, a few bruises, but everyone got out alive."

"Thank God! Where are they now?

"They found a hideout about twenty miles outside Pardis."

"The operational window closes in about two hours. Any chance they can pull it off?"

"It's unlikely, sir. The intel on the location was faulty, and we lost the element of surprise."

"Okay, pull them out before the strike levels the town."

"Yes, sir."

"Which leaves us with one question," President Rodriguez said. "Can we take on Iran and North Korea at the same time?"

Kate Simmons was a woman of few words. She only spoke when necessary and impactful. The former ranger, now chief of the army, had seen war and all its horrors. She understood the decision to go to war or not was not one to be taken lightly. Sons and daughters would say goodbye to their parents for the last time. Toddlers would grow up without their mom hugging them. Teens would live without their dads to guide them.

"Sir, we have prepared for that very eventuality. We can take them both at once and put an end to all major fighting in three months with a limited number of casualties. But if we wait, those conflicts will degenerate and require our intervention anyway. At that point, we're looking at a protracted war involving many regional actors on many fronts."

President Rodriguez looked at her straight in the eyes; she didn't flinch. He looked at the Chairman of the Joint Chiefs of Staff. The general nodded subtly.

"Prepare a joint strategic response plan with South Korea. Schedule a call with their president. Reach out to our NATO Allies. Let's build a coalition of the willing. Reach out to Israel's prime minister and let them know we're pulling our guys out. They have carte blanche for the preemptive strike."

He took a moment to capture the gravity of the moment.

"God help us all. You're dismissed."

They left the room, each with clarity on their next course of action toward an uncertain future. The president was still seated. He leaned back in his chair to ponder the recent events. He recalled the days of his campaign when he promised no more wars. This had been a pivot from his party's usual stance regarding foreign wars. He felt there was some truth to the adage, *you attract more flies with honey than with vinegar.* He knew how to resolve conflicts abroad through diplomatic channels and at home through political capital. But these turns of events were taking him into an unforeseen situation. He found himself wondering *how can we right the ship?* As he pondered these things, a silhouette could be seen further out the door. Before he could figure out who it was, his Chief of Staff broke the news to him.

"Sir, the directors of the FBI, the CIA, the DNI, and DHS are here. It's a matter of National Security."

"Have them come in."

The contingent of high-ranked intelligence officials and their key staffers entered with urgency. They joined the president at the table. The stocky man in charge of the FBI started the impromptu meeting.

"Mr. President, thank you for seeing us on such short notice," the director of the FBI said.

The commander-in-chief sensed this was no time for pleasantries. He leaned forward.

"Go ahead, Ray, what's going on?"

"Sir, a couple of hours ago, the Coast Guard San Diego sector intercepted what they thought were drug smugglers. Upon searching the vessel, they found something a lot worse."

The director's staffer handed the president a tablet with schematics of some sort.

"What am I looking at?"

"This, we believe, is an electromagnetic pulse device. Also known as an EMP device."

"What's the range?"

"Our experts are still analyzing it, but it looks like this could take down a city the size of Boston."

"Do we know who's behind this?"

"Not yet, sir. We are detaining the ship's crew in a rendition site in Mexico."

"What do we know?" The president asked, looking around the room at both directors and staffers. The CIA director responded,

"Sir, what we know is that there are more on their way, and some have already entered the country."

President Rodriguez's eyes grew wider, and a frown could be noticed on his forehead.

"How many?"

"We're still gathering intel, sir. But we estimate that five or six made it through New York, DC, Miami, LA, Seattle, and El Paso. And that another fifteen are on their way."

"So, if I understand you correctly, if any of those devices go off, a radius the size of Boston goes back to the Stone Age?"

"That is correct, sir. We estimate the blast radius to be about ninety square miles. Within which most electronic devices would stop functioning. No electricity, no cars, no communication, and complete darkness. Some portion of our infrastructure would survive. Most of our military bases are made to withstand EMP attacks. Many of our hospitals and shelters are hardened to withstand the brunt of an EMP. They might experience some disruption but would be able to provide limited services."

DHS Secretary Emilia Shaw continued.

"Our casualty projection models go from a few hundred to tens of thousands in the initial blast of one device. A well-coordinated EMP attack in multiple cities would cripple this country. If it occurs in winter, we're looking at an apocalyptic scenario."

"What are your recommendations?"

"Sir, we recommend you raise the threat level to DEFCON 3."

"DEFCON 3?"

"Yes, sir, if one of those things goes off, it'll make 9/11 look like a breeze in comparison."

"Okay, do it."

14

YOUTH FAIR

Balloons were floating high, and a giant bounce house was inflated, giving a festive feel to the modern place of worship. Kyle Boykin, the associate pastor in charge of what they called Next Generation Communities, had endeavored to make the church more welcoming to a diverse audience of all ages. He empowered his staff to reach out to the outcasts and marginalized and accept them in a judgment-free zone. They were preparing a block party culminating in a new style revival with intelligent lighting and real-life-like holographic performances by a host of contemporary bands. His efforts bore fruit. Having spent most of his youth on the wrong side of the tracks, he had genuine care and concern for the delinquents and downtrodden. Not one to avoid a fight in and out of detention until he had his *Come to Jesus* experience. Now, he was in and out of detention centers to assist in rehabilitating those premature inmates.

"Hey Batman, me ayudas por fa?" Kyle said.

"Pues no se me la estoy pasando bien con los cuates," Xaque, nicknamed Batman, said.

"Acuérdate güero me debes unas horas comunitarias."

"Wow, your Spanish is getting better, PK."

"Just tryin' to speak like you, man!"

"You're getting there," Batman replied, then pointed to the young man standing beside him. "Hey, this is my cousin Pepe, but we call him Tren 'cause he's *loco* motives, you know what I'm sayin'? This is Pastor Kyle."

"Yeah, I know I was *loco* too. Welcome, Tren. Good to meet you. They call me PK."

"Good to meet you, too."

"Yo, how many community hours you give me for this?" Xaque asked.

"Well, as soon as you help me set up these tables, it's an hour."

"Sweet. You think you can hook him up with some hours, too?"

"Yeah, for sure. Tren, you wanna help with setting up the stage? You look like you've got the muscles for it."

"Alright, I got you."

"Cool!"

Kyle led the way to the storage area inside the building. One of the volunteers received Tren and showed him what to do there. Kyle was heading back out when he heard the roaring sound of a loud crowd. He ran out. Not far behind him were Tren and a couple of volunteers.

When Kyle saw the source of the noise, he saw a small crowd gathered around what he deduced was a fight. When he arrived, he carved out a path to the center only to see *Batman* embattled with two other young men from a rival African American gang. The first one was holding him by the collar, trying to pull him to the ground, while the second one took out a knife to stab his Latino opponent. Before the blade could reach its intended target, Kyle grabbed the arm of the assailant with but a fraction of a second to spare. He twisted the wrist of the youngster, forcing him to drop the knife.

Tren came out of nowhere, blindsided the first one, and knocked him to the ground. He quickly got up, livid and ready to pounce back at Tren, but Kyle interposed himself between the two of them and shouted.

"Enough!"

They ignored him and kept moving forward. But he stood his ground.

"Back off! "He put his arm around Tren's midsection, pulling him away from the battle. Tren, though bigger, could feel that Kyle's strength was more than he had imagined. Though still on his guard, he always respected men of the cloth; he decided to stand down.

The other volunteers had arrived and interposed themselves between the other guys.

"Y'all have no respect for nothing!" Kyle said. This is a church!" What's wrong with y'all? Come on, everybody, go back to what you were doing." He turned to the two assailants.

"I should have you arrested. Come on, get out of here."

They left without any further incident.

Kyle went to Xaque. He had a cut over his left eye.

"Batman, what was that?"

"Sorry, PK, man, I didn't mean to bring this stuff here."

"Who were those guys?"

"They're from Triple P."

"Triple P? Really?"

"Yeah, you know them?"

"Something like that. Looks like they got you good. Go get it checked out."

About an hour later, Kyle called his right-hand man, Josh. And told him to take charge while he took a break. He headed straight to his car and drove three miles to the city's south side. This part of town was unwelcoming to outsiders. He parked at what seemed to be a down-and-dirty club. The guys hanging by the left corner stared at him suspiciously, but no one dared to do anything. On the opposite side, another group of young men was laughing it up until they saw him and stopped in shock.

"Yo, look, that's the dude from that church," Kinley, one of the two attackers, said.

"What's that fool doing here?" Retz asked.

"Yo, let's drop that fool!" But before he could take one step, another gangmate put cold water on his plan.

"I wouldn't do that if I were you."

Retz looked at him in surprise as if he was saying, '*What's your problem?*'

"He's tight with Ty G."

Kyle entered the empty club, and immediately, he heard.

"KB"

"Ty G"

Both together.

"K&G Keeping the style alive. Proud Power Posse"

They gave each other a manly hug.

"What's up, bruh?" Kyle said.

"We good, you? How you been?" Ty G replied.

"Can't complain," Kyle said.

"Haven't seen you around in a long time."

"Yeah, I know. I've been busy with church stuff, you know."

"Yeah, I feel you. How's Topher?"

"Topher's good. He just got engaged."

"What! Finally, good for him."

"Listen, why are your boys tryin' to beat people up at my church?"

"What are you talking about?"

"How about two of your boys came out and started trouble with one of my Latino kids."

"How did they look?"

"One had braids, and the other one got that bling around his neck."

"That's Kinley and Retz. They new around here."

"Well, can you make sure they don't bring that stuff to my church? If they want to come to pray, that's cool, but keep dem weapons out of there."

"Weapons?"

"Yeah, one of them almost stabbed my kid. If I didn't stop him, he'd be sitting in jail now. We really going back to those days, man?"

"Man, you been out of the game for a while now. Things be changin' fast. Now you have dem Latinos from *Lil' Mejico* stepping into the south side, dem Asian guys they comin' at us from the other side. You even have rednecks trying to get a piece of the pie too. We about to have an all-out war, bruh."

"You know what they say about war. War is old men talking and children dying."

"The way things are about to go down, it'll be everyone dyin' bruh."

"Thought you weren't gonna let that happen? Thought you said you'd do it differently. You forgot about Bishop and Big Pops?"

"Now you're tryin' me. They were my fam too, bruh. It hurt me, too."

"Then don't let it go down like that. We said no more drive-bys, no more blood in the streets, no more putting our bros in the ground. Just business, moving stuff around."

"You think I want this? You think I forgot?" Ty G lifted his shirt to reveal a bullet scar on his left abdomen. "There ain't a day that goes by I don't think about our boys, if I could be where they at instead of 'em."

Kyle stayed silent. He touched a nerve, maybe even went too far.

"You know Big Pop's daughter is turning five. Guess who been payin' her daycare? We about to throw her a big party. I'm her pops now. While you at church doing your pastor thing, I respect that, but I'm taking care of these people now."

"I feel you, man. So don't let it be like before. Do better now than we did back in the day."

"That's all I want, bruh. But if they come at me, I gotta make 'em pay otherwise, we all goin' down, you feel me?"

"Yeah, I feel you. Tell you what, if I can get them Latinos to stay on their side of town, can you tell your boys to stay outta trouble?"

"Yeah, if they don't come at us, we won't start trouble. I'll tell my guys to leave 'em alone."

"Alright. I'll take care of that. How's Mommy G?"

"She hangin' in there. Treatments and all."

"Yeah, tell her I'll come see her soon."

"Alright, she be askin' for you. Tellin' me I should go to church with you."

"You should!" Kyle said, smiling.

"One day. But now church ain't gonna pay her treatments. Besides, I know you be prayin' for your boy."

"Always, bro. You know I got you! Alright, man, Imma holla at you!"

"Alright, later, bruh."

Kyle headed out to the northwestern side of town, commonly called *Lil' Mejico* due to a significant immigrant community from Latin America, mainly Mexico and the North Triangle countries. He pulled up to Chapultepec, an authentic Mexican Bar and Grill. A couple of mid-twenties tough types headed his way to intercept him at the door.

"Sorry, we're closed," the alpha said while putting himself between Kyle and the Door.

"I'm here to see Rigo," Kyle said, looking at his counterpart straight in the eyes. The second one closed in towards his side, invading his personal space. Kyle could feel the upcoming pain. The only question going through this young preacher's mind was *should I fight back or turn the other cheek?* He thought, *If I don't act fast, there might not be another cheek left to turn.* Las Aguilas Gang was known to be swift and ruthless.

"Hey déjalo! Esta conmigo," Xaque shouted from a distance.

"Batman, conoces al gringo?"

"Si es amigo mío."

"You know Rigo is Busy," the henchman said.

"I spoke to him, we're good,"

"Sale pues, you can go."

Kyle, relieved, turned to his juvenile friend.

"You're late."

"Yeah, sorry, man had to drop Tren off." He paused a second. "You sure you want to do that?"

"Yeah, absolutely."

"You know these guys don't play."

"Yeah, I know, you know I'm not afraid to even die."

"Yeah, good for you, but I wanna live."

"Don't worry. God's got this."

Xaque looked at him unconvinced, but carried on anyway. As they entered the restaurant, they headed to the back, to the private party area. There, they found Rigo seated in the middle, accompanied by business partners and associates. The atmosphere was somewhat macabre: smoke in the air, stacks of money on the table, and a stockpile of illicit merchandise throughout the room.

"Come in, Little man," Rigo said.

Xaque came in first, followed by Kyle.

"Hi, Rigo," Xaque said.

"Xaque! Mi sobrino, come here and give your uncle a hug." Xaque timidly acquiesced to the request.

"You being good?" Rigo said.

"Yes, uncle."

"Who's your friend?"

"That's my friend Kyle."

"Kyle, huh?" He lit up a cigar and offered one to the guest.

"No, thank you. I don't smoke." Kyle said.

"That's too bad. You don't know what you're missing. I heard about you."

"Only good things, I hope?"

"I heard you ran the streets back in the day. Some even say that we wouldn't stand a chance if you were still in business."

"I had my moments, but I'm a pastor now."

"Ah! A man of the cloth. I respect that. Not much of a church guy myself."

"That's too bad. You don't know what you're missing."

Rigo chuckled.

"What brings you here, pastor?"

"I have a deal for you."

"I'm listening."

"Seems like things are getting hot between you, Triple P, and the other groups. If things explode, it's not good for anyone's business."

"We don't mind. We can defend ourselves."

"I'm sure you can. But would you rather spend your time buying bullets and caskets or bimmers and caddies?"

"It's just how these streets are: eat or be eaten. You know these people are snakes. They tough. But you know what is tougher than a snake?"

"What?"

"An eagle! They even hunt pythons. We are Las Águilas. We can take down anyone who gets in our way."

"I'm sure you can. But can you stop every bullet coming your way?"

"Are you threatening me, pastor? Cause that would not be a good idea."

"No, I'm not threatening you. There would be no point in that. All I'm saying is in all wars, there are unforeseen casualties. And you guys are right in the middle. Triple P to the south, the rednecks to the north, and the Asians to the west. They all have to go through you before they can get to one another. That can't be good. But what if you could run your business and even expand it without bloodshed?"

"Carry on."

"I'm proposing delimited territories, with areas for expansion and a non-aggression agreement from all sides. New people are moving to the area every day. The pie is big enough for everyone, and no one has to die."

"Pastor, you talk like a politician. You ever thought of running for office?"

"Nah. I'm good. I'd rather deal with street gangs. At least they have some honesty."

They both laughed.

"So, what do you say? Are we good?"

"Tell you what, preacher. If they don't step on our turf, we won't step on theirs."

15

AGAINST THE CLOCK

A secluded area outside of Pardis, Iran

"IT'S OVER. THEY'RE PULLING us out," Topher said. "We're going home."

"You're kidding, right?" Andy said.

"No, I'm not. Just got off the phone with General West. We're out. The Israelis are going to level the place. So, extraction is scheduled for two hours from now. Any time after that, it's going to start raining bombs."

"That don't make no sense," Andy whispered to himself.

"What about Gazelle?" CK asked.

"He's coming with us to Kuwait. Then they'll have transport ready to take us to our respective countries."

"If it's all the same to you, I'm going to see this mission through or die trying," Azael said.

"I told you so," Chad whispered to Topher.

"I'm with Gazelle on this one," Max said. "We didn't come all the way here to let these people die."

"I feel you, but you're in no shape right now. You lost a lot of blood back there," CK said.

"I've seen worse. I'll be fine."

"Guys, before we go any further, there's something we need to know," Topher said. "Gazelle, what's in it for you?"

"It's my job. I have to see it through to the end."

"I'm going to ask one last time. You tell us the truth, or we're going home."

"Fine. What I'm about to tell you could get me revoked from my position, but worse, it could get the love of my life killed." He took a deep breath. "Dr. Suri and I love each other. Because of our positions, our countries forbid our relationship. We are bound by duty to our countrymen, but are bound to each other through the heart. I'm not leaving here without her. I'm ready to go alone. But I could use your help."

The silence was deafening, each member speaking with their eyes. CK's were saying, *"This is touching, but to stay is crazy."* Max and Andy's were saying, *"We're good for whatever, just say the word."* Chad's were saying nothing. He was looking down at his guns, assessing their condition, as such actions spoke even louder. He broke the silence.

"Y'all know we're gonna go get them. I don't know why y'all are acting like we're going to let them down."

"Okay, hold up. One second," CK said. "You guys understand these orders came from Washington? As in the White House, right?"

The placid look on their faces said it all. They're ready to go regardless. But Topher put his foot down.

"Unfortunately, we have our orders. We're going home!"

"Very well then," Azael said. "I wish things were different, but I understand."

"All righty then, let's pack up," Andy said.

"Hold on now. Can I talk to you real quick?" Chad took Topher aside and whispered. "Listen, I know you want to go home. I want to go home too, we all do. But we have a small window to get these people back to their families." He paused for a second. "I know you want to be with Maddie and Ryan, but what would she tell you to do? What would she want?"

Topher didn't attempt to answer. He turned to the rest of the team.

"Everybody understands we do not have the support of HQ. We will be fully responsible no matter what happens. They will disavow us and maybe even court-martial us if we fail."

"So, let's not fail," Andy said.

"Alright then, let's get it done," CK said.

"Thank you," Azael said.

"So, what do we know?" Max said.

"Looks like they knew we were going to hit that building," CK said.

"That was the decoy location," Chad said. "Most likely, the hostages are held not too far. That's if they haven't moved them since our first attempt."

"When I did my reconnaissance before you arrived, I suspected another building, but it had less manpower, so I ruled it out," Azael said.

"That's probably where they are keeping them," Chad said.

"How can we know for sure?" CK said.

"Milkshake, can you still access the satellite?" Topher asked.

"I can try. The link is still active." He transmitted it through the Cube for all to see the layout of that part of town.

"This was my second option," Azael said. He pointed to a warehouse building about a mile from their first attempt.

"That looks about right," Chad said. "Lots of militants are guarding the place."

"How's your ammo?" Topher asked Chad.

"I don't have much left. Give or take, I have about enough for a quarter of them."

"And that's provided you don't miss." Andy chimed in.

"Come on, man, I never miss."

"Still, that's not enough to cover us," Topher said. "We can expect it'll be a tough fight. What about the rest of you? How are we doing on ammo?"

They all confirmed what Topher suspected: the ammo and power supply they had left were insufficient for a full-on frontal assault.

"That's encouraging," Andy said.

"There's got to be a way for us to get them without committing suicide," CK said.

"But unless you have a brilliant idea, that's just that, suicide," Andy said. "Don't get me wrong, I'm in no matter what. You guys know me, but the odds are not in our favor."

"What if we could even the odds?" Max said.

"What do you have in mind, Milkshake?" Topher said.

"What if we run a 'counter'?" Max said.

"American football," CK said to Azael to put him in context.

"You mean create a decoy?" Topher asked.

"Yes, what if we create a distraction and have them head to this other side of town, leaving the building less guarded?"

"How are we going to create that distraction?" Topher asked.

"I can hack their cell lines. I don't speak Farsi, but Mockingbird, and I'm guessing Gazelle, can help me figure out the messages."

"I think I like where this is going," Andy said.

Max continued.

"So Eager Beaver and Green Arrow would serve as decoys and draw their fire while Mockingbird, Gazelle, and Wave Runner would infiltrate the building, grab the hostages, and go."

"That's a no-go," Topher quickly interjected. "You can't give up your suit; it's proprietary equipment, and that's a court-martial for sure."

"What just happened?" Andy said.

"You didn't notice?" Chad said. "Milkshake wants to trade places with Gazelle. Let him use the suit and fly in the mission."

"Makes sense. He's pretty banged up."

"So is the other guy."

"Fair point."

"Hear me out," Max said. "As much as I love a firefight, let's face it, I'm not one hundred right now. The tech is proprietary because of the AI. I'll remove that because I'll need it anyway to run point. All he'll have is the operational commands and the comms. From here, I'll be able to direct you and create chaos for them."

"Plus, he knows the hostages that could come in handy in the field," CK added.

"I don't like it, but okay, let's do it," Topher said. Max switched the Cube projection to a 3D rendition of the town.

"Green Arrow and Eager Beaver," Topher said. "You will assume position over here by this red building. It's in a cul-de-sac. That will create a bottleneck effect, giving you the advantage."

"That's the Rouhani plant," Max said while tinkering with his suit.

"Okay, Arrow, Beaver, you're at the Rouhani plant. Mockingbird, Gazelle, and I will be posted here." Topher said and waited for Max to confirm the name of the location.

"The Saadi Center," Max confirmed.

"Okay, so we'll be at the Saadi Center waiting for the signal to breach this building," Topher said while Max added an overlay to the 3D display.

"What are those dots?" Gazelle asked.

"They're the active cell phone connections," Max said. "At this hour, those are most likely the militants."

"So that clump over there would confirm that's where the hostages are?" Chad asked.

"Yes, that's what I'm thinking," Max said. "So, I'll pick out one of them that is patrolling the area towards your position. From his cell, I will send a message out that they've spotted you, at which point, Arrow, you take him out so he can't reply. They will rush over in your direction. You light them up and keep them busy while you three infiltrate and get the hostages."

"That won't take care of everyone," CK said.

"No, you guys will have to fight your way through, but with most of them rushing to Arrow's position, it'll even the odds in your favor," Max said while handing Azael control of his suit. "Once they rush out, I'll shut down their cell connections. You'll just have to ensure they can't use their radios."

"Roger that," CK said.

"Okay, I need your help to decipher what they're saying," Max said.

CK, Azael, and Max go through the most recent messages to establish the hierarchical structure and night activity.

"So, what I make of this is that this guy, Omar, is their leader on the ground, but his geo location is away from the rest," Max said.

"Yes, that's right. And he's been going back and forth with this guy Attar. He wants to kill the hostages, but Attar said he'll take care of that matter when he comes."

"So, the good news is the hostages are alive. You must be relieved?" Max said to Azael.

"I'll be relieved when it's all over," Azael said.

"So, where is Attar now?" CK asked.

Max zoomed out of the image to see another clump of dots moving.

"He's on his way," Max said. "From the looks of it, they're about thirty minutes out."

"So, we'd better get going," Topher said. "Milkshake, you got what you need?"

"Yeah, I'm good."

"Gazelle, you're good with the suit?"

"Yes, I'll manage."

"Okay, let's go."

Still under the cover of night, they flew out. When they arrived in the vicinity of the small town, they split. Arrow and Beaver made a right inflight to take position at the Rouhani plant. Wave Runner, Mockingbird, and Gazelle continued straight to the Saadi Center.

About three minutes later.

"We are in position," Topher said. "Arrow, what's your status?"

"We're in position, ready to go full 300," Chad replied.

"What is he saying?" CK said.

"That's an old movie from like thirty-five years ago," Topher said. "In it, three hundred soldiers defeat an army of hundreds of thousands by positioning themselves in a bottleneck position."

"Ah, okay, got it."

"Can we please focus on the mission?" Azael said.

"Don't worry, Gazelle, we'll get them back," Topher said, not taking offense at Gazelle's rebuke. "Milkshake, do your thing."

"Roger that. The message is going out now. You should see movement soon. Mockingbird, I'm syncing your AI with mine to see the communication and reply in real-time."

While he said that, she started seeing the overlay of Max's interface as a couple of texts came in.

"The first one is from a Ghasem, and he's asking, 'Are you sure?'" CK said.

She continued.

"I'm replying 'without a doubt.' He replied, 'What about Attar? He said not to move until he arrives.' I'm going to say I'll clear it with Attar."

"No, don't say that," Gazelle said. "If he is his superior, he won't suffer insubordination. Say something like, 'Let me worry about Attar. Get all the men over here now. If we can get their suits' technology, the supreme leader will reward us handsomely."

"Got it," CK said.

"Looks like it worked. They're moving," Topher said as two pickup trucks filled with armed men, both in the cab and the cargo bed, sped out. "Okay, Arrow, we're waiting on your signal".

Before Chad could answer, Andy said, "Trust me, you'll know when to go."

"Cutting off their cell's reception," Max said.

A few seconds later, a big flash on the horizon quickly accompanied by a thunderous sound and an earthquake served as Beaver's signal.

"That's our signal. Let's go," Topher said. The trio with silenced handguns proceeded and took out one of the few henchmen at the front entrance. "I scanned the building with infrared. There's no activity in the upper levels. They must be in the basement."

They headed down a utility stairwell to the bowels of The Saadi Center. They systematically went door to door. Azael grabbed Topher's shoulder, stopping his progress. Azael pointed down to an invisible tripwire.

They cautiously avoided it and continued quietly, taking the presence of the booby trap as a sign they were getting closer.

They came to the end of the hallway with only a left turn possible. Azael peeked around the corner to see three henchmen guarding a door and sitting at a table. He signaled three with his fingers. In an unvocal communication at the count of three, they turned the corner like musicians in the flow. Each one shot one.

A fourth henchman turned the corner from what seemed to have been a bathroom run. Coming face to face with the reality of his comrades on the floor, three special ops agents looking straight at him, he grabbed his radio to call for help while attempting to hide back around the corner. CK shot him before he could utter a word.

Inside the holding room

"Did you hear something? "Suri asked.

"No, but we don't have much time left," Elisha answered. His head tilted downward, staring at the ground as if he were present in body but not his mind.

"What do you mean?"

"My country will not allow me to remain captive." He made eye contact with his cellmate. "They'll wipe out this zone."

"How? Why?"

"I know too much. They can't allow what I know to fall into enemy hands."

"Are you saying they will kill us?" Dr. Hiro said.

"I am saying they will do what needs to be done to ensure the survival of my people."

"If they know where we are, why don't they send help?" Suri asked.

"They might not know our exact location, but they'll know the town. That will be enough."

"But so many innocent people will die!" Suri said.

"Many more will die if our captors figure out who I am and break my will."

"Aren't you jumping to conclusions?" Dr. Hiro said. Maybe negotiations are going on as we speak."

"Our protocols require action within twenty-four hours of an existential threat event. By my count, we're getting close to that time. I'd rather not find out if I'm right—Ah, finally!" Elisha said while setting himself free from his restraints.

"Oh wow! How did you?" Dr. Hiro asked.

"With patience and consistency," Elisha said.

"You are an impressive man, Dr. Zvili," Suri said.

"Let's keep the compliments for when we are out of here," Elisha said while undoing her restraints. "Now, Suri, I need you to fake a panic attack."

"Okay, but why?"

"Trust me! Just do it!"

"Okay. "She started feigning a panic attack. Elisha then shouted out of the top of his lungs,

"HELP! HELP! She's going to die!" He paused. "Dr. Hiro, help me."

They both screamed at the top of their lungs,

"HELP! HELP! She's going to die!" The door opened. Ahmed entered.

"What is going on?" he said.

"I don't know. She just lost it," Elisha said. Ahmed got closer to her to assess the situation.

Continuing her performance, Suri pretended to lose consciousness. Ahmed hurried to her side, his senses narrowed to focus on the apparent crisis. In a sudden and decisive leap forward, Elisha ensnared his captor in a headlock, blocking blood flow to the brain. Ahmed attempted to get free, but to no avail. The old man's posture was too strong, and his counter moves too fluid to be broken. After a few moments, Ahmed's physiological reality overcame his resilience as he faded into a forced slumber.

Laying him slowly on the ground, Elisha took Ahmed's machine gun and searched his body for other weapons. He found a handgun, which he entrusted to Suri.

"Do you know how to use one of those?" Elisha asked.

"Yes, I do," Suri responded.

"Good, don't be afraid to use it."

He then pointed the rifle at Ahmed to finish the job.

"Don't do that!" Suri interjected. "He has a family too."

Elisha knew she was right, but the conflicting thoughts in his mind caused him to hesitate. Keeping Ahmed in the locked room should at least provide them with enough time to exit the building.

"Okay, fine. Let's get out of here before he wakes up," he said.

Suri undid Dr. Hiro's restraints. Elisha peeked left and right into the hallway, ensuring the coast was clear. No one in sight, he signaled the two scientists to follow him.

"Stay behind me." He said, aiming the rifle forward. The elder diplomat knew how to operate weapons of war.

Back in the Hallway

"I think he's dead," Topher said, assessing the fourth body at the end of the hallway.

"Which way do we go, left or right?" CK asked.

"I think we should split. Cover more ground," Azael said.

"No, let's stay together," Topher said. "We're short on time and ammo. If this gets ugly, we have a better shot together."

"You're right," Azael said. "Together is better." They made a right. After about thirty seconds, CK yelled, "GUN!"

The trio took defensive positions as they could, but it became clear that they were sitting ducks in the hallway. They fired shots in that direction.

"Mockingbird, let's do an old clock blitz," Topher said. "Gazelle, follow our lead."

Topher and CK got side by side, advancing rapidly towards the target with alternative shots, maintaining a constant flow of firing while preserving their ammunition. Gazelle picked up on the tactic almost instantly and joined the cadence. Their opponent was somewhat pinned down but attempted to take several shots. Bad mistake.

"Argh. I'm hit!" Elisha said.

"Elisha, are you okay?" Suri said. "Let me see that."

At the other end of the hallway.

"Stop! Stop! Stop shooting!" Azael said as he tried to listen. Topher and CK kept their weapons drawn, ready to engage as they advanced slowly. But no enemy fire was directed at them.

At the other end of the hallway, around the corner

"They're getting closer," Hiro said. "Can you run?"

"We can't outrun them," Elisha said as Suri attended to his wound. "We can fight, or we can surrender."

Hiro and Suri took about five seconds, which felt like five hours, to gauge the stakes of that decision.

"I say we fight," Suri said, drawing the handgun with a surge of adrenaline flowing through her body.

"Leave us ALONE!" She shot at the incoming threats. She took cover, expecting the return fire to come her way.

A couple of shots rang out, but the counterassault was abruptly cut short.

"STOP!" Azael shouted. "Stop, everybody, just STOP!"

Suri was puzzled.

"SURI! SURI!"

She turned the corner, her weapon drawn, about to shoot the incoming threat.

"Don't shoot! It's me," Azael took off the helmet.

Everything stopped, thoughts ran wild. Topher realized they had just shot one of the hostages. CK was thrilled about the reunion but fully aware that the celebration would have to wait a little bit longer. Azael was relieved to see her well, shaken but well. Suri was blank. The highly intelligent and accomplished scientist's brain ceased to function. It had never failed her before, but she had no point of reference, no equations, only emotions.

She stood still, not moving. Her eyes swelled with tears. Her body was shaking like a leaf, and the gun dropped to the floor.

"You're alive? You're alive. You're alive!"

She bolted towards him and embraced him with all her strength. She would have reopened his wound if it had not been for the suit.

"My love, oh my love," Azael said, tears flowing down his cheek, becoming one with hers.

Putting her hand softly on Azael's shoulder, CK interrupted the reunion.

"I'm sorry to break this up, but we have to go," she said.

"Dr. Hiro, Dr. Zvili," Topher said. "We are US Special Forces. We're here to take you home. Please come with us."

CK went to Elisha to assess his injury.

"How do you feel?" CK asked.

"I've had worse," Elisha answered.

"I can stop the bleeding, but you'll need surgery when we are safe."
CK applied a coagulating ointment and wrapped a military-grade compress
to her impromptu patient.

Turning to Hiro, she said, "Help me get him up."

"Yes, ma'am,"

Topher came closer to Azael and said to him,

"Are you ready to go?"

Azael snapped back into operation mode. He put the helmet back on.

"Yes, we're ready to go."

"Guys, you'd better hurry and get out of there. Omar and his minions
are here." Max said.

"Okay, guys, let's hurry, we have to go!" Topher said. "We can't leave
through the front door. Let's go through the eastern exit."

"Roger that," CK said.

"Okay, let's go," Azael said.

CK headed to the back of the pack to cover the rear and push
everybody forward. Azael and Topher were in the front of the pack. At the
eastern gate, Topher turned to the group.

"Okay, listen up," he said. "We are flying out of here in tandem. Mr.
Zvili, you're with Mockingbird. Dr. Suri, you're with Gazelle, and Dr. Hiro,
you're with me."

Each one was paired with their assigned partner.

"To fly out, we need to have an open sky and some room to
maneuver," CK added. "Once outside in the right place, we will tandem
using the rescue harness." She demonstrated succinctly how the equipment
functioned.

"Okay, stay close to your partners. Milkshake, are we clear?"

"Yes, you're clear, but hurry," Max said.

"On my mark. Three, two, one." Topher pushed the metallic door open, and he held it open while everyone exited. Then, he resumed his position at the head of the pack. About ten yards into the industrial yard, rapid-fire gunshots rang out.

"Pull back, head back, go back!" Topher shouted. As the words left his mouth, he saw the slowly closing door shut.

"Behind the truck!" Azael shouted, leading everyone to take refuge behind a construction vehicle.

"Milkshake, what happened? We're under fire!" Topher said.

"Must have been some lag in the system."

"How many are we dealing with?"

"Three, at least. But wait, it looks like the others heard the gunshots. They're all converging on your location."

The terrorists shot in their direction. Topher, CK, and Gazelle returned fire.

"I'm out," Topher said.

"Me too," CK said after firing another three shots.

"I am out, too," Azael said.

"Milkshake, we need an out. They're closing in on us!"

Chad and Andy had been holding off the militia about a mile away.

"Hold on tight, Wave Runner, we're on our way," Andy said.

"You won't make it in time," Max said.

"Hold on, I got this!" Chad said. Turning to Andy, "How many grenades you got left?

"Three."

"All right, that works. I need you to buy me about one minute."

"What are you doing?"

"Just cover me!" Chad said. Then, to his AI system, he said, "Sniper mode."

"Sniper mode enabled," the AI responded.

"Okay, Eager Beaver. Now!" Chad said.

Andy threw the first grenade toward their assailants and followed with rapid fire.

"Burst Stabilize 800 meters," Chad said to his AI.

Immediately, Chad's suit initiated a rapid launch sequence. Within seconds, he was airborne, and in about twenty seconds, he reached an altitude of 800 meters, about half a mile high. The suit stabilized midair. Andy looked at his partner and figured it was time for the second grenade and further distraction.

Looking through his enhanced AI assistance interface, Chad entered his own sniper mode, symbiotic with the machine, calculating the Pythagorean Theorem $a^2 + b^2 = c^2$, the gravitational pull, the windspeed, and the movement of the targets.

"Targets acquired," Chad said before unleashing three consecutive shots.

Bang! Bang! Bang! Thud, thud, thud.

The three militiamen fell to the ground with the breath of life departing their bodies.

"DROP!" Chad commanded the AI, prompting a rapid descent with a sharp deceleration right before hitting the ground.

Andy threw his third grenade to cover the sniper.

The landing was abrupt. It was more crash than landing. Chad smashed through the windshield of a car.

Back at the Saadi Center

"I love you, Green Arrow!" Topher exclaimed. "Come on, let's go!" The soldiers and the hostages made a run for it. Each soldier took hold of a militant's weapon and hid between a series of parked construction vehicles.

"Okay, strap up!" Topher said with a loud whisper as the rest of the militants turned the corner to find their comrades on the floor.

"Find them! "Omar shouted.

"Everybody set?" Topher said.

"We're set," CK said.

"Set as well," Azael confirmed.

"They're getting closer," Topher said. "We need a distraction to buy us enough time to get out of reach."

"At this point, we have to go 'shock and awe'. That's the only way," CK said.

"If that's what I think she's saying," Azael said. "I have to agree, we do not have much time."

Topher turned to the civilians.

"It's on you. Cause you have to shoot while we navigate our way out of here."

"I'm ready," Suri said.

"I don't know about this. There must be another way," Dr. Hiro said.

"There is no other way," Elisha retorted while extending his good hand to Topher for his weapon.

"I don't think I can do this!" Hiro said while CK put her weapon in his hands.

"Just point and shoot," she said.

"I don't like this."

"None of us do," CK replied.

"They are upon us!" Azael said.

"Okay, on my Mark...three, two, one. Launch!" Topher said.

They soared to the sky, making a barrage of bullets, forcing Omar and the militants to take cover.

"I think we're in the clear," CK said.

"Roger that!" Topher responded. "Green Arrow, Eager Beaver, get out of there!"

"Wave Runner, we might have a problem," Andy said. "Green Arrow came down hard. I'm en route to his location, but he has been unresponsive."

"Keep us posted," Topher said.

"Roger that. Beaver out."

"We might have to go back," CK said.

"I know. Let's get them to safety first," Topher said. "Milkshake, we're en route. Arrow is down."

"Yeah, I'm watching that on my screen. He hasn't moved for the past five minutes. Beaver has a head start, but about two dozen guys are behind him."

"You're hearing that, Beaver?" Topher asked.

"Loud and clear!"

Andy found Chad unconscious inside an old, beat-up European car. He broke the passenger side window and pulled Chad out of the vehicle, laying him down on the sidewalk.

"Arrow! Arrow! Are you alright? Arrow!" Beaver asked.

"What happened?" Arrow said while regaining consciousness.

"You went down pretty hard. Are you alright?"

Chad tried to get up.

"Yeah, I think I'm good," he said. "Yeah, I'll be fine."

"Good! 'Cause we gotta get out of here!"

"Yeah, let's go! Argh!"

"What's wrong?"

"I think I twisted my ankle when I landed. But I'm fine, let's go."

The militants made it to the eyesight of the soaring soldiers. They attempted to shoot them down, but their efforts were futile as the two shadows faded into the night sky.

"Wave Runner, we are airborne," Andy said. "ETA to rendezvous point, twenty minutes."

"Roger that," Topher replied.

About fifteen minutes in Chad said, "I don't think I'm gonna make it. My battery is about to die."

"I'm low, too," Andy said. "But I should be fine, I think."

"The burst must have depleted my stores."

"Let's go Tandem. Hopefully, we've got enough juice to make it."

"Okay, Tandem mode with Eager Beaver."

"Tandem accepted."

Automatically, the suits took over controls and joined midair, allowing Andy's suit to tow Chad's. They flew a few minutes before the inevitable.

"Yup! We're going down," Andy said. "Battery's about to die too."

"We're two minutes out," Chad said.

"Yeah, we don't have two minutes left of juice. We have another minute at best before it lands."

As Andy expected, the suits started to descend on their own. And landed them safely about two miles from their rendezvous point.

"Arrow & Beaver, you better get moving fast!" Max said. "I'm still monitoring Omar and his band of merry men. They're right on your tail. These guys don't give up!"

"As much as I like Omar and his guys," Chad said. "I'm not trying to see them again. Let's roll!"

"Yeah, let's roll. Try to keep up," Andy said.

The two soldiers made a run for it. Like shadows, they blended in the aphotic Iranian countryside.

"You all right, bro?" Andy asked.

"Yeah, I'm fine," Chad said.

"Your ankle still bothering you?"

"Yeah, a little bit, but I'll be alright."

At the hideout

"Welcome back!" Max said.

"Good to be back, but we have to get moving. We're running out of time," Topher said. "We're running low on energy. We can't tandem to the exfil point."

"Yeah, I figured as much," Max said. "I scanned the area and found twelve vehicles. I can hack the remote start system. The closest one is a Land Rover. About three hundred yards from here."

"Okay, let's commandeer it on behalf of the US government and the United Nations," Topher said.

"What about Arrow and Beaver?" CK asked.

"We've got to go get them," Topher said. "The sun will be rising soon. A black guy and a white guy in military suits in the middle of Iran's countryside, I don't like those odds. Gazelle, you take the hostages to the exfil location. We're going to get our teammates, and we'll catch up with you."

Gazelle walked towards Topher and extended his hand in friendship.

"Thank you," Azael said as they hugged. "Get your friends. We'll be waiting for you at the Exfil point." Though they had just met, they embraced as if they were brothers.

"We'll see you all in a few," Topher said upon breaking the hug.

"I'm going to need Betsy back," Max said to Azael.

The Israeli soldier was perplexed.

"His suit," CK said. "He wants his suit back."

"Oh, yes! I almost forgot about that," Azael said.

"Listen up, everyone," Max said while Azael took off the suit. "This never happened," he said, pointing to Azael and himself.

"Understood," Elisha replied on behalf of his fellow former captives.

"Alright, let's go," Topher said.

"Yes, let's hurry," Elisha said. Israel will certainly launch airstrikes before dawn. We must reach them before they do."

"You heard the man," Topher said as he and CK headed towards the door. Max followed them, but Topher turned to him and said, "Milkshake, I'd feel better if you went along with them. Make sure they get there safely, and maybe you can try to have them wait for us."

"You got it!" Max said.

The groups split as planned. Max, Azael, and the rescued hostages headed south, commandeered the vehicle, and made their way to the exfil location. Topher and CK headed back on their tracks to find their teammates.

A minute later, Topher said, "Arrow, Beaver, we're zeroing in on your location. We might have enough power to give you a ride."

"We sure could use a ride right about now," Andy said, panting.

"What? Don't tell me you're tired already," Chad quipped, hobbling on one ankle.

"Guys, do you see this?" CK asked. "Headlights heading your way. I'd say they're about half a mile out."

"Don't see anything yet," Chad said, looking back till the headlights rose on the horizon. "I see them now." The soldiers stood still, blending with the darkness of night. Topher and CK were hovering out of sight. Omar and his militants passed by them unsuspecting. Once they passed, Topher and CK made their descent.

"You all good?" Topher asked the two partners.

"Yeah. My ankle got hit when I came down, but I'll be alright." Chad said.

"That was one heck of a shot, man," Topher said. "We owe you big time."

"All in a day's work."

"How about we finish this day on a good note and head out of here," CK said.

"I second that," Andy said.

"At our current energy levels," Topher said. "We'll make it back to the hideout and commandeer another vehicle to hopefully make it to exfil in time."

They flew out. Topher tandem with Chad, CK had Beaver. They flew as far as they could before Topher's battery ran out, and they all landed.

"Milkshake, we're about a klick from the hideout. We need a vehicle. Can you assist?"

"Yes, sending you the location of a car not too far from where you are."

Milkshake sent them the location of a five-passenger pickup truck about a quarter of a mile from their location. It took them a couple of minutes to get to the vehicle.

"We're here, Milkshake," Toper said.

"Okay, let me unlock it for you."

A few minutes passed.

"What's taking so long?" Andy asked.

"Something's wrong," Max replied. "But almost there."

"Everybody take cover," Chad said, pointing to headlights turning the bend towards their location. The fully loaded pickup truck stopped, and about a dozen militants got out with machine guns in hand, scouting out the place.

Omar shouted in Farsi, "They are around here somewhere. Be alert."

"They know we're here," CK said in a low voice picked up by the suits' communication system.

"Somebody must have been watching us," Chad said.

"Okay, stay put," Topher said. "Right now, they're as blind as bats and can't see us—" Before Topher could finish his thought, another two pickup trucks arrived, equally loaded. They put on their high beams and positioned all three trucks to light up as much of the area as possible.

"How's everybody on ammo?" Andy asked.

"I'm almost out," Chad said.

"Whatever's left in this chamber," Topher said, still carrying the militant's gun he picked up earlier.

One random shot rang out. It hit a little too close to Andy. His instincts kicked in, and he fired back, exposing their position. Fire started pouring out from all directions, concentrating on the soldiers. Though they found refuge behind rock formations, it was just a matter of time before they were overtaken.

The sound of gunshots, as loud as they were, was suddenly overtaken by the blaring sounds of jet engines and the subsequent payload they unleashed on Pardis. The blasts temporarily lit the night sky just enough for Topher and the others to see the expression of terror on their opponents' faces. The fear that gripped the militants wasn't the fear of death; rather, it was the fear of loss. And for a second, they were not enemies but fathers, brothers, and sons contemplating the untimely loss of loved ones. Instantly, this conflict faded into oblivion. The combatants jumped back into their trucks and rushed out. Some fired desperate shots at the team. Those shots were in vain.

"Milkshake, what happened?" Topher said. "Tell them we have the hostages!"

"Wave Runner, we are at exfil point. They know we have them," Max said. "They fired anyways."

"NO! NO! NO!" Topher said. "Can you get us out of here?"

"I don't know. I think they shut me down," Max said, not understanding why a routine hack seemed so hard to perform. "You have twenty minutes before sunrise. They'll leave you behind if you don't make it by then."

"You heard that, guys. We have to run," Topher said. The quartet took off running. In normal circumstances, it would be a long shot for them to complete a five-mile run in twenty minutes, but after the night they had, it was virtually impossible, but they had to try.

About ten minutes in, headlights were approaching. Everyone knew they could not stop and hide. They would have to go through whatever was in their way, guns blazing if needed. Every team member drew whichever weapon they had available to them. The vehicle stopped.

"Don't shoot! It is me!" the driver said.

The team cautiously approached the vehicle until the face became visible.

"Suri? What are you doing here?" Topher asked.

"I heard you could use a ride. Besides, I don't think it's a good idea to leave my country after what happened. Come in!"

They all got on board the SUV.

"I'm surprised Gazelle let you out of his sight," CK said.

"He collapsed as soon as we made it, and he knew I was safe. It was a tough twenty-four hours for him. Probably the longest day of his life."

"I bet," CK said. "That's a good one. You better hold on to him."

"I intend to," they found each other smiling, a brief moment of normalcy, as destruction raged in their rear-view mirror.

"Would you explain my decision to him when he wakes up?" She confided in CK.

"Yes, I will let him know," CK said, understanding the weight on Suri's shoulders. "Don't worry, you'll be together again soon."

As they approached the rendezvous point, the Sun's rays lit up the Iranian sky. Soon, the local population and the world would wake up to a new reality.

"Albatross, this is Eagle Chick requesting access," Topher said as he saw the MI-26 Helicopter getting ready for takeoff.

"Access granted!"

16

FAMILY TIME

Point Piper, New South Wales, Australia, four miles outside Sydney

"HOLD IT REAL TIGHT," Robert said. "Go with the flow. Feel the waves. The sea is not your enemy. You just have to learn to negotiate its waters."

"I'm doing it, Grandad!" Ruby said. "I'm doing it!"

"Yes, you are! My little Captain Ruby! On to the high seas!" Robert said playfully. Turning to her dad, he said, "She's a fast learner."

"That she is!" Ethan answered. "She's the smart one in the family." Turning to his daughter, "Bibi, why don't you let me try it?"

"Here you go, Daddy." She ceded her place to her father. Now the eldest son was at the helm.

"That's a nice one, Dad. When did you get it?"

"A couple of months ago. It was time for a change."

"Indeed, it was," Ethan said pensively. "But I did like Ole Lizzie. I have found memories of her."

"We did have some good times with her."

"That we did. Like that time, we were in a storm and thought we would drown. But Ole Lizzie withstood the winds and the waves and got us home safe."

"Speaking of safety, did you talk to your brother?"

"Yes, Dad. I did. His mind is made up."

Robert sighed and stayed silent for a moment.

"He knows I'm not going to support him?"

"Yes, he knows you'll cut him off."

"How about Oliver? Did he speak to him?"

"We were both there. Dad, Wes is a grown man. If that's the way he wants to go, let him."

"It's not about him. It's about our family legacy. We have worked too hard for a spoiled kid to squander all that investment."

"I know you're talking about me!" Wes shouted from the back of the boat. "At least say it to my face!"

One stare from Ethan and Wes changed his posture and started to play with his nieces and nephews.

"Dad, the more you try to force him to follow in your footsteps, the more he'll rebel. Let him fly on his own for a while; when time comes, he'll return to the nest."

"Why can't he be like you?"

"That's because I'm like Mom, and he's like you," Ethan said with a smile.

Later, as the sun set over the bay in the early evening, the Russos returned to their parental home.

"Grandma! Grandma! I drove the ship," Ruby said.

"Did you now? I'm sure you did a good job," Mona said.

"It's 'steered the ship,' my dear. 'I steered the ship,'" Jackie, Ruby's mother, said.

"Let the child be," Mona said to her daughter-in-law. Turning to her husband, she said, "Robert, I can't understand this new cable system you got us. Why did you have to change it?"

"It was time for a change. This one offers more channels, streaming services, and VR channels at a cheaper price."

"For Pete's sake, Robert, you manage some of the biggest investment funds in the world, and you're worried about saving five ninety-nine a month?" The little banter caused everybody to laugh.

"Sorry, people, but I like a good return on my investment. More channels for less money. That's a no-brainer."

"It might be a no-brainer to you. But it takes a Ph.D. to figure this thing out."

"Oh, I can do that!" Ruby said while taking the remote from her grandma. Within seconds, the TV wall lit up with real-life holographic images of vintage Peppa Pig cartoons.

The little one brought smiles and laughter into the room.

"That's a smart one you got there," Wes said to his eldest brother.

Ethan chuckled.

"Why are you laughing?"

"Because that's exactly what Dad said on the boat. And you guys sound alike."

"We all sound alike."

"Yes, we do, but you two, it's to a whole other level. If I close my eyes, I can't tell you apart."

"Yet we couldn't be more different."

"Actually, you are more alike than you think. You're both driven and stubborn. You're just stubborn about different things."

"He wants to make money; I want to save the planet."

"Or you could say. He wants to ensure the well-being of the generations to come, and you want to ensure there is still a planet left for them to enjoy. Complementary goals."

"Forever the diplomat. Anyhow, thanks for getting him off my back."

"It's all good, mate. You're doing a good thing, and your heart is in the right place."

"Okay, everyone, dinner is served," Mona said.

The famished hordes made their way to the dining hall.

"Wow, this looks good!" Ruby said.

"You might save on cable, but you went all out on this dinner," Ethan said.

"Only the best for my dearests," Mona said.

Joy filled the room as only the aroma of delicious foods and the presence of loved ones could do. Everyone was joyous as they took their place at the table. Everyone except one. But before he could start preaching about the evils of consumerism and the inequities of this economic system, Ethan kindly put his hand behind his younger brother's back and whispered to him,

"Let it go. Think about Mom."

Wes made eye contact with his brother, then watched the jubilation on his mother's face. He nodded in acquiescence and sat quietly at the table as Mona said, "Before we say grace. This year in particular, with everything happening in this world, it's important to be grateful for the safety we enjoy, the things we have, and the people we love."

"I want to say grace!" Ruby said.

"Go ahead, my darling," Mona replied.

As the child closed her eyes and clasped her hands together, Robert excused himself to the dislike of his better half. As he walked to his den for a more private conversation, he could hear the fading sound of her prayer.

"Dear Lord, thank you for the food. Bless the hands that prepared it, and give some to those who do not have. Amen."

"Amen," everyone echoed.

Robert entered his den, shut the door, answered the phone,

"What took you so long? I called you yesterday."

"You called me at eleven twenty-five P.M., my time," Lawrence answered. "I sleep at that time."

"Save your excuses. The project is proceeding very rapidly. There are a lot of moving pieces. We need you and your peers to manufacture civil wars throughout the globe."

"I need you to be more precise," Lawrence said, knowing that any failure could cost him his life.

"Do you want us to activate militia groups?"

"No, we want you to create social chaos. Anarchy."

"How?"

"Use their poison of choice. For Europe, use labor disputes and terrorist attacks. For Mexico and other Latin American countries, use popular outrage against government corruption. For Taiwan, use Chinese patriotism."

"What about the US and Canada?"

"Use racial strife and anarchy. Pit everyone against their neighbor. Break it down to the most granular level possible."

"Isn't that what we've been doing for the past two decades?"

"We need you to take it to the next level. We need you— We need a total breakdown."

"Mind if I ask why? Why such destruction and mayhem?"

"Consider it a rebirth. It's painful now, but when the baby is born, all will be well."

"So, you say."

"So, I know. Hopefully, you live long enough to witness it for yourself. May I remind you, you wanted that position? You wanted the capacity to control messaging beyond your platform. Now you have that power and control. But we control you. Don't forget that. The minute we don't get what we want, what use are you to us? Please, always remain useful to us. Goodbye, Lawrence." He hung up and took a moment to regain his fatherly demeanor.

"Darling, what was so important for you to miss Ruby giving grace?" Mona said.

"Yes, Grandpa, you missed my prayer."

"I'm sorry, Bibi. One of Grandpa's brokers was being naughty."

"Did you send him to timeout?"

"No, but I spoke to him very strongly. He will behave now." He turned to the fully garnished table. "Let's dig in, shall we?"

17

VICTORY LAP

White House, Washington, DC/Jerusalem Joint Virtual Press Conference

"GREETINGS, EVERYONE, PLEASE WELCOME the president of the United States," the staffer said.

"Thank you all for coming," President Rodriguez said. He then addressed his virtual guest, "Thank you, Prime Minister Dahan, for your presence and your friendship."

"Thank you, President Rodriguez," Prime Minister Dahan said.

"As you are all aware. About thirty hours ago, a multinational convoy of IAEA Nuclear inspectors was attacked in Iran. The cowardly assailers ruthlessly killed everyone in the convoy except three. They kidnapped three of the world's finest scientists: Dr. Suri Mirzakhani, Dr. Hiro Ohira, and Dr. Elisha Zvili. As the world saw, the terrorists threatened to kill those innocent heroes of science whose only goal was to make this world a safer place. Immediately, my administration and Prime Minister Dahan's team worked tirelessly to bring them back to their loved ones. We dispatched a joint special forces team. Thankfully, through tremendous acts of courage and bravery, they rescued the hostages. They are currently under medical observation in Kuwait. Prime Minister Dahan." The president ceded the floor to his Israeli counterpart.

"Thank you, Mr. President. In light of this attack, our intelligence services obtained incontrovertible evidence of direct involvement of the Iranian regime. By doing so, the Iranian government has once again shown total disregard for the rule of international law and human life. They have decided to turn their backs on the Brotherhood of Nations and chose the path of violence over the shores of peace. As a result, we have no choice for the self-preservation of the Israeli State to address this existential threat head-on. A little before dawn, our military started operations in Pardis, Iran, to unroot the terrorist threat represented by this part of Iran. To the peace-loving Iranian people, we urge you to petition your government to abandon its belligerence towards Israel, America, and the world."

"Thank you, Mr. Prime Minister," Rodriguez said. "A friend always loves, and a brother is born for adversity. The United States stands with you and your people. The bond of brotherhood of our nations, with shared ideals of peace and freedom, shall endure beyond these trying times. We are ready to assist in any way necessary."

"Thank you, Mr. President."

"We'll take a few questions." The swarm of reporters' hands rose before he could complete his sentence. He called upon a familiar but often hostile reporter from the Affiliated Press, Connie Ostermeyer. "Go ahead, Connie."

"Thank you, Mr. President. What do you think the response of the Iranians will be? And supposing that they respond in kind, and considering the situation on the Korean peninsula, can the US be involved in two major conflicts at once?"

"To your first question. We would hope that the Iranian regime would reconsider its belligerent stance. We most certainly would prefer that they return to the negotiation table. But make no mistake, should they choose to escalate the situation and continue to blatantly violate the rule of international law, we are ready to take on both hostile regimes and swiftly restore peace to those respective regions of the globe. Our support of both our South Korean and Israeli allies is unbreakable."

"Reports on the ground indicate that US Troops have yet to engage the north. Why is that?"

"Connie, you know we can't discuss operational strategies. But I can assure you that every aspect of this conflict is being handled with full cooperation between our nations. Next question."

One hour later, in the Oval Office

"You did well, Mr. President," Sarah, the chief of staff, said. "In these times, the nation needs to see strength, confidence, and resolve. You showed them exactly that."

"Thank you, Sarah. I'm afraid we'll need more than a nice press conference performance."

"You don't think we can handle both conflicts?"

"No, it's not that. I know we can, but at what cost?" The president asked, but Sarah didn't dare answer. He continued, "When is the last time we've had a year without a single war?"

"I don't know. But I can find out."

"Don't bother. The closest one was the year 2000. Before you were born."

"Oh wow!"

"The strength of a country is in the spirit of its people. Our people are strong, but everyone reaches a breaking point."

"Do you think we're at that point?"

"I don't know. If it's not the Middle East, it's Africa. If it's not Africa, it's Eastern Europe. Same song, but a different tune. We believe in peace through strength, so we spend over one trillion dollars annually on our military. Yet we're always fighting. Why can't we ever seem to achieve perfect peace?"

"I don't know the answer to that, sir. But I can tell you this, if we don't resolve those conflicts quickly, our other enemies will be emboldened, and peace will be even harder to achieve."

"You're right about that, Sarah."

"What's going to happen to our boys?"

"That's a tough one. I told the brass they could handle it as they see fit. Don't get me wrong, we're proud they got the job done. They brought the hostages home. But they disobeyed a direct order. We can't have rogue units playing Rambo out there."

"Sorry, what?"

"Rambo?"

"I don't know what that is."

"Never mind. All that to say, there must be a punishment. But we can't lose one of our best units amid escalating conflicts. So, I guess they'll get two minutes in the penalty box and then return to the field."

Camp Buehring, Kuwait

"How's Max?" Topher asked CK.

"He'll be alright. They're working on him, but he'll be back on his feet soon."

"Speaking of feet, how about Chad and his ankle?"

"They injected it. He should regain full function in a few hours. "

"Good. Glad we all made it out of there."

"For sure. That was some crazy run, though."

"Yes, it was. But I have to say I think this is the best team out there. Best training, best people, best execution. You guys did good."

"Thanks, boss. You called Maddie?"

"I'm about to."

"Well, hurry. Or we'll be a member short. No amount of training is going to save you from her."

"Yes, ma'am! I'll catch you later."

"Later, Mr. Wave Runner." CK headed out of the room.

Now alone in the room, Topher dialed Maddie using the so-called *InPresence* mode from his mobile device. Once she picked up, half the room filled with a 3D rendition of her in her immediate surroundings.

"Honey! Thank God! "Maddie exclaimed, answering the call.

"Hey, babe. How are you?"

"I'm fine! How are you? And how's the team?"

"We're all good. A few bruises here and there, but nothing major. How's my little guy?"

"Ryan is fine. I just put him to bed. A funny thing happened today. The news was on. He heard the president speak about a rescue mission in Iran. Ryan asked if they were talking about his daddy."

"Oh wow, he did? That's a perceptive young man."

"Was he right?"

"You know I can neither confirm nor deny. But I'll say this: we've been doing this for a while now. Nothing official, but from what I see on the ground and hear in the grapevine, I think it's going to get worse."

"What do you mean?"

"I think these conflicts aren't going to stop. I think they are likely to escalate."

"Why are you saying that?"

"It's just my gut. Our enemies are more technologically advanced than before. They have more funds and more anger than ever. I just want you to be prepared if this escalates. A lot of good people we know will be dragged in."

"I get it. That's the life we signed up for."

Topher looked over his fiancée's shoulder to see Ryan peeking through the stair railing.

"I think you have a spy," Topher said. "Hey, Buddy."

"Ryan!" Maddie said. "You can come, Buddy, it's okay."

Ryan made his way to his mother's side, embarrassed to have been caught but glad to see his dad.

"Hi, Daddy!"

"Hi, buddy," Topher said, his face gleaming with the joy of a little child.

"Dad, when are you coming home?"

Topher's smile was subdued as he glanced at Maddie and then back at Ryan.

"Soon, buddy, very soon."

"I miss you, Daddy."

"I miss you too, Buddy."

"Okay, say goodnight to your dad," Maddie said.

"Goodnight, Dad."

"Goodnight."

"Okay, time for bed. Hop, hop. I'll come to tuck you in."

"Okay, Mommy," Ryan said, returning to his room.

"So, when are you coming back?" Maddie said, echoing Ryan.

"We're taking care of those few bruises I mentioned, but we should be heading home in about forty-eight hours."

"Good! Can't wait for you to be here. I have so much to show you for the wedding."

"Can't wait! Looking forward to agreeing to everything you selected," Topher said tongue in cheek.

"You know that's right! Still, you can choose your tux."

"Thank you, that is so kind of you!"

"Seriously, I miss you. I want you home."

"I know me too. I'll be home soon. I have to go. We have a debrief scheduled."

"Okay, be safe, hon."

"Roger that."

18

PRESERVATION

American University of Beirut, Lebanon

AS THE RISING SUN broke through the hacksaw ridge on the horizon, its glistening over the tranquil Mediterranean Sea contrasted with the frantic probing of forensic experts from the Beirut police department. Dr. Elenor Zalloua spent countless late nights in the lab, but this one was not what she had expected.

"I have been running the tests time and time again all night. I reviewed the data. I do not know how this happened, but this is not it. This is a fake sample," Dr. Zalloua said to the officers and her colleagues from the Virology lab.

"How did you lose this thing?" Detective Al Qazi said.

"Sir, with respect," Dr. Ghani, the director of the laboratory, said. "We do not lose viruses. Our safety measures are impeccable."

"Then how do you explain this?" The detective asked nonchalantly. He did not appreciate being dragged into what he thought was a frivolous investigation. *They most likely screwed up and blamed some mysterious forces,* he thought to himself.

"I do not know. That's why you are here! You're the investigator," the director replied.

"You do not seem to grasp the gravity of the situation, officer," Dr. Zalloua said.

"Enlighten me," he replied.

"This is a virology lab. We deal with viruses. Most of the time, they are harmless, but some are dangerous, and others are deadly. This one," she sighed. "This one is one of the deadliest." As the words departed her mouth, her mind drifted towards dreadful thoughts before she was pulled back to her current situation.

"How deadly?" the detective asked.

"If this were to get out. We could lose half of Beirut in weeks, maybe days."

Al Qazi's body tensed up. Now, Dr. Zalloua had his full attention. He grabbed his radio and started issuing orders.

"I need all available units to patrol the streets and stop everyone and everything that looks somewhat suspicious. Also, establish a communication protocol with the Internal Security Forces. Have them put Al Fahoud on standby."

"Sir. What is the description of the suspects?" An officer said on the radio.

"We don't have one yet. I will let you know when we do. But have all units patrol the city by sector. Let them be visible."

"Yes, sir."

He signaled the doctors to follow him while he headed to the detective in charge of forensics.

"Lara, what have you found?"

"Nothing, absolutely nothing of value."

"Come on, you must have found something."

"Nothing, the cameras show no signs of tampering. There are no fingerprints, fabric fibers, or signs of damage to the locks or equipment. There are pros, and then there are these guys." She moved closer to him and whispered, "Unless she made it up. Are we sure she's not lying? Cause we couldn't find anything."

"I don't know, but she doesn't seem to be. She's not showing any signs of deception. And the risks are too high."

"How high?"

"Think Covid meets Ebola high."

"I see. Okay, we'll keep looking. I'll let you know when we find something."

"Thank you."

He turned to the doctors.

"They have nothing yet, but they'll keep on looking."

"Ladies and gentlemen, we'll take it from here!"

The voice came from the main door as a small contingent of heavily armed soldiers donning military garb of the counter-terrorism unit made their entrance.

"What's going on?" Detective Al Qazi said.

"Detective Al Qazi, I suppose?" the commander of the squad said while presenting the detective with his identification. "I am Captain Kassir, Counter Terrorism. We will be taking over this investigation."

"But we barely got started."

"We appreciate your service. Please communicate all your findings to our liaison personnel. Also, we will conduct individual interviews with each

166 | D A V I D   E L I E   J R

member of the lab's staff independently." He looked around for a couple of seconds. "Starting with the director of the Lab."

"That would be me," Dr. Ghani said. Immediately, Kassir headed towards the lab's director.

"I'm Captain Kassir. Can we go somewhere private?"

They headed to Dr. Ghani's office. The professor sat in his chair, usually a position of power for the senior scientist.

"Dr. Ghani. Can you walk me through what went wrong?"

"Sir. It's unclear at this point. We run a very secure operation. Everything is done by the book."

"That's not what I'm referring to."

"What are you referring to?"

"You had one directive. 'Hide it in plain sight.'"

Ghani remained uncharacteristically quiet while Kassir continued.

"We gave you the funds to advance your research. Made you world famous. Brought this faculty to become one of the best in the world. In exchange, you had to perfect it and keep it safe."

"You don't understand-"

"No! You don't understand what you've done. Do you know who took it?"

"How would I know that?"

"You wouldn't, but we do. You have no idea what your incompetence has caused. Unfortunately, you won't be there to see this through. Goodbye, director."

Dr. Ghani remained speechless and motionless as Kassir walked out. After a few moments, he called the one person who mattered the most in his life. The line rang and rang, but there was no response. He tried again, no response. He tried a third time, she picked up.

"Hello, I'm in the middle of a lecture. Are you okay?"

"Amina, listen to me very carefully. I need you to get Dalia and meet me at the airport."

"What? Why?"

"Just trust me, we must leave Lebanon now. Take everything from the safe."

"Hamza, what have you done!"

"I will explain everything later. But head to the airport now, and do not forget the safe's contents. If you don't see me after one hour. Take the first flight to Canada. You will be safe there."

"Hamza, you're scaring me."

"Don't be scared. Everything will be alright. Just go now. I love you!"

"I love you too," she responded as a wave of despair grappled her heart.

19

REROUTED

Boeing C-17 Globemaster V Over the Atlantic Ocean

"THEY FIXED ME UP real well," Max said, rubbing the wound area.

"It's pretty incredible what they're able to do now," CK said, then turning to Chad, she asked, "What about your ankle?"

"Like new! I was shooting some hoops with some guys this morning."

"So, what will you guys do when you get home?" CK asked.

"I'm going to find me a good beer, my recliner, a ball game, and fall asleep two minutes in," Andy said.

"I'm with you on that one," Max said.

"How about you, Topher?" CK asked.

"I'm going to finish what I started before we left. Hopefully, we can get those wedding plans in motion."

"Come on, man, you know Maddie already has that covered. All you have to do is show up!" Chad said.

"Yeah, who am I kidding? She got it all figured out. Besides, I don't look forward to picking out table covers. Give me al-Saalihin all day."

"You might have your wish," The Co-Pilot said. "We've been ordered to reroute to Mexico. They'll brief you when you get there."

The team was stunned for a moment, even though they all knew better than to be surprised at this impromptu mission. They just hoped for a respite before heading back out. There were no complaints but rather wishes for a different timing.

"Any chance this mission is in Cancun?" Chad quipped.

"No such luck. You're going to Monterrey, Mexico. We'll let you know when we initiate the descent."

Mexico Aerial Military Base in Apodaca Nuevo Leon on the outskirts of Monterrey

On the tarmac, representatives of Mexico's State Department, the Centro Nacional de Inteligencia (CNI), and the US' Central Intelligence Agency (CIA) welcomed the team to the investigation. The introductions were brief, and so was the briefing. Time was against them. Every minute wasted could lead to a catastrophe of cataclysmic proportions. The CNI set up a state-of-the-art operations center in the Military base.

"We tapped in all CCTV footage." Agent Gomez of the CNI said. "We are monitoring all cellular communications. It's like we are chasing ghosts."

"Do we have anything on our side? "Topher asked CIA Agent Ellis, knowing that the Agency had a reputation for holding back vital information to protect sources and methods. This was not the time for turf wars. This was the time to save lives.

"We were blindsided as well," Agent Ellis answered. Topher didn't detect deception in the agent.

"Okay, then we divide and conquer," Topher said. "We are out of time, and the options are few. If we are to find this virus before it disappears or, worse, is released, we have to cover all the bases."

He continued,

"First, go to the source. CK, you speak Spanish, so you and Chad will head to the crime scene at the Virology lab and follow their trail."

"Roger that," she said.

Topher continued, "Andy, you will track the money movements. An operation this well executed has to be financed somehow. Follow the money."

"Sure, boss, but you know Max is better at that stuff."

"You speak Spanish?"

"Not a lick."

"So, I need him in the field."

"Good point."

"Max and I will work on the intercept. There are only two reasons for a heist like this. They either want to sell it or release it. Let's find them before we find out which one they are planning."

"What if they release it?" CK asked, turning to Agent Gomez.

"We have the military, regional, and local police assisting with the investigation and ready to initiate a lockdown if needed."

"But let's be clear," Agent Ellis said. "If this pathogen is released, the lockdown will only be for show. It won't stop it. We have to find it before that happens, or life as we know it is over."

"Understood," Topher said. "Let's get to it then!"

Each team left with representatives of the CNI, and the CIA. CK and Chad headed to the Institute of Virology. Topher and Max headed to Cartel country. Andy headed to the CNI to pair up with a team of analysts.

Institute of Virology

"This is where they kept the virus," Agent Gomez said as the cohort entered the most secure section of the facility. "Since the Wuhan leak, we have instituted major security reforms throughout the country's critical infrastructure. Especially labs and food processing facilities."

"Apparently, it wasn't secured enough," Agent Ellis said.

"At least we don't ship deadly viruses around," Gomez said.

"What is he talking about?" Chad asked Ellis.

"A few years ago, one of our labs accidentally mailed out a deadly virus not unlike this one to thirty labs worldwide. We issued a recall order. Twenty-eight came back. The missing two? Lebanon and Mexico. Connecting the dots yet?"

"So, this is ultimately our fault?" Chad said. Before Ellis could answer, CK put a stop to this finger-pointing exercise.

"Guys, can we stop playing the blame game? We have a virus to find. If we succeed, there will be plenty of time to determine who did what. If we fail, it will be the least of our worries."

"Fair enough," Chad said. Turning to Gomez, he continued. "Everything looks impeccable. Did they clean up after the heist?"

"No, we left it untouched as the investigation unfolds," Gomez replied.

"Were there any signs of tempering at all?" CK asked.

"Not at all. It's like they were ghosts. Until they encountered the unit on a routine patrol. They tried to fight them off but-"

"Come on, Gomez, that wasn't much of a fight," Ellis said. "Your guys didn't land a punch."

"Can we talk to them?" CK asked.

"They are under observation at the hospital," Gomez answered.

"Any footage?" Chad asked.

"No, the cameras were wiped clean."

"What's this?" CK asked, pointing to a peculiar-looking black box.

"I don't know," Agent Gomez said. Turning to one of his agents, he said, "Call the director."

A few moments later, the director, Dr. Nuñez, arrived.

"Director, thank you for coming," Gomez said, "We had a question."

"I already told the officers everything I knew, but sure," the director said.

"What is this?" CK asked, pointing towards the black box-looking piece of equipment.

"Oh! That's our holographic time-lapse camera," He responded. "It allows us to monitor the progress of the rodents during our experiments and allows us to review with precision the methods used by our team. It is so automated that I forget it's even there."

"Do you think maybe it captured whoever stole your virus?" CK asked.

"I do not think so. It's directed towards the rodents' enclosure and the work area. The viruses are held on the other side."

"Well, let's look and see what we find," Chad said.

"Okay, no problem," The director said.

He tinkered with a few commands on the box. The device's automated system took over the operation. It opened and revealed a state-of-the-art holographic projector. After a few seconds of warm-up, a perfect live 3D video image of the room was displayed in a preset workspace area.

"This is surreal!" Chad said, seeing their real-time-sized-down 3D projection in the room they were standing in. It wasn't his first time in this situation, but he marveled at the technological prowess every time.

"Can you go back to the time of the robbery?" CK asked.

"Sure," Director Nuñez said and proceeded to command the device. "Show yesterday at 2300 hours. Speed 2.5."

After a few minutes of watching footage of the dark, deserted work area, rodent enclosures, and some laboratory refrigerators, the hallway lights came on. The light streamed into the work area through glass windows.

"I think this was when our security patrol was making its rounds," Dr. Nuñez said.

"Is that when the intruders took them out?" Chad asked.

"Yes, that would be around that time," She responded.

"Do you have sound?" CK asked.

"Sound? Yeah sure. Play sound, volume twenty-five percent." Immediately after Dr. Nuñez gave the command, the high-definition audio feed filled the room, enhancing the immersive experience.

At a distance, they heard the guards engaged in casual conversation. Suddenly, they were screaming orders.

"¡Paran o dispararé!"

"Stop, or I'll shoot!" CK translated for Chad's benefit.

"Yeah, I kinda figured that," Chad said. "Oh, what just happened?" He said as a shadow could be seen flashing through the light stream.

"What was that?" CK said, equally shocked.

"I'm not sure," Dr. Nuñez said.

"Rewind it," Agent Ellis said.

They watched that portion five times before anyone attempted an explanation.

"It looks like that's what took out your guards. But what could be that fast?"

"I guess we have to speak to the guards. Can we visit them at the hospital?" CK said.

"I'll arrange for that. "Agent Gomez said.

Cartel Country, a mile away from the Sinaloa Cartel's regional headquarters

"Let's go over your covers again," Agent Flores of the CNI said.

"We're international weapons dealers representing European buyers. We have buyers looking for a weapon that would shift the world order. A shift that will benefit the cartel's activities worldwide." Max said.

"I'm the buyer. He is my Mexican contact. He is the cousin of Rodrigo Morales," Topher added, pointing to the undercover agent.

"Rodrigo has been working undercover for three years now. We are very close to bringing this whole operation down. Don't blow his cover."

"Just follow my lead, and we'll be alright," Rodrigo said.

"Understood," Topher said.

Monterrey Regional Hospital

"Thank you for talking to us. We know it has been a trying time. We will make it as brief as possible," CK said to Adolpho, one of the security guards.

"How can I help?" Adolpho said. "I told the officer everything that happened."

"Please tell us one more time. I understand you and your colleague were on your routine patrol around the facility, right?"

"Yes, we were on patrol when we stumbled on two guys coming out of the lab. We called on them to put their hands up or we'll shoot. But before we drew our weapons, I had a foot in my face, and everything went dark. I woke up here."

"Wait, how far were they when you called them out?" CK asked.

"We were about fifty feet, I would say."

"So, you're telling me they were able to hit you from fifty feet away before you withdrew your weapon?"

"Yeah, I've never seen anything like it. I do MMA on the side, but this was something else."

"What else can you tell me about them? Did they say anything?"

"They didn't speak. They just attacked." Adolpho said.

"What did they look like?"

"One was about five feet ten inches, I would say. One was light-skinned with hazel eyes. The other one had brown skin. He had sunglasses."

"Where were they from, you think?"

"Not sure...they could be from here, Latin America, Asia."

"Okay, tell me about the attack. How did they take you down so quickly?"

"Like I said, I've never seen anything like that. He did one of those moves. To think of it, he launched in my direction, got on his hand, and the last thing I saw was his foot in my face. Woke up here."

"Okay, thank you for your time," CK said.

CK reconvened with Chad to compare notes.

"So, what did you get from yours?" CK asked.

"Muy Tai," Chad said.

"What do you mean?"

"The guy who attacked my guard used a standard Muay Thai attack."

"Really, how did you figure that?"

"My guy said once they called out the intruders, his attacker took two leaps and lodged his knee in his face. I saw his X-rays, and they're not pretty. His facial bones' fractures are consistent with the size of a knee. It's whether that or a two-by-four hit him."

"That's interesting, you would say that. My guy said his attacker made one of those moves, got on his hands, and landed his foot in his face."

"Capoeira," Chad said. "That's a Capoeira move."

"So, you think maybe the one is from Thailand and the other from Brazil?"

"We can't know for sure, but it's worth the look."

"Okay, how do you explain their speed?" CK asked.

"I don't know, but they might have had a suit. Or some sort of enhancements. From what we saw in the footage, I don't think that normal humans can be as fast."

"Okay, let's call it in to Beaver. He might be able to trace something."

Cartel Country, Sinaloa Cartel regional headquarters

Nested in the hills of the Sierra Madre Oriental Mountain range was an imposing compound serving as both base and second residence to Don Demetrio, a shrewd outlaw with a penchant for life's finer pleasures. Topher, Max, and Rodrigo pulled up to the iron gate, where they were greeted by henchmen carrying weapons of war. Rodrigo was driving the SUV. He pulled down his window.

"Donde esta Don Demetrio?" Rodrigo said, asking for the location of the regional leader. His accent was heavy, as if he were a Sinaloa native.

"En la Piscina," the henchman said casually, indicating that his boss was by the pool. Topher, Max, and undercover agent Rodrigo rolled slowly into the plush premises adorned with immaculate landscaping. The trio parked the car in the driveway. There were a dozen cars, but the space could easily take double that amount.

They headed straight to the backyard. When they made it to the back of the mansion, even the hardened soldiers were stunned at the astonishing resort-like design of the outdoor décor. Equally stunning were the looks of the guests enjoying this paradisiac setting. Their chiseled bodies were cut out of a fashion magazine.

"Must be nice," Max quipped under his breath.

"Gigo!" Demetrio shouted from the poolside.

"Don Dem," Rodrigo responded as if they were old friends. They headed towards one another and embraced each other.

"How are the kids and Maricela?" Demetrio asked in Spanish.

"They are doing well. Thank you for the car. My little guy loves it!"

"Does he drive as fast as his dad?"

"He's trying! You should see him in this little SUV like he is the king of the road!"

"He's an adorable little kid. I should stop by one of these days."

"You should, Maricela, and the kids would love it! You should bring the whole family. We could go out for breakfast or something."

"Great, let's make it happen."

"Perfect. Listen, speaking of making things happen. I brought a couple of friends hoping you can make something happen for them. The gringo only speaks English."

"No problem, we can speak English." Don Demetrio responded in English.

"Don, this is Christopher Johnson and my cousin Max Becerra. Can we go somewhere private?"

"No need. We are amongst friends here."

"Perfect! They have something to ask you. And who knows, maybe we can do some business today."

"I like business. I'm all ears." Don Demetrio said while turning his attention to Topher and Max.

"Thank you, sir. I'll be brief," Max said. "My colleague and I represent an international conglomerate of security specialists. Our ears, like yours, are always on the ground."

"Good! What are your ears telling you?"

"They are telling us that there was a security breach at the Institute of Virology. And someone got a hold of a virus that, if weaponized, could change the balance of power in this world. Our employers want it. Rumor has it that nothing happens in these parts without your knowledge or consent."

"Rumors are often exaggerated."

"The world will be upended one way or the other by this security beach. If you help us acquire this virus. Our employers will ensure you get a seat at the big table."

"What if I like the table I'm sitting at now? Look around. What else can you offer me? This is just one of my houses. I have four more around the world. How bigger can that table be?"

"I'm sure you didn't reach this level by settling." Topher said. "I'm willing to bet your outlook has always been to attain the next big thing."

"True, but your mistake is to assume my eyes aren't already set on the next big thing," Don Demetrio said. Turning to Rodrigo, he said, "Gigo, your wife is Maricela, you have two children Ana and Pedro. Your dad was absent from your life, and your mom, Alessandra, has two sisters, Alma and Alana. Whose son is Max?"

Time stood still. Rodrigo was in an instant state of shock. Sure, Don Demetrio knew about his family, they became unfortunate contributors to the undercover operation. He knew the stakes were high, and if things took a turn for the worse, the Mexican government would be unable to protect his family, which was a risk he felt he could manage. *But how did Don Demetrio know about my aunts?* Rodrigo thought to himself. If he knew about his aunts, he certainly knew about their children. Lying about that would be futile. And did he know he was an undercover agent and was just playing along for the amusement? There were three of them with no backup in the vicinity against a compound full of ruthless killers. He felt those were as good odds as they could have, but would he be able to get to his family in time? One phone call, one text message, they would be dead. He had to improvise.

"My mom's cousin from Chiapas. They moved to the US when he was a kid." Rodrigo said, giving a performance worthy of the greatest motion pictures.

"Gentlemen, we're on the clock. Can we get back to business.?" Topher said.

"You heard the man. We're good for now. Thank you for the offer," Rodrigo said to Topher's surprise. He turned to Don Demetrio, seeking confirmation. "You good or?"

"It was a pleasant time but, indeed, we have business to attend to. Thank you for stopping by, gentlemen," Don Demetrio said in response.

"Very well then. Thank you for your time," Max said, then turning to Rodrigo, "Okay cuz, I will see you around." The two soldiers headed back from where they came.

"Let me walk them out," Rodrigo said. He caught up with them. Rodrigo approached Max to give him one of those family hugs as they were about to get in the car. As his head crossed Max's, he whispered,

"He's in on it. Security is tight at night, but they get lazy just make sure you hurt me." He continued louder, "Okay, *Primo,* I'll see you soon. Stay safe!" He went back to the pool area while Topher and Max drove off.

One hour later, at the military base

"While you guys were out playing Al Capone," Andy said. "I ran the search on those two who broke into the virology lab. It's inconclusive. I looked through countless bank records, flight records, and came up with about a dozen people who fit the profile. But they whether had solid alibis, and a few are dead."

"Did you run it through IRIS?" Max asked.

"Yes, the International Recognition & Identification System," Andy answered, annoyed. "We ran it for people from Brazil and Thailand with combat training and criminal background traveling into Mexico in the past year. The system came up with several names but, like I said, they were all dead ends. One guy was looking good, but he is part of a symposium in Mexico City, another is vacationing in Cabo, and on and on it goes."

"How about CCTVs red light cams, et cetera?" Max asked.

"It's running that as we speak, it's been getting hits but nothing putting those two guys in Monterrey last night."

"Okay, not bad," Max said. "We just need to keep looking. You're pretty good at this. You should do that more often."

"Nah, man, I'm more of the in-the-field action type."

"Speaking of field action," Topher said. "We had an interesting time with that Don Demetrio character. We think he might be in on it or at least know something about the heist."

"When we were trying to buy the virus," Max said. "We tried to bait him into getting into the next big thing. He then mentioned something about already focusing on the next big thing. He wasn't surprised or interested in what we had to say. But when we were leaving, Rodrigo, our contact, pretty much told us to come back at night."

"Night-time is coming soon," Chad said. "What about we suit up and pay him a visit? We'll see if he's more talkative that way."

"Alright, let's do it!" Topher said.

Don Demetrio's Mansion in the office den

The mansion, built in the 2020s, had large floor-to-ceiling windows. The design was immaculate. Don Demetrio was sitting at his large Italian Burlwood desk overlooked by a bookshelf containing some of the greatest military and crime classics of all times. Opposite his desk was a matching conference table overlooked by a holoscreen. Two comfortable sofas facing each other were between the executive desk and the conference table. Rodrigo was sitting on the sofa to the left of the executive desk while two of Don Demetrio's trusted associates were sitting on the other one. No one talked while Don was concluding business with two businessmen standing with four suitcases, one in each hand.

"Honey, I am so proud of you," Don Demetrio said. "You are doing so well! Ninety-six percent on your exam is so good! I will be coming home soon. Daddy is finishing some business meetings, and I will see you later tonight. Okay, baby, bye-bye now." He hung up the phone. "Sorry to have you waiting, gentlemen. But it's my baby girl. Always make time for your family, right guys?"

"Yes, Mr. Don. They are growing so fast," Enrique, one of Don's associates, said.

"Yes, they do grow really fast," Don Demetrio said. "I am trying to enjoy it as much as I can. Running a business here while they are home with my wife is not easy. But you should always keep business and family separate. Don't you agree, Gigo?"

"Absolutely, boss. Keep them home and keep them safe." Rodrigo answered.

"Why don't you come here to help me wrap up this business?" Demetrio said to Rodrigo. He then addressed the two men standing by his desk, "Thank you for your patience, gentlemen. I believe these are for me?"

They put the four suitcases on the desk and opened all of them to reveal stacks of cash.

"What a beauty. 2.5 million US dollars. Isn't this beautiful, Gigo?"

"Yes, sir. It's quite lovely," Rodrigo said.

"Do you mind helping me count these?"

"Not at all. Let's get it done."

"That's what I like about you, Rodrigo. Always ready to get your hands dirty. You're not afraid of hard work. By the way, which aunt did you say Max was the son of?"

"My mom's cousin Elvira, why?"

"Because I ran your family tree all the way to the arrival of the Spaniards, and I did find your mom's cousin Elvira. She does live in the US, but she doesn't have any children."

"Not biological. She was a foster care parent. Max is one of her foster children."

"Why, you're so good at this. Did you prepare that? Or does lying come naturally to you? Is it like second nature? You breathe, you lie type of thing?" Demetrio said while pulling out a taser gun. Immediately, his two trusted associates pulled out their weapons. Demetrio got up while still in the upward motion, and he discharged his taser gun, hitting Rodrigo in the leg, causing him to fall to the ground in shock.

"Thank you, gentlemen. There is no need to count; I trust you. You're free to go," Demetrio said to the two visitors. "See, when you trust people, you don't need to constantly check what they tell you. But for other people, the scum of the earth!" He kicked Rodrigo in the stomach.

Don continued,

"They try to gain your trust only to stab you in the back! And for what? A measly salary of a public worker! Look! Look! Look!" He pointed at the suitcases. "This is just another day at the office. With plenty more where that came from. I could have made you a rich, powerful man. Whatever Ana and Pedro want, they would get! College? Paid! Fancy vacation? Paid! Wedding? Paid! Rather, now they're going to live without a father." He grabbed a remote control from his desk. "Actually, I have a better idea. You're going to live without them and watch them die!" He turned on the Holoscreen, showing Rodrigo's family home in real-time with cameras in every room.

"No! Don! Don't do this! I'm right here!"

"You don't get it, Gigo! I trusted you. I loved you like my son! And you broke my heart. So now I will break yours!"

"Don't do this. I'm sorry."

"Don't beg. It's pathetic. Do you know what the most painful way to die is? I'm not sure cause I never died. But they say burning is the most painful. Either way, it'll do," he said while sending the order to his henchmen at the agent's house.

"No! No! No! Don't! Don't! Don't!" Rodrigo said, trying to get up and fight for his family, but Demetrio released another electric charge, immediately causing him to drop back down to the floor in pain.

"You're lucky I don't feel like dealing with the cleanup that comes with bullets, otherwise I would shoot you right now. But I'm in a hurry, I have to go home to MY family. So, as soon as this fire does the job, I'll be on my way. I wonder what is worse, watching your family die or knowing no one will ever be able to prove what happened? Look at the bright side. Soon, you all will be reunited in heaven or hell, whichever you prefer."

Outside the mansion, Sigma Team was creeping up on the location. Chad took up a sniper position on the hill opposite the mansion. Max and Andy were performing a ground approach, climbing uphill toward the side of the house, while Topher and CK were hovering in stealth mode midway between Chad and the Mansion.

"I think I have a lock on your mobster," CK said, looking through infrared vision. "Towards the northern side of the house. I detect six people, one of whom is on the floor."

"I have a visual," Max said while closing in on the mansion. "The guy on the floor is the undercover agent."

"Y'all went and blew his cover," Andy said while setting a small explosive charge on the floor-to-ceiling window. "He had a nice little thing going, and y'all had to go in and mess things up."

"Green Arrow, are you in position?" Topher asked, "We're not letting him die today. Not on our account."

"Yes, I'm ready when you are Eager Beaver, "Chad said. They knew the window was most likely bulletproof, so the soldiers coordinated the shot to be a fraction of a second after detonation.

"All right. Three, two, one, Go!" Andy said while detonating the explosive, shattering the armored glass. Before the glass could hit the floor, Chad fired a shot, hitting Don Demetrio on the right shoulder. He dropped to the floor in agony.

"Drop your weapons!" Beaver shouted.

"Suelta sus armas!" Max shouted. "Al piso! ¡Al piso!"

"To the ground to the ground," Andy continued while storming the room, guns drawn.

The two associates of Don Demetrio got on the ground face down while the two visitors got on their knees with their hands up. A few seconds later, Topher and CK entered the room, gun drawn. On the outside, four guards stationed on the perimeter rushed towards the office den, but their efforts were futile against Chad's marksmanship.

Topher and CK secured the weapons and the other entrance inside the den. Max got down towards Rodrigo to check on him.

"Are you alright?" he asked.

"I'm fine. But you have to get my family." He pointed towards the holoscreen. "Please go get them!" It took about two seconds for the soldiers to realize what was happening.

"Arrow! Get to this man's house now!" Topher said. "The house is on fire with children inside."

"I'm on it!" Chad said, taking flight heading towards the city.

"Milkshake, go with him! We got this," Topher said.

"I'm on it," Max said. He turned to Rodrigo and promised, "We'll get them out."

"That was a mistake," one of the two visitors said under his breath.

"Agent Gomez, we need coordinates to Agent Rodrigo's house. It's on fire with the children inside," Chad said over the common communication channel.

"This is Agent Ellis. Coordinates are being sent to your suits. And first responders are en route."

"Okay, Don Demetrio. Let's try this again," Topher said. "Where is the virus?"

"How would I know?" Demetrio said, still in pain from the shot.

"That's a nasty wound," CK said. "You might want to get that looked at before you lose your arm."

Topher took a couple of steps towards Demetrio to increase the pressure. Before his forward movement was completed, the room spun around him. Everything was blurry, and the sounds were garbled except for the ringing in his ear. That ringing was loud and clear. It took a good ten seconds before he could get his bearings back. When he came to, his gun was about three feet away. Beaver and CK were also down for the count. Demetrio's associates were looking around them in disbelief. One of them was heading towards his gun that had been kicked away from him. Topher was still somewhat disoriented, but he could tell that was not a good scenario. His gun was further away. He launched at the henchmen in a split-second move and slammed him down to the ground. By that time, Andy and CK regained consciousness. Andy's weapon had fallen within arm's reach. He grabbed it and pointed at the second henchman, attempting to get his weapon.

"Go ahead! Just give me a reason to shoot you," Beaver said.

"What just happened?" CK asked.

"I have no idea!" Topher said.

"I think we just got jumped," Andy added.

"Where are the two guys?" CK asked.

"It was by the two guys," Andy responded.

"Agent Gomez & Ellis," Topher said through the coms. "We have two extremely dangerous individuals on the loose. They just escaped the

Demetrio location. We need you to move in now!" Almost instantly, the hills were swarmed with *Federales,* K-9 Units & local police officers with helicopters overhead.

Topher continued, "That's it, Demetrio, you're going down. Make things easier on yourself and tell us where the virus is."

Though in pain, Don Demetrio said, "You just missed it," and grinned while looking at the Holoscreen. Topher noticed.

"Arrow, how far are you?"

"We're closing in on the location. We're about three minutes out."

"You need to make it in a minute. They don't have a lot of time."

"Roger that."

Rodrigo was back on his feet. He connected to his house's holosystem.

"Maricela, Ana Pedro! Listen to me, my loves," he said in Spanish. "Don't be afraid. Two men wearing black suits are on their way right now. They will get you out! Hang in there. You will be alright."

The words of comfort did little to diminish the distress and dismay they were experiencing. At this point, smoke filled the house. The only distinguishable things were the flames.

Maricela was going through her nightly routine in the upstairs master bathroom when the fire broke out. It took several minutes before she realized the house was on fire. When the smoke seeped through the door, she became perplexed. At first, she thought the kids might have burned something in the microwave oven. Upon opening the bathroom door to investigate the strange smell, she was welcomed by a blast of heat and smoke propelling her to the ground. Covering her mouth with the collar of her t-shirt, she crawled to the tub, turned on the faucet, grabbed a towel, and soaked it. She put the towel on herself as she crawled out.

"PEDRO! ANA!" She shouted.

The kids were at the ground level. She wasn't sure if they were in the kitchen, the living room, or the playroom. She wasn't sure they were still alive. Piercing through the smoke and the distance, she heard Ana scream.

"MAMA! MAMA!"

Though Ana was screaming out of the top of her lungs, Maricela could barely hear her from the second floor.

"I'm coming, baby! I'm coming," Maricela said. The stairs were engulfed in flames. The only path she could perceive through the smoke and the flames was through the banister overlooking the foyer. Without much hesitation, she straddled the handrail, hoping to move into a position where she would hang off the banister to shorten her fall. Before she could complete her movement, the structure collapsed, and she fell hard. The impact was blunt. Though she could feel something break, there was no time to assess. She tried to get on her feet to follow the voices of her children screaming her name. She was immediately thrown back to the ground. Her right leg refused to work. Her maternal instinct wouldn't let her quit. She crawled to get to her kids as the smoke and the heat grew more intense.

Outside the residence, Chad and Max were making their approach. Each one chose an opposite side of the house to make their entrance. They barely slowed down as they slammed through their respective windows. Chad entered from the second floor while Max went straight to the ground floor. The burning property had helpless bystanders watching from a distance, with the firefighters still far off.

"We're in," Chad said in the coms.

"The bathroom they are in the downstairs bathroom!" Rodrigo said. He had taught his children, 'If anything happens, the safest place is the bathtub'. A simple way for them to know what to do in an emergency.

"You heard that, gentlemen?" Topher asked.

"Loud and clear," Max said.

Chad headed outside Pedro's bedroom and walked through the hall overlooking the foyer. He saw Maricela crawling her way towards the bathroom. He rushed to assist her.

"Ma'am. I work with Rodrigo. We came to get you out," he said while getting closer to her. "I got you." He tried to lift her and bring her to safety.

"No!" She refused. "Get my children! Get the children!"

"Okay, I'll be right back for you, ma'am," he said, looking at her straight in the eyes.

By that time, Max had made it to the bathroom. He calmed the children down and got them to be partners in their survival. As Chad joined him, Max pointed to Pedro while giving Ana an oxygen mask. Chad did the same with Pedro.

"Hold on tight," Max said to Ana while covering most of her body with his own. Chad did the same as they dashed out of the restroom and followed the path of least resistance through the hallway, then through the living room to the window in the breakfast nook. Chad smashed through the window, absorbing most of the impact with his suited body. Max followed right through it. They lay the kids down in the backyard at a safe distance from the burning house. Chad headed back as fast as he could to rescue Maricela. As he reached the threshold of the window, he felt something like a bus hitting him at full speed, propelling him a few feet backward. He crashed to the ground with his ears ringing and the earth spinning around him. Max rushed to him and pulled him further from the structure. Chad sat up and was conscious enough to see part of the house collapse. The fire finally reached the gas tank, causing it to explode.

Chad took a deep breath. He was still dizzy from the blast but with enough wherewithal to launch one more desperate attempt to save Maricela. He hurled himself towards the house, but Max tackled him.

"It's too late, brother."

"Let me go!" Chad said as another portion of the house caved in.

"The firefighters are here. They'll take it over. We have to head back!"

Chad knew his teammate was right. Yet, he couldn't accept what he deemed a failure.

The paramedics, firefighters, and police officers took over the scene. They took the children to care for them. Chad and Max quietly disappeared in the chaos.

It took about ten minutes for them to make it back to Don Demetrio's mansion. When they arrived, the place was swarming with cops, agents, and paramedics. The latter were performing intensive care on Don Demetrio for what appeared to Max and Chad to be multiple blunt-force trauma injuries.

"What happened to him?" Chad asked.

Topher pointed to Rodrigo sitting down while being questioned by Agent Gomez a few feet away.

"Y'all didn't try to stop him?"

"Yes, we did," Andy said. "But our backs might have been turned for thirty seconds or so."

"Where are we with the virus?" Max asked.

"We missed it," Topher said.

"It slipped right through our fingers," Andy added.

"You mean it was here?" Max asked.

"We mean, the two guys that were here might be our guys from the virology lab," CK said, looking at Chad.

"You're kidding me, right?" he responded.

"Nope!" She said. "They fit the profile to a T. Didn't realize it at first, but after we got our heads handed to us, they were gone before we knew what happened. Yeah, they're our guys."

"So, they just vanished?" Max asked.

"They ran into the woods," Andy said. "The *Federales* and police are looking for them, but don't hold your breath."

"They're gone," Topher said. "Let's head back. We need to regroup with Command."

20

THE SHOW MUST GO ON

ASSEMBLED IN VARIOUS LOCATIONS worldwide, for the high society members to be gathered again in such short order was peculiar, to say the least. Surely, things were not going as planned. Yet, to be part of the group, one had to come from a lineage of overcomers or defy the odds and ascend to the pinnacle of a mission-critical field. The mission, preserving humanity and the supremacy of their fraternal order. That mission was facing unprecedented headwinds.

"Ladies and gentlemen, thank you for attending this meeting with such short notice," Robert Russo said from the encrypted holofeed. "Dear friends, the hour is late. Our mandate is facing uncharacteristic opposition. I will not bore you with platitudes. Neither will I insult your intelligence with euphemisms. Rather, let me get straight to the point. The two virus samples have been stolen."

He then waited a few seconds to let everyone grasp the enormity of the announcement and catch their breath after the initial shock. Then he continued.

"This is a setback, to say the least. But worst, it's also a threat to our agenda and to ourselves."

Though the situation was cause for alarm, Russo's candor was reassuring to the cohort assembled. They were used to winning against all odds and rose to whatever challenge they faced. They owned the world and would deal with whatever was thrown at them. "Therefore, we are implementing new protocols to ensure everyone's security and propel our agenda forward. Tertius, the floor is yours."

"Thank you. As Quartum stated, the threat we face is significant. Our operatives and intelligence assets have identified the source of our troubles. We are dealing with an alliance amongst the dregs of this world. They call themselves The Arachnid Network. A reference to the eight secret societies and criminal enterprises from unallied regions of the globe."

"With respect, could you please elaborate?" Erika Kaiser asked.

"Sure. From what we know, the heads of The Python Society out of India, Leech in Eurasia, Tarantula in Brazil, Dragon from China and Southeast Asia, Crimson Moon out of North Africa and the Middle East, Panther Society Sub-Saharan Africa, Orchid Japan and Hoja Blanca South America, have formed an alliance with significant operational efficiency. As a spider weaves a web, these organizations have banded together to weave a web to destroy us and the civilization our order has protected for centuries."

Some group members with more exposure to those organizations were starting to feel concerned about the outcome of this emerging confrontation. Tertius could sense the uneasiness rising in the audience. Yet, he didn't feel any anxiety; quite to the contrary, he welcomed the challenge and reveled at the possibility of gaining full control of those regions as well.

"But like any bug," he continued. "We will crush it and resume our agenda stronger than ever. The first step is to protect each one of us. For that purpose, everyone will be assigned a security detail as appropriate for their circumstances. For those whose profile warrants it, your security detail will be upgraded with our elite team, the Arm. For those of you with a lower profile, they will be embedded within your staff, whether as VPs, EAs, or students, based on your situation. Quartum," he ceded the virtual stage to his colleague, more habituated with being the center of attention.

"Thank you, Tertius. Let us use this as a reminder as to why our preservation policy is the right path. We are outnumbered, but thankfully, we are not outgunned. To perpetuate our order and continue our civilization's way of life, we must press forward with our common goal to rebalance the Earth's biome, conserve its resources, and adjust its population downward."

"What happens if they release the viruses?" Prince Albertsen asked.

Quartum flinched for a fraction of a second, barely perceivable to the untrained eye.

"At this stage, our teams of scientists are still working to develop therapeutics and an antidote. It is unlikely that their scientist would be further ahead than ours. Therefore, we consider that at this stage, releasing the viruses would be suicide regardless of where in the world they'd release it. But if they were to do that, get your affairs in order!"

21

DEBRIEFS

Tehran, Iran

SHE HAD NEVER BEEN in a police station before. Let alone in the interrogation chair.

"Dr. Suri Mirzakhani, thank you for joining us. My name is Detective Zarif. I was assigned this case from the time you were abducted. First off, let me say, on behalf of the nation, we are glad you are safe. Several investigations are open regarding the activities surrounding your capture and subsequent rescue. More precisely, the involvement of foreign operatives on Iranian soil without the consent of our governmental authorities."

"Thank you, Detective. Anything I can do to help?" Suri said.

"Can you please walk us through what happened the day you were abducted? Where did they take you? What do you remember? Any information can be useful."

"Sure, we were going to the nuclear site for the IAEA inspection. Suddenly, somebody yelled 'rocket'. Everything after that was a big blur. They tried to get us from one SUV to the other, but it was blown up. Before we knew it, the place was swarming with militants. They killed all the security personnel, grabbed us, and bagged our heads to blindfold us."

"Sorry you had to go through that," Detective Zarif said. But those were hollow words to Suri. Her bones still ached from the trauma of the abduction. The hurt of seeing Azael shot down still lingered in her soul.

"Do you know this man," the detective continued, handing Suri a folder with several pictures of Azael in action. From the time he entered the hospital on a stretcher to when he entered the Golestan Gym. The pictures were mostly inconclusive. Except for the one taken at the hospital, the others were of his back or a blurry part of his face.

"I think he was one of our security officers, right?" She said.

"Yes, he was."

"Did he survive the attack?" Suri asked, knowing full well the answer to that question.

"He did more than survive. He stole the ID of the dead driver, Mahmoud Hosseini. Pretended to be him while getting his gunshot wound taken care of at a local hospital. He then escaped the hospital and headed here to Tehran. We can trace him to the Elahiyeh neighborhood."

"Why would he do that?"

"That's what we're wondering. Why do you think he would do that?"

"I couldn't tell you. I'm a scientist, not a detective. This is your field of expertise."

"Well, in my 'experts' experience, only one thing brings a man to such extremes: love. Love of woman or love of country." He took the pictures back and put them back in the folder. He continued,

"After Elahiyeh, we lost track of him, but not a long time later, you guys are rescued in Pardis. And not long after that, Israeli rockets started falling down, and now we're in a full-out war."

"So, what are you thinking happened?" She asked.

"I'm still trying to piece it all together. But this is a highly trained individual roaming the streets of Tehran after getting shot. I would bet he is Israeli special forces. Maybe one of their spies. Which means I must escalate it to the Ministry of Intelligence. No need to tell you that at that point, it's out of my hands, and they will consider any collaboration with the enemy an act of treason punishable by death."

"Are you calling me a traitor?"

"No, ma'am! You are one of our brightest scientists. I am simply asking you to help me piece it all together. Anything you might have heard while on duty with Elisha Zvili or while in captivity could help us determine what happened and thwart our adversary's attacks."

"Elisha Zvili was a gentleman throughout our time together. I don't know how much more I can contribute to your quest. Like everybody else, I'm on edge with the hostility and would love for it to stop so we can live in peace. Whatever I can do to help, I will. But I'm not sure what that would be at this time."

"Well, for one, you could confirm if this man was part of the team that rescued you." He said, pointing at Azael's picture.

"They were wearing some sort of combat suits covering their faces. So, I couldn't tell you either way." She used all her inner strength to maintain her composure. "I couldn't tell if you were one of them. That's how blurry everything is," she continued. Then she performed.

"I'm sorry, sir. I wish I could be of more help. I'm trying to remember as much as possible, but it's difficult. Sometimes, all I can see are the dead faces and blood everywhere." Her eyes swelled with tears. She gasped, put her hand on her mouth, sniffed back some snot, and continued. "And when we were in captivity, the guards sometimes would—" She broke down crying.

"Ma'am, it's okay. I think we are done for now. We will be in touch if we need anything else. Thank you for coming," he said, not wanting to hear her melodramatic stories, which would do little to further his investigation.

"I'm sorry...it's just...can I go?"

"One last thing, my contacts at the Ministry of Intelligence believe your words to the world could go a long way towards creating goodwill from the international community."

"What do they want me to say?"

"They want you to attest to the peaceful nature of the nuclear program. Do you think that's something you can do?"

"I don't see why not. Like I said, I will do whatever I need to bring peace back to our people."

"Very well. Yes, you can go. We'll be in touch."

She sniffed back some snot several times, picked up her purse, and walked to the door. He opened the door for her, let her out first, looked back to the one-way mirror in the room, walked her out to the entrance, said a final goodbye, and headed back towards the other side of the interrogation room. Two agents from the Ministry of Intelligence were waiting there for him.

"What do you think?" Detective Zarif asked.

"We don't trust her," the agent replied. "Keep an eye on her."

"I already am. I have one of our best on the job. If there is anything to find, he'll find it."

"Good, process all the information through the Ministry. Because of the war, we are spread thin right now. But I want this case prioritized. She's not telling us everything."

"I agree. If she's hiding something, we will find it."

Tel Aviv, Kirya Compound

"How long am I going to be pushing papers?" Azael asked his mentor and friend.

"As long as it takes!" Aluf Boaz Tishbi said. "You don't seem to realize our predicament. First, they know I lied to protect you. They know we know there's a mole. That mole is powerful and connected. Before we take it down, we need a rock-solid case. Second, you disobeyed orders-"

"I saved lives! They would have killed Suri and the other scientists. We were right to stick to our guns and get them out of there."

"Be it as it may, the military doesn't work like that. The success of any military organization is predicated on soldiers following orders. They can't allow you to be creative or have a conscience. For a lot of our colleagues, you should have been court-martialed. That's still a possibility, by the way. So, for now, the best thing for you to do is lay low, help me find the mole, and you'll be back in their good graces in due time. In the meantime, we have a war to win. That's the only thing that matters."

"If winning the war was the only thing that mattered, wouldn't the brass want all their soldiers fighting that war?"

"Yes, they would. But that's the question, isn't it? Would you fight 'that' war?"

"Meaning?"

"War is you shooting whoever from the other side comes through your crosshairs."

"Don't you think I know that?"

"What if Suri came through your crosshairs? Are you pulling the trigger then?"

"Are we killing civilians now? Is that what we do?"

"No, it's not what we do. But wars have collateral damage. They also have highly valued civilians working towards their war efforts. Which makes them de facto soldiers for their side. Some would say her most recent speech would be enough to—"

"What speech?"

"Oh, you didn't know?" The elderly pulled out his holophone and put it on the table. He started playing footage of Suri as she said,

"Good morning. My name is Dr. Suri Mirzakhani. Thank you, Mr. President, for your presence, and thank you to the ministers of defense and intelligence for putting this joint press conference together. As you know, our country was attacked recently. This attack was unprovoked and unjustified. As a scientist first, and second, as the nation's envoy to the International Atomic Energy Agency, I can attest to the peaceful nature of Iran's nuclear program. Though our latest inspection was cut short due to the cowardly attack by members of the terrorist organization known as al-Saalihin, I have been deeply involved in all aspects of our regulatory compliance program. For years now, I have observed, reviewed, and openly critiqued Iran's nuclear program. They have always complied with our requests. Why? Because it is a peaceful program. Nuclear energy offers safe and unlimited energy for our country and partners' needs. It allows us to reduce our dependence on fossil fuels and increase our children's chances of inheriting a healthy planet with the promise of a better tomorrow. Access to reliable energy for their education, healthcare, and future careers. Everything we do, we do for our children. Therefore, I respectfully ask for the leaders of Israel to immediately cease the hostilities. Let's sit down at the table of the brotherhood of nations and come to a peaceful resolution to this conflict. I will leave you with the words of one of the greatest advocates for peace this world as ever known, Martin Luther King Jr. 'Darkness cannot drive out darkness, only light can do that. Hate cannot drive out hate, only love can do that.' End of quote. Thank you for your time."

"I must say she's very good," Aluf Tishbi said. "This is well played. I'm not sure what my favorite part is. Bringing up the children or the King quote at the end. From the look on your face, I suppose you didn't like it as much."

Azael was speechless. He knew her. He knew she joined those inspections to make sure the IAEA inspections because she was concerned the program was not peaceful, and she was afraid foreigners wouldn't be able to see through the subterfuge. He finally summoned the strength to speak.

"Aluf Tishbi, I know her. I can't explain why she gave that speech. But I know her. She will stand for what's right no matter what."

"I'm sure she will. But in the meantime, here she is giving moral high ground to our adversaries, and here we are scrambling to make our case to the world."

"That is not on her. That is not on me! We told the brass not to attack! They did not listen to us. We got Zvili out safe."

"Yet some people now wish you hadn't."

"You can't be serious!"

"Well, we think he didn't say anything, but do we know for sure? And the person you risked your life to save is now advocating for our enemies. Some consider her an enemy of the state. So, I ask again. As a soldier, now that she is aligned with her government, if she came into your crosshairs, would you pull the trigger?"

Persian Plaza Hotel Tehran, Iran

The Persian Hotel Plaza was well regarded amongst diplomats, *hommes d'affaires*, and foreign nationals sojourning in the country's capital with impeccable lobby, luxurious amenities, and succulent meals. She was not a foreigner but might as well have been. She did not recognize her country. The events catapulted her into the center of an international armed conflict. Yet, the hostilities on the outside were overshadowed by the raging war on the inside. Her love of country versus the love of her life. Her patriotic duty versus her professional ethics. All these competing interests kept her from paying attention as she entered room 514 of the five-star establishment.

"That was a nice speech," Azael said from the shadows in the back of the room.

It took a moment for her mind to catch up to her ears. When her mind confirmed what her heart had hoped for so long, she dropped her purse to the ground and embraced the beloved intruder. There are no words. He thought of a smart quip, but nothing came. There are some moments in life when no words are needed. The sheer flow of emotion said it all.

"I thought I might never see you again," she finally said.

"Nothing would keep me from you, my love." He responded with tears flowing down his cheeks. He was surprised by that but didn't try to stop it. He didn't try to hide it. He didn't have to pose. He could just be. "Nothing, you hear me?"

She thought of asking him how he made it inside the country with the military running everywhere and intelligence services on high alert, but it felt like an exercise in futility. He was the best at what he did.

"You have to leave." She said. It's not safe for you here. They're watching my every move."

"I know," he said. "I was watching them watching you."

"Why did you come?"

"I had to see you. I had to look you in the eye and ask, "Did you mean what you said?" He pulled back a little bit to look her in the eyes.

"I had to say these things."

"You're not one to be forced to do anything. Tell me the truth."

"I did it for you. They're on to you. They're on to us. If they haven't pieced it together yet, they will soon. So, I gave the speech they wanted me to give to assuage their suspicions. But you must leave. It's not safe."

"I'm not leaving without you."

"You must."

"Why don't you come?"

"I have unfinished business here."

"What business is more important than us being together?"

"Preventing a nuclear showdown. If I'm here, maybe I can influence them in downgrading the nuclear program."

"Do you think that's possible? "

"I must try. Because if this war continues, everyone loses. There are no winners."

"Take this." He handed her a small device, a little smaller than a peanut.

"What's this?"

"It's a two-way communication device you put in your ear. With it, we can talk. If you whisper, I will be able to hear you. You can be anywhere in the world. I will find you." He showed her how the device works.

"I have to go before they realize I'm gone."

She held him tight, not wanting this moment to end. She was tempted to urge him to stay. Maybe they could escape this world's madness, just the two of them. But she knew better. There was no place on earth where they would be at peace unless this war ended.

"I know my love, I know. Be careful soldiers are everywhere."

"I will. I love you."

She managed to mumble those words back to him. "I love you too". The tears were streaming down her cheeks. Her heart hoped they would be together again, but her mind worried this was the last time she would see him. War had a way of taking lives indiscriminately. The best-trained soldiers and the plebes fell in combat just alike. Peasants and aristocrats felt the cruelty of its wrath. There were no guarantees, only hopes and dreams easily snatched away by the harsh realities of war. She knew that full well, but she chose to hope in her heart of hearts. Now was her turn to pull back and look him in the eye and say, "I will see you soon. My love."

Tel-Aviv, Israel, the next day

"You need to come with me now," Tishbi said to Azael from the parking lot of his apartment building. "In the car now." Azael complied immediately. Tishbi continued, "Are you out of your mind?"

"What is going on?"

"Are you out of your mind? You must have lost your mind!"

"What is going on?"

"What would possess you to go into our enemy's territory without clearance? You must be out of your mind. You must have known they would find out. We have spies. They have spies. Everybody knows everything. Sorry, they know almost everything. The one thing they don't know is, what in the world were you doing in Iran?"

"Aluf, I was—"

"Oh, I know what you were doing. You went to see her. Of course. Okay, she's beautiful, I get it. I would want to see her too if I were you! But they don't know that. As far as they are concerned, you might have gone to see the Ayatollahs!"

"I had to know."

"You had to know what?"

"I had to know why she said what she said."

"You had to know why she said what she said," he repeated sarcastically. "What you had to do was to keep her safe. I'm afraid you put her and yourself at great risk. And for what?"

"So, I could know."

"And what did you find out?"

"She was buying time to keep our relationship under the radar."

"And now, our leaders suspect you of treason. Who knows if the mole didn't alert them of your whereabouts inside their country? Putting her at increased risk." Tishbi took a deep breath. "Listen. Love is about trust. In times like these, you're going to have to trust her. You need to lay low now."

"Understood."

"Good. Speaking of laying low. We're going to Lebanon."

"What? Why?"

"I have a mission for you."

22

LIKE THE GOOD OL' DAYS

Columbus, Georgia

"WE HAVE NO TOLERANCE for looting and vandalism." Police Chief Powell said. "We respect everyone's right to protest peacefully. It is the bedrock of our democracy. But no one has the right to destroy or steal someone else's property. Effective immediately, we are imposing a nine p.m. curfew in the city. We are actively investigating the incident. Officer Solano has been placed on administrative leave until the investigation is completed. We want to reassure you we will follow the facts and the law wherever they may lead. But we need the public to give us some time to get to the bottom of this. We'll take a few questions."

He looked at the press gathered on the steps of the police headquarters and pointed to Ashleigh Williams.

"Ashleigh."

"Thank you. It's been a week since video footage of the killing leaked through the media. What do you say to people wondering why it takes so long to press charges against Officer Solano?"

"We certainly understand the frustration of some of the public, but we can't let emotions guide our decision. If we take this to trial, it will be because we have a solid case. So, we are asking for your patience. When investigating police-involved shootings, it is paramount that we gather all the facts."

"Sir, if I can. In the case of Erin Davis, your officers were able to find and charge the perpetrator within the first forty-eight hours. What do you say to those who feel that these always seem to take longer when a black man is killed as opposed to a white woman?"

"I can assure you we treat every case with the same expediency regardless of race. In Erin's case, we had a killer on the loose. There is an added sense of urgency when more lives are at risk."

"Are you saying that there is no urgency when one of your cops kills a black man?"

"Come on, Ashleigh, I think you know better."

"Do I? We have been seeing these killings for decades now. I'm sure you saw the latest Paribus poll that said seventy-five percent of people in the black community of this city trust their local drug dealer more than your department. What are you going to do to gain back the trust of this community?"

"With due respect, Ashleigh, Paribus is a satire organization. This so-called 'poll' doesn't reflect what we see on the ground. We have invested large amounts of funds and working hours in developing a community-based approach to policing. We have made great progress in building trust in the communities we serve and are determined to maintain and build upon that trust. Thank you all!" He walked away, visibly frustrated by the line of questioning.

A few hours later

"Ashleigh Williams is joining us from City Hall, where thousands of people have gathered in protest," Allen Terrier said from the WDTD studios.

"Thank you, Allen. Yes, I am here at City Hall, where people have protested peacefully for hours. I have been talking to several people, and they did not like what they heard at the press conference by the chief of police and the mayor. One of these people is Pastor Kyle Boykin." She turned towards her infield guest.

"Pastor Boykin—"

"Call me Kyle."

"Okay, Kyle, obviously you're white, but you are marching here today. Why is that?"

"Well, for us, it's not about race. It's about the value of every human life and being treated fairly by those who are meant to protect us, not harm us. On a personal note, I knew Retz. Yes, he was from the 'wrong' side of town," he said air quoting his words. "But he was turning a new leaf. He started coming to church. He was moving away from the streets and making new friends with people from different backgrounds. Here I have his acceptance letter from CSU." He pulled the letter from the inner pocket of his jacket. "He was going to college. He didn't have to die. That's personal to me because I knew him and because I'm from these streets too.

I got a chance to turn my life around. Why not him? This is wrong! And we will not rest until he can rest in peace."

"I can feel your passion and commitment towards this cause. So far, it looks like everything has been peaceful. But as you can see, the sun is coming down. Once nightfall comes, things tend to be different. Acts of vandalism, looting, and violence seem to break out regularly. Is that your way to send a more direct message?"

"Not at all. We are here protesting peacefully. As you see the sun going down, we will pack our stuff and go home. The people who come at night are not a part of this movement. We don't know who they are. They are most likely not even from here. If you keep your cameras rolling, you'll see everybody here start leaving and heading home, and a bunch of other people will come and cause chaos. That's not us. And the Retz I knew wouldn't stand for it."

"Thank you for your time. This was Ashleigh Williams for WDTD. Allen, back to you." She turned to her crew, "All right, guys, let's wrap it up."

"Why don't you stick around and keep these cameras rolling to find out who those people are and where they come from?" Kyle asked.

"Oh, we already know."

"So why don't you expose them?"

"I can't."

"Why not? You're Ashleigh Williams. Why don't you break the story?" She chuckled.

"You think that's how it works? I find a story and run with it. I have news for you, pun intended. There's a blackout on this topic. The execs don't want us to cover it. End of story. So, my hands are tied."

"Just like that?"

"Listen, I'm from these streets too. Why don't you call me, and we'll talk. But not here. Maybe we can go for coffee or something." She handed him her card.

"Okay, I'll take you up on that," he said with a small grin on his face.

Yoki's Café the following morning

"Thank you for coming," Kyle said.

"I wasn't sure you were going to call," Ashleigh said.

"You said you had information about the people destroying our city. And after last night, this has got to stop."

"I agree it's heartbreaking to see all those businesses, people's hard work trashed like that."

"So, what do you have?"

She pulled out an oddly folded-to-fit file folder from her purse.

"In there, you will find what we have so far. We identified at least thirty people from out of state. We looked into their recent movements, where they stay, and political affiliation."

"We? Whose 'we?'"

"I can't divulge. But let's just say I'm not the only reporter who doesn't like what's going on. But, like me, most hands are tied. The big bosses run the show. When it came to this, they decided that no one would talk abo—" her phone vibrated. She took a quick look, and her eyes grew big. She put her hand over her mouth and let slip a faint, "Oh my God! I gotta go!"

"What? Why? We just started. You can't leave now."

"Officer Solano was just shot. They think Triple P is behind it. So yeah, I gotta go!"

"Triple P? Are you sure?"

"That's what the wire said. I'll know more when I get to the station. But anyhow. The micro-SSD drive in the folder has everything we got on the troublemakers."

He stayed silent a little longer than normal. "Okay, thanks. I gotta go, too."

He grabbed two twenties from his wallet, more than needed to cover the tab, and dropped them on the table as he got up.

"Thank you, Ashleigh. We'll be in touch." He headed for the exit.

Ashleigh was slightly stunned by his sudden urgency to leave, but she couldn't worry about that now.

About twenty minutes later, Kyle arrived at the Triple P headquarters. In normal times, the facade of legitimate businesses held up pretty well. But these were not normal times. The place looked more like a military base than a business establishment.

"I need to see Ty G now!" Kyle told the two henchmen.

"He busy. Come back later."

"Y'all need to step aside and let me talk to my bro, like now! I ain't asking you twice."

"He meeting with people."

"I don't care!"

One of the henchmen leaned to the ear of the other and said, "Yo, it's KB. you better let him through." They moved to the side and let Kyle through.

"Ty G! What in the world is wrong with you!"

"Watch yourself, Preacher! Don't be coming here and making accusations."

"It's all over the news!"

"Come here," Ty G said, signaling to his former gangmate to come very close and look at him in the white of his eyes.

"It wasn't us."

Kyle paused for a second. He knew Ty G more than his brother. They had lied countless times to get out of trouble, but they also had been real with one another. He knew Ty could lie his way out of anything, but this was not one of those times. He believed him.

"You got to turn yourself in."

"I know you didn't come up in here and say I got to turn myself in for a crime I didn't commit! You must be trippin'."

"Nah, man. You hear the sirens. I bet you they're coming here. I bet you they're coming here guns blazing and hope you sneeze wrong to put you six feet underground."

"Look at this," Ty G said, pointing to an arsenal worthy of a small army. "If I'm going underground, they comin' with me. You know I don't sweat the SWAT!"

"Yeah, I know, I know. And a lot of people are gonna die. Your guys, their guys. Good cop, bad cop, it doesn't matter. They all die. Except those who did it. That's exactly what they want."

"You think I don't know that? But I'm not going down like a chump."

"How about you don't go down at all?"

Ty could hear the blaring sirens getting closer and closer. In a matter of minutes, maybe seconds, a small army would be at his doorstep. Looking around at his own little army and the considerable arsenal at his disposal, he was ready to wage war. Regardless of the outcome, people would die. Surely, he would die fighting till the bitter end. Quite a few of his soldiers were a little more than children with no life experience. They would die too. The one person who would surely live is the one who framed him. Whoever that was would never be caught if he took the fall for it. Maybe Kyle was right after all. Maybe going peacefully and fighting the battle in the court rather than the street could allow him enough time to find the culprit and exact his justice.

"Yo Ty! They around the corner!" One of the henchmen posting watch shouted. Everybody in the room except Ty and Kyle took up their weapon and headed to the fortified windows.

"Looks like the whole CPD is rolling up!" The same henchman said.

"Listen-up! I need everyone to stand down. We're not gonna play it like that," Ty said. "Put down your weapons. We gonna play it smart. Jimbo, call Shapiro, tell him to get bail money ready. KB, you're gonna negotiate with them. Tell them I'll turn myself in on one condition: everybody else walks. Period."

Kyle was stunned. He had pleaded with Ty in the past, but seldom was he successful in changing his mind. The current turn of events was either a testament that miracles still exist or the first step towards their funeral.

"I got you, bro!" Kyle said, choosing to believe the former over the latter. He pulled out his holophone and sent a message to Ashleigh Williams. The message said, "*Loved meeting with you today. Would love to do that again. Might not make it past today tho. Need cameras at this location NOW to make it out alive.*"

She replied.

"We're already on our way fully equipped. Don't do anything stupid, Pastor. Your community needs you...and yeah, another coffee meet would be nice!" Kyle let a smile peek through his face. Ty snatched the phone from his hand.

"I know you're not hitting on no girl right now, bruh!" Ty said while looking at the text exchange on the phone, "Holup, the TV girl? Alright, I ain't mad at that. My boy's in the big leagues now! You better put your head in the game if you want to see her again, bro."

"Don't worry. I got you," Kyle said while grabbing his phone back and dialing 911.

"911, what's your emergency?" The operator said.

"My name is Pastor Kyle Boykin. I am with the leader of Triple P. He wants to talk with the SWAT negotiator and avoid a deadly downtown shootout in the broad daylight."

"Hold on, Mr. Boykin," the dispatcher said.

"This is CPD SWAT. We have the building surrounded. Come out with your hand up!" The megaphone said loud and clear.

"Ty! They got mad snipers on the buildings. There's like tons of them," the watchman said as their CCTV cameras showed SWAT members on the roof and approaching the building from every conceivable angle.

"Alright, boys grab your guns! This is our house!" Ty G said.

"No, Ty G! Don't do this! There's another way," Kyle said, then addressed the dispatcher "Ma'am, are you there? I need the chief of SWAT now."

"I apologize for the hold. Please wait."

"It don't look like they tryin' to negotiate. They want a fight they gon get it!" Ty said.

"No, No, No. There's another way. Ashleigh just pinged me. They outside cameras rolling. Come out with me. I'll go out first. They ain't gon shoot me on live TV. You come out hands up with me as close to me as possible. No sudden movements and get down on the floor outside."

"Ty don't listen to this fool, man. We can take them," Jimbo said.

"Actually, listen to me. My way, we can live another day and win the long game. His way, we all die."

"Alright, little bro. Lead the way."

"Take off your shirt," Kyle said while he took off his shirt.

"What the what?"

"Trust me on this. We won't give them any excuse."

"Whatever, man," Ty said while taking off his shirt. "Alright, guys, while we go out the front. Y'all know how to get out of here. Jimbo split them up between the safehouses. Lay low till I'm back."

"We have to go," Kyle said. They headed to the front door. Kyle put his hands out first and shouted, "Don't shoot! We're coming out unarmed! Don't shoot!"

"Oh my! Are you getting this?" Ashleigh said as she saw her new acquaintance coming out of the compound shirtless.

"Yes, we're rolling," the cameraman said.

"Good! Don't miss any of it. Mickey, are you tapped in the cops' frequency? I want to hear what they're saying."

"You already know I am!"

"That's why you're the best! You know that?"

As she looked unto the center of attention, Kyle and Ty G were on their knees with two dozen tactical lasers pointed at them and countless service weapons pointed in the same direction. No officer had attempted to approach them.

"Ashleigh! The execs are ordering us to head back to HQ."

"What? Who's taking over? Mindy?"

"They didn't say. But I don't think anyone is taking over. GPS shows all the vans are at HQ. Hold up," Mickey said while raising the volume to his illicit police radio.

"What happened?"

"Nothing...they're not very chatty."

"OMG! Mickey, I don't care what you have to do, get this on the air NOW!" She ran to Kyle and Ty G in the middle of the action.

"Ashleigh, what are you doing?" Kyle said once she kneeled between him and what felt like a firing squad.

"I'm making sure we get to grab that second coffee. What's your friend's name?" She said with her mic away from her face. After he answered, she pulled the mic to her face and addressed the two suspects.

"This is Ashleigh Williams for WDTD. I am downtown with Pastor Boykin and Tyrone Green. Gentlemen, you're about to be arrested by CPD's finest. Anything you want to say?"

"Yes, there's something I'd like to say," Kyle said. "This man is not the man you are looking for. He did not kill Officer Solano. He is fully willing to cooperate with the police investigation to clear his name."

"Ma'am, please step aside," the SWAT agent said to Ashleigh, having been surrounded by five agents. The agents took both Kyle and Ty into custody.

"This like the good ol' days, bruh," Ty G murmured to Kyle before officers took him away. "Like the good ol' days!"

23

POINT OF NO RETURN

Nukus, Karakalpakstan, Uzbekistan

"THIS IS THE POINT of no return," said Egor Bulka, deputy minister of Russia for agro-industrial complex, natural resources and ecology. "After today, there will be no communication between us until the Day of Reckoning. Li Jing Hua will review the operative procedures."

"Thank you, Mr. Bulka. After decades of hard work, we are finally at the point where we can break free from Western imperialism. As you can all see, Western society is falling apart at the seams. Our operatives on the ground have performed well. They have fomented divisions to levels we could only have imagined. They have successfully divided every segment of American life. Racial, religious, and political tensions are extremely high. We have politicians working for us at every level of government. Our special forces are stationed throughout the country. The morale of the American people is at an all-time low. Now is the time to strike the fatal blow to this dying society."

"How can you be sure this will be a fatal blow? Americans have proven resilient," said Binh Pham, Vietnam's deputy minister of information and communications.

"Yet your people have proven more resilient and defeated them soundly. You were able to stop these imperialists from taking over your land and carved your own destiny. It's time for the rest of the world to be masters of their own destinies. This blow will be fatal. The EMP devices are being put in place all over the major American cities. Our agents have secured the pathogens the imperialists had planned for us. They will be released in the US and Israel in thirty days. At that point, the pilot union will declare a strike in the US. The pilots will refuse to fly internationally until their demands are met. By the time those demands are met, the first symptoms will start to manifest. The incubation period is seven days. So, the pathogens would have spread all over the US, Canada, and Mexico. Once symptoms are revealed in those countries, our countries will impose travel bans from North America. When all countries have announced their travel bans, that will be the signal to detonate the EMPs. That will be the Day of Reckoning.

"Sorry to interrupt," said Antonio Cardozo-Abalos deputy minister of tourism and foreign trade of Venezuela. "With no communication how will we know if everyone is doing their part?"

"Very good question," Li Jing Hua said. Everyone joined the Alliance of their own accord. The plan has been laid out and crafted with each country's principals and military brass. Some of them before they came to power. At this point, we expect and require flawless execution. Anyone who misses their part of the plan will be deemed to have joined the enemy. There is no neutrality, you're whether with us or you're against us."

"Understood," Antonio Abalos said.

"Good. As I was saying. Once the EMPs go off. Our special forces on the ground will secure high-value targets across America and the West. Those targets include the seats of governments, police stations, media stations, telecom companies, and the like. At the same time, a second wave of troops dissimulated in cargo ships at all major ports will be deployed. At which points your countries will deploy their troops at your designated targets. As for the countries already engaged in conflicts, we have many assets already positioned to be put at your service to turn the tide in your favor. You must prevail, and we are putting our resources at your disposal. Are there any more questions?" She waited a few moments.

"Very well. Let's execute."

24

MÊLÉE À TROIS

Monterrey, Nuevo Leon, Mexico

"DON DEMETRIO WAS PARANOID apparently," Andy said. "We have some good footage from our two MMA enthusiasts. IRIS is running their profile right now, so we should get results in a little bit." A few seconds later, comprehensive profiles of the targets populated the holoscreen. "Here we go."

"Antonio Bustamante," CK said, reading off the giant holoscreen. "From Porto Alegre, Brazil, former special forces dishonorably discharged for insubordination. Continued in his dishonorable ways with a life of crime. Died in a prison riot five years ago."

"He looked very much alive to me," Topher said.

"Narong Channarong," Andy said, taking his turn reading the second target's profile. "Born in Chiang Mai, Thailand. Had a short-lived MMA career. Spent most of his time on the wrong side of the law. He is also 'dead'. He died in an explosion linked to Chao Pho, which is how they refer to organized crime syndicates in Thailand."

"So, we're dealing with the Night of the Walking Dead?" CK said.

"Of course not," Max said. "The reality is we're dealing with people who faked their deaths. It's the best way to operate in the shadows undetected. If you're dead, no one is looking for you."

"The question is. How deep does this go? How many of those guys are there?" Chad said.

"We'll need answers for those. But the more urgent question though is where are they now?" Topher said.

"I'm on it," Max said. "Now that we know who we're looking for, it should be a breeze... gotcha! IRIS has a lock on them. Just a question of time before we get their current location...oh, that's not good."

"They are almost at the US border," CK said.

"Yes, and they're heading there fast," Max said.

"We have to alert the locals," Andy said.

"No, that wouldn't do any good," Topher said. "Look at what they did to us, and we're special ops. What do you think will happen to the Border Patrol agents or the Laredo police? Nah. Let them go home to their families. We have to take care of that ourselves." Turning to Agents Gomez and Ellis. "Can you guys spare a chopper?"

"Yes," Agent Gomez said, "we have a couple of Bell V-280 Valor. But these guys will be long gone by the time I clear the paperwork."

"Is there anything you can do to speed it up?" Topher asked.

"Hold on. I know a guy." Gomez said while dialing a phone number on his personal phone. He stepped a few feet away to get some privacy.

After a few moments, he came back closer. "Okay, pilot is on his way. He'll be here in ten minutes."

"Okay, let's suit up," Topher said. "Make sure you're fully charged. This is going to be one for the ages."

Forty minutes later, eight thousand feet over Laredo, Texas

"We're closing in on them," Andy said, looking through a high-performing monocular device from eight thousand feet in the air.

"Guys, let me state the obvious," Topher said. "A lot is riding on this mission. We're facing an enemy we were not trained to fight, Individuals with enhanced capacities."

"Enhanced abilities or not. A sniper's rifle is a great equalizer," Chad said.

"I'm counting on it," Topher replied. "You'll stay on overwatch and take out the driver. Max, Andy, and I will take on the passenger. CK, you find us that virus and secure it no matter what. Do you understand me? No matter what happens to us, you find it, secure it, and go."

"Roger that," she replied.

"Alright, let's execute!" Topher said.

The team, fully suited, locked and loaded, got in motion without hesitation. The pilot released the hatch. Wave Runner jumped first, followed by Milkshake and Eager Beaver, Green Arrow followed, and Mockingbird went last with her mind set on the viral prize. Green Arrow stayed on overwatch, tracking the vehicle and preparing for the kill shot.

"Holdup!" Stop! Everyone stop! We have a situation," Green Arrow said. "We have three black SUVs approaching our target. Two from the front and one from the back."

The vehicles stopped in a standoff position. Two Arm agents came out of each SUV wearing dark-colored t-shirts and spring jackets.

"Looks like we're late to the party. Who are these guys?" Beaver asked.

"I don't know, but how about we find out after we get the vials?" Milkshake said.

"Okay, change of plans," Wave Runner said while assessing the situation.

Channarong got out from the passenger side to face the four assailants coming from the front. Thirty seconds later, Bustamante got out from the driver's side to face the opponents coming from the back of the vehicle.

Topher continued, "Green Arrow, stay on overwatch and cover our sixes, but let's try to bring some of them in alive so we can know what we're dealing with."

"Roger that!" Chad said.

"Beaver, Milkshake cover the front."

"On it," Andy replied.

"Mockingbird, you and I, we're heading to the back. You go for the vials; I'll cover you." Topher said.

Beaver and Milkshake took defensive positions behind the van's open doors. While Bustamante was battling the assailants, one broke free from the struggle while the other three kept Bustamante engaged. The one who broke free headed towards the van but was intercepted by Beaver and Milkshake.

"Put your hands—" the opponent's fist came millimeters from connecting with Beaver's suited face. Beaver barely dodged the impact of the attacker's fist; the van's body wasn't so lucky. The hit dented the side of the van as if a baseball bat had hit it. Without flinching, the attacker launched a second attack towards Beaver, causing him to fall to the ground. Max launched to the aid of his partner, but in a judo-like move, he used Max's momentum against him, sending him flying to the ground. With the two special operators on the floor, he initiated what could be a fatal attack on Beaver. A high-velocity strike on the destabilized soldier, but right before impact,

BANG!

A shot rang through the air, stopping the attacker's momentum and sending him in the opposite direction.

"Like I said, the great equalizer." Chad quipped.

"He's still alive," Andy said.

"Tie him up," Max said.

"On it," Andy replied.

In the back of the vehicle, Wave Runner opted for a shock and awe approach. He threw an impact grenade at the pack, disorienting them. Then, he posted himself between the van's back door and the pack while Mockingbird went into the van looking for the virus.

"Hurry! That's not going to hold them for long," Wave Runner said.

"I'm on it," Mockingbird said.

Channarong was the first to get back on his feet and launch an attack on Wave Runner. The latter anticipated the move and did a judo move of his own, using Channarong's momentum to slam him against the van. He proceeded in, unleashing a fury of punches at him. That tactical advantage was short-lived. Channarong broke free with a kick to Wave Runner's abdomen, sending him flying a few feet backward. He landed amid the approaching assailants. A two-to-one brawl ensued. Wave Runner was on the receiving end of several suit-damaging blows, but he also drew blood from his opponents.

Channarong took the opportunity to head towards the inside of the van to take on Mockingbird.

BOOM! Another shot rang through the air. This time, Channarong dodged the bullet, which only grazed him. He continued his charge into the van.

A second shot rang, this time from inside the van, sending Channarong to fall on his back outside the van with a bullet in his chest.

"I got it," Mockingbird said while coming out of the van with a metallic suitcase.

Rat-a-tat rat-a-tat several rapid-fire shots rang out of nowhere.

"I'm hit!" Green Arrow said, "My suit isn't responding."

Mockingbird looked up and saw a dot falling from the sky. Without thinking twice, she dropped the suitcase and launched towards her falling brother-in-arms. In a race against time, she pushed her boosters to their max capacity, hoping to reach him before he reached the ground. At this altitude, the suit's shock absorption system would be of little help, if any. She tackled him like a football player and broke the momentum of his fall. The landing was brutal, but they would survive.

On the ground, Topher's opponent pushed him to create some separation between the two. Before he could counterattack, bullets started raining down, forcing him to take refuge behind the opponent's SUV. The Arm agent took hold of the suitcase. As he did, Channarong got back on his feet to confront the Arm agent and retook possession of the suitcase. He fought valiantly, but with a bullet in the chest, he was no match for the Arm, which knocked him out with a perfectly executed Krav Maga combo.

"Package retrieved initiate exit," the Arm agent said.

Understanding his cause was lost for the moment, Bustamante took advantage of the chaos to steal one of the Arm's SUVs, leaving Channarong behind.

Rat-a-tat rat-a-tat

Rapid fire from the enemy drone forced Wave Runner, Milkshake, and Beaver to take refuge behind the TAN's van, providing cover for the Arm operatives to make their exit using the remaining two SUVs. Once the vehicles were on their way, the drone took off.

"Mockingbird, Green Arrow, what's your location?" Topher said. Mockingbird, do you copy? Green Arrow, do you copy? I repeat, do you copy?"

"Yeah, we copy," Mockingbird said.

"What's your location?"

"We're about half a mile north of you," she said.

"Okay, we're on our way," Wave Runner said.

They reunited about two minutes later.

"What's the status?" Wave Runner asked his two teammates.

"My suit is busted, but I'm alive thanks to her," Green Arrow said.

"That was some fast thinking," Wave Runner said.

"Yeah, but I dropped that suitcase. I should have..."

'Nah, don't do that," Beaver interjected. "You did the right thing. You saved our brother. We'll take our Ws where we can."

"Command," Waver Runner said, contacting his superior officers. "We encountered significant highly trained operatives. They escaped with the parcel. We are unable to pursue this due to severe damage to our equipment. We request immediate trace on vehicles leaving in multiple directions from our location. We are returning to base."

"Trace initiated. But negative on the return to base."

"Requesting permission to return to base," Wave Runner repeated, unsure what he had heard the officer say.

"Request denied. Significant civil unrest in the city and surrounding areas impedes operational efficiency. Unrest is echoed nationwide. Please report to the Joint Base in San Antonio-Fort Sam."

"Roger that." Addressing his teammates, "Looks like we're not going home yet."

25

MANDATORY COMPLIANCE

TAN Meeting Holoscreen

"THANK YOU FOR COMING," Li Jing Hua said. "I know we just met with the operational guidelines, but some new developments require your immediate attention and adaptation. Mr. Burka will go into more detail."

"Thank you, Chair Hua. Earlier today, our agents carrying the pathogen on US soil were intercepted by US Special Forces and our rivals at the Arm. One of our operatives was captured, and the other one escaped."

"What about the pathogen?" Binh Pham asked.

"Unfortunately, he left it behind, and he thinks it is in the Arm's possession."

"So, our enemies have our secret weapon?" Antonio Abalos said.

"Yes, they do," Burka said. "And for that reason, we have to move up our timeline. We must initiate the attack in seven days rather than thirty."

"That's not possible!" Binh Pham said. "How can this plan even work without the pathogen?"

"Before the confrontation, Agent Bustamante infected himself with the virus as a fail-safe. He laid down his life so we can complete our mission."

"But don't we risk them unleashing the virus in our countries?" Abalos said.

. "Yes, we do," Burka replied. "That is why we must strike first, and we must strike hard. It will take two days for him to be contagious. So, we ordered him to hide for that time. After this, he is to spend the next five days going to as many public places as possible, including clubs, churches, shopping malls, and airports. After five days, he will start showing symptoms; a few days after that, they will become unbearable, and sometime after that, he will die having given the ultimate sacrifice for our cause. By the time the authorities figure out what happened, it will already be too late."

"This is a significant change of operations," Abalos said. "What if we can't meet this timeline adequately?"

"All our governments have considerable resources," Li Jing Hua said, retaking control of the conversation. "If you need further assistance, please let us know. We will be happy to increase our contribution to your efforts. But make no mistake, this plan will go forward and will be executed flawlessly. The way we see it, we will have to spend considerable resources on dealing with your countries. We would much rather do so with you as allies rather than enemies. The time for indecision is over. Now is the time for action. Thank you, that is all."

26

KUNOICHI IN PLAY

Beirut, Lebanon

"THIS IS AZAEL AZOULAY, destroyer of worlds," Tishbi said smiling. "Azael, this is Detective Al Qazi, former Lebanon Special Forces. We often found ourselves on opposite sides of conflicts, even sometimes on opposite sides of each other's gun barrels. But it seems now we are both looking down the barrel of a common enemy. How are you, old friend?"

"I am well! Nice to meet you, Azael," Al Qazi said.

"And who are the lovely ladies?" Tishbi asked.

"This is Dr. Elenor Zalloua from the lab in question. She filed the police report. And this is Lara, head of our forensic team. You can trust her."

"Nice to meet you ladies," Tishbi said.

"Nice to meet you as well," Dr. Zalloua replied.

The five were sitting casually in a cafe in downtown Beirut. The hazelnut wallpapered walls meshed with contrasting apple-red light fixtures. The aroma of fresh ground coffee fused with the scent of spices and baked delicacies. The sounds of the hustle and bustle and background music covered their conversation.

"Why don't you fill him in?" Tishbi said to Al Qazi.

"Sure. A few days ago, Dr. Zalloua was working late at her lab when she noticed something was off."

"What was off?" Azael asked. They both looked at Dr. Zalloua.

"So, we routinely inventory our pathogens and update logs that sort of thing. I didn't think much of it at first, but the labels of a couple of the vials looked slightly different."

"How so?" Azael asked.

"Like they were newer. So, I pulled out their chart, called in some colleagues, and we ran some level four biochemical tests. The results were at odds with the charts. So, I ran more and more tests until it became clear that this wasn't the original pathogen."

"That's when they called us in to investigate," Al Qazi said. "We canvased the lab through and through, but we couldn't find any lead."

"We applied state-of-the-art forensic techniques," Lara continued. "But before we could finish our work, agents from the federal government showed up and took over the scene,"

"Did you alert them?" Tishbi asked.

"No, we did not," Al Qazi answered. "Furthermore, the director of the lab has been missing since that day."

"You think he is part of this?" Tishbi asked.

"Hard to tell. But if I were a betting man, I would bet he is."

"I think it's quite clear that he is related to it somehow," Lara said. "If we would've had more time in the lab, I'm convinced we would have found more evidence."

"No, you wouldn't," Azael said. "From what you're telling us, this was done by some of the best operatives in the world."

"What makes you say that?" Lara asked.

"First, they had to know this virus even existed. How many people in the world with that kind of information?"

"Not many."

"Then, they had to know the lab had it in its possession. Then, they had to be able to swap this highly infectious virus for a fake one without anyone noticing and anyone getting infected. If that wasn't enough, once you figured something was wrong, they dispatched the federal authorities to squash any investigation. Which means they were watching you. Which means they might be watching us now."

An uncomfortable silence set in amongst the group. The level of awareness rose as they pondered Azael's words before he continued.

"As good as they may be, your forensics would most likely not render any viable results."

"So, how do we track them down?" Lara asked.

"You have to understand, these people play the long game," Azael responded. "So first, you need to figure out who knew of the existence of the virus. How did it come into your possession in the first place? Second, who had access to the building in the past year or so? From staff members, government inspectors, and cleaning crew to maintenance calls. They would have put in place whatever they needed for a successful operation. And third, who has a use or a motive for such an item to be under their control?"

"Looks like we have our work cut out for us," Tishbi said. "Perhaps we can find somewhere more discreet to continue our conversation? "He said, looking at Al Qazi.

"I have somewhere we can go," Al Qazi replied.

Forty minutes later, outside Beirut

"This is not what I expected," Tishbi said.

"What were you expecting, old friend?" Al Quazi asked.

"I was expecting something more modest, more inconspicuous, less glamorous."

"Lebanon must pay its public servants very well," Azael quipped.

"It is quite the opposite," Lara said. "We are underpaid and overworked," she said, smirking.

"So, to remedy that situation, we created our own retirement fund," Al Quazi said. "While we seize assets from corrupt criminals and turn them over to more corrupt officials, we decided to put some aside to make sure our families and the families of our fallen comrades are taken care of."

"Don't worry, we're not judging," Azael said. "We all have skeletons in our closets."

"Some skeletons are nicer than others," Tishbi said.

"If you think this is a nice skeleton, wait till you see inside," Lara said. "Besides, who would think a counterterrorism investigation is underway in a mansion on a mountain overlooking the sea?"

The lobby was elegant, with pristine tan marble floors, a Persian rug, and Middle Eastern motifs gracing the walls and doors of the residence.

"I would love to give you a tour, but we have more pressing matters," Al Qazi said while leading them to a room with a conference table, whiteboards, projection screens, and computer stations.

"Welcome to the Operations Room. We are good to conduct the investigation from here."

"Okay, let's get started," Tishbi said, wasting no time. "Dr. Zalloua, who has access to your lab?" he said while grabbing a dry-erase marker and writing on a whiteboard.

"The people who have access to this part of the lab are few. We have five staffers, one administrative assistant, and four researchers."

"Okay, we need their names and employment files," Tishbi said. "Do you have access to those?"

"I do," Zalloua said, but we need proper authorization to access the files. Detective Al Qazi, would you be able to get that?"

"Hum, "Al Qazi cleared his throat. "Doctor, this operation is off the books. We need those HR files to find this virus. Don't worry about liability. If it comes to it, we'll get you out of trouble. We have experience with this sort of operation."

"I don't like this," she said while sitting at one of the workstations. "I'm in the system."

"Okay, we will need a few things," Azael said. "We can start with the lab's access logs for every employee and visitor. Previous associations, employee files. If they did anything wrong in the past, we'll find it."

"Okay, I'm not sure I can do all of that. I can give you the files."

"That's fine, I'll take over from here," Azael said.

"Okay, here they are," she said while getting out of the chair.

"Thank you," Azael said while getting in the chair. "Okay, let's see." After a few minutes of tinkering with the system, Azael conceded, "I'm not finding anything out of the ordinary so far."

"You have to be kidding me," Al Qazi said, looking at his holophone in personal mode.

"What?" Lara asked.

"Dr. Ghani was just found dead. He committed suicide."

"Oh wow! Do you believe that?" She asked, but Al Qazi turned his attention to Dr. Zalloua.

"Are you okay, Doctor?" he asked.

"I knew it," she said.

"What?" Lara asked.

"I knew he was connected to this. He was acting frantic when I broke the news, almost panicked. He is not usually like that in stressful situations. I dismissed it because this is such a dangerous pathogen. I thought he was worried about a breakout and the potential liability."

As everyone's attention was on Dr. Zalloua, Azael took a leave from the room.

"Where are you?" he said, "I can't hear you very well."

"I'm in my bathroom with the shower running," Suri said. "I think they're going to kill me."

"Are you sure? We knew they were going to follow you."

"It has gotten more intense," she said. "They changed the people following me. They used to be more like police officers, but now they seem military types."

"How many?"

"Probably five or six. Also, they were females."

"Females?"

"Yes, they followed me to places where men couldn't go. At some point, I was alone with one of them. I felt like she was going to make a move, but thankfully, people came in. It's getting to be quite intense. And these females look fierce."

"Kunoichi."

"What?"

"Kunoichi. Female ninja assassins inspired by the Japanese. Your government has been training them for decades to carry out some of the most secret missions against my government. You need to run."

"Run? Where? How?"

"Listen to me carefully. When we hang up, you'll pull the fire alarm. That will create a distraction. Then your building has a service elevator for the maintenance staff. Use that one to get to the ground floor. Use the staff exit to get out of the building. Follow the tall bushes. They will lead you to the adjacent building. There, you can steal a car."

"You want me to steal a car?"

"My love, you have no other choice."

"I don't like this! I don't even know if I can do that."

"I showed you how. Don't you remember?"

"Yes, I remember, but it was just for play."

"Well, now it's for real."

"You know what will happen to me if I get caught?"

"I know what will happen to you if you don't leave. They'll kill you. You don't have a lot of time. Once you have a car, head straight to the Swiss embassy. I will have my friend wait for you there. He'll arrange for you to leave the country tonight. Take nothing other than your documents."

"Hey, Azael, are you okay?" Al Qazi yelled from the operations room. "We found something."

"Okay, I'm coming," Azael responded. "I have to go. Stay strong, stay focused. You'll do great. I'll find you."

She took a deep breath.

"Thank you. I will let you know when I'm safe."

He texted Nikolas.

"She's coming to you. Exfil ASAP. Kunoichi in play."

Nikolas replied, *"Roger that."*

Returning to the room, Azael asked, "What did you find?"

"Okay, we're still piecing things together, but it looks like our director was being very well compensated," Al Qazi answered.

"By whom?" Azael asked.

"We don't know yet. But his wife and kid went missing on the same day we started investigating the lab breach."

"We also found out the lab where the virus came from doesn't work with that level of pathogens," Dr. Zalloua said.

"Someone is trying to hide the virus's origin," Lara said.

"The director had a custom to take work home. Maybe we can find something there?" Dr. Zalloua said.

"I guess that's our next stop," Tishbi said.

While they headed towards the exit, Tishbi took Azael aside and asked, "What happened?"

"She said they're trying to kill her."

"Are you sure?"

"From her description, they're sending the kunoichi after her."

"That's not good," Tishbi said, visibly concerned. He continued.

"What did you tell her?"

"I told her to create a distraction and make a run to the Swiss embassy."

"Good. Then?"

"Once she's there, we'll have to figure out what's next."

Tehran, Iran

The fire alarm was blaring. Suri mustered her courage to open her apartment door as the other dwellers flooded the hallways. To create a sense of panic, she yelled,

"Fire! Everybody out!"

She achieved her goal of creating a flood of people heading out of the building. The unintended consequence of her tactic was that she now had to go against the flow of people. Her heightened alertness made her look at every face as a potential attacker. Even children seemed threatening.

She made it to the end of the hallway unarmed. She pushed open the door marked 'employees only'. She was surprised no one tried to escape her make-belief fire through this exit. There was an elevator and another door leading to the staircase. She called the elevator but hid in the staircase in case of an ambush. The coast was clear in the elevator, and she headed to the ground floor. She could feel a sense of relief. *Maybe this plan would work*, she thought to herself. Maybe she could finally be free.

On the ground floor, the door opened to two of her pursuers. She pushed the closed-door button, hoping it would close fast enough, but that was futile. The air was sucked right out of her upon impact of her assailant's foot on her diaphragm. She tried to throw a punch to repel the second strike, but her strength failed her. In the blink of an eye, one attacker had her in a chokehold, trying to snuff out her last breath. Standing in the doorway, the other was holding her legs midair to prevent her from kicking. Suri saw her life flash before her eyes. But before she could see the end of her story, she got her right leg loose and kicked her would-be assassin repeatedly right between the eyes, breaking her nose and causing her to drop Suri's other leg. Suri pulled her taser and stroked the head of the killer choking her, forcing her to let go. She then tased the other one, about to launch back at her. The two attackers' temporary paralysis wouldn't last long, but hopefully could give her enough time to get to the embassy.

She ran out of the elevator and cautiously exited the building through the staff service door. Still out of breath, she looked left and right for signs of the other kunoichi. The coast seemed clear. She looked for an older car, and she figured it would be easier to steal. She hated the idea, but it was a life-or-death situation. Everything was a blur. Before she knew it, she was driving towards the Swiss embassy. In a few minutes, she would be safe. Traffic was light as she raced through the streets; every pair of headlights looked suspicious.

She didn't notice at first. A car pulled up to her side. The car in front of her slowed down, attempting to bring her to a halt. She almost rear-ended it. That's when she realized she was cornered, a car to her left, behind her, and in front of her. The car in front slowed down almost to a halt when Suri saw the barrel of a gun aimed at her from the car beside her. She sped up and squeezed between the car to her left and the one in front of her, using the sidewalk as an escape route. She tore the road and clipped the side mirror of a parked vehicle. She swerved back onto the road dodging pedestrians.

The embassy's street was coming in about a quarter of a mile. She waited until the last possible moment before making the right turn, burning rubber and scraping a parked car. She raced through traffic, zigzagging between vehicles. Her chasers caught up to her. They attempted to corner her, positioning themselves on both sides and behind her. The vehicle to her right slammed into her. To dodge that hit, she veered left and slammed into the vehicle on her other side, causing it to crash into parked vehicles.

Her vehicle took a beating, but the airbag did not deploy. Her adrenaline flowed as fast as her car was racing to the umbrage of Swiss sovereign territory.

The embassy appeared in the distance. She put the pedal to the metal. She let hope come through her mind, *this could be the end of this nightmare*. She could see the gate, Nikolas, and armed guards waiting behind it.

She was about a hundred yards from the gate when the kunoichi slammed into the back of her vehicle. The second vehicle was spraying bullets toward Suri's vehicle with total disregard for collateral damage. Glass shattered in the cabin, and holes popped up on the side of the vehicle. The rear passenger tire blew, destabilizing the car. One last hit from the back sent the vehicle flying and tumbling through the street at sixty miles per hour. It tumbled and crashed into the embassy's gate, crossing the line into sovereign Swiss territory.

The kunoichi's vehicle screeched to a halt. They stepped out of their vehicle to finish the job. They approached the crash site. Nikolas and the soldiers gathered around the vehicle. Paramedics were in the background running towards them. The assassins were resolute on getting their hands on Suri, but faced with rifles of Swiss soldiers, they stopped in their tracks. Nikolas was standing there holding a handgun in his right hand. Not saying anything, he took a few steps forward to the edge of the property with a stare daring them to do something.

They were seething with anger and frustration, police sirens blaring in the distance. They stood down. Their leader spat on the floor, aiming right in front of Nikolas' feet, and they drove off. The paramedics secured Suri and took her to the medical bay.

One hour later

Two vehicles pulled up near Director Ghani's mansion. Azael and Tishbi were riding in the second vehicle, Al Quazi, Lara, and Dr. Zalloua were leading the way in the first one.

"Let's see what we're dealing with," Al Quazi said while pulling a little pouch out of the glove compartment. Lara, in the driver's seat, pulled out her monocular scope.

"Can you guys see?" Al Quazi asked while calibrating his fly-size surveillance drone.

"Yes," Azael answered. "We see the bug's view and yours."

"Okay, perfect. We'll do a small recon. If the coast is clear, we can infiltrate the property. Otherwise, we'll have to get a search warrant."

"That might be more complicated," Lara said.

"Yeah, but I know a judge. He is clean." He maneuvered the drone closer to the house. The drone had enhanced audio and video capture, infrared, a biometric scanner, and night vision. "Looks like someone made it before us." The bug rendered three-dimensional video images of two individuals foraging through the house.

"What do you say if we crash this party?" Lara said while cocking her gun.

"I don't think that's a good idea," Azael said through the holoscreen from the second vehicle.

"Why not?" She responded.

"We wouldn't make it out alive."

"Are you scared?"

"Not at all. I just know how to calculate the odds."

"There are only two of them, and we have them off guard," Lara said, looking through her monocular scope.

"There are also only two of us," he said. "The doctor and the elder do not count. No offense, Tishbi."

"None taken," Tishbi responded with a smirk, enjoying the banter.

"And your boss, well, I'm sure he was quite the operative in the past, but how would he fare today?"

"You know I'm right here?" Al Quazi said. "And if it were back in our day, we'd show you a trick or two."

"I'm sure you would," he said, directed at Al Quazi, then turned to Lara. "But that leaves you and me to take the fight to them."

"We have guns, badges, and the element of surprise," she said.

"That's true, but before you engage in combat, it's good to know your opponents." He leaned closer to the window and focused on the intruders. "First, look at the door. It looks like authentic cedarwood, yet it's busted, even slightly off the hinges. But from this angle, I can't see any tools, no door ram."

"Okay," she said.

"Second, Al Quazi, can you pull closer to the second-floor window?"

"Sure."

"Look at this guy's hands, they have some sort of dust or plaster on them. It looks like they smashed a wall or something. I'd bet they're after the safe. Third, look at them moving. They're fluid, precise, and faster than your average thief—"

"Four, another car just pulled up," Lara said.

"That's getting interesting," Tishbi said.

"Indeed, it is. Still want to crash the party?" Azael quipped.

"Let's keep watching," Lara replied.

Four Arm agents got out of the vehicle. Their suits and ties, though inconspicuous, reeked of wealth and style.

The two men exited the house through the side window, jumping from the second floor without hesitation. They cautiously waited until the four were inside the house to go for their vehicle, leaving the Arm agents none the wiser in the house.

"Al Quazi, you stay on these four. We'll follow those two," Azael said while maneuvering his vehicle to trail his mark.

"You got it."

"Hey, Quazi, can you run these guys through biometrics?" Tishbi asked.

"Yes, but we have to be in the office. Our leadership restricted our access to IRIS for in-office use only. We could go back to the safehouse, but we would lose our targets."

"I'm going to regret this," Lara said. "I have a way in the system."

"Really? Why am I not surprised?" Al Quazi said.

"Well, sometimes you need information right away," she said while taking over the spy bug's controls. She interfaced the controls with her holophone, gave them back to Al Quazi, and started tinkering on her device.

"Our four stooges are moving. We will have to pursue them," Al Quazi said.

"Don't," Azael said. "You need to search the house. Maybe you can find what they were looking for. Can you lodge the *bug* somewhere in their car?"

"Yes, sure can!" Al Quazi said.

He hid the bug under the car. Once the quartet of Arm agents opened the doors, he navigated the *bug* from under the car into the cabin and landed it under the passenger seat.

"Well done boss," Lara said. "By the way, I think I have something. Azael, one of your two guys works as an attaché to the ambassador at the Syrian embassy."

Azael didn't immediately answer. A message from Nikolas came in. It read, *"Package damaged but secured...she's okay :-)"*

"Azael, are you there?"

"Yes, I'm here. Syrian embassy? Do you think he might be Syrian Special Forces?"

"*Idarat al-Amn al-'Amm.* The General Security Directorate?" she said. "I don't know. He doesn't register anywhere else, and this match is sixty-four percent accurate."

"Any way to find out?"

"Not without raising red flags. But if they are Syrian Special Ops, this might get more complicated than we expected. Whatever you do, do not lose them."

"That might prove harder than it seems," Tishbi said. "We're heading towards a military checkpoint. I don't know about Syrian agents, but I'm sure Israeli ones are not welcome here."

"You are correct," Lara said. "I don't need to tell you what happens if they figure out who you are."

"This road leads to the airport." Al Quazi chimed in. "Looks like our two fellows might want to leave the country."

"They just pulled to the checkpoint," Azael said. "They went right through. We are five cars behind. Our cover credentials should hold, but stand by."

"Okay, we are here with you," she said, followed by a short silence. "We are entering the house." She led the way through the dismantled but somehow still majestic cedarwood doors.

Professor Zalloua was between the two agents. Al Quazi scanned up and down the street to ascertain if any other interested parties were observing them as they observed their predecessors.

"Your boss lived the good life," Lara told the scientist. Dr. Zalloua did not reply. She was stunned by the grandeur of the mansion.

"I'm sure directors make good money," Al Quazi said. "But I don't think they make that much money. What was your boss into?"

"I am as shocked as you," she replied. "I wish I could tell you more."

"Don't worry, we'll get to the bottom of it." Turning to Lara, he said, "Okay, do your thing."

"I'm already on it," she said. She put down her work utility bag and pulled out her multifactor forensic scanner. The scanner allowed her to digitally detect and process common forensic elements like fingerprints, gunshot residue, and other biomarkers.

"What are you finding?" Al Quazi asked.

"So far, multiple fingerprints, hair samples, and footprints. I'll run it all through IRIS in a few."

"I found the safe," Dr. Zalloua shouted from the second floor.

The two agents joined her and saw the safe open on the ground. The hole in the adjacent wall indicated it had been ripped from its hinges in the wall.

Al Quazi stooped down to peek inside. There was some jewelry and a couple of Rolex watches.

"Look," Lara said, putting on her gloves and grabbing the late director's passports from Australia, France, and South Africa.

"Look at that," Al Quazi responded, making a discovery of his own. Three envelopes containing the related currencies and bank cards of local banks to those nations.

"We might need your help," Tishbi whispered in the coms. "These guys don't seem to be buying our story."

"That's not good. Hold on. Let me make some calls. What's the name of the agent?

"El Khoury," he answered.

"Okay, give me a second."

"Hurry, we do not have that long. He's asking us to get out of the car, and some other agents are coming our way. They must have been tipped."

"Okay, don't do anything crazy. Just play along. I'll get you out of this," Al Quazi said.

Al Quazi made a call to General Hariri, a member of the Cabinet whose portfolio encompassed National Security and Counterterrorism.

Five minutes later, Azael and Tishbi were hand-tied in the holding area of the checkpoint. They could see El Khoury talking on the phone, nodding his head. He hung up and headed towards them.

"Untie them," El Khoury said to his subordinate. He didn't have time for introductions, even less for apologies and formalities. "Follow me," he said to the two Israeli agents. He didn't like them and knew they didn't like him.

"We grounded all the flights," El Khoury said. "The official reason is a temporary outage of the communication infrastructure. Plainclothes officers on the ground are initiating a search. More are on their way."

"I'm Tishbi—"

"I know who you are," El Khoury said. He handed him a device. "Here, going forward, use this holophone to communicate with us. Get in your car, follow me. While en route, give us your best description of the targets."

Ten minutes later, they arrived at the airport.

"Everybody, spread out. The description is on your devices," General El Khoury said as the plain-clothed and uniformed soldiers spread out in the airport. "You two are staying with me," he told Azael and Tishbi.

"Of course," Tishbi said.

"Follow me," The general said as the chief of security walked up to them. "Please take us to the command center."

"With all due respect, sir," Azael said. "I understand the logic of the command center, but we might be out of time."

"I beg your pardon?" The general replied.

"I think we would be wasting time looking through footage."

"You have a better option?"

"I believe I know where they are," Azael said, turning to the Chief of Security. "If my memory is correct, you have chartered flights departing from this airport, right?" he asked.

"Yes, we have quite a few private flights and Air cabs coming in and out. They have all been grounded."

"Can we head to that terminal?"

The chief of security looked to the general, who shook his head in the negative.

"Tell you what. Why don't the general and I head to the command center, and you two head to the terminal?" Tishbi said. To which the general reluctantly nodded in the affirmative.

Once at the terminal, Azael, with his holophone in hand, visually scrutinized all the faces he came in contact with. None of which came close to the suspects. A mix of business types and wealthy vacationers. No one carrying one of the most infectious pathogens on earth.

"How can we help?" Asha, the terminal's administrator, asked.

"Can you gather the staff and run these images by them?"

"All the staff received the notice already. No one has come forward,"

"So, no one flew out in the past ten minutes? What were the last three flights out?"

"Come with me to the log… Let's see, we have a flight under the Mbili Entertainment Corp, the president of Cedar Capital, and the last one was a diplomatic flight chartered by the Syrian embassy."

Azael picked up the device provided by the general.

"General, the pathogen left the airport. Can you intercept?"

"Are you sure?"

"I'm positive."

"Our fighter jets would not make it before they leave Lebanese airspace. Any indication where they are going?"

Azael turned to the Administrator and asked,

"Destination?"

She took a second look at her log.

"Tel Aviv," she answered. "The flight is headed to Israel."

"You heard that, general?"

"Yes," he answered.

"Take IDF. I will take the prime minister," Tishbi told Azael over the holophone.

"Copy that," Azael responded.

"Excuse me," Tishbi said and stepped away to dial the prime minister. The general could still hear him.

"I need the prime minister… Take him out of that meeting now! Have his chief of security patched through as well. Do it now. I don't care! Do it NOW!"

It took about thirty seconds to get the prime minister on the line. As soon as he picked up, Tishbi blurted out.

"Mr. Prime Minister, you need to head to safety now! Sir, I am in Lebanon with agent Azael Azoulay. We have credible intel of an imminent terrorist threat heading towards the country. A virus, sir. It can potentially cause an extinction-level event— Minutes, sir, we have minutes. Twenty-five minutes if we're lucky. Agent Azoulay is notifying IDF and Mossad." Pulling aside even more and almost whispering, Tishbi continued.

"Sir, do it discreetly. I believe we have a mole in the inner circle. I'm not sure who yet, but we do not want to spook the suspects. That could prove to be catastrophic... Thank you, sir." Tishbi hung up and dialed Azael.

"Status update?" he asked.

"IDF, Mossad, and Shin Bet are notified. They are enacting an immediate high-response covert intercept protocol."

"Okay, good. Let's reconnect with Al Quazi," he said while linking the call with his old friend.

"Hello," Al Quazi said, but did not wait for an answer. "Did you catch them?"

"We located them, but they flew out on a private plane heading towards Israel. Our agencies have been notified, but now more than ever, we need to know everything about this thing. What did you find?"

"Not much...but it's more what we did not find."

"We're listening," Tishbi said.

"The director was quite the meticulous man. We found a small notepad hidden under his nightstand, containing lists of addresses and numbers. Turns out these are banks, houses, and storage units in various countries. Also, there was a list of items like passports, passport numbers, and driver's licenses for the same countries. We found most items on the list except their Canadian passports and currency."

"We went through their closets, bathrooms, and bedroom, and it looks like they were leaving in a hurry," Lara said.

"So, you think she went to Canada?"

"Yes, per Dr. Zalloua, they have ties in Canada. Montreal, to be more precise."

"It should be easy to find out if that's where she was headed," Azael said. Turning to the Chief of Security, he continued, "Do you have access to IRIS?"

"Yes, we do,"

Addressing Al Quazi, Azael continued, "Can you send me her pictures? If she boarded a flight from this airport, we'll find her."

A few moments later, IRIS confirmed she had boarded a plane to Montreal. But her trail went cold after she arrived in the *city of a hundred steeples*.

"They caught them!" Azael said. "Our liaison confirmed. They retrieved the vials, and the suspects are in custody."

Tishbi and the other agents sighed a sigh of relief.

An hour later, after debriefing with General El Khoury, and clearing from the Israeli embassy and the Lebanese State Department, Tishbi, Azael, Al Quazi, Lara, and Dr. Zalloua huddled.

"Mission accomplished?" Lara asked.

"I wouldn't be so sure," Azael answered.

"Me neither," she confessed.

"What is the status of our four intruders?" Tishbi asked.

"The federal authorities took over the surveillance," Al Quazi answered.

"Not surprising," Azael said.

"Now you can expect increased scrutiny every step we take," Tishbi said.

"This thing might be going deeper than we originally thought," Al Quazi said. "We might never know who these four goons were. I hope your government can get more information from the two guys in custody. But I respectfully ask, can they be trusted?" he said, looking at Tishbi.

Tishbi did not answer immediately. Rather, he looked for the proper answer.

"I hope so," Tishbi said. "I hope so."

"This virus cannot be allowed to be released. It would spell disaster for the entire planet," Dr. Zalloua said. "It should never have existed in the first place."

"How can we prevent an outbreak?" Lara asked.

"It's out of our hands now," Al Quazi said.

"Any antidote?" Azael asked.

"None that I know of," Dr. Zalloua answered. "My boss was the expert in that regard."

"Can we access his files?" Lara asked.

"Not anymore," Al Quazi answered. "Now you can expect every move we make to be under the microscope. And we don't know who our enemy is."

"There might be a way," Tishbi said. "Can I talk to you for a second?" he said to Azael, taking him aside and whispering to him. "What about her? She has to get out of her country anyway. Would she agree to go to Canada? She could track down the director's wife and be out of her government's reach."

"She's been through a lot. I'd rather have her come to us in Jerusalem."

"You forget, we're still in an active war with the government that she was a part of just a few days ago. She'd be too exposed."

"Good point."

"She's not on their radar; we know we can trust her."

"Guys, care to fill us in on your little party?" Lara asked.

"What do you say?" Tishbi asked Azael before rejoining the others.

"Okay, let's do it."

"We have an asset we can send to find the director's wife in Canada," Tishbi said. "Maybe she can help put the pieces together. It's a long shot, but it's our only play."

Azael sent a text to Nikolas, *"Prep Exfil to MTL."*

27

NIGHT NIGHT

"YOUR HONOR, MY CLIENT is not a flight risk," Shapiro said in the filled courtroom. "The evidence against him is flimsy at best, downright slanderous at worst. Therefore, we respectfully petition the court to let him go on his own recognizance."

Ty G was sitting next to his longtime attorney, Shapiro. Behind him was his former gangmate turned pastor, Kyle Boykin. He was hoping for the best, but regardless of the outcome of this bail hearing, he knew that had it not been for Kyle, this would have been a more somber gathering, his funeral.

"Does the state object?" Judge Chao said.

"Your honor," the prosecutor said. "This is a hardened criminal with a long rap sheet. We respectfully ask that the bail be set at five million dollars."

"Your honor, with all due respect, this is preposterous. The prosecution knows full well that my client is innocent. He has a solid alibi and doesn't own a passport. With this mysterious flu outbreak, several countries have banned travel from our country. He is not a flight risk at all since there is nowhere to fly, too!"

"First, counselor, we do not know if your client is innocent. That is why we have these proceedings," Judge Chao said. "Second, your client is facing some serious allegations. Anyone can be a flight risk under these circumstances. That being said, it is late. The court would like to see as many people as possible before the lockdown takes effect tomorrow. So, here's what I will do. If you can take care of it immediately, I will set the bond at half a million dollars."

"I can certainly do that, your honor," Shapiro said. He took out his holophone and entered a few taps and clicks. "Done through the Bail App, your honor."

"Okay, then adjourn—"

The light flickered, sounds of electric zapping could be heard, and sparks burst out of the electronic devices in the courtroom. The room went pitch black for about two seconds until the emergency lights kicked in.

Shapiro's phone sparked in his hand, causing him to drop it. He picked it back up.

"What just happened?" he said. A sense of wonder and annoyance filled the room. He attempted to check the news on his holophone. "My phone does not work."

"Order in the court," Judge Chao said, striking her gavel. "Order in the court. Bailiff, please find out if the outage is only in this building or if the whole block is out. In the meantime. The court is in receipt of the bail. Therefore, Tyrone Green, you're free to go for now. Adjourned."

"Thank you, your honor," Shapiro said, tapping Ty G in the back as both a congratulatory gesture and a signal that it was time to go. The second bailiff removed his restraints. "Let's get you processed out," he said, leading the way out of the courtroom to the clerk's processing department to retrieve Ty G's personal items. The clerk found his items. Shapiro said his goodbyes, and then Ty G reverted to his normal street clothes.

"You good, bro?" Kyle asked him.

"I'm still here, bro. Let's get outta here."

Rat-rat-rat.

"Shots fired! Shots fired!" The bailiff said into his military-grade radio. They peeked around the corner. The lobby was being overtaken by what looked to be a paramilitary group of about a dozen. The bailiff pulled out his gun to fire back at the attackers. Kyle pulled him back and lowered the gun.

"Don't do it. You'll kill us all." Kyle whispered. The bailiff didn't say anything. He realized Kyle was right.

"We have to get out of here," Kyle continued.

"What about that door y'all brought me in from?" Ty G said.

"Yeah, the backdoor for high-profile perps. This way," the bailiff said, leading the way.

"Holup! Where do y'all keep y'all guns?" Ty G asked.

"Nah, man, I'm not about to hand you a gun." The bailiff said.

"You'd rather shoot your way out by yourself? How long do you think your community college training is gon last?" Ty G retorted.

"I'm pretty sure these guys are special forces," Kyle added.

"How do you figure?" The bailiff said.

"I'm a military brat. My dad and my brother are both special ops. Trust me on this one, give us the guns."

"Follow me," the bailiff said, conceding the point. They ran to the court's armory, which didn't have much of an arsenal. Kyle and Ty G took handguns, and the trio headed towards the secret backdoor used for high-profile and high-risk suspects. They opened the door slowly, ready to defend themselves if needed. The door opened to the back of the building into a narrow alley. They headed to the eastern corner. They froze in place at the sight of mayhem. The streets were dark with inoperative streetlights and multiple car crashes. All the buildings were dark. The main sources of light were the moon and the fires burning throughout the hellscape. They could hear shots being fired in the proximity.

The bailiff fell to his knees. "Oh my—" he did not finish his sentence but started crying. Kyle put his hand over his mouth, holding back his own tears. Ty G stood there in disbelief until his fighter's instinct kicked in.

"Y'all, we got to get out of here," Ty G said.

"How? How?" the bailiff said. Whoever did this is everywhere. They'll find us."

"If we stay here, they'll find us," Kyle said. "Listen, I don't know what's happening, but we don't have time to stand still. We have to move. I don't want to leave you behind. Are you coming with us, or are you staying here by yourself?"

"I'm coming."

"Okay, y'all follow me." Ty G said.

Ty G led them out of the downtown area through back alleys and private properties.

"KB, I betcha you forgot about these parts," Ty G said.

"It's coming back, though. I guess our time running from the police is coming in handy,"

"I guess so," Ty G said. "Hol'on, hol'on, hol'on." He stopped abruptly and gestured to his companions to be quiet. He pointed to a faint light heading their way on the road they were about to cross. The light became brighter and brighter. The trio took cover under bushes. They stayed still and watched as military trucks rolled through. Kyle counted about twenty armored vehicles. As a precaution, they stayed down after the vehicles were out of sight. In the distance, they could hear the thunderous sound of explosions and gunfire reverberating.

"What in the world is happening?" the bailiff whispered.

"I don't know, but we have to keep moving," Kyle said.

"Alright, let's go," Ty G said. They walked for two hours under the cover of night until they arrived at Triple P's safehouse on the outskirts of town. A quarter mile off-road, the compound was dark and not visible from the road, hidden behind the tall grass. About fifty yards from there, Ty G could see some shimmer through the window, and he let the thought go through his mind, finally home. He let his guard down. Maybe it was the ruffle in the grass or a shadow in the pitch-black night. He sensed something was wrong. The cold metallic cylinder of a gun's barrel pressed against the back of his head. Gunmen surrounded them.

"I wouldn't take one more step if I were you," the voice said.

"If you were me, Jimmy, you would know this is my house and this is my crew." Ty G responded. Immediately, Jimmy put down his weapon.

"Oh, my bad boss. My bad! Things are getting crazy. We better get inside."

The place was an old farmhouse repurposed to accommodate Triple P affiliates needing to lay low. The place was dark, lit by candlelight.

"What in the world is going on?" Ty G said.

"Man, we don't know. We was watching the news on your trial on the TV. When it just cut off."

"You lost power, too?" Kyle asked.

"Nah, we didn't, but all the channels were dead. We was comin' to get you, but when we was about to get to the main road, we saw them big, armored cars with military rolling down the road. We killed the lights."

"They spotted you?" Ty G asked.

"Nah, they didn't."

"Were they our guys?" Kyle asked.

"Nah, man, they looked foreign like they from China or Korea or something'. Who's your cop friend?" he asked, looking at the Baillif.

"He not a cop, he the bailiff from the court," Ty G said.

"Y'all buddy buddy?" Jimmy said, wondering why Ty would bring a law enforcement figure in their midst. He tolerated the preacher, but a policeman was pushing it.

"He saved our lives," Kyle said. "We saw some of those foreign fighters storming the courthouse right after we made bail. He got us guns and got us out of there through a back door. We might be dead otherwise, who knows?"

"Okay, then," Jimmy said. "Anyways, we got some signals with the radio. Some guy was saying America is under attack. Looks like the whole world turned against us."

28

ONSLAUGHT

Joint Base San Antonio, Texas, a few hours earlier

"THE GOVERNOR IS COMING to town," the base commander said, sitting at his desk. Behind him were off-white shelving garnished with a mix of books and memorabilia. In the left corner of the room was a US flag, and a Texas flag stood in the right corner. "Due to the ongoing protests and the outbreak, we are concerned with the safety and security of the governor and everyone at the event. We would like your team to assist with security. We are under an active statewide lockdown, so that should reduce the variables, but still, we can't lock down the protests."

"Of course, sir," Topher answered.

"We are deploying the Texas National Guard along with some US National Guardsmen. But we could use your expertise on the ground. Also, I know you want to head back to your home base. I requested an authorization on your behalf."

"Thank you, sir,"

"The governor's press conference is scheduled for nineteen hundred hours at the Children's Hospital of San Antonio. He wants to be in the epicenter to project confidence. Which means it'll be a logistical nightmare. You will liaise with Captain Duncan. We need all hands on deck."

"Understood, sir."

"Dismissed."

Children's Hospital, San Antonio

A small crowd gathered in the lobby of the pediatric hospital. Reporters and top-tier medical staff were readying for the governor's announcement. Wave Runner and Eager Beaver were leading the security detail. They were wearing dark suits and ties.

Green Arrow and Mockingbird were in civilian clothing in a protest for justice at Milam Park, a block away from the Children's Hospital.

"Whose brilliant idea was it to hold a press conference in the middle of an outbreak, five minutes away from a massive protest?" CK said.

"I'm asking myself the same question," Chad said. "NO JUSTICE NO PEACE!" He then shouted along with the crowd.

"Lightened up, you two. Soon, it'll be over," Max said on overwatch duty.

"Easy for you to say from up there," Chad said.

"Can't always be you. Let other people have fun sometimes!"

"Stay focused," Topher said. "This could get bad fast."

"Roger that," Chad replied.

Governor Gauff took to the podium.

"Thank you all for coming. My fellow Texans, once more, we are faced with an unprecedented threat from which we know very little. A virus that spreads fast and far. A virus that is treacherous and merciless. But make no mistake, we have the best medical staff and the best scientists in the world right here. We will prevail. I know these times can be scary, I know these times create a lot of uncertainty. I'm not going to disrespect your intelligence and sugarcoat the situation. These times will be challenging. But we are strong, we are resilient, we are Texans!" The Governor said to the applause of his supporters in the room.

"Now, my fellow Texans, we will not hang you out to dry. We will not leave you to weather the storm by yourself. We are in this together…"

"Guys, things are getting pretty agitated over here," Chad said. It seems we have some professional troublemakers stirring the pot. The protest is fast turning into a riot."

"I can see the action spilling into the street," Milkshake said, perched on top of a building fully suited up. "Beware, more agitators might be coming your way. I'm spotting a van… make that three vans by city hall. They are unloading a small army. "

"Things are out of hand here,'" Mockingbird said. "We're heading back to the vehicle to suit up. I advise getting the governor to safety."

"…This is why I am signing the Texans' Health Resilience Economic And Treatments Relief Bill, known as the THREAT RELIEF Act. This legislation immediately deploys state resources to deal with the first wave of this crisis. This is the first step. It will provide additional funding for hospitals like this one and ensure our children have the best healthcare possible. It will increase unemployment benefits for people economically impacted by this virus-"

Topher leaned into the ear of the governor's chief of staff.

"We have to go. Significant threats are incoming."

The chief of staff nodded when the place turned dark for about ten seconds before the backup generators kicked in.

"Well, ladies and gentlemen, it seems we have a power outage," The chief of staff said. "We will end this press conference here. Thank you all for coming. Stay safe."

Everything in the city went dark. Streetlights turned black, lights shining through the windows disappeared, traffic lights stopped, and cars ceased to work. The sounds of the few cars still on the road crashing into one another popped up throughout the area. The police helicopter providing aerial surveillance spiraled out of control. It crashed half a mile from the hospital. Downtown was completely dark except for the sporadic accidental fires. It took Milkshake a moment to make sense of what he was witnessing until gunfire broke out at City Hall and the police departments.

"Wave Runner, do you copy? Milkshake to Wave Runner, do you copy?"

The communication was choppy and faint at first.

"I copy. I copy," Topher said.

"This is not a power outage. Both buildings and vehicles have lost power," Milkshake said. "This is an EMP attack. I repeat, we are under attack. Secure Big Bear. Several hostiles engaging at City Hall and local police departments. Shots fired. I repeat, shots fired."

"Roger that," Topher said. "Sir, we have to leave now!" Topher said directly to the governor.

"Yes, right after some pictures with the staff," Governor Gauff said.

"Sir, we're under attack. We have to leave now!" Topher said in the Governor's ear, firmly guiding him towards the back exit.

Milkshake flew up in altitude to gain a better vantage point. He could see as far as the three highways converging downtown.

"Milkshake to Bengal Tiger, do you have incoming assets converging to the central theater?"

Milkshake said to the National Guard's field commander.

"Negative, Milkshake. All assigned units are on location," he replied.

"Bengal Tiger, please confirm, no additional units are on the way to this theater," Milkshake repeated.

"Confirmed. All expected units are on location."

"Bengal Tiger, ready troops for active confrontation. Multiple presumably hostile military-grade convoys are incoming from Highways 10, 35, and 37 from both directions. Convoy also on the 410, presumably heading to Fort Sam. Civil unrest swelling towards Big Bear's location."

"Roger that, Milkshake," the field commander said. "All troops to take defensive posture, ready for combat. Wave Runner, secure Big Bear now!"

"Guys, you might want to suit up for that one," Milkshake said. "From what I can see, we have a war on our hands."

"That's a negative for us," Topher said. "Securing Big Bear is the first priority."

"Roger that. Mockingbird and I just made it to our vehicle. Stupid thing won't open! Whose idea was it to make everything electronic?" Chad said. He took off his jacket and wrapped it around his handgun to muffle the sound. He shot the trunk's lock several times until it popped open. "We got it open, suiting up now."

"Arrow, Mockingbird, you have incoming," Max said as four foreign soldiers turned the corner. Chad and CK took refuge behind the vehicle.

Without issuing a command or engaging in conversation, the soldiers opened fire.

"We're taking fire," Arrow said.

"I'm coming to assist," Milkshake said.

"No, it's okay. We got this," Mockingbird said. "Focus on Big Bear." She aimed at a soldier's foot beneath the vehicle. She fired and hit him in the lower tibia, forcing him to the ground, where she welcomed him with one between the eyes.

The other three stopped firing for a split second, seeing their comrade fall to the floor. That's all Arrow needed to dispatch three shots in three seconds. Each one hit its intended target.

"Problem solved," Arrow said.

"That was a nice one," Mockingbird admitted.

"Yours was pretty cool too."

"When you guys are done complimenting each other, do you think you can suit up?" Milkshake said." Some people from the crowd are getting closer to the hospital. They have assault rifles. They are not civilians. I think it's fair to assume they are after Big Bear. No need to tell you this will go south fast unless we act swiftly."

"Roger that," Topher said. "We are heading to the back exit with Papa Bear, Mama Bear, and the Cub. Meet us at the western exit by the parking garage."

"Our suits would be nice right about now!" Eager Beaver said.

"Suiting up right now, hang tight. We're coming with your suits," Arrow said.

"Bengal Tiger, the crowd is pulling to the perimeter, ready guardsmen to engage," Milkshake said. "The enemy convoys are circling the downtown quadrant."

"Guardsmen ready to engage," Bengal Tiger answered.

"Roger that," Milkshake said. "Be advised, enemy forces outnumber our troops two to one."

"Why would they come so short-staffed? They would need to be at least four times as much."

"Sir, I think they have air support."

"You don't stop with the good news, do you soldier? What are we dealing with?"

"Radar has two UAVs heading our way."

"How are these drones even flying after the EMP blast?"

"They either staged them outside the blast radius or, just like our suits, they're made to withstand an EMP blast. Either way, they're coming fast." Milkshake's warning was as fast as anyone could expect, but it was too little, too late.

BOOM!

The first drone on site fired a low-capacity missile, hitting the northern portion of the perimeter. All the guardsmen at that post were killed or severely wounded.

Ratata-ratata.

The second drone fired rapid machine gun rounds on the soldiers posted on the southern portion of the perimeter, killing several and wounding many more. The crowd heading towards the southern post shouted a battle cry towards the guardsmen.

"Perimeter breach, perimeter breach," Bengal Tiger shouted to his troops. "Fall back! Fall back! Keep formation, I repeat, keep formation."

The guardsmen pulled from their respective positions to form a narrower shield around the hospital's points of entry.

"The UAVs are coming back. I repeat, UAVS are making a loop back," Milkshake said. "Arrow, Mockingbird, are you good?"

"Affirmative," Arrow said. "We are en route."

"Wave Runner, be advised, hospital breach is imminent," Milkshake said.

"Copy that," Wave Runner answered.

"I got the rocket drone," Max said. "Arrow, get the machine gun drone. Mockingbird, get to Wave Runner and Beaver, and get Papa Bear and his family out of there!"

As the fighting exploded from all sides, Milkshake aimed at the missile-yielding drone. The first missile strike was destructive, but a second one would prove to be devastating. Arrow perched himself in a sniper position on top of the closest high-rise hotel building. He aimed at the socket, joining the machine gun to the drone, causing the machine gun to fall out of its bearings and destabilizing the UAV. The second was to the rudder, causing the device to go into a tailspin, crash into a building, and then to the ground.

"Beta drone down," Chad said. "Milkshake, you need assistance on Alpha drone?"

Boom! A flash explosion in the night sky.

"Milkshake, do you copy? Milkshake, do you copy?" Arrow said.

"I copy, alpha drone down. Heading to the hospital now."

"Command, this is Bengal Tiger requesting immediate backup. The hospital has been breached. I repeat, the hospital has been breached."

"Mommy, I'm scared," Krystal, the governor's daughter, said.

"Don't be afraid, my love. We will be okay," Mrs. Gauff answered, her shaking hands and voice betraying her words. "These men will protect us."

"Mockingbird, how are we doing on these suits?" Beaver asked.

"Just made it to the roof of your location," she said. "They really need to make a lighter version of these!" She said, dropping the one case she was holding to the floor and detaching the other one she had tethered to her suit.

"Good!" Wave Runner said. "Can you meet us at the western exit?"

"Negative," she said, peeking over the ledge. "The crowd—actually, let's call it what it is, the militia made it to that side of the building, and they're trying to gain access. You're surrounded from all sides. Your best bet is to meet me on the roof."

Wave Runner took stock of the situation and assessed the people under his charge. He felt it was a lot to ask of them, but there was no other viable option.

"Sir, ma'am, we need to move. We need to get you to the roof." He said.

"Okay, whatever you need us to do," Governor Gauff said. He turned to his daughter. "Honey, I need you to be strong, okay?"

"Okay, Dad, but what about the children?" She said. Governor Gauff had no answer for his daughter.

"My friends will take care of them," Wave Runner said to reassure her. "Milkshake, Arrow, prioritize protection of civilian staff and children."

"Roger that," Arrow said.

"Okay, we have to move," Wave Runner said.

"The elevator is this way," Governor Gauff said.

"Will it even work?" Mrs. Gauff asked.

"It should, they're made to withstand these types of events."

"We can't take the elevator," Wave Runner replied.

"Don't you think it'll be faster?"

"Yes, but we don't know how many hostiles have entered the hospital. If they get to us while in the elevator, we'll be sitting ducks with few options. We have to take the stairs."

"Don't worry, sir. Wave Runner will be in front, and I'll be covering the back," Beaver said.

"Alright, let's go," the governor answered.

"Clear," Wave Runner said as they started climbing the stairs. The cacophony of bangs & blasts was becoming louder and louder. The pounding sounds engulfed the staircase's reverberating acoustics. "Talk to me, team, status updates."

"Trying to hold off the assault on the east wing," Arrow said. "Heavy casualties sustained. We're outnumbered and need backup, and we need it now!"

"Hostiles are swarming the streets," Mockingbird said, still on the hospital roof. "They're infiltrating the building from all sides, Wave Runner. You better make it up here fast."

"Roger that," Wave Runner replied. Turning to the governor, he said, "Let's speed it up!"

Eager Beaver joined Wave Runner at the head of the pack and whispered, "We might want to reconsider the elevator option. We're not going to make it at this pace."

Wave Runner thought about the option. In minutes, they could be on the roof, suiting up, or the long grind up the stairs with exhausted civilians.

"Sir, ma'am," he said. "Change of plans. We'll have to go through the fourth floor to the elevators." The governor felt a sense of gratification that his original idea was being adopted. The glimpse of satisfaction was wiped out when Wave Runner handed him a gun.

"In case you need it," Wave Runner said. "Stay close to us, but whatever happens, keep your family safe. Don't worry about us. Getting you to safety is the only thing that matters. Understood?"

"Yes, sir," the governor answered.

"Alright, let's go."

Wave Runner opened the door. The floor was dark, dimly lit by the generator-powered security lights that survived the EMP blast and the glare coming from the hallway windows. The staff and their patients were hunkering down in place. They shut all the doors and pulled the blinds to the room windows. Doctors and nurses were going in and out of rooms, trying to keep as many patients alive and stable as possible.

Wave Runner was at the front of the pack with his weapon drawn. Eager Beaver resumed his position in the back. Krystal let go of her mother's hand and ran to the large hallway window overlooking the hospital's entrance.

"Krystal!" Mrs. Gauff said, running after her daughter to bring her back into the fold. The child arrived at the window first. Her silence was uncharacteristic. The mom arrived second, and the other adults followed.

They were silent at the scene unfolding before their eyes. Mayhem and destruction engulfed the city. Smoke billowed from burning buildings, flashes of gunfire and explosives lit the streets like an infernal Fourth of July. The charm and beauty of the city were ravaged. The cruelty of war was on full display. Eager Beaver spoke first.

"Come on, we have to move," he said. Before that point, his priority was to keep the governor and his family safe. Now, it was to get them out of the way so he could get out there and make whoever was behind this pay.

"Who would do something like this?" Betty Gauf asked.

"I don't know, honey, but we have plenty of enemies." The governor replied. "What's important now is th—" Governor Gauff hunched over and grabbed his chest in pain.

"Daddy! Daddy!"

"Honey, what's wrong?" The state's first lady said. "We need a doctor!"

Wave Runner found the resident doctor on the floor. He and his staff set the governor in the best available room on the floor and started working on him. Topher took the gun he had given the Governor and handed it to his wife.

"Ma'am, do you know how to use one of those?"

"Don't insult me, son. I'm Texas-grown."

Rat-ta-ta

Machine gun fire erupted at the other end of the floor.

"Good, you might have to use it," Wave Runner said. "Do not let anyone in this room unless it's one of us. The blinds are pulled, and no one knows you are here."

"What's your name, son?"

"I'm John Smith, ma'am," he replied. She knew he was lying. Being from a military background, she knew members of Delta never gave their real names.

"Well, Mr. Smith, I understand the assignment. Now, you go out there and make this country proud."

"Yes, ma'am." He exited the room, then said through the com unit, "Milkshake, Mockingbird, Arrow. Papa Bear is incapacitated; exfil is not possible. Hostiles are on the floor. We need all available backups on the fourth floor now!"

"Roger that, we're coming," Chad said.

"Follow our geo location. We'll be on the move," Wave Runner said.

"You're not waiting for your suit?" Mockingbird asked.

"There's no time. Fire is rapidly getting closer to Papa Bear's position. The best way to protect him is to take the fight to them," Topher said.

"Besides, I have some extra bullets I need to discharge," Eager Beaver added.

The duo, weapons drawn, hurried towards the gunfire. Upon approaching the hostile squad, they took covert positions.

"I count ten," Eager Beaver whispered.

"Sounds about right," Wave Runner replied.

"So, what's the plan?" Andy asked.

"Let's go for a bait and shoot," Topher replied.

"Okay, just don't shoot me."

"Can't make any promises."

Wave Runner stayed at one end of the hallway while Eager Beaver crawled through the neuro-oncology department's testing waiting area to make it to the midpoint of that hallway. He waited for the squad to pass his position. Wave Runner fired a few rounds, taking down two of the squad's soldiers. They replied with a shower of bullets and raced towards him. It took them a moment to make out that some of the gunfire wasn't theirs. By then, Eager Beaver had shot down five. Confusion overtook the three remaining. Wave Runner shot two, and Beaver shot the last one.

Milkshake had joined Mockingbird on the roof and grabbed one of the cases. The team and a handful of soldiers converged on the fourth floor and joined Runner and Beaver at the shootout site.

"Let me guess. bait and shoot?" Chad said, looking down at the formation of the enemy's fallen soldiers.

"You know it," Beaver answered. "But next time, you need to be here. This guy almost shot me."

"Yeah, you're lucky I missed," Runner replied in jest. "But all joking aside, more are coming. We need to get this place ready."

The fighting went on all night. Bursts of gunshots followed by lulls of hustle and bustles that felt like silence in comparison to the thunder of battle. Betty Gauff was hunched over her resting husband, gun in hand. She was praying for his recovery and their very survival. Over the years, she had constantly prayed for men and women of the military to make it back home safely. Most of the time, those prayers were answered, but a few too many times, they had to bury loved ones. That night, she felt that too many would be buried. The thought came to her several times that this time around, she might be one of those being buried. She had thoughts of the funeral; they would probably bury all three of them together in a closed casket ceremony. Her mind was drifting in and out between prayer and slumber when the door opened. She jumped up, cocked that gun aimed it squared at the light brown face coming through the door. Her finger was tensing up on the trigger.

"Are you one of us?"

"Yes, ma'am, I bleed red, white, and blue," Milkshake replied. "Mr. Smith sent me."

She put the gun down.

"Did we win?"

"Why don't you look for yourself?" he said, pointing towards the blinded window.

She pulled the blinds open. Tears swelled in her eyes as she saw a sea of pickup trucks, SUVs, and cars all flying their version of the Star-Spangled Banner.

"It was a rough night, but our people came through," Milkshake said, coming to her side. She had never met him before, but she wrapped her arms around his side and lay her head on his chest. He responded by putting his hand on her shoulder. Looking through the window, she saw pain and destruction, but she also saw hope in the thousands of people who came to defend their community.

"Honey?" Governor Gauff said faintly.

"Oh, honey," She replied, rushing to his side.

"Papa Bear is awake," Milkshake said in his coms. "Send the medical team in."

"What happened?" the Governor asked.

"These men saved our lives, honey," she replied.

"Actually, Texans saved all our lives," Milkshake said. "We fought like there was no tomorrow, sir. But this was a very well-planned attack. We weren't prepared for it. We were at a disadvantage all night. It didn't look good. Their troops kept pouring in from who knows where."

"How come? We have a base right here."

"Not sure, but from what I can make out at this point, they took it out before we could mobilize. They had us pinned downtown. Their forces overwhelmed ours. Until about three in the morning, we felt like we'd lose the city. That's when the tide turned in our favor. I don't know how, but thousands of trucks poured in from all over the area. Veterans, farmers, cops, you name it, they came and fought with us."

As Milkshake was recounting the story, the doctors and nurses arrived in the room. They checked the governor's vitals and IV fluids. They looked good. A few moments later, Wave Runner and the rest of the team came into the room with Krystal.

"Daddy! Daddy," she said, running to hug her dad. The governor became overwhelmed with the feel of his daughter's embrace.

"Oh, my love," he said, crying. Turning to the soldiers, he said, "Thank you! Thank you!"

"It wasn't only us, sir," Wave Runner replied. "A lot of people came and fought. They fought for their country and community, but also for you. It would mean a lot if you could greet them."

The governor looked at the doctor. The doctor nodded in approval and gestured for the nurse to assist the governor's movements. He was barely visible when he arrived at the window, but it was enough for the crowd to explode in cheers. Were it not for the burning buildings and war-torn streets, this would have been mistaken for a sports event of some kind, as someone started the national anthem.

He spoke no words, only waved at the crowd and raised his fist. The message was unequivocal: *we are here, and we will fight.*

29

ENEMY HONORS

"HOW LONG HAVE YOU two been together?" Prime Minister Dahan said.

"Four years, sir," Azael answered.

"Your people didn't object?" Prime Minister Dahan asked Suri.

"They didn't know," Suri answered via holoscreen. "When they found out, they had me followed and almost succeeded in killing me. That's why I'm in Canada right now."

"Good thing they failed. The world needs more people like you." Dahan said. "We are very happy for you. True love is hard to find in this world. Once you find it, hold on to it, regardless of the consequences. Hold on to her, son. You are lucky."

"I will, sir," Azael said.

"We are also very grateful to you two for your invaluable efforts in stopping this terrorist attack. The consequences would have been dire for our country and the rest of the world. Our prayers are with our American friends who were not so lucky. Now for the ceremony. Suri, you will be the last recipient. Azael, your honors will come when your active service is complete."

"Sir, with respect, my honor is to serve my country," Azael said.

"And you dispense with your duty admirably," Dahan said. "Suri, once you receive your medal, you can give your remarks to the nations of the world. I read your transcript. It is good. Any questions?"

"Yes, sir, what happens after?"

The prime minister remained quiet, waiting for her to expand on her line of questioning. She continued.

"I'll give my speech and receive your medal, and then what? Our countries keep killing each other until no one is left?"

"That obviously is not the goal. We hope this gesture might appeal to the Iranian people to pressure their government to come to the peace negotiating table."

"With respect sir, I don't think this is going to happen. We are a proud people with a long legacy of warriors. Might I remind you, Israel struck first?"

"Yes, we did under extreme pressure while facing an existential threat."

"I understand. Given the right information, I know what my government is capable of." She took a deep breath. "I guess what I am saying is that today's ceremony might touch the younger generation, but will not move the authorities. The generals and other leaders live for war. Coming to negotiations after being hit would be admitting defeat. They have one goal. It's to see you gone."

"What are you saying?"

"All I'm saying is that a new generation of Iranians embraces its cultural heritage. They are more modern and consider themselves part of the community of nations. They wish for the days when the country was more open, and the promises of freedom and prosperity were within reach."

"Are you suggesting a regime change?"

"I'm suggesting that you consider that today's goodwill might be a step, but more will be needed to gain the hearts of the people."

"Sir, if I may add," Azael said. "We are the best trained in the world. Our military and special ops are amongst the top in the world. But I agree with Suri. We must find a fast end to this conflict. We are better, but they are a lot more than us. Even with the Bahrainis and the Emirates on our side, how long can we last?"

"You forgot the Americans?"

"No sir, I did not forget them. Their army is formidable indeed, and their support is invaluable. I saw them in action more than once. But we must think ahead. For how long can we count on their support? They are entangled in conflicts all around the world. They have conflicts in North Korea and Europe, plus we can expect them to go after whoever was behind the release of the plague on their country. I am concerned that even they might reach their limit. When that happens, who goes first, us or the South Koreans?"

"Thank you for your observations. You both make good points. Rest assured, our generals and cabinet members are considering all the options. We will protect our people and come out of this stronger than ever. Please excuse me. We will reconvene in two hours for the ceremony."

Two hours later, the ceremony unfolded as expected; a handful of people of value, all heroes in their field, were honored by the prime minister. The event culminated with the virtual medal being awarded to Suri. She was presented as a patriotic Iranian who loved her country and dedicated her scientist's life to maintaining world peace. After he awarded her the medal, the prime minister let her say a few words.

"Thank you, Mr. Prime Minister. It is with great joy that I humbly receive this unexpected honor. I know some would question my judgment in accepting such an award while our countries are at war, but make no mistake, I'm a proud Iranian woman. I love my people and my country. I dedicated my life to making it better. Furthermore, I dedicated my life to making this world a better place. A place where children can grow up free from the horrors of war. A place where the nations of the world can sit down at the negotiating table rather than barrel down the road to destruction. A place where armed conflicts don't threaten the very survival of our species and all other species of this planet. A place where cooler heads prevail. This is what this is about for me. Iran and Israel do not need to fight. We have more in common than what sets us apart. For the sake of our children, we can do better. We must be better. Thank you all."

The prime minister retook center stage.

"Thank you for these eloquent words. We certainly hope—" Dahan's words were cut short by his aides and security detail. An aide to the prime minister took to the podium.

"Ladies and gentlemen, we apologize for the abrupt interruption. We have just received word that America is under attack. We do not know much at this point. But it is a full-scale invasion. When we know more, we will communicate it with you."

Eight hours later in the Israeli war room

"Our intelligence officials are having a hard time assessing the extent of the attacks," The prime minister said to his cabinet, intelligence officers, and military officials. "Who is involved is unclear, but here's what we know so far. Based on the current flow of information, America is being invaded." An eerie silence filled the room. "Like all of you, I wonder how this was possible. It looks like the plague was the first strike, closely followed by localized EMP attacks to cripple their infrastructure. Major cities have fallen under the control of the invaders. The death toll is unknown. The number is certainly in the hundreds of thousands and maybe the millions. As we speak, the fighting is still happening. When possible, we will provide more information. But as of now, we must conclude that we cannot expect the Americans to contribute to our war effort."

"Were you able to speak to the president?" one of the military officials asked.

"Unfortunately, as of now, the whereabouts of the US president are unknown."

30

LIVE ANOTHER DAY

Air Force One, thirty thousand feet above the earth

THE CUSTOM-FITTED BOEING 848, serving as the president's personal vessel, was headed to an undisclosed location in the Rocky Mountains. At that altitude, all was calm except for the squadron of fighter jets escorting the leader of the free world to the most secure location in the nation. The seven-story-high airborne mastodon sped through the night sky. It had three decks. The top deck contained the most advanced mobile communication center in the world. The bottom deck had a cargo hold. The middle deck housed the living quarters, the president's office, and the situation room.

In the latter, navy blue panels accented the ominous white walls. The center of the room was fitted with a blue-grey holographic conference table, which served as a command center. The national security team gathered around the table. Present on board were Sarah, the Chief of Staff, DHS Secretary Emilia Shaw, Chief of the Army Kate Simmons, General McIntyre, Chairman of the Joint Chiefs of Staff, and General Dunn.

288

"Give it to me straight," President Rodriguez said.

"We are being attacked on all fronts, Sir," The chief of staff said. "Tonight, around 2100 Eastern Time, as we feared, a series of EMP devices were detonated throughout the country. LA, New York, Chicago, Atlanta, and the list goes on. Hospitals and Military Bases are hardened against EMPs, but military towns surrounding them were affected. Fort Bragg, Fort Benning out of Columbus, Fort Hood, Texas, and that list also goes on. The full list is in your briefing packets."

"Casualties?" the president asked.

"Too early to tell. The EMPs have severely hampered our ability to communicate with people on the ground. But from what we can gather, this is a full-on invasion with multiple points of entry. Our most critical international allies are also facing similar assaults. For instance, before boarding, we received news that China launched a full-scale invasion of Taiwan."

"Sir, if I may," Emilia Shaw, DHS secretary, said.

"Go ahead, Emilia."

"We believe this is a coordinated attack involving several foreign agents leveraging multiple systemic pressure points."

"Keep going," the president said.

"Sir, we have intel that suggests that foreign troops have been pouring into this country undetected for years. They were the advanced teams being stationed at strategic locations. Cargo ships were bottlenecked at various ports during the holiday rush, concealing the assault force. Our attention and resources have been focused on dealing with the social unrest and the EF2 epidemic ravaging our country."

"What's the latest on that?"

"It's not good, sir. Infections are increasing at an alarming rate. We fear we will have a full catastrophic system failure in less than three months."

"This can't be a coincidence," the president said while waiting for Emilia's confirmation.

"We don't believe that it is, sir. All evidence leads us to believe that both the social unrest and the outbreak are part of the attack. They used an infected individual as the delivery mechanism. He went through strategic gathering hubs around the country. Those included clubs, churches, and especially airports. We know, for instance, that he went to the Dallas and Atlanta airports. They are also leveraging the nationwide mass protests as dispersion vehicles. "

"Who are the culprits?" the president asked.

"Sir, we are dealing with an axis containing a coalition of unallied countries. And in all candor, some allied countries as well. China, Russia, North Korea, and Iran are the big ones, but other medium-sized powers are in on it too."

"How did we miss this?"

"We got complacent. But we think they used operatives posing as low-level officials to evade our surveillance protocols."

"Our response?"

"We're stretched thin," Emilia continued. "We have a significant number of troops engaged in foreign theaters. The North Korea and Middle East deployments are taking considerable resources. Reinforcing NATO-allied countries against Russian aggression is also taking its toll. Between all those, half of our active forces are abroad."

"Bring in the other chiefs," the president said, looking at the chairman of the Joint Chiefs. General McIntyre remained silent, deferring to the chief of staff to address the commander-in-chief.

"Sir, we also found that their infiltration of our country went deeper than we thought," Sarah said. "They also occupied critical positions. At this moment, we are not in contact with any of them. For some, it might be due to the loss of communication, but we fear some might have been captured or even killed."

"Where is Steve?"

"On Air Force Two," Sarah replied. "It was a close call, but he is en route as well."

"Let's go back to Washington. I need to address the Nation from our Capital."

"Sir, that is not possible," Sarah said. "Fighting is raging in DC, Virginia, and Maryland. Our troops are standing strong, but enemy fighters are flooding in. If we go back, we cannot guarantee your safety. Even now, we have six planes that look exactly like this one flying around the country in case our enemies try to take you down."

"I don't care! We must head back and face the enemy head-on! Americans need to see their leader standing strong and unafraid."

"Sir, two were taken down by enemy forces. If they make another attempt, there's a one in four chance they will succeed in taking you out and us in the process. America would be left without its leaders."

"Sir, with all due respect, Americans need their commander-in-chief alive." Kate Simmons interjected. She knew her president was a fighter. He never backed down. That's what she liked about him. But she also knew how to sacrifice battles to win wars. "Our priority is to keep you safe so you can lead this country through its darkest hour."

"If our people don't stand up and fight, there might not be a country left to lead!" President Rodriguez said.

"Sir, our troops and our people are resilient," General McIntyre said. "They will withstand this onslaught. Right now, the enemy is giving it their best shot. The real war starts tomorrow. We just have to make sure we make it there. We just have to live another day, sir."

31

DOWN, NOT OUT

"WHOA, THIS IS SURREAL," Kyle said, walking the city's devastated streets with Ty G. The winter breeze chilled their bones. "Never thought this would happen here. I can't believe this."

"Well, believe it, bro. We at war," Ty G replied as a wave of smoke struck their nostrils. "The sooner you realize that, the easier it'll be to adapt and fight back. You feel me?"

"Yeah, I feel you, but I still can't believe my eyes. This could have been us." He pointed at a makeshift mass gravesite in the park behind Columbus Memorial Hospital.

The crematorium was working around the clock, burning enemy bodies. Bodies of locals were lined up at the morgue or in climate-controlled trucks, those that survived the EMP attack. The deceased, who were unrecognizable, were buried. Their personal items were cataloged and stored to be remitted to their next of kin if anyone asked for them. Grief filled the streets as relatives discovered the grisly fate their loved ones suffered on that fateful night. The stench of death was everywhere.

"How do you know she's gonna be there?" Ty G asked.

"I don't, but if she's not there, that means she's dead. Cause that girl works a lot." They approached the barricaded hospital entrance.

293

"Do you have a medical emergency?" the soldier asked.

"No, I'm here to see my sister-in-law. She works here," Kyle said.

"Only staff, medical personnel, and immediate family members of patients are allowed."

"I just need to see if she's alive."

"Sorry, no exceptions. Now, please step away from the perimeter."

"Come on, it'll just take a—"

"Please step behind the barricade, sir," the soldier said, tightening his grip on his weapon.

"Okay, okay, no problem," Kyle said to diffuse the situation. "Let me just ask you. Are you in Ranger School?"

"Sir, please move past the barricade."

"My dad was a ranger, and my brother is a SEAL. General Boykin is my dad."

"Let me see some ID."

"My brother is deployed. I just need to check on his wife and my nephew. Make sure they're okay."

The name Boykin reverberated through the halls of the military base. From stories of exploits long ago to techniques taught to recruits and aspiring special operators, that name was legendary.

"You should have started with that," the soldier said. "Let them through," he shouted to his colleague manning the entrance.

"Look at you droppin' names," Ty G whispered to Kyle as they walked to the entrance. Once inside, he continued. "How did you know he was in Ranger School?"

"Honestly, it was just a Hail Mary. I figure they all want to be rangers, so they all know my dad and maybe my brother. So, it was worth the try."

"For sure! We're in. Where's your sister-in-law at?" Ty G said, looking at a chaotic scene of people on gurneys, nurses running to and fro, the PA system calling on doctors and surgeons. The burning smell from the outside gave way to a bleach-like smell of disinfectant.

"I have no idea. But she works the maternity ward."

"Alright, let's go."

After roaming the hospital for about twenty minutes, peeking through room windows, they finally heard,

"Kyle! Kyle! It's really you!" Maddie said, hugging him tighter than he had expected. "Thank you, God!"

A little stunned, he replied.

"Are you okay?"

"Yes, I'm fine. The last time I saw you, you were on the news getting arrested. Then this happened, and the courthouse was one of the first places they attacked. I hadn't heard from you since I thought maybe-"

"It was close, but we're okay," Kyle said, looking at her teary eyes.

"Come on, Maddie. You know it'll take more than some commies to take your boy out," Ty G said.

"Hey Ty," she said, letting go of Kyle and moving to hug Ty G. "I'm glad you're okay."

"I'm glad you're okay too."

"Any word from Topher?" Kyle asked.

She looked at him and shook her head. He saw fear in her eyes.

"I'm sure he's okay," Kyle said while pulling her in to hug her. They stayed there for a moment until she took a deep breath.

"Yeah, I'm sure he's okay. Last time we spoke, he was in San Antonio. From what we heard, they repelled the invasion."

"If Topher and his crew were there, the enemy never had a shot."

"Yeah, I know. It's my parents I'm most worried about. Not sure California was so lucky."

"There's no way the enemy took out a navy base. But if they did, I guarantee you, your dad will be amongst the leaders of the resistance. He's a tough one, just like his daughter."

"You got that right. It's that McAdams cloth we're made of."

"How's Ryan?"

"He's okay. He's in the pediatric playroom with some other staff's kids."

"Do you want me to take him to church? It'll probably be safer for him there with all the virus thing going around."

"You don't have to. He's on a different floor. He's safe." Maddie said, her maternal instincts kicking in.

"You're sure? We have power, food, and set up a makeshift Vacation Bible School. Some call it 'Invasion Bible School.'" He smiled.

She thought to herself, though the equestrian flu ward was several floors apart and the protocols were solid, viruses have a way of spreading far and wide.

"Okay, take him. I'll pick him up when I'm done here. Drop him at your parents' house if I don't make it in time.

"President Rodriguez is coming on air." A Nurse shouted. Everyone paused what they were doing and congregated around the closest TV set.

"My fellow Americans, last night, our country was viciously attacked by insidious enemies who sought to destroy us from within. They abused our civil liberties to carry out their perverted attack. In a matter of hours, they have killed thousands of innocent people. Their plan was multilayered and perfected over time by multiple countries, which can only be described as the Coalition of the Sinning. For decades, they infiltrated every aspect of American life, gaining the trust of our institutions, climbing the ladders of the American edifice to better demolish it. They took out most of our power grids and electronics through a series of virtual assaults and EMP attacks on several key cities, after which they targeted the leadership structures of our federal and local governments. There were hard-fought battles throughout the country. To put it bluntly, they sucker-punched us. But America has a strong chin. They planned to take over our country, and they failed. We are here, and we are standing! Our administration has started to repair the power grids and is working around the clock to restore power to every corner of the nation. FEMA is distributing food, water, generators, EMP-proof electronic devices, and emergency vehicles. Many of our military bases survived the attacks and are assisting in the recovery effort, and they will ensure the safety of our homeland.

"The news is not all good. Currently, most of the Eastern Seaboard and the West Coast are under enemy control. Therefore, if you are in those areas, hang tight. We will not abandon you. The battle will be long, but we will win. Earlier today, Congress met in an undisclosed location and at my request, authorized the suspension of habeas corpus starting tonight at nine p.m. Eastern. Accordingly, if you are a co-conspirator or partaker in this heinous attack, we will find you and bring you to justice. Also, at my request, Congress authorized the unleashing of our military against the countries that planned this attack, including Cuba, Pakistan, Venezuela, Russia, and China. Two of the culprits, namely, North Korea and Iran, are already facing the might of our military. We are coordinating with NATO and other allies for a unified response against this wicked alliance.

"I assure you, we will not stop until we have restored the full territorial integrity of our great nation. Our enemies made one fatal mistake; they hit us but did not finish us. We are down, but we are not out. We are hit, but we are not done for. We are hurt, but now we are on the hunt. We did not start this fight, but we will finish it.

"The Good Book says, 'Though he slay me, yet I will hope in him; I will surely defend my ways to his face. But as for me, I watch in hope for the Lord, I wait for God my Savior; my God will hear me. Do not gloat over me, my enemy! Though I have fallen, I will rise. Though I sit in darkness, the Lord will be my light.'

"In other words, we're coming! To every country that had a hand in this, we're coming! We're coming to every world leader who authorized, advised, or facilitated this treachery! There is nowhere on earth where you can hide. We will not leave a stone unturned until all are brought to justice. You're either with us or against us! This is our home, this is our land, we will defend her till the bitter end! God Bless you, and God bless the totality of the United States of America!"

"What's habeas corpus?" Maddie asked.

"Habeas corpus. It's martial law," Ty G answered. "It means now the military is in charge. They can arrest and detain anybody they want."

32

BAD OPTIONS

Rocky Mountains, undisclosed location

"DO NOT SUGARCOAT ANYTHING. Just give me the facts," President Rodriguez said.

"That was a good speech, Mr. President," General Dunn said. "But the reality is, our military is stretched thin. Our forces are already involved in two conflicts. Both Iran and North Korea had a part in this, so they must pay. But so did so many other countries. We are vastly outnumbered."

"Can't we compensate our human deficit with equipment and technology?" the president asked.

"Only to a certain extent," General McIntyre, the Joint Chiefs' Chairman answered. "We increased our naval assets along all the major trade routes. But we are met with significant opposition. We have Aircraft carriers and Destroyers in the Panama Canal and the Suez Canal coming under fire. But the opposition is the fiercest in the Strait of Hormuz and the Taiwan Strait. Our equipment is the best in the world, but they have much more than we do."

"Let me put it this way, Mr. President," General Dunn said. "Even the best MMA fighter is retrained by a few other athletes. Individually, they can't stop him, but together, he can't beat them all."

"What is the ratio?" President Rodriguez asked.

"It's hard to tell, sir," Dunn responded. "The reports from the field indicate that we are often attacked by cargo ships retrofitted into full battleships. Under a scenario where civilian vessels are, in reality, military assets, we are looking at maybe a ten-to-one ratio."

"Ten battleships for every one of our destroyers and aircraft carriers?"

"We don't want this to be a protracted war," Steve added. "The more we fight, the more we stand to lose."

"You don't sound very optimistic," the president said. "Generals, in your professional assessment, what are our chances to win this war, regain the fullness of our territory, and remain the dominant power in the world?"

"In all honesty, sir, there are too many variables and unknowns at this stage to give a definitive answer," the Chairman said. "First, we don't know how deeply they infiltrated our societies. Second, we don't know the full extent of that alliance. Third, we don't know how committed our allies really are."

"First, how deeply do you think they infiltrated our society?" the president said, echoing the Joint Chiefs' sequencing.

"Sir, the general used his words carefully," Emilia Shaw, DHS secretary, said. "He said *societies*. As always, we have been monitoring our enemies and allies' cabinets. But it seems that operatives groomed, sometimes from birth, have been systematically injected at all levels of all the major countries in the world, to a level that frankly we did not anticipate."

The president leaned forward without saying a word. She continued.

"Think about it this way. Imagine someone gets diagnosed with breast cancer, and after a few tests, they find that it has metastasized all over their body. Last night's attack, that's the breast cancer. Our intelligence agents are uncovering how deep the infection goes, and it's not good. Several countries which we thought wouldn't pose a threat are, in effect, Chinese outposts."

She took a sip of water and continued.

"We're talking Caribbean and Latin American countries a stone's throw from the mainland. We're talking African, Asian, and Eastern European countries, which jeopardize European allies."

The president clasped his hands together, pursed his lips, and then asked, "Second, what about your second point? How deep does this alliance go?"

"This is a tough one, sir," the Joint Chiefs said. "All we're able to find linking all those countries together were a few meetings here and there with low-level officials. It's hard to know who the co-conspirators are versus the collaborators."

"Third?" the president asked.

"Third," Steve said. "Our allies have expressed outrage, but none have committed troops to combat. My guess is that, at best, they want to see if we get back up. At worst, they're infiltrated so deep that they're in on it."

The president sat back on his chair, resting his face in his left hand.

"What are our odds of winning?" he asked again.

"With NATO & Pacific allies by our side, sixty percent, but without them, twenty percent," General McIntyre said.

"I guess now we'll see if they are as eager to help us as we were to help them," Steve said.

"In that case, until further notice, we have to assume that we're on our own," the president said. "Our response has to be decisive."

"Yes, sir," the joint chief said. "We are deploying the Seventh Fleet in the Pacific. Also, we have the carrier strike groups heading to the coasts. They're patrolling at large the East & West Coasts to prevent any further invasion and are ready to retake our land at your command, sir."

"We have to strike Beijing," Kate Simmons blurted out.

"Of course, we're going to strike Beijing," the joint chief said, surprised by the abrupt nature of her comments.

"No, I mean we have to destroy it in one sweep hit." She responded.

"You're talking nuclear?" Emilia Shaw asked.

"What level of casualties are we looking at?" the president interrupted.

"Best estimate a full-on war of this magnitude without the use of nukes, we are looking at anywhere from 100 million to 300 million people," The joint chief said. "With the use of nukes," he took a breath. "It's an extinction-level event, sir. They have nukes, too. And we must assume they are very well prepared for this eventuality."

Silence gripped the room as the top officials looked down at a set of what they felt were bad options.

"Maybe we should consider a peaceful surrender," Steve said, breaking the silence. "That move would save millions of American lives, not to mention human lives worldwide."

"But that would subject our children and their children to live under tyranny, and that's not something I'm ready to live with," General Dunn said. "That under our watch, this American experiment, unprecedented amongst nations, the beacon of freedom would be extinguished from the face of the Earth is unconscionable to me."

"I'm with General Dunn on this," Emilia Shaw said. "Surrender is not an option."

The president looked at General McIntyre.

"Dunn's right. This fight is not only for us but also for future generations."

"We must take out the capital," Kate Simmons repeated. "It's the only way. If you take out the giant, our allies will gain confidence, and it will strike fear in our enemies."

"What are you suggesting?" the president asked.

"A strike team to hit right at the heart."

"Do we even have that capacity?" Steve asked. "Our military bases have been severely damaged. We are still assessing our nuclear arsenal's structural integrity."

"Are we even ready to launch a nuclear strike?" the president asked.

"No, sir, our arsenal is questionable at best," General McIntyre said. We are awaiting final reports, but part of the assessment is the readiness of our arsenal. Our experts fear we might be infected with Trojanware."

"In English?" the president said.

"In English, it means if they infected our systems, a launch of our nuclear missiles would detonate them in their silos or redirect them to one of our cities or that of our allies."

"How? How? How did it come to this?" the president said. "You mean to tell me we are fighting for our very existence, and we can't use our most powerful weapons! This is unacceptable!"

"Sir, I know it's a long shot," Kate Simmons said. "But the team that freed the hostages in Iran. Reports from the ground indicate they were responsible for saving Governor Gauff and his family when San Antonio was attacked. They're amongst the best we have and are fully operational. Sir, if you give the go-ahead, we can coordinate with our assets in the Pacific and turn this tide around in a matter of days."

"And what would they fight with, bayonets?" the president asked.

"No sir, our current arsenal is compromised, that is true. But we have old World War Two weapons, the so-called backpack nukes, we still have them in our repository. If we can refit four or five. The team could infiltrate the city at night, and each one could detonate their package in a strategic location simultaneously. The war would shift in our favor immediately."

"Just so we're clear, this is a one-way mission, correct?" General Dunn asked, though he already knew the answer.

"Yes, sir. If we go forward with this mission, we would be requiring of them the fullest measure of valor for the service to our country. Their sacrifice would save countless American lives."

"Or we could just be signing off on the end of our species and life on earth," Steve said, exasperated.

"It's your call, Mr. President," General McIntyre said.

The president pondered this decision, looked at the reports on the table in front of him, made mental calculations, and said,

"Do it. Go ahead and get it done...and God help us all."

33

SUNDAY IS A GOOD DAY TO DIE

"YOU CAN'T SPEAK HERE," Kyle said to the army recruiter. "This is a church. We don't get involved in politics."

"This is beyond politics. Within a few hours, the enemy will be upon us again. We need all able-bodied men and women to join the fight. To preserve our freedoms and restore our country."

"I understand all of that. My family is military, but you have to understand this is a community of peace, not war. Can't you go recruit on TV?"

"I don't think I made myself clear. This was not a request. This is mandatory under article—"

"Yeah, save it, I get it. It's martial law. But martial law doesn't mean people have to violate their conscience, now does it?"

"Is everything okay here?" Reverend Riveira said.

"Pastor, your associate pastor refuses to let us address the congregation to bolster our recruiting efforts. We have incoming enemy troops from Macon and Hogansville. So far, we've been able to rebuff them, but that might not be enough. We need all able-bodied people to join us in the fight for our land."

"Would you give us a moment?" The senior pastor said.

"Sure."

The Reverend signaled to Kyle to follow him a few steps away from the recruiter.

"Pastor, we can't let him speak."

"Why is that?"

"The pulpit is not made for recruiting people to kill other people. We're already operating a shelter. Helping people? Yes. Recruiting for the military? That's not our job. Besides, you know how they've treated us for the past few years. Now they want to ask for our help? Nah, I'm straight."

"Yes, I know how we've been treated. I was there, Kyle, but how do you think the invaders will treat us if they take over? Do you think it's going to be audits and bad-mouthing? You're in for a treat. You know, I lived several years in restricted nations where they can imprison you or even kill you for being Christian. What do you think happens if we lose?"

Kyle did not answer the question. Pastor Riveira continued

"When this country was founded, they recruited people from everywhere, including the church, to fight for the common cause of freedom. Of course, we want peace; we do not want war, but this fight was brought to our doorsteps. Either way, our lives changed forever. I saw Ryan play with the other kids. They don't understand the extent of what is happening. Now, it's up to us to make sure they never do. It's up to us to answer the call. I will make the announcement. I'm sure several of our young people will answer the call, but I'm too old to fight. I think it'd be best if you stood with me on stage and stood with them on the battlefield.

These will be hard days. They will need their pastor by their side. Can I count on you?"

Kyle's heart said no, but his mouth said yes. He rationalized that the kids joining the fight could barely carry a weapon, let alone conduct warfare. Maybe by being there, he could keep them safe.

"Yeah, I'll be there, pastor. I just don't know how I feel about shooting at people we're supposed to save."

"Thank you, son. Maybe if we save this country, we can then save the world. These are tough times. May God give us wisdom to navigate them." He walked back to the recruiter. "Officer, do you have a copy of your announcement? I will make it from our pulpit. You can count on our support. We're going to get our country back."

"Thank you, pastor." He handed him a patriotic leaflet giving the locations of 24/7 recruiting posts throughout the area. "We have incoming enemy convoys headed our way. They'll be here soon. We need all the help we can get."

"Understood. I will refrain from giving long-winded remarks." The pastor said in jest.

Pastor Riveira gave the announcement. A host of young adults and many older minors answered the call. Before the hour was over, Kyle and his young parishioners found themselves in a makeshift training facility, a tent with a whiteboard, weapons, and uniforms. The room was packed with civilians soon-to-be deputized soldiers. People from different walks of life were present.

The wealthy and those from humble means were all ready to take up arms to defend their home. Even some of the criminal elements of the city showed up, each on a separate side of the tent. Ty G and his Triple P crew were at the very back on the right side. Opposite to them were Rigo and Las Águilas. The Asian Syndicate led by Fanbo Zhizhi, commonly called Fanboy, & local rightwing militia members, were halfway through the front while Kyle and his people were towards the middle of the room. Ashleigh Williams pulled up next to him. The police officers who survived the initial attack were upfront, eager for payback. The instructor illustrated on the board the positioning they would take to repel the enemy attack. The drawing was reminiscent of high school football Xs and Os, with the exception that it wasn't yards and plays they would lose; it was lives and loved ones. The trainer then demonstrated how to use the weapons and gave instructions that could be summed up as 'point and shoot' at anyone with a gun who's not wearing this uniform.

"Sir, can I speak to you?" Kyle asked the instructor. "My name is Kyle Boyk-"

"I know who you are," The instructor said. "What's on your mind?"

"Sir, with respect, where's the rest of the troops?"

"Deployed. It turns out retaking New York and LA is more important than what happens to Columbus."

"Sir, these kids aren't ready for this."

"Ready or not, the enemy is coming."

"Excuse me," Ty G interrupted. "Y'all not worried about these Asians joinin' the fight. As far as we know, they might be part of it."

"Everybody here has been vetted before being admitted," the instructor said.

"With due respect, if that were true, he wouldn't be there," a police officer said, pointing at Ty G. "He is one of the city's most notorious gangsters. So is this guy." He pointed to Rigo at a distance.

"From where I stand, sometimes the only difference between a criminal and a cop is the badge," Ashleigh said.

"The news lady is not wrong," Rigo said, having gotten closer. "But I have to say right now, I'm not worried about the police. I'm more worried about the *commies* shooting me in the back." He pointed at the Asian syndicate.

"I know you're not talking Hugo Chavez," Fanboy said.

"What did you say to me?" Rigo responded, moving closer to Fanboy.

"That's enough!" Kyle shouted. "This is worse than middle school! I don't care if your ancestors came from Europe, Africa, or Asia, right now, we're all Americans, and we're fighting for our homes, our families, and our freedoms. The bullets won't care where you're from when the battle starts. This enemy wants us all dead! I don't know about you, but I'm not going to make it easy on them. As a matter of fact, I say we send them packing wherever in the world they came from! Now, I know we all come from different backgrounds. Some of us have been on different sides of issues, but today we're all one. I've been in the trenches with this man right here." He pointed to Ty G. "There's no one I trust more to cover my back. We don't always see eye to eye, but we're family at the end of the day. Today, we're all family 'cause we're all Americans! Alright?"

"Yah!" Rigo said, taking two steps back.

"We got you," Fanboy said.

"Okay, good, "The instructor said. "Suit up. We're out of time. "

The volunteers were embedded in units of the remaining soldiers. The units were camouflaged throughout the woods and the overpass overlooking the southbound I-185.

"Wait on my signal," Captain Alexander said to the troops through his radio. "Wait for it—unit Alpha, go now!

About a mile from the overpass, advance team Alpha fired nails at the wheels of the last vehicle of the convoy using high-powered nail guns. The driver slammed the brakes before he realized what was going on. Five soldiers and volunteers were upon them. Each one took down a passenger. Once all the soldiers inside the vehicle were neutralized, team Alpha followed the convoy in one of the few surviving gas-powered SUVs. Team Beta took down the second-to-last vehicle. By the time the convoy was approaching the overpass, five out of fifteen vehicles had been taken out without the head of the convoy realizing it.

Rigo, Xaque, and Captain Alexander were stationed on the overpass. Kyle, Ashley, and Ty G were hidden in the woods, ready for an up-close ground assault.

"On my signal, be precise, aim, and shoot. No friendly fire." Captain Alexander said. "Now!"

Rat-ta-ta.

The troops positioned on the overpass sprayed the convoy with bullets. Almost instantly, the convoy came to a stop. The ground troops started shooting from the woods. They were staggered on both sides of the road and took turns shooting and reloading.

"Stop!" Captain Alexander said. Everyone in the convoy was dead.

Xaque ran down to the enemy trucks. "They're all dead, sir," he said as he cautiously approached the vehicle. Several other foot soldiers followed suit, confirming.

"Regrésate a tu posición! Return to your position," Rigo shouted at his nephew. As he said that, the hatch of the truck opened. Machine-gun-enabled drones came out flying.

"Take cover, everyone!" Captain Alexander shouted from the top of his lungs. "Take cover! Drones!!!" As they scrambled to return to their defensive positions, the second truck hatch opened and released machine gun-enabled Robodogs."

The troops on the overpass were sitting ducks for the drones, while the troops on the ground were prey to the robodogs. The troops returned fire towards the machines while retreating. Fanboy at the wheel of the gas-powered truck mowed down some robodogs, creating a barrier between the incoming threat and Kyle's team. The truck was riddled with bullets. Fanboy and his team crawled out of the vehicle from the passenger side and ran into the woods with Kyle's team.

The robodogs launched into the woods in pursuit of the soldiers. After about two minutes, Ty G grabbed Kyle by the shoulder.

"Stop! Stop!" Ty G said. "We can't bolt like that. We got to take these things down."

"Yeah, but they're machines," Ashley said. "How are you going to take them out?"

"From where I'm from, there's nothing a bullet can't do," Ty G replied. "We're gon shoot them down."

"Ty G is right, "Kyle said. "We can't run forever. We're faster than them, but they are more precise."

"Then we have to level the playing field," Ashley said.

"We need a decoy," Fanboy said. "These things probably use heat sensors and biometrics. If we multiply heat sources, we can confuse them long enough to take them down."

"I got flares," Ashley said.

"I got them too," Ty G said.

"Okay, good," "Fanboy said, "I think if we tie them to these trees, we can create a cone of confusion."

Ty G took the few flares he had and handed them to Fanboy. "Alright, y'all, set that up, KB. Let's go slow these things down."

"Alright, let's go!" Kyle said.

They backtracked until they saw robodogs methodically roaming the woods. They lay on the ground behind a tree elevation.

"You ready?" Kyle asked.

"Oh, I'm more than ready." Ty G said, revealing two hand grenades.

"Alright, now you're talking," Kyle said. "Door dash?"

"Yeah, let's do a door dash, "Ty G responded. They would shoot at the Robodogs, causing them to converge on their location and throw the grenade hoping for maximum damage when they had enough of them a proximity. The plan worked; they took out eight of the enemy machines.

"Alright, guys, we're coming in hot with tons of those evil dogs on our tail," Kyle said through the radio.

"No worries, preacher boy, we're ready," Fanboy said. Kyle and Ty G came in sprinting at full speed, jumping for cover behind the tree line.

"Okay, wait for my signal," Fanboy said as the robodogs started arriving. Fanboy gave the signal when about twenty of them were in the cone of confusion.

"Now!"

Soldiers lit tree-tied flares all around the robodogs, causing them to be disoriented.

"Everybody down!" Ty G said, throwing his second grenade amid the robodogs. Most of the robodogs were blown to pieces. The soldiers opened fire on the surviving machines.

"Alright, guys, let's take back what's ours," Kyle said as they marched back to the interstate.

When they arrived back at the edge of the woods, the carnage was beyond what they could have expected. Bodies of soldiers scattered on the overpass and the highway below, too many to count. The enemy drones also sustained losses. Carcasses of the now obsolete machines littered the road and the edge of the woods. Captain Alexander was pinned down under a truck. He could be heard screaming on his radio,

"Command, where is that helo? We need that helo!" The answer was invariably the same,

"Helo is incoming."

Kyle looked at Ty G, then at Ashleigh and Fanboy.

"Y'all want to crash this party?" Fanboy said.

"Yeah, we don't have a choice," Kyle said.

"Okay, but what's the plan?" Ashleigh asked.

"Plan is pick a drone and shoot at it, then duck when they shoot back," Ty G said.

"I'm afraid he's right," Fanboy said. "Each one pick one and try to take it down,"

"I don't like this plan," Ashleigh said.

"None of us do," Ty G said. "But Sunday is a good day to die."

"How about we stay alive?" Kyle said. "Everyone, just spot where you're gonna take cover when they shoot back, and we should be fine."

"All right, y'all ready?" Ty G said.

They all said,

"Ready."

"Let's do it!"

Rata-tata.

Two drones went spiraling down. The rest retaliated, spraying bullets in the woods. Branches went flying. The dirt spattered a thousand times. The targets took refuge as they could. Some hid behind the more massive trees, others behind a rock formation, and others were not so fortunate. The drones were unrelenting. It was just a question of time before they would all be mowed down by the machines.

BOOM.

A deafening sound pierced the sky, and the drones dropped dead to the ground. Three helicopters from Fort Benning flew over, turned back around, and landed near the battleground.

Kyle and the crew ran to the road. It was chaos. The bodies lying there were too many to count. There were as many wounded. Captain Alexander himself had several non-life-threatening injuries. Amidst the mayhem, Kyle noticed Rigo on his knees, bleeding.

"Rigo!" He screamed, running towards him. "Are you all right, man? You need to get to a medic—" Kyle stopped cold in his tracks and saw Xaque Flores, the young man they affectionately called Batman, lying there lifeless, his body riddled with holes. As a military kid, Kyle was raised to be tough. Subsequently, as a minister, he was taught not to show too many emotions to project confidence rather than despair and weakness. For a moment, he tried to hold it in, but before long, he found himself overwhelmed with soul-crushing pain. He got on his knees and cried with a man he barely knew over a common bond that was now lost. The paramedics came and dragged a dazed Rigo to attend to his wounds. Ashleigh came and took Kyle to Ty G., he was standing by an Ambulance as they were taking Jimmy's body away.

They were brothers in the streets. Now they're brothers in arms, sharing the bond of pain.

34

EAGLE WRATH

San Antonio Joint Military Base SCIF

THE SENSITIVE COMPARTMENTED INFORMATION Facility, commonly called SCIF, increased security to the highest level. Sigma Team was vetted and cleared. The room was practically empty. Topher and the team were awaiting their next orders. The general in charge of the Base and the Air Force lieutenant were there. A heavy silence covered the room until the door opened. Immediately, the air was sucked out of the room, everyone stood in salute.

"At ease," President Rodriguez said as he entered with General Dunn and Kate Simmons.

"Ladies and gentlemen, thank you for being here," General Dunn said. "We appreciate your service to your country. You already sacrificed a lot, but we are here to ask you to do it again."

"This war is exacting a heavy price on our nation," Kate Simmons said. "We have lost many lives fighting to regain our full territorial integrity. We reclaimed most of New York, but Manhattan is still under enemy control. The story is the same throughout the country. LA, Chicago, and Seattle are all partially or totally controlled by our enemies. Our people are fighting bravely, but we're just outnumbered. There seems to be no end to their troops.

"We continue to fight over the high seas," General Dunn continued. "But I'm not going to lie to you, they have the upper hand. Our ships are bigger and better, but theirs are faster and pack enough punch to keep us on the defensive. In the air, we have superiority. Their planes and, more importantly, their pilots are no match for ours. So, we are taking the fight to them. As you can imagine, they are ready for our retaliation."

"But where we are at a total loss in space and cyberspace," Kate Simmons continued, "We estimate that our cyberspace operators are outnumbered twenty to one. As such, we cannot confidently deploy some of our more strategic and impactful weapons."

"Let me put it to you simply," General Dunn said. "They hacked our nukes, all of them. The subs, The planes, and the silos. If deployed, all bear the risk of detonating instantly or being redirected. We could aim for Pyongyang but hit Paris."

"That's where you come in," Kate added. "We were able to refurbish World War Two era backpack bombs that are analog and unconnected to any modern systems. They have a lower potency than our modern arsenal. But we believe that if we detonate five of them in the heart of the enemy's empire, it will shift the momentum of the war in our favor and give us a puncher's chance. We will launch a full-on aerial assault on several cities ahead of your arrival. That should keep them busy while you sneak into the capital and deliver your payload."

"There is a catch," Dunn continued. "There is no remote detonation. We anticipate that any remote signal would be intercepted by enemy AI technology. You must drop the package in a strategic location within a highly monitored city during a period of active conflict and start the timer. You will have twenty minutes to get at least twenty miles away. If you can't get away, you will have to detonate the bomb yourself."

"What you're telling us is that it's a one-way ticket," Chad said.

"For any other unit," Kate said. "Yes, it's a one-way mission with very little chance of success. For your unit? It's a toss-up. Nevertheless, if you succeed, you give your country a chance to turn the tide and preserve our freedoms, and our children's freedoms for generations to come."

"I know that we are asking of you the full measure of devotion to our country," President Rodriguez said. "We chose you because your valor is legendary. If anyone can get it done and come back, it's you. As you know, I also wore that sacred uniform. I too lost sworn brothers in the line of duty. I looked into mothers' eyes as they laid their children to rest. I do not ask this of you lightly. We have been in many wars as a nation, but this is our darkest hour. Never have we faced an enemy that threatened our very existence. If they had their way, the United States of America would cease to exist. But I believe they have misjudged us. When she's faced with peril, America's children will defend her till the end. We look the suckers in the eyes and make them regret they came at us. I am asking of you to defend her, make them pay, and come back to tell us all about it."

"We got you, Mr. President," Topher said. "I think I speak for all of us when I say I'm not getting buried in Beijing. When my time comes, I'll be buried as a free man in the land of the free and the home of the brave."

"From your mouth to God's ears," the president said with a mix of admiration and aspiration. "From your mouth to God's ears." He ceded the floor to General Dunn.

"Thank you, Mr. President. Operation Eagle Wrath will launch at 0600. You're dismissed."

"Chris," Dunn said, addressing Topher. "I remember when your father and I were deployed in one of our special missions. All he wanted was to get back to you. Make sure you get back to your boy. I don't have it in me to look your father in the eye and tell him his boy isn't coming home. So, you make sure you come home, you hear me?"

"I hear you, sir," Topher said. "I hear you."

Bohai Bay, the Northeastern coast of China

"This is it," Lieutenant Ross said. "The USS Bush, JFK, and Miller are unleashing on them now. Keep coms to a minimum, deliver your packages, and get out. The timer is set for five hours, after which you'll be considered killed in action. Remember, guys, this is Beijing, not Beirut. Failure is not an option!"

"It never is sir!" All said in unison.

Under the cover of night, with bombs bursting in the air, Wave Runner, Milkshake, Green Arrow, Mockingbird, and Eager Beaver flew out. The in-suit low-altitude flight took less than two hours. At the edge of the megapolis, they split five ways. Beaver headed to the Fengtai district, Mockingbird to Shijinshan, Arrow Haidian, Milkshake Chaoyang, and Wave Runner to Xicheng. All spread about forty miles from one another.

Wave Runner was flying in the same general direction as the US attack. Looking straight ahead, he saw payload after payload altering the Beijing skyline. The Chinese air defense system could stop many of the incoming fire. When he was nearing his target, he peeked up ahead and saw three B-23 stealth bombers crash to the ground.

"How did that happen?" he asked himself. Before the answer spurred into his mind, his suit stopped responding. He plummeted into Zhongnanhai's Lake in the Imperial City, the seat of the Chinese Communist Party and the Central Government. Though the water and the suit's built-in shock absorption diminished the blow, he still felt pain on impact. He was half-conscious, disoriented, and hurt. Wave Runner's AI console's flickering screen indicated a catastrophic system failure with minimal functionality. Thrusters and geolocators were inoperable, but more importantly, the air management system was defective.

Dozens of light beams pierced through the waters, followed by streaks of machine gun fire in his general direction. Waver Runner swam away from the surface. He wasn't sure if they saw him fall from the sky or if the splash alerted some of the soldiers guarding the heart of the Chinese government. From the randomness of their fire, he figured they couldn't see him yet, but they would be elite soldiers entrusted with protecting the inner sanctum of the country's highest authority.

The deeper he swam, the more the barrage of bullets kept flooding the waters. With his air system compromised, he estimated he had minutes left before he suffocated to death. He kept swimming deeper and further, trying to get away from the soldiers, but the more he swam, the more intense the shooting became. He could feel the air supply becoming scarce. He thought of surrendering to save his life and become a prisoner of war.

But what would that cost his country? The military tech in the suit? Exposing this mission, considered the last hope for his nation, would he give up his teammates' location? If he did surrender, would his dad, the great general, be disappointed? What model would that set for Ryan, his son? Would Maddie still love a coward? So, he thought to himself. Surrendering wasn't an option, but the only other option seemed to be making peace with God. He didn't have a religious bone in his body, but for the first time in his life, he felt he was about to meet his maker. He wasn't ready for that. Not yet, not before kissing Maddie at the altar, not before raising Ryan to become a man.

The bullets kept pouring in the water. He could feel some hitting him. Were it not for the waters and the suit, they would have pierced his skin.

God, if you're out there. If somehow you get me out of this. I'll walk straight.

For the first time since his childhood, he prayed. The bullets kept raining in. Even more beams of light started shining through. The only thing keeping him alive seemed to be the Vantablack suit, which was nearly impossible to see at night.

He kept swimming and swimming and swimming. The lights became sparse, and the bullets fewer and fewer. Finally, he was out of their search area. He kept going until there was no more recyclable air, and then he had no choice. He had to get out of the water. He pulled to the retaining wall adjacent to the exit stairs. With only his head sticking out of the water He retracted his helmet and gasped for breath. Though the air was filled with smoke from the Coalition's strikes, it felt to him like a breath of fresh air from the hills of Georgia.

Chinese air defenses were repelling most of the rocket fire. The Antimissile Defense Artillery System (TADAS), commonly referred to as

The Great Wall, intercepted most of the missiles unleashed on the ancient city. Yet the Coalition could still hit several significant targets and keep the military and security apparatus on their toes. Wave Runner looked up to the billows of smoke rising throughout the city and could envision the mushroom cloud he would detonate and the chaos ensuing. He swam to the stairs, and right about when he was about to step out of the water, a strong beam of light blinded him. An unarmed drone was hovering a few yards from him. The light combined with the blaring siren were disorienting. The drone shouted in between siren blasts.

"Surrender now. Do not attempt to escape. We will not hesitate to shoot on sight. Surrender now. Do not attempt to escape. We will not hesitate to shoot on sight."

Topher could see the flashlights agitating and heading his way. He thought of diving back down, but the suit would be useless. He ran out of the water, pulled his sidearm, and shot the drone down. The shot blended in with the sound of war, but the flash-bang gave up his position. There were several parks and buildings nearby. He calculated that if he hid in one of the buildings, he might have enough time to detonate the bomb. Even if he couldn't get away from the blast, at least he would tip the war in America's favor. He wouldn't see Ryan grow up to become a man, but at least he would become a free man.

Wave Runner dashed onto the street and darted towards the first building structure he saw for some cover. Then, he ran towards a garden with multiple structures reminiscent of a maze. He thought hiding in one of the buildings could buy him some time. He calculated he was two minutes and forty seconds from the fourth structure. The group of soldiers pursuing him were further out. He estimated their arrival time to be about five minutes and thirty seconds. The bomb would take five minutes to set up for detonation. He was short two minutes. It seemed to him the soldiers were highly trained and most likely wouldn't need much time to find him. He peeked up and could see five drones in the distance homing in on him.

"I need two minutes! Give me two minutes!" he said, shocked to be praying once more.

He got to his targeted building without slowing down and jumped through the glass window, gun drawn. He quickly scanned the room. It looked empty. He made his way into the building and picked a room at random. He knew the soldiers would see the broken window, but that was irrelevant since the drones were tailing him. All that mattered was whether he could set this bomb up in a record time of three minutes. It had never been done. He retracted his helmet and got to work immediately. About two minutes in with one to spare before his estimated time for the arrival of rival forces. He felt the barrel of a gun on the back of his head.

"I don't think that's a good idea," the voice said in a slightly accented English. "You won't make it in time." Wave Runner was taken aback. How did this soldier get the jump on him? He couldn't communicate with the others, but their bombs didn't go off either. *"Did we fail?"* he thought to himself. *"But failure is not an option."* Complying with the stranger bore no benefit. He figured he was going to die either way.

He quickly pivoted with a back strike to knock the gun out of his opponent's hand. The stranger saw the move coming, dodged the blow, and charged Wave Runner, pinning him against the wall with his right forearm on his neck and the gun in his left hand pointed at Topher's face.

"Don't be stupid. We don't have a lot of time. They'll be here soon," the stranger said. The words did not register in Wave Runner's mind. He attempted to disarm him again. The attempt was futile.

"Okay then, have it your way," The Stranger said, as they could hear the shouts of the incoming soldiers approaching.

BANG!

35

MEETING OF THE MINDS

Concordia University, Montreal, Canada

"THAT WILL NEVER WORK," Kian-Amir said. He was sitting back on his leather chair behind his cherrywood desk opposite the now-famous scientist. "The country is at war. They will rally behind their government against the foreign enemies."

"Don't be so sure about that," Suri said. "Yes, the war rallies people behind their government. But the war doesn't erase the discontent against decades of repression and isolation. The people are tired, they want peace, and they want freedom."

"But is it freedom if their ruler came from their adversary?"

"It's freedom if the ruler carries out his duty with justice and equity,"

"But the ruler would always be indebted to the powers that installed him. Is that really freedom?"

"All the powers in question would do is to give a push to a train that's already in motion. Iran will be free."

"What makes you so sure?"

"It seems your family has been outside the country for too long. There is a new generation rising. They have a strong Persian identity. An identity embodied by your grandfather's legacy."

"What is my grandfather's legacy?"

"Does it matter? What really matters is what your legacy will be. You have a golden opportunity to lead our great civilization into the future. A future of prosperity, justice, and equity."

"What an opportunity! Taking over a country destroyed by war! To be a foreigner's puppet! Sorry, but I'm doing pretty good here. Canada is so far barely affected by the war."

"Is that what you think? The world is already in disarray. What do you think happens when two billion Muslims start an all-out war against one another? What do you think happens once Saudi Arabia and its allies engage Iran and its allies head-on? Do you think Canada will remain unaffected? How long do you think it can hide behind its policy of neutrality? We cannot stop what is happening in America, Europe, or Southeast Asia, but you can stop our people from being destroyed. You can bring peace to the Middle East."

"Peace in the Middle East is a pipe dream. Something we tell the children at night so they can go to sleep. We have been at war since the dawn of time. Nothing is going to change that."

"So, all your lectures about the future of Iran and the potential of its people, that was for naught?" That was for what, a meager stipend?"

"I didn't speak because of greed; I spoke because of grief. I hate to see my country as the pariah of nations. We have a great culture and a great people—"

"Then do something about it! Lead your people into a new era of peace and prosperity with its place amongst the brotherhood of nations. The door is open, but you must walk through it." Her disposable holophone notified her. The message read, *"We think we have a breakthrough."* "I have to go. Think about it carefully. We'll be in touch." She got up and left.

McGill University, Downtown Montreal

Scientists from around the world filled the room both physically and virtually. Dr. Earhardt, one of the first civilian scientists to encounter the virus, led the multidisciplinary task force. The room was large with holoscreens and holographic modeling stations.

"Dr. Suri, thank you for joining us," Dr. Earhardt said. "As you know, the pathogen stems from the equine flu modified to rapidly mutate." Since we first encountered it several years ago, my late mentor, Dr. McMaster, and I have tried to replicate it to find an antidote, but to no avail. Whoever produced it implanted an encrypted algorithm in the virus's genome and threw away the key," she paused. "Until now. Thanks to Dr. Ghani's notes, we were able to sequence its atypical genome, and we made progress in decrypting the underlying algorithm. How the virus works, it mutates so rapidly that our immune systems cannot keep up. By the time it figured out how to fight the initial virus, it had already mutated so much that it might as well be a totally different virus."

"So, we need to slow down the replication process to give the body a fighting chance," Suri interjected.

"Exactly," Dr. Earhardt said. "But this virus has been modified to evade the commonly used antivirals.

"When a nuclear reactor is out of control, we have a *scram* which releases, one way or the other, high levels of negative mass reactivity. This absorbs the neutrons, causing immediate cessation of the fission reaction." Suri said. "This virus behaves much like nuclear fission. If we can identify its core and release appropriate opposite ions, we can stop the replication or at least slow it down so the body can build the appropriate immunity."

"This could increase the effectiveness of Bellumavid," Dr. Earhardt said. "Currently, Bellumavid's effectiveness rate is between twenty to thirty percent. We could improve these numbers threefold if we could slow down viral replication. Now it's just a question of breaking the code of this virus."

"We do think, like you do, that stopping viral replication is promising. But we are running out of time," said Dr. Zarza from the La Paz Hospital University in Madrid, Spain. "This virus is spreading as fast as SARS-COV-2 but is far more lethal. Some of our international partners are sidelined due to the fighting going on worldwide."

"What are you suggesting?" Dr. Earhardt asked.

"I suggest that we apply a multilayered approach. Yes, we need therapeutics to slow the virus's progression and work with Bellumavid. Yes, we need a permanent prevention method, like a vaccine, to eradicate this disease. But we also need something to deploy rapidly to stop the ravages and slow the spread. We need a viral interference protocol."

"That's risky, Dr. Zarza," Dr. Earhardt said. "In case you're not familiar, viral interference is when a person is infected with a virus which prevents another virus from infecting the host. In simple terms, it's like filling the bus with people at an earlier stop so when the bus arrives at your stop, there's no more room, and you can't come in."

"It's like using potassium iodide during a nuclear disaster," Dr. Suri said. "When someone is exposed or at risk of being exposed to radiation, we give them iodide, so it fills their thyroid glands, which then prevents the radioactive iodine from entering their glands. This gives them a fighting chance to survive the ordeal with a less severe outcome."

"But there is a risk of double infection in some cases," Dr. Earhardt added.

"Yes, there is, but it might be our best chance to slow down the virus. What spreads faster than a virus, if not another virus? The question what is the right one to use?" Dr. Zarza said.

"Zika!" Dr. Amina Ghani said. "My husband was doing extensive research on a modified Zika virus. I didn't know why at the time, but now it makes sense. It's non-lethal for the most part and can spread in various ways, including mosquitoes. If we modify it and map it to bind to the same receptors as the *EFlu*, this might block it from infecting the host."

"I concur," Dr. Zarza said. "The profile of the genus Flavivirus makes it a prime candidate for the interference option."

"Okay, so we'll divide it into three working groups," Dr. Earhardt said. Group one, Dr. Zarza, will work on the interferer to prevent Eflu infections with another milder infection. Group two, with Dr. Suri, work on the Interceptor cocktail to flood the infected body with opposing ions, causing the virus to slow down, giving the immune system a chance to fight. My group will work on injection, a deployable vaccine. Thank you, everybody. Let's get to work."

36

THE DEATH OF A MAN

Macon, Georgia, about ninety miles northeast of Columbus.

"YOU SURE ABOUT THIS, bro?" Ty G said. "It's not a very preachy thing to do. Actually, it's quite ungodly. You sure you want to cross that line?"

"What other choice do I have?" Kyle answered. "What's ungodly is charging thirty thousand dollars for a medicine they make for pennies while people die. So today, we're going Robin Hood on these criminals."

"Tell you what. Let me go in there. I'll take care of that business, and you can wait for me at the base or the church if you prefer. You know I got you."

"Nah, man. You told me you been takin' care of Big Pop's daughter 'cause you're her pops now. Well, until my bro comes back, I'm Ryan's pop. And I ain't about to let no disease take him, not when right behind that counter is the medicine that can make him better."

"Okay, I feel you. Robin Hoodlum, I like that, Robin Hoodlum. Alright then, mask up." He cocked his handgun. Kyle took a deep breath, put on his mask, and cocked his gun as well.

Ty G entered the building first, fired two bullets into the ceiling, and said, "Nobody moves, nobody gets hurt!" He stepped to the pharmacy counter and said, "Bellumavid now!"

The technician froze. The pharmacist sped from the back, took the whole rack of Bellumavid, and put it on the counter. Ty G chuckled.

"I just need two," he said.

"Put the gun down and put your hands up," the undercover guard said, pointing his gun at Ty G. He complied.

"Why don't you put your gun down?" Kyle said with his gun behind the guard's head. The guard hesitated.

"Put it down now!" Kyle yelled. The guard complied. "On the floor with hands behind your head."

"I got them," Ty G said.

"Alright, let's go," Kyle said.

They ran out and drove north towards Atlanta for about thirty minutes. Then, they parked by the side of a river in the countryside. The night was pitch black. They took out their outer clothing, threw them in a metal barrel, doused it, and burned it. Then, they put the vehicle in neutral and put three sanitizing foggers in the car. After the foggers discharged their content, they doused the inside with gasoline and lit up the vehicle. Once they felt the fire erased any DNA trace or other evidence that could lead the authorities back to them, they pushed the vehicle into the river. They looked around a couple of times, then drove off in a second vehicle they had hidden.

"You know, we could've sold this car for half the price, right?" Ty G said. "Then sell this one for the rest and buy the thing clean."

"What is done is done. No point double-guessing," Kyle said, looking out the driver's window.

They drove on local roads for about one hour until they stumbled on a military checkpoint.

"That's not good," Kyle said.

"Just play it cool," Ty G said.

They stopped at the checkpoint and rolled down the driver's window.

"Good evening, gentlemen," the soldier said.

"Good evening, sir," Kyle said.

"Where are you coming from, and where are you going?"

"We came from Atlanta and are heading back to Columbus."

"It's late to be traveling. It's past curfew."

"Yeah, sorry, sir. The outreach took longer than we thought. There are a lot of hurting people out there."

"I thought I recognized you. You're Pastor KB. General Boykin's son."

"Yes, sir,"

"Thank you for what you do with the kids. My boy has completely changed because of you. You do some good work."

"That's what we're here for. Serving the community."

"That's good. Keep it going. But be careful. We've had a lot of crimes lately. Not everybody has your heart." The soldier said. "Let them through," he shouted to his fellow soldier. "Have a good night, gentlemen."

"You too sir," Kyle said.

As they drove off, Ty G said, "That was smooth. You're a natural, bro."

"Hopefully, not too natural," Kyle said.

They drove for more than an hour without much conversation.

"You alright, bro?" Ty G asked.

"Yeah, I'll be alright," Kyle said. "Thanks for comin' through tho."

"It's all good man. You know, sometimes I think maybe it's time to get out the game. Do investing or somethin' like that, you know? But it's always somethin'. My mom's medical bills, or some kid can't afford treatment or daycare. It's like, that's what I know how to do, and I'm real good at it. Don't know if I could get out if I really wanted to. But you, you got out. I respect that. I guess what I'm tryin' to say is don't beat yourself up, bro. We all do what we have to do for the people who matter to us."

"Yeah, I get it, man. I appreciate that."

They kept quiet for most of the way.

"Bro, what's happenin' at your church?" Ty G asked while they were passing Kyle's church.

"Not sure," Kyle said as he looked at the crowd gathered outside the church. Candles were lit, and flowers were laid at a makeshift memorial. He spotted his dad towering in the crowd. Once he got closer, he saw his mom beside him. Pastor Riveira was close by.

"Dad! What's happening?"

"Your brother's unit was on a mission in China. They went radio silent for some time now. That mission failed. They are presumed dead." General Boykin said, his eyes were light red, but his face stoic.

Kyle didn't respond immediately. Numbness invaded his mind. He looked at his mom. Her eyes were worn and watery.

"I'm sorry, Mom," he said as they approached and embraced each other. Kyle held his mother tight. He tried to hold back the tears but couldn't. His dad put his hand on his shoulder.

"Maddie?" Kyle asked while pulling away from his mom.

"She's in quarantine with Ryan," his mom replied.

"I don't think that's a good idea," Kyle said. "She shouldn't be alone right now.

"Why don't you go check on her?" The dad said.

"My condolences," Pastor Riveira kindly interrupted. "We are here for you."

"Thank you. I appreciate that," Kyle replied. A steady flow of other parishioners of all ages came to Kyle to offer their condolences as well. Once the flow died down, Kyle decided to head to his brother's house.

"Alright, let me go check on Maddie," Kyle said, looking at Ty G to see if he was okay with it.

"Won't you drop me at the base, and you can keep the car to take care of what you got to take care of?"

"Thanks, man," Kyle replied.

"My condolences again, Mr. & Mrs. Boykin," Ty G said to the grieving parents.

"Thank you," The general responded.

"Be careful," Mom said to her son.

After Kyle dropped Ty G off, he headed to Topher's house. The place was dark. He knocked on the door. There was no response. He tried to peek through the window. Finally, he saw a silhouette approaching.

Maddie opened the door.

"Hey, Kyle. What are you doing here?"

"I came to check up on you and Ryan."

"We're fine."

Her tone and demeanor were confident, but the bottle of bourbon on the table said otherwise. Kyle walked over to the table, picked up the bottle, and read the label.

"Redemption Straight High-Rye Bourbon. I didn't know you were a bourbon girl."

"I wasn't till this darn war. You're not afraid to catch the virus?" she asked rhetorically. He was in the living room, not far from where his brother had proposed to her before everything started to go awry.

"After all we've been through, I ain't scared of no virus. Besides, I brought some reinforcements." He showed her the medicine bottles.

"What's that?" She said, getting closer and taking one of them. "Bellumavid! Whoa! Where did you get that? They run for 30k each."

"Let's just say I have good friends. I think you can adjust the dosage to give it to Ryan. But you're a nurse, so you already know that."

"I sure do! Thank you so much!" She said while giving him a heartfelt hug. "Thank you, thank you. Gimme a second. I'll be back." She went upstairs to administer the medicine.

Kyle picked up the bourbon bottle. He hadn't held one of those in years. After he left the gang life, he vowed to stay sober and never drink hard liquor again. But liquor had a way of alleviating the pain. The pain, the pain, the pain of losing his brother, the pain of seeing his nephew suffer and slowly fade towards eternity, the pain of betraying his faith for his desired outcome. A little drink couldn't hurt. He got a glass from the cabinet and poured himself a drink up to half the glass.

"Don't drink all of it," Maddie said, coming down the stairs and overlooking the scene.

"You didn't leave me much to work with. But don't worry, there's still some left." He poured some into her glass and handed it to her. "How's Ryan?"

"He's hanging in there. He took his medicine and fell right back asleep."

"He's a trooper. He'll be fine. Does he know about Topher?"

"What is there to know? Did they find a body? Topher and his team are the best in the world."

"I hope you're right," Kyle said, admiring her optimism. "I hope to God you're right."

"Come on, you know I am. You don't remember the state championship? We were down twenty-one at the half. People counted us out. But did your brother give up?"

"Nah, he never gives up."

"That's right. He threw a Hail Mary like I had never seen, and we won by two."

They spent the next hour reminiscing on childhood memories and Topher's exploits. As time passed, Kyle could feel the blood flowing through his veins, his heartbeat racing. Like a magnet, an invisible force was pulling him to her. He had known her for many years, even before his brother had known her. She was like a sister to him. For all intents and purposes, she was his brother's wife. He felt staying any longer could lead them down a treacherous path they would not recover from.

"Maddie, I got to go. I'll check on you tomorrow."

"Alright, I'm glad you came by." She walked him to the door and hugged him goodbye. "Thanks for coming. Stay safe."

"You, too, be safe," he said, stepping onto the porch. She closed the door. Suddenly, she felt a cloud of darkness coming over her. The light was lit, but the room was dark. The silence in the house amplified the cacophony of her mind. The voices that started as whispers in her head grew louder and louder.

What if they were right? She thought to herself. *What if I had seen the love of my life for the last time when he left for that undisclosed mission?*

She would not feel his strong arms hold her anymore. She would never know the sadness of seeing him leave for a mission, nor the joy of seeing him walk through the door after an eternity apart. Without a body, how could she know for sure, and with a body, all hope would be lost. Maybe hope was already lost. Maybe the only thing to do was to join him. *But what about Ryan? Uncle Kyle, grandma, and grandpa would be there.* She held the bottle of Bellumavid in her hand. Surely, half of it would make the pain stop. Surely, half of it would reunite her with Topher. But if he was alive, he would never forgive her for giving up. *But it's so hard and painful,* she thought. She grabbed a blanket from the ottoman, lay on the couch holding their couple's picture, and cried herself to sleep.

The next day at Kyle's church, Maddie was sitting in the back. The band played a hymn, and the lyrics talked about a hiding place.

You are my hiding place

You always fill my heart

With songs of deliverance

Whenever I am afraid

I will trust in You

I will trust in You

Let the weak say

I am strong

In the strength of the Lord

Except for weddings and funerals, she hadn't been to church since her childhood. She was at a loss for words and didn't know how or what to pray. She just wanted Topher back. She wanted the pain to stop. Those words felt right. They felt real. They felt like they were hers; they were her prayer.

"Thank you, band, for this amazing rendition," Pastor Riveira said. We know we can find refuge in Jesus Christ, the rock of ages during these perilous times."

The congregation responded with *Amens* and other signs of approval. He continued.

"This pandemic is severely impacting our community. But we serve a God who answers prayers. I'm glad to announce that a team of international scientists based in Canada has arrived with treatments for the virus. If you have a loved one suffering from the illness, or want to learn more about how to protect yourself. Dr. Earhardt and her team will be headquartered at the GW Carver High School."

When the service ended, Maddie walked out the back. To her surprise, there were military police vehicles with their flashing lights. She was in disbelief when she heard the words,

"Kyle Boykin, you're under arrest for armed robbery. You have the right to remain silent. Everything you say can and will be used against you in a court of law."

Kyle, hands cuffed behind his back, glanced at the entrance, his young students looking at him in shock, their parents with shame. But there in the small crowd was Maddie. That, more than anything, was a gut punch. For so many years, he tried to minister to her and his brother, make them see the light, but now all she would see is a failed felon. He was back to being the troubled son of the general. The black sheep once again.

Inside the car, the arresting officer commented.

"Was it worth it, Boykin?"

Kyle didn't answer.

"You must feel really dumb right about now. These scientists are here from Canada and brought tons of Bellumavid to treat patients for free. So, you're going to rot in jail for nothing."

Kyle remained quiet.

"Why aren't you like your brother? He's gone now, but at least he made your family proud. Now your mom is going to lose both her sons. That's a shame."

Kyle remained quiet.

"You know, your dad was my training officer. He showed me all I know. He's a great man. But apparently, the apple does fall far from the tree."

Kyle remained quiet.

"You're in for a treat. We're in war times, so no more cushy cells. You're in for a world of pain, my friend."

Kyle remained quiet.

The officer rambled all the way to the processing center. Once inside, they took Kyle's mugshot, processed his file, and locked him up in an overcrowded cell.

"I wish I could throw away the key," The arresting officer said.

Kyle remained quiet.

37

ALL THE WRONG QUESTIONS

Beijing, China

BANG!

THE STRANGER OPENED FIRE next to Wave Runner's ear, causing him to be disoriented. He then pulled a Taser and shocked him under the chin. Topher fell to the ground. The stranger put a black bag over his head, tied his hands behind his back, and pulled him back up.

"Okay. let's go!"

Still dazed from the shock, Wave Runner couldn't distinguish what he heard or where he was being dragged to. He was thrown in the back of a vehicle. From the sound of the doors slamming and the feel of the ground, he figured he was in a van or a truck. The vehicle drove off.

A few hours later, Wave Runner was tied to a chair. He could barely hear the footsteps heading towards him. He felt a hand slightly touching his head to remove the sac. The place was dark. The stranger walked away from Wave Runner and headed towards a control console on the wall. He entered a quick command. and the steel blinds across the room automatically opened. Light flooded the room, blinding Topher for a moment.

"I apologize for all of this," the stranger said as he walked towards his captive. He pulled out a knife. Topher could barely see as his eyes were adjusting to the ambient light, but he made out the knife in the hands of his captor. As the stranger got close to him, Topher's body tensed up, and his mind prepared for excruciating pain. The only thing he didn't want to do was to betray his nation.

Whatever happens, stay strong. Do not flinch, he said to himself. Keeping his honor and making his son proud was all that mattered at this point.

The stranger leaned towards Wave Runner and said.

"Watch out, we're not going to need this," he cut off the ties binding him. "Mr. Boykin, can I trust you? Or should I put those back?" Wave Runner remained silent for a few moments as the stranger was unbinding his feet.

"How do you know my name?"

"I know many things."

"Why am I alive?"

"You have many questions, but you ask the wrong questions."

"What are the right questions?"

"Well, you could start with my name. I know your name, Ryan's, and Maddie's, but you know nothing about me. That doesn't seem fair, does it?"

Topher's eyes widened. His fist clenched.

"Don't worry, we mean them no harm."

"What's your name?" Topher said as he decided to play along.

"Zang Yongsheng. I work for the Ministry of State Intelligence."

"So, you're a federal agent. Why didn't you let the soldiers catch me?"

"Once again, the wrong question." He gestured to Topher to follow him to the large window.

"Is it not beautiful?" Zang said, pointing to the view outside the window. Hills of manicured gardens with majestic mountains in the background.

Topher did not answer but rather looked toward Beijing.

"Are you looking for mushroom clouds? If you don't see any, your friends were not as fortunate as you."

"Where are they?"

"I wish I could tell you. Our military most likely got them. So, they are either dead or in custody, which nowadays is as good as dead. Let me ask you a question of my own," Zang continued.

"Before the attack, did Americans want war with China?"

Topher took a moment to process what he had just heard. He ignored the question at first. The possibility of failure captured his thoughts. *Could it be that it was the last time they would see each other when they split heading to their respective targets?*

He imagined heading home, consoling their families. It was bad enough that he got caught, but at least one of them should have been able to detonate their package. Then there was hope. Maybe they were lying low. Maybe they were looking for him, or maybe, at this point, they're just watching over him from a better place. Maybe now it's up to him to finish the mission.

"No," Topher answered as they stood at the window overlooking gorgeous gardens in the forefront with a stunning mountain view as the backdrop.

"I can tell you, the Chinese people did not want war either. Therefore, the question you should ask is, who wanted the war? Who decided that the best way forward was the destruction of our beloved countries?"

"Who?"

"To know 'who', you have to ask, 'who benefits from the carnage?'"

"Who?"

"Look at this scenery. Isn't it beautiful?"

"Very."

"If you carry out your mission. Do you think this view will matter?"

"How do you know about my mission?"

"You have no idea how much we know about you. How do you think they found you so fast? How do you think we found you so fast?"

"How?"

"That's not what matters at the moment. What matters is that we have a short window to stop the world's destruction." He took a deep breath and turned away from looking through the window to looking Topher in the eyes.

"If your mission were to succeed, what do you think our response would be?"

"I would think that you would respond in kind."

"And then, what would you do?"

"We would most likely figure out a way to retaliate."

"So, you bomb Beijing, my home, with nuclear weapons. We then bomb DC or New York—" He paused. "Then, eventually, you regain control of your nuclear arsenal and go for Shanghai, Guangzhou, and Shenzhen." He stopped looking into Topher's eyes, stared into the air, and continued.

"We go for LA, Chicago, and Atlanta. Millions of people die on both sides. Both countries have been rendered inhabitable for decades. That's only in our two nations. You can imagine what happens in our respective allies. Paris, London, Moscow, Saigon, all gone. Radiation contaminates everything, and a nuclear winter finishes what's left. Is that what you want?"

"I just follow orders."

"What happens when the orders are based on false premises? What happens when orders threaten our very existence on this planet? What happens when the orders threaten life everywhere, even in a small town like Columbus, Georgia?"

"If you're so concerned about life, why did your country attack mine?"

"Like I said, the people do not want war. The question is really, who wanted the war? Who benefits from it?"

"I don't think anyone benefits from a war that brings us to the brink of annihilation. Weapon manufacturers will make a lot of money. But what's the point of money if everyone is dead?"

"You assume that the only thing people want is money. You assume, rightfully so, that it is the main driver of human endeavor. Yet, what if I told you some people have all the money they could ever want? What they want now is legacy."

"What kind of legacy is that?"

"What if you view the Earth as a limited resource needing to be preserved? And you view the billions of humans on Earth as expandable parasitic lifeforms. What would be the logical course of action to preserve your main resource?"

"You eliminate the parasites. Who would want such a thing?"

"Now you ask the right questions. Unfortunately, that's the question we're all asking."

"What do you know?"

"We know that groups of powerful people operating in the shadows are pulling the levers of power not only in your country and mine but worldwide. This war is a direct result of their efforts. I love my country, and I'm sure you love yours. I don't want to see it destroyed. I know it's just a question of time before your country regains control of its nuclear arsenal. We estimate that we have at most three days until they regain control. Once they do, the world as we know it is over."

"What do you want from me?"

"I need you to convince your president to stand down and negotiate peace."

"You're out of your mind! We were hit hard in our homeland. There is no way they will accept to surrender! No way!"

"I'm not asking you to surrender, but to give peace talks a chance. To give both our nations a chance. To give our children a chance at life!"

"Listen, I only want to go home and be with my family. But what you're asking is impossible. I'm a soldier, not a diplomat."

"That is true. You are a soldier. But you're a soldier with enough connections to get close to President Rodriguez and get him to listen. That's all we can ask for."

The door opened, and a young man with a clean haircut and a nice shirt said.

"Deacon, they're getting close."

"Who's getting close?" Topher said.

"The military," Zang replied. "They're looking for you grid by grid, all over the city and surroundings. They'll be here soon. We have to go."

"Where?"

"The city is too hot. We have to take you further in the countryside until things cool down, and we can get you out of the country."

"Isn't that treason if they catch you?"

"Don't worry about me. My duty is to save my country. Getting your president to stand down will save yours. Take off the suit."

"What?"

"Take off your special ops suit. We have some clothes for you."

"I can't leave this suit behind."

"You must. That's how we found you, by the way. Now, please hurry! We must go!"

Topher traded the suit for inconspicuous clothing. He looked at the suit and said, "What if I refuse?"

"You can come with me, or you can go with them." He pointed to the bottom of a neighboring hill to a multitude of Chinese soldiers canvassing the hillside. Reluctantly, Topher engaged the self-destruct function on the suit. "Engage the self-destruct function to detonate in thirty minutes from now."

"Okay, let's go," Zang said, leading the way through the room's main door.

On the other side of the door, Topher noticed seven men with automatic weapons. He figured they were there to intervene if he attempted anything. They walked to the end of the hallway. On both sides were rooms, most likely offices. They went down the stairs into the lobby of the building, they passed a series of tall doors leading to an auditorium. Passing those doors, they made a turn and exited to a door on the side of the building leading to the back of the structure. Pulled right to the door was a van with its back open.

Zang threw Topher's suit in the back and closed the doors. He told the driver, "Hurry, you have twenty minutes left before the self-destruct sequence completes." The driver nodded and drove off.

Zang took Topher to a Sports Utility Vehicle parked about thirty feet from the door. They drove off.

38

IT'S GOING TO HURT A LITTLE

MADDIE HAMMERED THE DOOR as if she were a federal agent. As the door opened, she barged in past her general father-in-law.

"They arrested Kyle," She blurted out.

"Yes, we know, dear," Mrs. Boykin said.

"You know?" Maddie replied. "Aren't you going to do anything about it?"

"Sit down, hon," Mrs. Boykin said tenderly. "Did Kyle give you some Bellumavid by any chance?"

"Yes."

"They're accusing him of armed robbery at a pharmacy outside Macon. The robbers took two bottles of Bellumavid. So now we know why."

"Oh my! I still have them. Can I return them and vacate the charges?"

"It's not going to be that easy," General Boykin said. "He made his choices, and now he has to face the consequences. But if you give them to me, I can see what I can do."

"In the meantime," Mrs. Boykin said. "Ryan is the priority. Take him to the medical camp they set up. Those scientists are his best shot."

"My longtime friend Colonel Blaine is in charge of that camp," General Boykin said. "He'll take care of you."

The medical camp had only been operational for a few hours, but was already overwhelmed. People came from as far as Atlanta, and some crossed state lines from Alabama. Maddie reached out to Colonel Blaine, he bumped her to the front of the line.

"Hi, my name is Dr. Suri Mirzakhani. I am a nuclear scientist with the IAEA."

"Hi, I'm Maddison and this is Ryan," Maddie said, shaking Suri's hand.

"Nice to meet you. My colleagues and I have developed several protocols for treating and preventing Eflu. We mapped out the progression of the disease in four phases. From what I see in this chart, your son is at stage two of that progression."

"I'm familiar with the phases," Maddie said. "I'm a nurse at Columbus Memorial Hospital."

"Okay, good," Suri responded. "We are now in an in-field clinical trial. In your son's case, since he is already infected, we need to slow down the viral mutative replication so his immune system can get acclimated to the virus and fight it. This drastically improves the efficacy of Bellumavid. Do you have any questions for me?"

"Yes, why do you look familiar?" Maddie asked. "Weren't you the scientist kidnapped in Iran?"

"Yes, that's correct."

"Oh wow, what are the odds?" Maddie said. "I know now is not the time, but I have so many questions about that."

"Well, maybe when we close for the day, we can go out for a drink or something."

"I'd like that," Maddie said.

"Okay, Ryan, it's going to hurt a little," Suri said.

39

A LONG SHOT

Chinese Countryside

"WHAT IS THIS PLACE?" Topher asked.

"Our operations center," Zang said.

On the top side, the facility processes food for the entire region. Underneath the processing plant, the room was filled with computers and holoscreens, manned by staffers gathering data, compiling profiles, and monitoring individuals. Topher tensed up. He felt the operation was quite impressive. He thought he was in the lion's den.

"Isn't bringing me into your government's operations dangerous?"

"You think this is the Ministry of State Intelligence?" Zang said, chuckling. "No, their facilities are twenty times better." He started walking towards the biggest holoscreen.

"So, if this is not for the government. Who are you then?"

"All you need to know is that we are a group of people who love our country, want to see it thrive, and raise our children in peace."

"对不起，先生。 **你可能想看看**这个。" An agent said. Topher didn't understand the words, but understood the body language and context clues. He thought the analyst told Zang there was something that would be of interest to him. The analysts stopped at his station, entered a brief command, and projected it onto the central holoscreen. They walked towards it. The analyst continued to speak to Zang in Mandarin.

"Wanna fill me in?" Topher asked.

"That man we suspect is the key to all of this," He pointed to the holoscreen. Drone and satellite footage of a man with an entourage paraded on the screen. "We just located him in Chengdu."

"Where is that?"

"That's further inland, far from here, far from the fighting. We have had an eye on him for a while, but what is he doing in China? Why is he here?"

"Who is he? Why are you monitoring him?"

"Let us worry about that for now. You worry about reaching out to your president to stop this war."

"And how do you suggest I do that?"

"One of your brother's friends, Tyrone Greene, has been dealing contraband satellite phones. He uses one himself. We will call him and have him reach your brother."

"Ty G? Your hope for mankind is Ty G's side operation? You gotta be kidding me!"

"I'm not kidding. This is quite a serious plan."

"How do you even know who Ty G is?"

"As I told you—"

"Enough! Enough with your riddles! How do you know all of this?"

"It is better if we keep our cool," Zang said while an analyst pulled out his gun and aimed it at Topher.

"No! You can tell me what I want to know, or you can put a bullet in my head right now!" Topher said while positioning his head right on the barrel of the analyst's gun.

Zang gently put his hand on the hands of his colleague and lowered the gun away from Topher's forehead. He nodded, signifying that he had it under control.

"Follow me," he said to Topher, leading him into a separate room. He poured himself some coffee, offered some to Topher, who declined, and continued into his office. He sat down and asked,

"What do you want to know?"

"Everything," He replied. "I want to know why you know so much about us, Columbus, my family, even Ty G! How did you know about my top-secret mission?"

"It's actually quite easy, demanding but easy." He took a sip of his coffee. Over the past four decades, we invested in a ubiquitous intelligence-gathering infrastructure in every corner of your country and frankly, the world. We have psychological analysis algorithms. We know who's going to be a leader before they know they're going to be leaders. To put it simply, every piece of technology in your country that we manufacture can potentially be used to gather information."

Topher started connecting the dots of the implications of this.

"What do you mean by every?"

"Every single thing that we made or one of our subsidiaries made can be used to collect information on the users and the people in contact with them." He took another sip. "For instance, your mission, though the conversations of your leaders were well protected, the antiquated Nukes were stored in a facility using security equipment, some of which we manufactured. Your suit had components manufactured by us. We can track those. Couple that with holophone data and surveillance cameras, we can create a realistic assessment of the situation. We don't always get it right, but we have gotten very good at it."

Topher didn't say anything. Still processing the implications of this information.

"You seem shocked. Don't worry. Your CIA, NSA, and other three-letter organizations have been doing the same for decades. I'm sure they have a dossier about me somewhere."

"I'm not shocked. I'm frustrated that we let our guard down."

"And that you did. Every time your mom posted a picture of you, the son of a general, we were there. The historic high school championship victory, we were there. The commencement ceremony at West Point, we were there."

"Okay, I get the point."

"Okay, but I need you to understand that, when it's my government or yours engaging in spying, that's expected. But when it leads to world annihilation, that's something else entirely. Normal governments are not in the business of extermination. Domination, yes, but extermination?"

"So, who's behind it?"

"That's what we are trying to figure out. The guy you saw on the screen, we think, is the key."

"The key to what?"

"To unravel who is behind the war and how to stop it from ever happening again. But until then, you're the key to stopping the upcoming onslaught." He started projecting drone footage on his holodesk. "

"Whoa! Where is this?" Topher asked.

"This is in the Atlantic Ocean." The drone footage showed a flotilla of warships hoisting China's Five-Star red flag, as far as the eye can see. "They're heading to your country's East Coast. And these are heading to the West Coast." He changed to a different drone footage of the Pacific Ocean fleet. "But conversely, this is also happening on this side of the world." He showed a fleet of Aircraft Carriers hoisting the Star-Spangled Banner. "These are heading our way."

"This makes Normandy look like a walk in the park."

"We don't have much time, but we can stop it. Listen, I know it's a long shot, but it's the only one we've got right now. Can I trust you?"

"Trust is a two-way street. If you want me to trust you, you will have to trust me. I want this insanity to stop as much as you do."

"Okay then. This is your gear." He handed Topher a duffle bag with weapons and tactical gear. Topher took the bag and inspected its contents.

"What's that for?"

"Field trip." Zang grabbed his own duffle bag. "We're going to Chengdu."

Columbus, Georgia Detention Center

"Wake up, sunshine!" The guard said to Kyle while clanging his baton on the cell bars. "You're getting out of here."

Kyle felt like telling the guard a thing or two, but he knew that was a bad idea. He held his composure, held his hands up, and turned around for the guard to slip his handcuffs on him.

"Someone paid my bail?" Kyle asked while they were walking out of the cell.

"Nope," the guard said. "You are being released into Captain Alexander's custody. You and another fifty inmates."

Kyle didn't like the sound of that.

"Why? What happened?"

"There's a massive fleet of commies on their way. It's like nothing we've ever seen. All able-bodied men and women of combat age are being called to the coast, and inmates like you are going to the front of the line. While people like me are deemed essential workers, so I'll be right here. They're going to put you right in front, bullets flying your way. But, hey, thanks for your service."

They gave Kyle his belongings and had him sign a few forms. An old yellow school bus was waiting for him and the other inmates. Kyle conversed with a few others on the bus, no one was afforded legal counsel.

"A trip to the graveyard" is what one inmate called their journey.

Within the hour, they were back at the military training facility. The inmates were handed light beige camouflage outfits, which differed from the standard darker green issue. Kyle figured they'd want the inmates to go first. As he glanced at the crowd, his gaze caught Ashleigh's from the other side of the room. His heart sank, but he looked away to the captain taking the stage. The captain laid out the defensive tactical operation.

"The best defense is offense," the captain said. "So, we're going to meet them on the high seas. We'll hit them before they can hit us. Across both coasts, a tenth of the force will be in naval squadrons with far deployment. They will be deployed with one objective: search and destroy. They are to sink as many enemy ships as they can."

Once the captain was done with his speech, the leadership assigned the positions. Most inmates were assigned to the tip of the spear. Which amounted to not much more than a Kamikaze mission. Kyle knew once he boarded that boat, he would not be coming home.

Mess Hall

Kyle was sitting with other inmates. Not too far from him was Rigo and some other newly appointed sergeants. He laughed at the thought that he would soon be taking orders from a gangster turned soldier. As he was lost in thought, a gentle tap on his shoulder.

"Can we talk?" Ashleigh said while sitting down next to him.

"Yeah, sure. What do you want to talk about?" Kyle responded.

"Well, let's start with why you're avoiding me."

"Not sure if you noticed, I was literally tied up."

"Yeah, I noticed. I came to see you, but they said you refused to come."

"I thought you were there to do one of your interviews."

"Really? That's what we're doing now? You know full well why I came. I don't know what's wrong with you, but you better figure it out quickly."

"It's all figured out. I don't know what you want me to say. I don't even know why we're talking right now."

"Really?"

"Yeah, for real," Kyle said and got up and left.

Triple P hideout

"Hey G, the sat phone," the gangmate said, handing Ty G the old yet still functional device. Ty G took the Satellite Phone and answered.

"Yo! Dis Ty"

"Tyrone, this is Topher,"

"Topher who?"

"Kyle's brother."

"Nah, man, that can't be 'cause he died. We had service for him and all his crew."

"I'm alive."

"So, if you alive why aren't you here?"

"Listen, we don't have a lot of time."

"How did you get this number anyway?"

"Listen, I'll answer all your questions when the time comes, but now I need to speak to my brother. Can you reach him for me?"

"Your bro? Your bro's in jail, bruh."

"How? Why? You got him in one of your schemes again? I thought he was done with that life."

"Well, not sure I like your tone, but Imma let that pass, for once, I didn't get him in trouble. He got me in trouble."

"My pastor brother got you in trouble? Really? That's a hard one to swallow."

"Well, swallow this. While you out there playin' GI Joe, he out here takin' care of everyone. He be takin' care of your fam too. Ryan got sick with that flu thing. The meds are like thirty Gs. He ain't got that type of bread. So, we went and got some meds the good old-fashioned way, you know what I'm sayin'. We got the meds to Ryan, so he got better. Now these scientists from Canada are here treating everyone for free. Go figure."

Topher didn't say anything.

"Don't worry tho, Maddie and Ryan, they alright now. It's just your bro that's kinda stuck right now."

"You guys didn't post bail for him?"

"They don't do that no more. They don't have the resources. So now you're in until they get to you."

"Can you get to him? I need to speak to him."

"They arrested him not too long ago, but now they takin' all them inmates to go fight in that war on the coast. There's a boatload of ships headin' our way. They gon' put them right in the front."

"You're not going to fight?"

"Nah, man, they be looking for me too. They caught your brother 'cause he don't know how to lay low. He be out in public and at church. He made it easy for them to find him. Besides, Imma be honest with you, I don't know if we can win this thing. They had drones and machine gun dog-like robots attacking us. We beat them, but it wasn't as many as what they got comin' this time."

"Listen, with what I have to tell my brother, we can save everyone and stop the fighting, but I need you to get to my brother. Can you bust him out of there?"

"What? Dude, what part of laying low didn't you get? The laying or the low?"

"Ty, this is the most important thing you can do right now. When was the last time I asked you for anything?"

"At least ten years ago."

"Right. I need you to bust my brother out so I can speak to him."

"That'll be hard. They gettin' shipped out the day after tomorrow. Why do you need him so badly?"

"'Cause he's the only guy I trust to get this done for me."

"What do you need done?"

"I can't tell. And trust me, you don't want to know. You think they're looking for you now? If I tell you, all eyes will be on you. Besides, I thought you guys didn't leave anyone behind?"

"I thought you guys didn't do that either. But here you are talkin' to me."

"Fair point, but it's more complicated than that."

"Yeah, alright, if you say so. Okay, tell you what, Kyle's my boy. I don't want him to be shipped out to die. I'll get him outta there. Gimme twenty-four hours, then call this phone."

"What's your plan?"

"Don't worry about my plan. I got some of my guys on the inside. We'll get it done."

"Okay. Pull through."

"Bruh, I always do."

It took some creative thinking on Ty G's part, but a few favors later, Kyle walked out unnoticed while some other chap slept in his bed. The chap would claim to have been assaulted and knocked unconscious.

Triple P hideout, twenty-four hours later

"It's your bro," Ty G said, handing the satellite phone to Kyle.

"Hello," Kyle said, skeptical of Ty G's story.

"Hey, little bro," Topher said.

"So, it's real you're alive?"

"It came close, but I'm still here."

"How about the rest of your team?"

"MIA, most likely KIA. But they're a tough group, so who knows? Listen, I know what you did for Ryan. Thank you, it means a lot to me."

"Don't mention it. Ryan is my nephew. He's family, so we look out for our own."

"I need you to do something for me. It will sound crazy, but I think it's the only way out of this mess. I can't get into the details, but I have a dossier that I need you to show to the president."

"Which president?"

"President Rodriguez."

"Are you out of your mind? How am I going to do that?"

"You have to use—"

"Nah, I don't have to do nothin'. You have to come back, decorated soldier that you are, and petition to speak with your commander-in-chief."

"I can't. Believe it or not. I'm in the doghouse with our leadership."

"That's hard to believe."

"Trust me on this one, I know these things. Let's just say that the Iran hostage situation would have ended differently if we followed orders."

"You went rogue?"

"Keep that to yourself, it's top-secret info. But let's just say we valued the lives of the hostages over our military careers. We disobeyed orders. What saved us was that, against all odds, we succeeded. It's the type of results that the press and politicians like. But since then, the world has exploded, and they've been putting us in the most dangerous situations. Even this mission was a one-way ticket."

"There seems to be a lot of those going around. Still, a rogue hero is better than a criminal."

"Even if I could, I'm way too far away. Access to what gets to the president's desk is highly controlled. The only way to get this done is to get him alone and show him what I'm about to show you."

"I trust you with my life, but you're asking me, a recidivist felon and now a fugitive of the law, to meet with the president of our war-torn nation. It can't be done."

"I know it's a long shot. I never told you, but I was and still am really proud of you for becoming a minister. I remember parts of the sermon of that day. Something about Jesus using unlikely people to do his work. Maybe this is one of these times, 'cause, I'm not going to lie to you, it's a long shot, but it's the only chance we have."

"I don't know, bro. I really screwed up. Like I never thought I'd go back there."

"Isn't your faith all about forgiveness? Maybe you need to forgive yourself. I called you because, in a sense, we're the same. I lay it all on the line for the country I love. You lay it all out for the community you love. I do it in the military. You do it in the ministry. Even you getting in trouble was laying it all down for Ryan when I couldn't. For that, I'm forever grateful to you, but I need you to do it again, not only for Ryan, Maddie, or me but for the whole world. Cause if those boats reach the shore, this world isn't going to survive."

Kyle closed his eyes and took a big sigh.

"What do you need me to do?"

"I'm going to give you an encrypted IP address. When you access it, you will find a comprehensive investigation into the cabal that orchestrated all the events leading to the war. It goes deep. Both presidents think they're acting of their own volition. But they're being manipulated into destroying their nations and the world. We need Rodriguez to step towards a ceasefire so diplomacy can resume, and peace can have a chance."

"Whatever is in that file, Rodriguez isn't just going to pull back and let the Axis keep pounding us," Kyle said.

"Let me deal with this. No one loves America more than I do. Everything I do is for her."

"Alright, I got you."

"Thank you, I appreciate you."

"Same, alright, give me that address."

Topher gave him the IP address, with strict instructions on whom to trust to get to President Rodriguez. They hung up. Kyle turned to Ty G.

"Bro, I need to use the terminal."

"Nah, bro, you trippin'. Yesterday, your bro said they'd be coming after me if he told me about this thing. This place is the only thing between me and them prison bars. You poking around online for national secrets on my terminal, illegal at that, that ain't gonna happen."

"Really, bro, after—"

"Don't even try that. I just busted you out for this. I did my part. You need to go to your girlfriend. Her office got one too. They be harder to take down. You feel me."

"Bro, me and Ashleigh, we ain't talking like that no more."

"We? Who's we? She be talkin', you just ain't listenin'. You got that guilt trip going. Listen, bro, ain't no shame tryin' to save your nephew."

"That's not true. A crime is a crime. And for what? Dem scientists are here giving it out for free."

"Yeah, but you sure your nephew would've been able to hold on till they arrived? All I'm sayin' is, you did what you thought was right with what you knew at that time. But now you pray, ask for forgiveness, and move on. Ain't it how it's supposed to work?"

Kyle didn't have an answer. Ty G continued.

"Now, a lot is riding on you pulling through. So, you better get your head straight and get it done!"

"Alright, let's go get this thing done." He got up and grabbed a hoodie, and headed toward the door. Ty G stayed seated.

"You ain't comin'?" Kyle said.

Ty G gave it some thought, sighed.

"Might as well, I got to make sure you don't get yourself caught again."

40

TIME FOR A CHANGE

Tehran, Iran

LAST TIME HE WAS HERE, he was being hunted, trying to save his beloved. This time, he was the hunter trying to save his people. Azael was with three handpicked fellow Sayeret Matkal operators. Yonatan, Avi, and Naftali were all seasoned in the field. The black van stopped outside the protest area, behind an inconspicuous older building. On the fourth floor, two field intelligence officers, Meir and Yossi, were waiting for them.

"How is it looking?" Azael asked.

"It's looking good," Yossi said. "We have eyes inside the chambers and on the streets."

"Six minutes into the speech, we will detonate two small explosives at the front gate," Meir continued. "Then two more explosives in the back of the crowd. This will cause panic in the crowd, which will charge the palace. The security will then rush the leaders out through the emergency exit where the last two explosives are located. This is when you will take your shots."

"PR machine?" Yonatan asked.

"Assets are on the ground, ready to tell the story of how the crowd rose and loose gunmen dealt the fatal shots," Yossi answered.

"Okay, let's get in position," Azael said.

The four operatives each set their sniper stations at a separate window with a clear view of the palace's back exit. After setting up his station, Azael stepped away for a moment.

"Are you there?" he said.

"Yes, I'm here," Suri said, holding her earpiece. "I wasn't sure you were going to make it."

"I wouldn't miss it. Not even for the most important mission of my life. Where are you? There's a lot of background noise."

"Believe it or not. I'm at a bar," she said, shocked to hear those words come out of her mouth. "We just closed for the day. So, we came to decompress."

"A bar? A bar in America. I guess a war would get you to drink."

"It's not the war. I made friends here. The other scientist we run the trials with, and a nurse. Her husband is deployed. So, we're just a few women hoping their men come home in one piece." She stepped out to a quieter spot.

"Well, after this, I'm done. I'm coming home to you. Wherever in the world that is, I'll be there. Whatever happens with this war, we'll face it together."

"I would like that more than anything," she said.

"How are you?" he said softly.

"I'm exhausted, physically and mentally. The treatments are working. We saved so many lives, but many more are coming from all over the country and some from other places in the world. They brave the war and conflict to be able to save their loved ones."

"I'm proud of you."

"I'm proud of you, too."

"Killing someone is nothing to be proud of."

"I don't see you as someone who will take another man's life, but as someone who will help restore freedom to my country and peace in the world. A few days after you're done, Kian-Amir will be installed. And we can turn the page on this dark chapter. Our future will be better because of it."

"You're so positive. That's why I love you."

"I love you too. Hurry and come back to me."

"I will."

They hung up. Azael went back to his station and looked towards the rest of the team. Everyone was in position, ready to execute.

Pok, pok, pok.

"GRENADE!" Yossi screamed, but too late.

BANG!

The bright flash and loud sound hit them as if they ran into a brick wall. Azael tried to go for his handgun, but couldn't make out the ground from the ceiling. The room was spinning around him. Before he could regain control, Iranian special forces flooded the room, shouting incomprehensible orders. But he got down on his knees with his hands up.

Columbus, Georgia, the day after the failed assassination attempt.

With a clear path towards sealing this pandemic's fate, Colonel Blaine and the city leadership loosened curfew rules. The sounds of revelries overpowered the growl of the generators. Pool and dart competitions had regained popularity. The old jukebox, deemed unworthy of scant energy resources, ceded its throne to spontaneous group chants. American classics and patriotic songs served as collective therapy holding the community together. The lights were dimmed out, as much to conserve energy and to provide a calming, intimate atmosphere. Portraits of iconic music artists peppered the interior brick walls. Only two TVs were on. Both tuned in to whatever news channel was able to broadcast at that particular time. The levity of an establishment with an all-you-can-drink tap policy offered a semblance of normalcy.

"How's Ryan?" Dr. Earhardt asked, bringing a glassful of lager to her lips.

"Ryan is doing really good," Maddie answered. "Thanks to you guys, he's almost out of the woods."

"Glad he's okay," Dr. Earhardt said.

"You must be proud of what you guys were able to accomplish?"

"Not really, it's just part of the job."

"Don't minimize your accomplishments. You and your team found successful therapies for a once-in-a-lifetime pandemic. You saved countless lives."

"That's very kind of you, Maddie. But the truth is, if I had been a better researcher, this pandemic would have been avoided.

"What do you mean? I don't follow."

"I encountered this virus before," the doctor said, sipping her beer. "Years ago, I was working at the University of Vancouver when we received a version of this virus. It was sent to us by mistake. I think it went to two dozen other labs worldwide. What we saw that day terrified us. We spent the next few years advocating for safer lab practices and trying to come up with a protocol that would stop viruses like this one cold, no pun intended. Unfortunately, we failed on both fronts, which is why we're here today. You can argue that none of this would have happened if we didn't fail."

"Oh, don't blame yourself. The people who released it knew exactly what they were doing. If you had the treatment for this one, they would have released another one. You did good here. My son is alive. Take that W doc. They don't come often nowadays. With that big battle brewing on the high seas, I feel some Ls are coming. We're going to need hospital beds."

"When are you heading down there?"

"In two days. I'll be headed to the coast for the battle royal." She took a sip.

"Suri, you're awfully quiet. Are you alright?" Dr. Earhardt said.

"I am fine, ladies."

"I know that look," Maddie said. "That's the look of a woman who doesn't know if her man is coming home." She put her arm around Suri's shoulder. "I'm right there with you, sister. I'm right there with you."

Dr. Earhardt felt somewhat out of place. Maddie and Suri had a bond that was hard to understand. Suri put her head on Maddie's shoulder and cried. Maddie peeked over to Suri's holophone. It was tuned in to what seemed to be Iranian expat news. The chyron read, *"The Supreme Leader vows swift justice against his would-be assassins."*

After a few moments, Suri took a deep breath and said.

"Thank you for everything, ladies. I have to go." She got up and rushed out the door. Maddie and Dr. Earhardt were taken aback by Suri's abrupt departure. Suri walked out of the bar, took another deep breath, pulled out her holophone, held it without dialing, and put it back in her purse. She went to the hotel room and started putting essentials in a duffle bag. She lay on her bed staring at the ceiling as tears fell down her cheeks. She took her holophone and made the call.

"Alo"

"Sayed, It's me,"

"Suri?"

"Yes."

"Don't tell me you have something to do with that assassination attempt," Sayed said.

"They're going to kill him."

"So, you do have something to do with that."

"You have to help him."

"Are you trying to get me killed too?"

"No, I'm trying to save the man I love."

"Why should I? If he dies, maybe, you'll come back to me?"

"Please don't make this more difficult than it already is."

"What exactly are you asking me? "

"Finish the job. Kian-Amir is in Bahrain ready to take over the government."

"That will never work. Even if you kill him, the rest of the government will not just fall apart."

"It already has!" She said. "The dominoes are all in place. The only thing missing is for the first domino to fall."

"You're asking a lot."

"I'm asking you to save our country," she paused. "Don't ask me how I know this, but I know for a fact that Israel has their nuclear weapons pointed at you right now. If we cannot get this done. This war will become nuclear. This is your chance to save the country you love."

"And the man you love at the same time."

"The two are not mutually exclusive."

"I get you left me, but why did you have to go for a special forces soldier from our rival country?"

"I guess I like dangerous men."

"It seems you like to put them in danger too."

"Will you help me?"

"You know I could never say no to you."

"Thank you," she said. I'll be there in sixteen hours."

Tehran, Iran

There were no bombings in the capital that night. Israel knew it had a better chance of letting the people turn the tide. Sayed looked out the window, and all he could see was a sea of people calling for change in their country. In a few rooms down was the handful of people preventing that change. Sayed was not an ideologue. Rather, he was a pragmatist. He knew when the writing was on the wall.

"We have a breach at the east gate," he said through the security radio system. "The east gate is overrun, all units to the east gate." Half of the soldiers posted at the front gate followed orders and hurried to the eastern side of the building, leaving the front gate undermanned. In a separate radio, he said,

"You're clear."

The once peaceful crowd became agitated and violent. They overpowered the guards at the front gate. The barriers fell. Sayed ran into the room where the leaders were gathered.

"The building has been breached. We must evacuate."

"I will not leave my seat," the leader said.

"If you do not leave, we cannot protect you," Sayed said.

"I think we should go," one of the aides said.

"It's now or never, sir," Sayed said. The leader got up and followed Sayed towards the back of the building, where three military helicopters were waiting.

"You are not coming with us?" the leader shouted to Sayed over the clamor of the spinning helicopter blades.

"No sir, this is my base, and these are my men. I must defend them to my last breath."

"We have to go," the pilot said.

"Okay, go," The leader said.

Sayed took out his gun and shot towards the mob that had just broken into the yard. They shot back at him, and before long, he was on the floor, and they were standing over him.

"Okay, I think we're good," One of the men said while giving Sayed a hand up.

"Thank you," Sayed said. "Your work will be felt for centuries. Now to Evin prison, we have no time." Sayed and three other security officers ran to a detached hangar. They boarded a black van. They took off to the infamous Evin prison. They navigated around the chaos unfolding in the city. A mix of celebration and destruction were commingled and hard to differentiate. They arrived at the detention facility within minutes.

"Why are we freeing the Israelis?" one of the security officers said.

"Consider it a peace offering," Sayed said. "One step towards ending this war. One step towards a peaceful Iran." He took his holophone and called Suri.

"It's done. The leader is on his way to Egypt."

"Why did you let him live?"

"It's an insurance policy. We're not trading one dictatorship for another. Your guy better do good by the people."

"What you call an insurance policy, I call a Damocles sword."

Inside Evin Prison

Azael was in solitary confinement, his body bruised all over and his face looking like it had seen better days. He made ridges in the soap to keep his mind tethered to reality. He wondered if he would ever see Suri again. How would she find out what happened to him, and even more, what was happening to her? How could he get out of here to get to her?

He was rummaging through his thoughts when he heard a loud bang on the door. A guard barked orders. Azael didn't make out what he was saying, but he knew the deal. He got on his knees, facing the wall with his hands on his head. When the door opened, he could hear widespread commotion. Azael thought to himself, this must be it. This must be when they make a public example of him as they did his brothers in arms.

This was also his last chance to make a move, escape or die trying. One guard entered the cell. Azael timed his approach with precision. When the guard was a few inches from him, Azael made a volte-face pivot, striking the guard in his diaphragm and landing on his feet. The guard felt the air sucked out and couldn't breathe. Azael took him by the neck, trying to use him as a human shield. The guard used Azael's momentum against him, pushing in the same direction he was pulling, and slammed his back against the wall, causing him to lose his grip. The guard bent to get out of the way of his colleague's aim; the second soldier shot a Taser round at Azael. He fell to the ground in shock. The guard handcuffed him, put a black bag over his head, pulled him up, and rushed him out of the cell.

Azael was still disoriented, but could sense he was outside the prison. He thought this might be when they would execute him. He decided to focus on the last time he saw Suri and took solace in the fact that she was far away, away from all this.

"Here's your prisoner," the guard said. "Be careful, he's a feisty one."

"We'll take it from there," Sayed said. He grabbed Azael by the arm.

"Watch your step," Sayed said to Azael as they entered the vehicle. The ride took about twenty minutes.

They parked behind what looked like an apartment building to the outside world. They went up two flights of stairs.

BAM! BAM! BAM! Sayed knocked on the door. An operative opened the door. As they passed the threshold, Sayed removed the black bag from Azael's head. Everything looked blurry to him while his eyes adjusted to the light. He could feel the handcuffs coming off. His first thought was to fight, but he was immediately disarmed when he discerned the silhouette running towards him.

Suri embraced him with all her strength. Her words, though unintelligible, were as profuse as the tears flowing down her cheeks. Azael was speechless. During his special operations career, he had been trained to respond to any situation, but this time, he was at a loss for words. He had a hard time processing what he was experiencing. All he could do was return the embrace and hold her tight. His tears mixed with hers; somehow, that was all that needed to be said.

"I'm sorry to break your reunion," Sayed said. "But we have to go. We have to get you out of the country before they realize the subterfuge."

The couple pulled apart. Azael looked at her in the eyes and said.

"Thank you. I love you."

She wiped some of her tears away.

"Don't thank me. I was just returning the favor," she said, smiling.

"I'm sorry I failed," Azael said.

"Don't see it that way," Suri responded. "It is better that a true son of Persia took care of it," she said, looking at Sayed. "Now our destiny is in our hands, not that of foreigners. Iran belongs to its people."

"We're ready," the operative said.

"Okay, let's go," Sayed said.

41

WORST CASE SCENARIO

"NEW YORK, WASHINGTON DC, and Miami are gone. So are LA, San Francisco, San Diego. Chicago, Houston, Dallas are gone too." Emilia Shaw, DHS secretary, said. "We lost millions of people. The surviving hospitals can't even make a dent in caring for the injured. Therefore, we can expect to lose even more people to injury and nuclear fallout."

"That's your worst-case scenario?" President Rodriguez asked.

"Yes, sir. If the Axis were to launch a nuclear assault, this is the most likely scenario. They would go after our more populous cities and finish off what they started. Many of our cities are crippled because of the previous EMP attacks. A nuclear attack would take us out entirely."

"Could we intercept their missiles?"

"They have hypersonic missiles," General Dunn said. "We can't intercept. The only thing we can do is to retaliate in kind. Beijing, Shanghai, Moscow, Pyongyang, Tehran would all be gone."

"Can we stop the attack from taking place?"

"Cyber Command is actively undermining our adversaries' capacity to use their nukes like they did ours."

"Right now, sir, the momentum is on our side," Army Chief Kate Simmons said. "We retook most of our territory. The regime change in Tehran gives us some breathing room to focus on the Pacific and Atlantic theaters. We regained full control of our arsenal. We have a short window before their fleet arrives at our shores. If we strike now, we can cut the head of the snake. Stumping the impact of their naval attack. But it will be too late if we wait till their boats get to our waters."

"What's the estimated death toll under that scenario?" the president asked.

"We estimate the immediate casualties resulting from a full-on nuclear attack on the Axis key cities to be between three hundred to five hundred million people,"

"You're asking me to kill half a billion people?"

"We're asking you to fulfill your constitutional duty and save American lives against all enemies, foreign or domestic." Kate Simmons said.

"Actually, sir they're asking you to destroy the human race," Steve said. "You see, they omitted the part about nuclear winter."

"What do you mean?" President Rodriguez asked.

"Everything they said about the nuclear impact and the fallout is true. But that's not all. The aftermath of a full-on nuclear confrontation would create so much smoke that it would block the sun. This would plunge the entire planet into a decade-long dark winter where agriculture would be impossible. So not only would we be killing our enemies, and our allies but also people who have nothing to do with the conflict. The human race would be done."

Columbus, Georgia outside the WDTD studios

"Can we talk?" Kyle asked.

"What is there to talk about?" Ashleigh said. "You made yourself very clear. Well, message received. Let's move on."

"Come on, don't do this," Kyle said.

"Don't do what? Ignore you? Treat you like a piece of trash?"

"I deserve that," Kyle admitted. "Do you know how hard it is to see everything you worked for go down the drain?

"You mean like a relationship you invested in? Yeah, I think I know."

"I messed up, I get it. I wasn't in the right space. I spent years trying to stay clean. Only to go right back to that life."

"We all understand you did that for your nephew. It wasn't right, but we all do things sometimes that aren't right, especially now. What I don't understand is what I did for you to treat me like that?"

"You didn't do anything to deserve that. It's all on me. I think I did that to you so you wouldn't do it to me. Who wants to be with a felon?"

"But isn't that my choice to make? Aren't you the one preaching 'let he who is without sin cast the first stone?'"

Kyle didn't say a word.

"How do you want people to take that seriously if you can't forgive yourself?"

"Can you forgive me?"

Ashleigh didn't respond.

"Truth is, I owe you my life. The night of Ty's arrest, you stepped in and stopped them from shooting at us. That took courage. You risked your life to save ours. You didn't deserve what I did. Can we get a do-over?"

"Nah, I'm sorry. Fool me once, shame on you, fool me twice, shame on me. You had your chance."

"I messed up, I get it. But I need your help."

"Find someone else."

"There is no one else."

"You should've thought of that before you -"

"Topher is alive," Kyle blurted out.

"Huh? No, he's dead. We had a funeral."

"Listen, what I'm about to tell you is highly classified. You cannot tell anyone, and you cannot report on it under any circumstances. Okay?"

She tried to resist the pull, but her curiosity got the best of her.

"Okay. You have my word."

"Topher is alive. He was sent to China on a combat mission. We thought he was killed in action. He wasn't. He was gathering intel about the true origins of the war. He told me it goes deeper than we think. He uploaded a full dossier for us to take to President Rodriguez—"

"Oh, whoa! Things went from 'I'm sorry' to 'let's see the president' pretty fast."

"I know this is a lot to take in, but we don't have a lot of time. We are facing annihilation. If my brother is correct, what is on this server can prevent that from happening. It can give peace a chance. I think it's a risk worth taking."

"Okay, Imma need more than that. Access to those terminals is restricted. I could lose my job."

"You see that flotilla heading our way? If it gets here, we lose everything. Topher said that the dossier has evidence as to the origins of the war. He said both sides were being goaded into it. If we can show the president that he and his counterparts are being manipulated into mutually assured destruction, maybe we can get them to halt the fighting and negotiate peace. Will you help me do that?"

"Ok, for the sake of the planet, I'll help you." She grinned.

Chengdu, China

"Careful. Be very careful," Zang said. "This is TAN territory."

"What is TAN?" "Topher asked.

They were riding in a black Aston Martin DBX courtesy of the Chinese government. The luxury SUV blended perfectly with the surroundings. It was like the war never started. It was like there was no fighting. Las Vegas had nothing on Chengdu. People from all over the world, having bought their place to safety, bet that China and the Axis would emerge victorious, so they ensured their position in the New World Order. Billionaires and centimillionaires were a dime a dozen. The place was sprawling with dignitaries, elites, and heirs to unimaginable fortunes. Topher noticed a subset of individuals mingling with the elites. They were young, with fine clothes and hard faces, like MMA fighters on vacation.

"TAN stands for The Arachnid Network," Zang replied. "With the advanced state of surveillance, various crime organizations and secret societies realized it was too costly to fight one another and law enforcement organizations. They decided to join forces and agreed that the network would solve any differences. They have representatives from every crime syndicate from around the world. It's very hard to determine the extent of their associations. From what we know, TAN includes the Pythons from India, Orchids from Japan, Crimson Moon of North Africa and the Middle

East, the Panther Society of Sub-Saharan Africa, Hoja Blanca of South America Leech from Eurasia, and our own Red Dragons. Those also represent multiple organizations and crime families within their regions. As technology progressed, it became more difficult for them to stay one step ahead of law enforcement. So, they teamed up. They infiltrated every power structure of their societies. They're in governments, industries, and so forth."

"Sounds like the UN of organized crime. What do you think Russo is doing here?"

"That's what we are trying to figure out. As you know, the cabal Russo is a part of is very powerful. They run the world in the shadows. We're not sure why he would risk exposure by meeting with TAN."

They rode for a few minutes, tailing Russo's convoy from a distance.

"You see these guys here." Zang said, pointing to a group of young people at a street corner, and these guys right there?"

"Yeah, I see them."

"They're TAN foot soldiers. They're as lethal as they come."

"I think we tangled with them back in Mexico."

"Yeah, they're the ones who unleashed the virus on your country."

"So, they're the ones who almost killed my son."

"Yes indeed. But to be fair, Russo's group was going to unleash it here. TAN outdid them."

"It's all the same to me. As far as I'm concerned, we can take them all down."

"That might prove more difficult than you think. We don't even know how deep they all go. Hold on—" Zang paused, listening to his com device. "They went in the St. Edwiges Casino Hotel."

Zang and Topher followed Russo and his entourage into the opulent establishment. Zang was dressed in a fine suit fitting the setting, and Topher wore a suit befitting a bodyguard of sorts. They went through tables of baccarat, roulette, craps, and the like. The bars were full of people reveling and having a merry time. Russo arrived at the back of the casino, where there were gigantic mahogany doors. A pair of dragons were crested in the doors, and the handles were sculpted king cobras. Passed that point, even his entourage was not allowed to follow. Two TAN soldiers escorted Russo.

Zang and Topher sat at the nearest bar.

"We need eyes inside that room," Topher said.

"Working on it, "Zang replied. He then spoke softly in Mandarin in his com's unit. The voice on the other side responded. Zang then translated, "They're narrowing in on that room." He signaled a bartender. "Cognac," he said. "Order something and look happy," he told Topher.

"Martini," Topher ordered.

"Okay, we have access to five holophones and two hidden cameras.

Zang pulled out his holophone and put it in private screen mode. He smiled as if he was watching something interesting. It was as if they were in the room.

The henchmen had taken Russo to their leader. A man by the name of Tang Lang. His Rolex Volcano 18k Ruby and Diamond watch matched his flamboyant red velvet suit and crimson hair.

"Mr. Russo, I hope you liked our gifts," Tang Lang said.

"Mr. Tang Lang, a.k.a. the War Wolf. Bodies of dead people at my doorsteps, not exactly my idea of Christmas gifts, but I get your point."

"We were impressed with how you concealed the matter from your family. You are quite an astute man."

"You seem to know a lot about me. I presume you know why I'm here?"

"Enlighten me."

"It seems we are engaged in a mutually assured destruction scenario. You kill our people. We kill your people."

"Isn't that what you wanted? What did you call it? Depopulation, or Preservation?"

"Preservation, but that's beside the point."

"Would you be that concerned with lives if your plan had succeeded? Were you not planning on unleashing the plague on our populations?"

"A necessary evil for the preservation of humanity as a whole."

"Well, consider this our contribution to world preservation. I am going to be honest. Many on our side reveled at the sight of the once great American empire on its knees like a child squirming for her mommy. Australia is not far behind Mr. Russo. Maybe your children will be next. For, what is Australia without America?"

At the bar, hearing the conversation, Topher had flashes of Ryan, what he went through, and of Kyle going to jail, and the suffering inflicted upon Columbus. He subtly reached for his gun in his suit jacket with his right hand.

"Not now," Zang said, putting his hand on Topher's left hand, still resting on the bar counter. "Your time will come."

Inside the chamber, Russo said, "Eventually, the war will come here."

"I doubt that. But if it does, we have contingencies, as do you. The only contingency you didn't count on was the plague being released in your lands. So now you want a truce."

"What we want is a mutually agreeable settlement that ensures the prosperity and posterity of our respective orders and legacies."

"Why would the dragon negotiate with the ant?"

"You cannot think you are going to win this war?"

"Oh, but we are winning. Soon, the Atlantic and Pacific fleets will be in position to crush the head of the snake and unleash the fury of a nuclear holocaust on Western powers."

"You think President Chen will order the killing of hundreds of millions of people?"

"Hundreds of millions? Billions is more likely. Total destruction of America, Europe, and their vassal states."

"President Chen will never go for such levels of destruction. It would destroy China as well."

"President Chen will do whatever we want. The ego of that man is so big, we can get him to kill his own mother to satisfy it."

"You're insane," Russo said.

"Please save me from the moral outrage. Is it different from what you wanted to do to our populations?"

Russo had no response.

"But fear not, you will not have to witness it. I hope your house is in order, Mister Russo. Little Ruby will surely miss her grandpa."

"Let's not be hasty now. Surely, we can come to an agreement?"

Back at the bar, Topher said, "They're going to kill him. We need to get in there."

"Can you help?" Zang said in his com unit.

"Yes, earplugs now," the operator said.

Zang pulled out two pairs of earplugs and handed a pair to Topher.

"Put these on and cover your face," Zang said. They put the earplugs on, laid their faces on the counter, and covered their heads.

It took about twenty seconds before a sonic deflagration sent everyone to the floor in agony. All the glass in the blast's radius shattered.

"Are you okay?" Zang asked Topher.

"Yeah, I'm good," Topher responded. "A little shaken, but I'm good."

"Okay, let's get him out of there before they get back on their feet."

Topher and Zang, guns in hand, headed for the VIP room. Everybody was on the floor in agony. Topher spotted Tang Lang on the floor. He stood over him, his gun aimed squarely at his forehead, finger on the trigger.

"Not like this," Zang said, putting his hand on Topher's shoulder and then pointing to Russo on the floor.

Topher grabbed Russo and put him on his shoulders like he was one of his fallen brothers in arms.

"Vehicle is waiting for you on the back of the building," The coms said.

Topher and Zang made their way through the kitchen area and walked around floored personnel throughout their exit route. The Aston Martin DBX was waiting for them in the back of the building. The blaring sounds of police and ambulance sirens were getting louder every second.

"Get us out of here now," Zang said.

"Where are we going?" Topher asked.

"Back to Beijing."

Undisclosed location in the Rocky Mountains on the tarmac

"Thank you, Steve, "General Boykin said. "Getting us here on such short notice was a 'tour de force.'"

"Don't mention it, General. Getting you here was the easy part. Getting you to the president is the hard part. But we'll have to figure it out." Steve said.

"Pardon my manners. Steve, this is Ashleigh Williams. Her outlet provided the terminal for the dossier.

"Pleased to meet you, Ashleigh," Steve responded.

"This is Tyrone Greene. Our communications analyst. He provided the sat phone we reached you on."

"Nice to meet you, Tyrone."

"Nice to meet you, too," Ty G said.

"And you know my son,"

"Yes, nice to see you again, Kyle."

"Nice to see you too. Can I ask you? Where is the president's head at now?"

"As you can expect, the president and the war cabinet are bent on fighting this war till the bitter end."

"Even if that means the end of mankind?" Ashleigh said.

"Yes, as long as we're the last ones standing," Steve replied.

"And that's what they're counting on," Kyle said. "Big powers bent on winning no matter the cost."

"What are the casualty assessments?" General Boykin asked.

"We're looking at a billion people worldwide at least."

"How about this side?" Ty G asked.

"If all our defenses fail, twenty-five to one hundred million."

"Oh my—" Ashleigh said, stunned.

"That's just with the initial hits. The following radiation, societal collapse, and nuclear winter could triple that number. Our people are barely adapting to life post-EMP attack. Nuclear strikes would couple the EMP, kinetic destruction, and long-term radiation."

"So, if we get hit, the nukes would take out our remaining electronics, destroy wherever they fall, and make those places uninhabitable for generations," Kyle said.

"Exactly. We won't recover." Steve said as silence fell upon the group.

The vibration of a government-issued holophone broke the silence. Steve took a look at the device. "We have to go. Urgent war room meeting. This might be our chance."

They boarded two black full-size SUVs. Five military-grade Hummers escorted them to their destination. The ride through the winding mountains took about twenty minutes. Nested deep within the Rocky Mountains hid the Fortress, the last stand of the US Government.

"No unauthorized civilians allowed," the guard said.

"They're with me," Steve said. "The president cleared them." He handed the guard and executive authorization stamped with the President's Seal.

The guard reviewed the authorization letter, confirmed with his terminal, and let them through.

They went through vehicle scanners, several protocols and checkpoints. The vehicles entered the underground compound. Steve led them to the secure war room.

War Room

"Good to see you, old fox," General Dunn said to General Boykin. "I'm sorry about your boy. He was one of our finest. He will be truly missed."

"Thank you—"

"Ladies and gentlemen, let's start," President Rodriguez said, entering the room with a heavy Secret Service presence. Everybody rose to their feet. "Please be seated," he said. "I understand that we have civilians joining us. General Boykin, thank you for your service and your sacrifice. This nation is in your debt."

"Thank you, sir." General Boykin answered.

"Steve, I authorized this because it came from you," the president said. "But we don't have a lot of time. So please make it quick."

"Thank you, sir. I believe they have intel, which you should consider before we make our next move. The fate of the world depends on it."

"With due respect sir," General Dunn said. "We are in the middle of military operations. We do not have time for this."

"Let them speak," President Rodriguez said.

"Kyle the floor is yours," Steve said.

"Thank you. Mr. President. This war is fake," Kyle said. He was an experienced public speaker. He knew that starting with a shock statement would get their attention. "How do I know?" Kyle asked rhetorically.

"I know because my brother, Sergeant Major Christopher Boykin, is still alive." He continued as Ashleigh handed the president a copy of the dossier.

"My brother reached out to me with evidence that this administration, NATO, and our opponents were goaded into this war that nobody wants." He paused and took a sip of water. "Sir, what if I told you that despite every country thinking they are acting of their own accord, they are controlled by hidden forces? What if I told you that your next move, which you think is yours, is already predetermined? What if I told you that you are unknowingly doing the bidding of unelected, extra-governmental individuals who frankly run the world?"

"I would ask you for the evidence of what you are alleging," the president said.

"In your hands is a dossier detailing people, places, and methods applied to get us to where we are today, which is the brink of annihilation."

"To what end?"

"Power and depopulation. They believe the earth's finite resources cannot sustain the current population growth projections."

"So, they're trying to destroy the earth to save it?" Kate Simmons said incredulously, glancing at Steve. "And aren't they in the world they are trying to destroy, I mean save?"

"From their standpoint," Kyle said. "It's a controlled destruction. The cities being destroyed are already depleted of their natural resources. The radiation fallout will go out over time. They have set cities and retreats to wait it out and restart in their utopia."

"And who are the members of that group?" Emilia Shaw asked.

"We don't have the full roster, but in the dossier, you will recognize some prominent names," Steve answered. "All significant leaders holding the levers of power. Media, energy, technology, and the list goes on."

"Enough!" Dunn said. "Steve, I am sick and tired of you undermining this administration and this country at every turn!"

"I'm protecting this country," Steve said.

"Mr. President, we are in a kinetic war against the biggest nuclear power and the biggest army in the world. We do not have time for conspiracy theories," Dunn said.

"Excuse me, but you have to see this," a military aide said, turning on the holoscreen.

"What now?" the president said, looking at the live rendition of the Atlantic war theater. "What's this? Are we infested with locusts?"

"No sir, those are Chinese drones," The aide said. Countless drones, as far as the eye could see, were reminiscent of a swarm of destructive locusts.

"Sir, they're about thirty minutes' flight from our fleet." General McIntyre said. "We need authorization to deploy HAARP overtly."

"But that would open a can of worms and raise questions we might not want to answer," Emilia Shaw said.

"If we don't, we might not be around to answer those questions."

"Get them out of here," the president said, pointing at Kyle and his cohort.

"Sir, it doesn't have to be that way," Kyle pleaded.

"You heard the president. Get them out of here," Dunn said. "All of them." He looked at General Boykin.

An aide brought them to their temporary quarters within the bunker.

"Patch through the General Thompson," Chairman of the Joint Chiefs McIntyre said. "General, as you know, the swarm of drones is heading your way. But the weather forecast changed in your favor. Get ready for some rough seas and high tailwinds."

"Roger that," General Thompson replied.

In the Quarters

"What is HAARP?" Ashley asked.

"It's classified," General Boykin said. "Don't worry about it. Worry about convincing the commander-in-chief to resolve this conflict as quickly as possible with minimum casualties."

"Looks like they want the maximum casualties," Ty G said.

"I just don't know what else to do," Kyle said. "They're not trying to listen to what we have to say."

"I've been in these rooms," General Boykin said. "We're trained to do one thing and one thing only, and that's to win. We don't look at total casualties, just American casualties. We do whatever it takes to minimize them. So, they won't stop until China is defeated, or we are, and we can't be."

"So, what can we do?" Kyle asked.

"Son, you're a pastor, not a soldier. There's nothing you can do at this point. You did what you could. But now it's out of your hands. So, you do what you preachers do. Pray for a miracle 'cause that is the only thing that will stop this catastrophe."

On the high seas of the Atlantic Ocean

"Brace for impact!" General Thompson said as the first shots were fired from the swarm. Live ammunition and rockets were unleashed at the American fleet. The ship sustained a direct hit from a rocket.

"Fire at will!" General Thompson ordered the gunmen. "Where is that hurricane?" he said to his second officer.

"Sir, we have meteorological disturbances heading our way," a shipmate said.

"All non-fighting personnel below deck now." The general ordered. "Gunmen keep firing at will. Hold the line and wait for my signal."

The gunmen kept spraying bullets at the sky. The more drones they shot down, the more seemed to be coming. At first, there were a few drops of rain, then it drizzled, and within five minutes, the winds intensified.

"Pull everyone below deck!" General Thompson said. "All gunmen below deck now!"

A few minutes later, the second officer said, "Everybody is below deck."

"Okay, good," General Thompson said.

"Now what?"

"Just hold on tight and watch," The general answered.

The wind rocked the ships like they were ping pong balls. After a few minutes, tornado cells formed about a quarter mile from the fleet. The meteorological anomaly caused the drones to be wind-damaged and disoriented, and the added resistance depleted their batteries. An hour later, the shipmates were on deck looking at the remnants of countless lifeless drones floating.

"What was that?" the second officer asked.

"It's classified," General Thompson said with a grin.

In the war room

"Sir, the drones are down," the joint chief said as they cheered.

"Good job, everyone," President Rodriguez said. "How long before the Fleets come face to face?"

"About forty-eight hours, sir," the joint chief said.

"Let's recess," the president said. "Get rest. You will need it."

42

LEVERS AND TRIGGERS

THE PRESIDENT RETIRED TO what served as the presidential residence in the underground compound. Every time President Rodriguez opened the door, he was taken aback. He had a sense of awe that never got old. The pristine marble floors perfectly matched the wallcoverings, working in concert with the Brazilian rosewood furniture to convey serene opulence. The grand piano brought a sense of order amid chaos and beauty amid the horrors of war. Every time he needed to escape the burden that was his to bear, he would sit at this timeless work of art and do it justice. He would play with abandon, performing equally magnificent musical pieces. But today, the place was already taken. His little genius was already there, playing to her heart's content. She stopped when she saw who was at the door.

"Grandpa, Grandpa!" the seven-year-old Aurora said.

"Ha! How's my cupcake!" President Rodriguez said.

"Hey, Dad!" Esperanza said.

"Hi, Honey," the president said to his daughter. The first lady approached the president with a look on her face. President Rodriguez recognized that look. She hugged him.

"What's wrong?" the president asked softly in her ear.

"I'm sorry," she said.

"What are you sorry for?" he replied.

She walked him to his office. The room was reminiscent of the Oval Office.

"I think you should listen to him."

The president didn't say a word, wondering how that was possible and pondering what his next move should be. Finally, he said,

"How did you get in here?" As soon as the words left his lips, he realized it was a useless question to ask.

"This is what we do, sir."

"I'm glad you're alive."

"You have to stop this."

"So, your brother told me."

"It's true, sir."

"I should call the Secret Service."

"Don't do that to them. They have families."

"Are you threatening my family and me?"

"No, sir. You are the commander-in-chief. I followed my orders to the grave and back. But everything my brother told you is true."

"How do you know? Last time I checked, you are special forces, not CIA."

"I just flew a clandestine flight back from China. While there, we caught one of them."

"One of who? The cabal?"

"They call themselves the Consortium. We got one of their top guys. I can show you."

"Go ahead."

Topher put his holographic device down on the desk. It displayed a three-dimensional rendition of Topher & Zang questioning Quartum back at the operations center.

"Start talking," Topher said on the holographic projection.

"We know you're with the Consortium," Zang said. Quartum, seated on a chair with his hands tied behind his back, stayed quiet.

"Okay, here's what we know," Zang continued. "Robert Russo, to the outside world, you're the CEO of Lithosphere Capital, one of the biggest investment banks in the world. You sit on various philanthropic boards and think tanks. But who are you really? What is your position in the Consortium?"

"I don't know what you're talking about."

"Save it. You're wasting your time. Right now, here are your options: you can talk to us, or you can talk to them," Zang said, displaying surveillance images of TAN soldiers searching Chengdu and other cities. "They're all looking for you."

"From how that conversation was going, it doesn't look like they like you a lot," Topher added. "It'd be a shame if they got their hands on you."

"So, let's start with—"

"How about we start with you removing those restraints? They're hurting my wrist," Robert said. "I'll give you the information you want if you give me what I want."

"What is it you want?" Zang asked.

"It's true, I'm part of the Consortium. At least, I was until recently. They turned on me. I need protection. They're all over the world. There are only a few places where it would be harder for them to get to me. China happens to be one of them.

"Political asylum?"

"More like disappearance. A new life for me and my family."

"An international witness protection program?" Topher said.

"Sure, call it what you want," Robert said dismissively."

"Okay, we will arrange for that," Zang said.

"How do I know you have the power to make me disappear?"

"Because we already did. Where are you right now?"

Russo did not answer.

"Who knows you're here?" Zang continued. "If we were to pull the trigger, who would find your body?" He removed Robert's restraints. "Yes, we can make you disappear, but we can also make you reappear right back in a TAN stronghold."

"Fine, what do you want to know?"

"Who is the Consortium?"

"Easy, open the Journal. All the biggest corporations in America, Europe, and the so-called West are represented. Then flip the pages of the Post. Most big-name politicians, senators, congressmen, and ministers are on our payroll. Some knowingly, others unknowingly, but we control them. We have people in most cabinets of world governments."

"There must be thousands of companies, politicians, and so on," Topher commented.

"Yes, but when you go up the chain of ownership, it all comes down to a few of us in control."

"Is that where you come in? A world-renowned investment banker?" Zang said.

"Yes, I coordinate the contact between the stakeholders and the principals."

"What are you saying in plain English?" Topher said.

"You're military?" Russo asked.

"Yes,"

"Okay, so you are a soldier, I presume. We have soldiers, too. They are politicians, media figures, athletes, celebrities, and anyone with influence. They push our narratives. We tell them what to stand for and what to fight for, and they do it. The masses look up to them, so they follow them. When needed, we have the ARM. Our version of special ops. They do the dirty work that no government agency can do. Up that chain, we have generals, basically CEOs of companies, high-ranking politicians, etc. I would be considered the chairman of the Joint Chiefs. I am the link between the generals and the commander-in-chief of our organization."

"Who is that?"

"I don't even know. Never saw him outside our organization. He's not a CEO or founder of an NGO or think tank. But what he says goes. We refer to him as Primus."

"How do they refer to you?"

"I'm Quartum."

"So, he is the first, you are the fourth. How many are there?" Zang said.

"Seven. Each with oversight of a critical sector of our operations. We are the Council."

"What is your purpose?"

"Simple, maintain the world order and the perennity of the human race within that order."

"How do you achieve that?" Topher asked.

"Control of the masses."

"Humans can be unpredictable. How can you control billions of people?"

"You are correct, soldier. People can be hard to control, but you would be surprised how easy the masses are to control. All you have to figure out is the right levers to push and the right triggers to pull."

"Let me guess, that's where the media comes in?" Topher asked.

"Very good soldier, very good. The public doesn't understand that the job of the media is not to tell them the truth, the whole truth, nothing but the truth. But to tell them what to believe and when to believe it."

"Do you tell them how to vote?"

"Of course, sometimes this side, sometimes that side. A young face when we need it, an old face when it suits us."

"So, you got Rodriguez elected?"

"Rodriguez? Ah, this one slipped through. Every now and then, you have one of those unknown quantities that upset the apple cart. Rodriguez is his own man. By the time we realized he would win, it was too late. But that's okay. We have enough soldiers throughout his government and his opposition to keep him under control."

"How?" Zang said.

"Levers and triggers," Russo said. "It's all levers and triggers. Rodriguez is a proud man. He wants to make the history books. Be amongst the greats. Maybe get carved on Mount Rushmore. The first Hispanic president of the United States. Men with egos are the easiest to control because you know exactly how they'll react."

"What happens when they don't react as you expect?" Topher asked.

"It depends, but if they pose a serious problem to our operations, they might commit suicide, car accident, or get cancer. Remind me, how did Senator Woods die?

"Heart failure," Topher replied.

"Ah, yes, congenital heart failure. The cleanest way to remove a threat."

"You killed Woods?"

"We granted him his wish. He was tired of wars and opposed what was shaping up to be our most critical operation."

Images of Woods and his dad flooded Topher's mind.

"You murderer—" Topher said, but Zang stopped him from hurting him.

"Why did you kill Woods?" Zang asked.

"He was getting sentimental. He openly opposed our plans. We had to send a clear message. To be fair, I tried to save him, but he went too far too fast."

"So, you killed him because he opposed the war?" Topher asked.

"That's right. We had to send a clear message."

"So, you orchestrated this war?" Topher asked. "All of this destruction, a pandemic that nearly killed my son!"

"The pandemic didn't go as planned."

"What went wrong?" Zang asked.

"We intended the pandemic to hit Asia, Africa, and South America and be contained there. But TAN beat us to it and, unfortunately, released it in America. Which is a shame. The order I mentioned is threatened because if America loses the war, all the allies fall with her."

"Is that why you're seeking asylum? You think America will lose?"

"No, I think America will win. I seek asylum because the Council blames me for the setbacks. They are not very forgiving. But America will win because Rodriguez will not want to go out as the one who presided over the fall of an empire. He will use the last tool in his arsenal."

"Nuclear weapons," Zang said.

"So, destroy the world to preserve your order?" Topher said.

"So overly dramatic. The world won't end. Some places will be rendered inhabitable for some time. But the upsides are that the world population will be reduced, and we will maintain the order."

"You're sick!" Topher said.

"Enough!" President Rodriguez said. "You can turn it off."

"Are you sure?" Topher said. "There's more."

"I heard enough."

"What are you going to do about it?"

"What can I do about it?"

"As commander-in-chief, you can order the troops to stand down and diplomats to step up and talk to the Axis."

"You think it's that easy?"

"It's that easy, sir." You give the order, and the soldiers follow. It's that simple."

"What if they don't reciprocate, and that posture leaves us vulnerable?"

"You don't leave our defensive posture, but you can signal peace."

"What about these invisible armies of Consortiums and Councils, or whatever they call themselves? Do you think they will take it lying down?"

"Probably not. But it's worth the fight. You're the leader of the free world. If your grandchild is to grow up in a better world, it's a fight you must take. I'm right here, ready to fight with you. I know it's scary. They killed Woods. He was your friend."

"He was more than a friend. He was my mentor."

"They killed him because he opposed the war. They killed him because he decided to stand up for what's right. All I'm asking is that you do the same. You stand up for the millions of people who will die. You said you would be a voice for the voiceless. Please, I beg of you, stand up for them. Just stand down so peace can prevail."

"Okay, fine. You'll come with me." He picked up his desk phone.

"Convene the whole team in the command center in thirty minutes," he said to the dispatcher.

"Sir. Can I see my father and brother?"

"Of course."

Secret Service agents led Topher to his family's quarters. The walk was a few minutes. Topher updated them on the situation. After short goodbyes with his family, he returned to the presidential section. The president and Topher headed to the command center with a Secret Service escort. The president was the last one in the room.

"You may be seated," President Rodriguez said. "Thank you all for coming. What's the status?"

"Sir, the fleets are still hours away from the initial impact," General McIntyre said.

"What's our posture?"

"We are outnumbered ten to one, sir. Between the Chinese, Russians, North Koreans, and many other Axis countries."

"Any word from our allies?"

"No sir, just platitudes, no serious commitments."

"What about Article Five? 'An attack on one is an attack on all?'"

"Our biggest NATO allies are fighting in their own lands, the smaller ones are sending us blankets and extra batteries."

"We spent trillions of dollars and countless American lives delivering countries from tyranny," President Rodriguez said. "No one is there for us when it matters."

"We do have good news, if we can call it that," The joint chief said.

"Cyber command has a high level of confidence they have neutralized the Russian and Chinese nuclear arsenals," General Dunn said. "We can hit them hard. Cut the head of the snake before it can bite."

"What does 'high level of confidence' mean?" the president asked.

"It's eighty percent, sir," General Dunn answered.

"So, there's a twenty percent chance that they can respond in kind? So, there's a twenty percent chance of mutually assured destruction."

"Yes, sir," General Dunn said.

"If I may, sir," Emilia Shaw, DHS secretary, said. "If we don't proceed with the nuclear strike, we face a ninety percent chance of our destruction."

"Understood," Rodriguez said. "Here's what we're going to do. We are going to stand down."

"Sir, I don't think that's a good idea," General Dunn said.

"We are going to stand down, reach out to the Chinese and Russian administrations, and negotiate a peaceful settlement."

"Sir, are you sure about this?" Emilia Shaw said. "We have lands that are still not back under our control. Like New York and San Francisco, to name those two."

"We will keep our nuclear posture. Negotiate a full return of our lands, and we will return the lands our troops are currently occupying.

"So, we're going to surrender, we're going to lose this war?" Kate Simmons said.

"We are not surrendering and definitely not losing this war. We are winning the future. The future of our children and our children's children."

"Sir, with due respect, this is not one of your rallies. It is war," Dunn said. "We do not surrender. We do not back down. We have our shot. We take it."

"I appreciate your sentiment and your dedication, General. But the decision is made. Get the Axis presidents on the line." The president gestured for the dispatch to make the call.

The dispatch went through the communication protocols to get the presidents of Russia, China, and North Korea together.

"I'm afraid I can't let you do that," General Dunn said.

"I beg your pardon?" President Rodriguez said.

"Sir, I'm afraid you are not in a position to make the right decisions for this country."

"How dare you?"

"Agents, please escort Mr. Rodriguez and Mr. Boykin to their quarters and await further orders."

"Yes, sir," Agent Brown said. "Please follow us, gentlemen."

"You better not touch me," Rodriguez said.

"Sir, I think it's best to comply," Topher said. The soldier knew that sometimes retreat was the best way to win.

The secret service escorted Rodriguez back to his quarters and Topher to the quarters where Kyle and his father were being held.

"What happened, son?" General Boykin said. "Are we putting an end to this madness?"

"I'm afraid not," Topher replied. "After seeing the evidence and receiving confirmation from Zang that the Chinese president was ready to talk. Rodriguez agreed to pause the fighting to start negotiations. But then the true colors came out."

"What does that mean?" Kyle said.

"General Dunn unilaterally removed the president and me from the room."

"What?" Kyle said.

"They can't do that," Ashleigh said.

Ty G chuckled and shook his head.

"You find that funny?" Topher said.

"Nah, man. But y'all think this country is based on laws. It's always been based on power. Right now, that Dunn dude has the power. If y'all want to stop this thing, y'all got to figure out how to get the power back to Rodriguez."

43

LOCKED AND LOADED

"HOW IS THAT POSSIBLE?" Ashleigh said. "They can't just remove the president. He's the commander-in-chief."

"Apparently, they just did," Kyle said. "How? I'm not sure, but it's crazy."

"It's simple, son," General Boykin said. "We let corporations run our lives, from the Fed to the Internet to our weapons program; corporations run everything. The problem is that corporations can be bought, so they were, and here we are."

"How do we stop it?" Kyle said.

"Ty G is right," Topher said. "We have to give the power back to Rodriguez."

"How?" Ashleigh asked.

"The ultimate power in this country is with the people," Topher said. "I'm not sure how to do it, but we need to get to Rodriguez. Have him address the people of the world and the Axis presidents in the same breath."

"I have my broadcast kit, and I can contact the station to stream it and broadcast it on the airways."

"Yeah, but as soon as we get out of here, they'll spot us on the cameras," Kyle said.

"I took them out," Topher said. "In about thirty minutes, these guys will wake up with a bad headache tied up in a closet."

"What about Dunn and the rest?" General Boykin asked.

"We need to stop them from ordering the nuclear strike," Topher answered.

"Looks like y'all gonna need some guns. How y'all gonna get that?" Ty G said.

"Leave that to me," Topher said. "Ashleigh and Kyle, you got Rodriguez. Pops, Ty G, and I got the command center." Topher then gave Kyle a holophone and instructions on how to contact Zang.

"Everybody get back," Topher said and then shouted, "Help! We need help!" When secret service agents opened the door, Topher, in one fluid motion, struck the first agent with a slap to the carotid. He instantaneously collapsed unconscious. With his left hand, he stopped the upward motion of the agent's drawing his weapon and knocked him out with his right hand. He tied and gagged them up.

Each agent had a machine gun, a sidearm, and an ankle pistol. Topher handed a gun to his dad, Kyle, and Ashleigh, then handed the machine gun to Ty G. He kept the remaining ankle pistol.

"Here are your guns," Topher said. Ty G didn't say anything. He just grinned at Topher.

"Thank you, son, but it's only Americans in this building. Are you ready to shoot your own?" General Boykin said.

"I swore an oath not to any one man but to the country's constitution. Right now, the duly elected president of the United States is held against his will in an illegal coup. As a result, billions of people stand to die, and the world as we know it will be destroyed. So, listen carefully. This is it. There's no easy way out of this one. The only way out of this is through it. On the other side of this door are tons of agents. They will converge on this position as soon as the first shot is fired. If they're shooting at us, find cover. When they reload, shoot back. Whatever happens, keep moving forward. We are out of time. The only thing that matters right now is the mission. For some of us, that means we might have to say our goodbyes on the other side of this. Are you all good with that?"

"Yeah, we're good," Ashleigh said.

"We got this, bro," Kyle said, cocking his gun.

That is when Topher realized something had changed in his brother, and he could tell Ashleigh, the TV girl, had changed too. But it turned out he had changed as well.

"Kyle, pray for us before we head out," Topher said.

Kyle was not expecting this request from his brother, but obliged without skipping a beat.

"Father God. Be with us, protect us, help us save this planet. In Jesus' name. Amen."

All said, "Amen."

"Alright, let's execute," Topher said.

"Hold on," General Boykin said. "I'll buy you some time. I'll create a diversion to pull some of their forces from your path. Like that, I won't slow you down either."

"Okay, be careful, Dad," Topher said.

"I will. You'll know when to go."

General Boykin headed to the entrance of the compound. He was able to walk around unimpeded as a man in uniform. When he made it to the entrance elevator. He was stopped by the guards.

"Sir, can we help you?" One of the guards asked.

"I need to get out of here, son," the general said.

"Sorry, sir. At this time, no one gets in, and no one gets out."

"You don't understand. I need to get out of here," the general yelled. He started to act upset and panicked. He then pulled out the gun.

"Gun!" The guard said as he pulled out his gun.

"Code black, we have a code black. Entrance elevator." The other guard said in the comms. Immediately, a swarm of guards and agents converged on that position. Surrounded by guards and agents, the general put his hands up, laid the gun down on the floor, kicked it toward a guard, and said,

"I surrender."

Upon hearing the commotion, Topher said,

"Okay, let's go!" The coast was cleared until they approached the presidential suite.

They first went to the presidential quarters. Topher peeked around the corner leading to the presidential suite. Four agents were guarding it. He signaled the rest of the team to be quiet and wait. One of the agents ventured too close to the corner, and then there were three. Preferring not to spill the blood of fellow Americans, Topher whispered to the team, on his signal to point, not shoot.

"Put your hands up!" Topher shouted as the team overtook the guards. In record fashion, the agents drew their weapons. "Don't do anything stupid," Topher said, still moving towards the guards. "We're not here to hurt the president. Do not lose your life for nothing. Dunn is making a big mistake. We can save this world. It doesn't have to end this way. President Rodriguez can stop it. But for that, I need you to stand down. I need you to let us through. Remember your oath."

The math was simple: they were outgunned, and to pull the trigger would be certain death. One by one, the guards laid down their weapons and put their hands on their heads.

"Turn around," Topher ordered. He gave zip ties to Ty G. "Tie them up." When Ty G was done tying them up, Topher banged on the door, calling to the president. He opened the door.

"Mr. President, we can broadcast your message to the world," Topher said. "Chen is willing to do the same."

"What about Dunn? You know I'm willing to do it. But it won't mean a thing if the nukes start annihilating cities all over the world."

"Sir, let me take care of Dunn, you take care of delivering the message," Topher said. "Kyle, Ashleigh, you're up. As soon as we close that door, barricade it. Trust no one but us."

"All right, Boykin, whenever you ready," Ty G said.

"Okay, let's go," Topher said. They headed towards the command center in the underground maze.

"Holl up," Ty G said. "Gimme the extra gun,"

"What?"

"We need to split up," Ty G said. "In them streets, we do that a lot. We got a guy do a little somethin' so the police or other gangs go after him while we take care of business on the other side of town."

"So, what are you thinking?"

"You said you took out the camera, right?"

"Yes, they're blind."

"Imma draw them this way while you go up one floor and back down the other side close to the command center. For that, Imma need firepower 'cause I ain't tryin' to die down here. My mom's still alive. She can't lose her boy like that. You feel me?"

"Yeah, I got you. That might actually work," Topher said, handing the handgun to Ty G.

"All right, I'll see you on the other side."

Ty G headed towards the command center. Topher went up the flight of stairs a few feet from them. Ty G gave it a few minutes, then shut the lights in the hallway leading to the command center. He drew first blood, shooting a guard in the shoulder.

Not bad, bruh, he thought to himself. The response was swift; bullets started flying toward him. He could feel the wind of a couple of them barely missing his face. He took cover around the corner and ran as fast as he could in the opposite direction. He could hear the agents shout,

"Code Black, Code Black. Sublevel four. Section A."

Ty G found a machinery room he could take cover in with only one way in. As long as he had bullets, he could hold them off. He took a cover position behind some heavy machines. As he heard the footsteps, he fired a barrage from the machine gun. He didn't hit anyone but sent a message to his would-be assailants.

"Come out with your hands up," an agent said. "There is no way out."

Ty G responded with a few more shots. Then he said, "I want my lawyer."

"That's not how it works," the agent responded. "An assault team is on its way. I suggest you surrender now because when they arrive, they won't ask nicely."

"I know my rights. I want my lawyer," He shouted back. He acted defiantly, but he knew time was not on his side.

"Make a hole!" another agent said.

Ty G knew that meant the strike team had arrived. He fired random shots towards the entrance and ran to the back of the room. He heard the clanging sound of the impact grenade hitting the ground. He covered his face and ears. The distance and his countermeasures decreased the impact, but not enough. He was still disoriented. He fired towards what he thought was the entrance, but his shot was off to the side. When he paused, the strike team stormed in and shot back. The heavy machinery served as Ty G's fortress. Most of the shots ricocheted, but one somehow found its way through the machinery into Ty G's chest. His right pectoral burned with intense pain as he fell on his back, barely able to breathe. He saw the room spin around him, and everything became blurry. He saw lights coming all around him. His breath was becoming fainter. He said,

"Sorry, Momma."

Ty G's plan worked. Topher made it to the command center unimpeded. There were five agents on guard. With the element of surprise on his side, Topher calculated that the first two would not stand a chance. For the third one, it would be a contest of speed and precision. The fourth and fifth ones would have a clear shot. He could maybe dodge one, or maybe they could both get him. There was no time to come up with a better alternative. When he signed up for military service, he thought he would be fighting foreigners. He never thought so many Americans would be at the end of his gun barrel. He repassed his oath of enlistment in his mind.

"I, Christopher Boykin, do solemnly swear that I will support and defend the Constitution of the United States against all enemies, foreign and domestic; that I will bear true faith and allegiance to the same; and that I will obey the orders of the President of the United States and the orders of the officers appointed over me, according to regulations and the Uniform Code of Military Justice. So, help me, God."

"God forgive me. When you see them, tell them I'm sorry."

Bang! The first agent fell to the ground.

Bang! The second agent fell to the ground.

The other three drew their weapons. *Bang! Bang! Bang!* Topher rolled to the ground and dodged the first barrage while shooting down the third guard. He caught him falling and used him as a human shield. He protected Topher from two shots, but the third one went through the body and hit him on the side of the stomach area.

Bang! Bang! The fourth and fifth guards fell to the ground.

Topher felt the pain. He assessed the damage. He thanked God it was a flesh wound. It hurt, but he would be okay. He placed the third guard's hand on the biometric reader, opening the door to another hallway leading to the command center.

Inside the Command Center

"First contact is imminent, sir," The operator said to General Dunn.

"Warheads?" General Dunn asked.

"Warheads engaged cyber command, ready to initiate launch. We have locks on Beijing, Moscow, Pyongyang, and Tehran. For the first wave."

"On my signal," Dunn said. "Five, four, three, two, one. Do it,"

"Don't!" Topher shouted, guns drawn. One towards the operator, the other towards Dunn. "Step away from the terminal."

"Son, look around you," Dunn said. "You're hurt, and you're outgunned. This launch is going to happen. It will happen with you dead or with you alive. The choice is yours. Stand down now!"

"I might die here today. Trust me, if I do, I'll take you with me. This is your last warning. Abort the launch. Do it now."

"Drop your weapons," a voice said.

Topher heard the order as he felt the barrel of a gun against the back of his head.

"Drop your weapons," the voice said again. Topher put his weapons down on the floor.

"As a matter of fact, everybody put your hands up," Steve said, entering the room with a contingent of soldiers and agents. "By order of the rightful and duly elected president of the United States, Fernando Ismael Rodriguez-Estrada, you're under arrest for seditious conspiracy and treason."

"Steve, you're making a huge mistake!" Dunn said. "If we don't act now, we are done! They will take us out."

"No, you made a mistake when you thought you could overthrow the president," Steve replied. "And you're wrong about this. We do not have to destroy the world to protect our country and our values. Thankfully, I'm not the only one thinking that."

The emergency alert alarm blared for a few seconds before a composite image of the presidents of the United States, China, Russia and the NATO commander appeared from their respective offices.

"This is a joint broadcast of the presidents of the United States, China, Russia, and the NATO commander." Ashleigh's voice said.

"Fellow citizens of the world," President Rodriguez started. "The past few months have been trying. All of us fought, suffered, and experienced loss. We lost loved ones, we lost belongings, and we lost time. But we did not lose hope. We keep faith in a better future. A future where our planet is safe, our people prosper, and our children thrive. All people share the hope that tomorrow will be better than today. Whether they live in Miami or Moscow, Boston or Beijing, New York or New Delhi, all the citizens of the world want is to live in peace and prosperity. That is why I am ordering all American troops at home and abroad to stand down. As leaders of the world, we are announcing a multi-lateral cessation of hostilities. This will allow us to sit down and negotiate a more enduring peace with level heads and clear minds. To the American people. I know this has been difficult for all of us. It will be tempting to seek revenge and retaliation. But I urge you not to give in to bitterness and seek justice on your own terms. Rather, redeem the time, rebuild our country, honor our departed, and cherish the loved ones still with us. May God bless you, and God bless the United States of America."

President Chen then spoke in Mandarin,

"Distinguished presidents, comrades, brothers, and sisters of this beautiful planet. We spent a century building a world of innovation and prosperity. Technological advances in agriculture, medical care, and industry have improved the lives of many. Yet billions felt left behind. This divide fully expressed itself through various conflicts, culminating in the most devastating event in human history. We went to the precipice of annihilation. We looked into the abyss, we saw the void, and said, 'Not today'.

Today, we take a step back to chart a better course for mankind. Today, we choose fraternity over hostility and cooperation over elimination. Today, I, too, order all Chinese troops to stand down. Wherever you are in the world, cease the hostilities and cooperate with the local populations. We will hold multi-lateral meetings and start the healing process in the coming days and weeks. We will tend to our wounded and heal our lands. As President Rodriguez said, we all lost something in this war, but I believe we can win the future together. Join us in this reconstruction; join in building a better world where no one is left behind, and everyone has a stake in our common well-being. Thank you."

The Russian president and the NATO commander also gave their remarks, ordering their troops to stop the bloodshed. All over the world, in different conflict zones, white flags began to rise up. It took days and weeks, but eventually, fighting was reduced to a few skirmishes.

44

WITHOUT FURTHER ADO

"Now to you, Christopher," Pastor Riveira said. "Scripture said husbands must love their wives like Christ loved the church. There is an old song titled *'What is love?'* This is the old age question. Here's the best description of love you will find. First Corinthians Thirteen says, *'Love is patient and kind; love does not envy or boast; it is not arrogant or rude. It does not insist on its own way; it is not irritable or resentful; it does not rejoice at wrongdoing, but rejoices with the truth. Love bears all things, believes all things, hopes all things, endures all things. Love never ends.'* You want to have a successful marriage? Love her like this, and I promise you, the two of you will have a beautiful life together. Amen"

The crowd replied, "Amen."

"Now, would you please stand?" Pastor Riveira said to Topher and Maddie.

Christopher, will you have Maddison McAdams to be your wife? Will you love her, comfort and keep her, and forsaking all others, remain true to her, as long as you both shall live?"

"I will."

Maddison, will you have Christopher Boykin to be your husband? Will you love him, comfort and keep him, and forsake all others, remain true to him, as long as you both shall live?"

"I will."

The ring exchange followed. They both said,

"With this ring, I thee wed, and all my worldly goods I thee endow. In sickness and in health, in poverty or in wealth, till death do us part."

"By the powers vested in me by the State of Georgia, I now declare you husband and wife. You may now kiss the bride."

A few hours later, as the small, intimate reception was winding down.

"I just want to thank you all for sharing this moment with Maddie and me. Over the past few months, this has been the only thing that kept me going, for Maddie, Ryan, and me to build our family. We're hoping for better days ahead. But whatever comes, we'll face it together as a family. Thank you all."

Topher and Maddie then went around the room, greeting all the guests personally.

"Dr. Earhardt, thank you so much for coming," Maddie said.

"Wouldn't miss it for the world. You look so beautiful."

"Thank you for all you did for us while I was gone," Topher said. "It means a lot to us. You kept her sane in this insanity."

"We kept each other sane," Dr. Earhardt said.

The couple moved on in the room to the next guests.

"Thank you, guys, for coming," Maddie said.

"Thank you for having us," Suri answered. "It's our honor to be here."

Topher didn't speak but rather hugged it out with Azael.

"I still can't believe my eyes," Topher said to Azael. "Thank you for coming." He then turned to Suri, "Thank you for saving our son."

She smiled and said, "Thank you for saving me. Actually, thank you for saving us because that one would have died trying." She put her arm around Azael's.

"That is the truth," Azael said. "But I'm glad I didn't have to. Because I want to spend the rest of my life with you." He turned to Topher and Maddie and said, "Thank you for everything. When our turn comes, we hope you can make it. It would be an honor to have you as guests."

"The honor will be ours," Topher replied. "Who knows, maybe we'll see each other before that if duty calls."

"Hopefully, duty doesn't call too soon," Maddie interjected. "You, sir, owe me a honeymoon."

"Indeed, I do," Topher answered as they moved on to the next guest.

"Ty G," Topher said, smiling. "Thank you for coming man."

"Thanks for havin' me."

"I heard you saved the day," Maddie said, all smiles.

"Nah' I just did my part. Your hubby here, he the hero."

"Couldn't have done it without you. Glad you pulled through."

"Come on, man, you know it'll take more than a bullet to take me out." He pointed to the site of his gunshot wound. "But y'all make a beautiful couple. All the best."

The night went on with laughter and fun stories. It was as if the war never happened. That's until Kyle and Ashleigh stepped out of the reception on a cool spring night. The temperature was in the mid-sixties. The sky had scattered clouds. The moon was bright. The city bore the scars of conflict. Its buildings served as the bookmarks of a book filled with pages of trauma.

"Do you think we'll ever fully recover?" Ashleigh asked.

"I don't know. We lost a lot of people. Everywhere you go, there's a reminder of something or someone gone. So, I don't know. But tell you what, whatever the future holds, I want to face it with you by my side."

"You're not going to ask me to marry you, are you?"

"Oh, absolutely not! There's no way I would ask you to marry me at my brother's wedding. You must be crazy."

"Okay, good."

"Don't worry, when I do pop the question, you won't see it coming."

"Oh really? You better not do anything stupid, cause I might just say no."

"Oh yeah? Really? By the way, that's what Maddie did to Topher, so that would be incredibly predictable. So, you might want to be a little more original and say yes."

"We'll see. You better make it good."

White House, Washington, D.C., two weeks later

After a secret Medal of Honor ceremony honoring Topher and other valiant soldiers for their bravery during the war. Kyle, Ashleigh, and Ty G were awarded the Presidential Medal of Freedom a week prior. President Rodriguez called Topher into the situation room with a few other trusted advisors.

"Congratulations on your medal," the president said.

"Thank you, sir," Topher replied.

"It's well deserved. But I didn't call you here to congratulate you. We were on the brink. We came so close to losing everything. This cannot happen again. As you saw, the Council's reach goes deep. We need to dismantle the Council and bring its members to justice. I'm not talking about a kill squad. Investigate, build a case, and bring them to justice."

"By myself, sir?"

"Actually, glad you brought that up. We've been in constant negotiation with Beijing on prisoner swaps. Here are some pics that might interest you." The president handed Topher two letter-size pictures.

Topher stayed stunned for a moment. "Chad, Andy."

"They were captured. We'll get them back."

"Max, CK?"

"We're still looking. But don't worry, we'll find them. We'll bring them home."

"I spoke to President Chen, and we both recognize we have a problem. We need it solved immediately. He's going to take care of TAN, but we have to take care of the Council. We cannot risk the fate of humanity to people operating in the shadows. I will put at your disposal the full power of the government of the United States of America. You need to find them and bring them to justice."

"Yes, sir."

THE END!